"With its gripping premise and non-stop action, *The Blue Hour Sanction* delivers a thrilling narrative that will captivate fans of both *The Hunger Games* and *James Bond*. Prepare for a wild ride through a world of deadly secrets and high-stakes missions—you'll be hooked from the first page."

—Andrew Watts, *USA Today* bestselling author of the Firewall Spies series

"Landon Beach's *The Blue Hour Sanction* is everything you want in a thriller. The vividly imagined, fast-moving plot pulls you along at breakneck speed. Strong writing, nonstop action, stunning twists, and a female lead who will take your breath away. You won't want to put it down."

—Susan Hunter, author of the Leah Nash Mystery Series

"A fresh take on telling a story within a story, *The Blue Hour Sanction* dives into the past of one of Beach's most fascinating characters, bringing her to life for a rip-roaring origin story that's different than anything else out there."

—Ryan Steck, The Real Book Spy, and author of *Lethal Range*

"*The Blue Hour Sanction* is my number one fiction read of 2023."

—Wendi Flint Rank, top NetGalley reviewer

THE BLUE HOUR SANCTION

Landon Beach

Cover designed by Design for Writers

This book is a work of fiction. Names, characters, places, and incidents either are products of the author's imagination or are used fictitiously. Any resemblance to actual persons, living or dead, events, or locales is entirely coincidental.

Landon Beach
Visit my website at landonbeachbooks.com

Printed in the United States of America

First Printing: July 2023
Landon Beach Books LLC

ISBN-13 978-1-959783-00-8

blue hour
\\'blü\\ \\'aú(-ə)r\\

—the period of time just before sunrise or just after sunset when the sun casts a diffuse light from below the horizon and the sky takes on a vivid blue tone

sanc·tion
\\'saNG(k)SH(ə)n\\

—a measure designed to enforce a law or standard

"You know I . . . had a speech prepared for you. I'd been rehearsing it for three months. It was pretty good, as a matter of fact. All about the betrayals and dead friends—a kind of passionate requiem. And naturally what a . . . filthy, cold-blooded monster you are, et cetera . . . et cetera. That part was very eloquent. It even went into the philosophical implications of the relationships between the mercenary and his employer. You would have been impressed. But right now, face to face with you, I don't really want to go . . . through all that. You see, I don't mind taking money from you. But having you offer me money for your life with all those *bodies* littering Africa, is . . . actually . . . degrading. So I . . . turn down . . . your arrangements."

—Colonel Allen Faulkner, *The Wild Geese*

She possessed no distracting or debilitating conscience and felt no remorse.

She would not miss him, but she would miss Gstaad—the skiing, the walking paths, the famous winter hiking trails, the mountain air. And the promenade in the middle village, which was lined with art galleries, historic restaurants, hotels built out of wood, and designer-label stores such as Louis Vuitton, Ralph Lauren, Hermès, Brunello Cucinelli, Moncler, Prada, and Cartier—he had purchased gifts for her from each shop. Then, there were the smaller boutiques, which her cover as a socialite demanded that she profess a hunger to roam through. And she had, remarking how they carried her favorite labels: Chloe, Dolce & Gabbana, Tod's, Dior, Marc Jacobs, and Oscar de la Renta. She had spent hours and hours walking the picturesque promenade both with him and by herself. That part of the mission had been enjoyable, even memorable, but it was time to leave.

Her cobalt dinner dress flowed like water in a river's current, moving around a fallen tree, smooth and undeterred toward its final destination. The top of the dress ran straight across her chest, exposing no cleavage, with the right side tapering to a one-inch-thick strap that ran over her pale shoulder; her other shoulder was bare. Her cobalt heels, specially ordered from Bergdorf Goodman, sunk into the plush carpet with each stride. When the time to act came, she would take them off.

"Haven't tired of this, have you, Justine?" Junius said, emptying the wine bottle into the second glass. His blue-green eyes sparkled—contacts, of course, to match his king's.

She had three full legends—aliases—that she used. Justine Iris, a wealthy socialite from the Outer Banks of North Carolina, was her current legend, which would be retired after the mission. Flo would miss her. She liked being Justine, and she had enjoyed the weekends she had spent at the beach house in the Outer Banks earlier in the year, building up her cover.

Flo reached the bar and rested her forearms against the strip of polished brass that bordered the top. It was cool, and she almost shivered. "Not at all," she said with a sheepish grin—one that always caused his eyes to survey her agile form. She had him trained, and that would be to her advantage in a short while.

He handed her the glass and moved his eyes up and down her body, then raised them to the ceiling. "Well," he said, shrugging, "it's only money, and money is one vast plain of annoyance."

The words were delivered in his Richard voice, which he slipped into occasionally. She still wondered how much he had paid for the voice lessons to imitate his idol. *Hundreds of thousands, perhaps, maybe more.* He continued to train with his vocal coach three times a week. *"Mustn't let my grasp on the old Welsh boy slip, Justine,"* he said, imitating the stage and screen legend who had been dead for nearly twenty years. He delivered the line every time he left her to attend one of the voice sessions. As peculiar as his fascination with the deceased actor was, his behavior aligned with what she had learned from studying his dossier before the mission. He was drenched in wealth, still headed his family's shipping company, StarLine, but no longer *worked* and, therefore, had decided to keep busy by devoting himself to recreating the celebrity he most admired—from the iconic voice to the Swiss residences to the jet-set lifestyle. She theorized that there had been some plastic surgery but not enough for him to pass as a double . . . just enough to be intriguing—to someone—when he became the character, moving like him and somewhat sounding like him.

He bit his lower lip and met eyes with her. "Still—it beats the *hell* out of working, no?"

And like the snap of a finger, *Victor* was back, and Richard was tucked away for later use.

Flo signaled her agreement that enjoying wine with him was better than working with a pleasant tap on his hand. The brief sentiment was a lie, though. She had been working for months and was working right now. And she neither relished having wine with him nor savored being in his company.

4

She had arrived at his magnificent chalet in Gstaad in the early weeks of October when the winds from the Alps came down like a whistle from a giant and cooled the country's lower terrains, signaling the coming on of winter. And since then, she had gathered enough intelligence on Victor Lars Junius to know that the Greek shipping magnate's company, passed down to Junius from his father, had started out as a respectable operation but had now become a front for an international criminal conglomerate. The kickbacks he received had put him near the top of Forbes's annual list.

And yet he can't share a real *bottle of wine with me.*

After *staring* at their glasses of wine—*"An amateur skips the visual assessment, the weighing and considering,"* he had said—they toasted and went through the same tasting routine they had performed for every new bottle opened together, which had been many, over the previous eight weeks: noses in the large glasses, deep sniffs followed by sips of more liquid than swishes of mouthwash, and then the tactile exploration—the ample use of their tongues to evaluate the flavors, textures, and surprises. She would swallow first, then grin, then say something like *"nice."* He would hold the wine in his mouth longer, squinting as if to assess it on a deeper, more sophisticated level. The precursor to his swallow was always either an act of closing both eyes or a quick raise of both eyebrows. Finally, he would look at the glass like he was disappointed in it and mutter, *"disjointed,"* or *"not as silky as I would have thought,"* or *"a bit on the flabby side,"* or *"too aggressive,"* or *"simple in the mid-palate . . . I lost interest."*

Flo slid the fingers of her right hand down the sleeve of his tuxedo jacket, the red polish on her nails making it look like four rivulets of blood were streaming toward the bar. He observed and then went through his tasting ritual once more.

After she had sent her coded message back to the company last night, stating her intentions to sanction—assassinate—Victor Lars Junius and her plan to do so the following night, she was surprised to get a message back within an hour;

usually, she received a reply no earlier than two hours after she sent a communication. In the reply, the company's administrative triumvirate made their position clear: They felt that although she might be able to gain some more information in the next few days about who the major players were in the illicit empire—specifically, the ones *above* Junius—they agreed with her assessment that she was now at the crucial vertex of her mission. Better to eliminate him now and see what it stirred up rather than lose their opportunity . . . and possibly lose *her.*

She was in the middle of a one-week window to sanction Junius and get out, and the arrangements to bring her home had been in place for three days now after two employees from the shell company Kross, Inc. had arrived in Marseille in the company's private jet. Staying any longer at the chalet meant risking her cover being blown, which would mean immediate torture followed by execution. Hence, the three administrators agreed with Flo's move to kill Junius immediately. The reason they had replied so soon was that they wanted to have one more exchange the following afternoon when Junius had his daily massage and then took his nap.

Five hours ago, she had received the message—a final go-ahead and a confirmation of her route out of Switzerland and back to the United States. Little had changed from the original plan that had been presented to her in her final mission pre-briefing. The head of the company's weapons division, Albert Munny, was staying in a small home, about an hour away, that the company had purchased four years ago to serve as one of its central hubs for European operations. For this mission, it proved to be a serendipitous purchase as the company had closed on the property a few months after Junius had built his grand chalet. Tonight, Munny would be waiting in a truck eight-hundred meters up the road from the northern entrance to the chalet. There was no video surveillance beyond the perimeter of the estate, and after four-hundred meters along the road, heading south or north, beyond the chalet's gated entrance, there were no traffic

6

cameras. And at the four-hundred-meter mark, the road bent to the east before straightening out northwards again, which provided an opportune place to tuck the truck into the side of the road three-hundred meters past the bend. Munny would approach from the north; in the original plan, he was to approach from the south and be parked eight-hundred meters away in that direction. The communication said that because of the heavy snowfall during the past twenty-four hours, the northern roads were a safer bet to get out of Gstaad—the resort town's snowplows always started north and worked their way south. The liability with the northern pick-up point was the bend. Munny would have no visual of her until the last three-hundred meters. If she experienced trouble before then, she would be on her own.

After she made it to the truck, she would hide in a specially-designed, hidden compartment until they were within a half hour of the French border. Then, she would change her appearance at a cabin the company owned, and they would get into a different vehicle with French plates—all hail open borders—and travel to Marseille where they would stay for two nights in a safe house. There, they would both change appearance to look like the two Kross, Inc. employees and arrive at the Nice Côte d'Azur Airport to head back home to the United States after a wonderful stay on the French Riviera. The two company employees who had arrived three days ago would stay another week at a different hotel and then fly coach back to the United States. 9/11 was still at the forefront of everyone's mind; security would be tight.

There could be no mistakes.

The company had arranged for false message traffic—that could never be traced—to reach StarLine, stating that the woman who had been staying with Junius would be attempting to board a merchant ship out of Rotterdam, Antwerp, or Hamburg to cross the Atlantic to the port of Callao in Peru. Naturally, unaware of what had happened to Junius, StarLine's management would be confused by the information and try to reach Junius. Flo's superiors predicted that whomever Junius had worked for would have already sent a clean-up crew to his chalet and created the narrative that Junius had died of an unfortunate accident; the organization would make sure that it was never known that Junius had been assassinated because of the attention it would draw, which was what the organization wanted to avoid at all costs. For Flo's company, the prospect of learning more about the secret organization by observing how it dealt with StarLine, the cleanup, the local police, and the media was worth the bold move to have Flo sanction Junius. And just when it appeared that the secret organization had the situation under control, Flo's company would leverage her second legend and notify StarLine—again, through a series of cutouts—that Justine was not a socialite from the Outer Banks but that her "real" name was Darby Brisbane, a ghost writer for a major author in the states, and that Darby split her time between a beachfront penthouse in Miraflores, an upscale district in Lima, Peru, and a penthouse in Manhattan's Upper East Side.

Hopefully, the confusion and questions caused by this leak would cause Junius's organization to make a mistake, which would provide even more information.

Of course, Flo lived at neither of the residences nor in a beach house in the Outer Banks. Her home was in the suburbs of Raleigh, North Carolina, where the company she worked for, Worth-Gideon, Inc., was located. She and Munny would fly into Charlotte, North Carolina and then drive the three hours to Raleigh. There, she and Munny would provide a complete debrief at the company's headquarters, and the company would continue to monitor what was happening in the illegal organization since Junius's assassination. After her out briefing, she would be getting some well-deserved time off: the mandatory company vacation after an operation concluded. She thought she might catch the newest *Harry Potter* film, which had only been in theaters for a month.

If anything happened to Munny, or if their primary escape route became compromised, then she had her insurance policy: two full legends, beyond her

8

three with the company, known only to her, that she had set up two years ago. One was French, Iva Jolie, and one was English, Ilda Johnson—the initials of her current legend in reverse. She had a safety deposit box in Paris and one in London, which would help her survive if she had to disappear. In each box was $50,000, a birth certificate, a driver's license, and other documents she could use to substantiate who she was once she took on the new identity. Both passports were hidden in the soles of her running shoes, which she had concealed earlier underneath the canvas log carrier with leather straps that was next to the full cord of wood stacked on the ground level, ten feet below the terrace's floor.

"We must visit the Christmas Market again tomorrow," she said. This was yet another aspect of Gstaad she would mourn the loss of. There was festive, and then there was Christmas-Market-Circus-in-Gstaad festive. Beyond the lights and décor, there were stalls all along the market street that had something for everyone—gifts and gift bags, socks, hats, food, desserts, upholstery, ornaments, decorations, keepsakes, and other novelties that fit the occasion. Every stroll had lifted her spirits; every stroll had made her miss home.

"If you like," he said.

She giggled. "I like."

Junius pressed a button below the countertop, and the room went dark except for the oatmeal, milk, & honey candle that flickered at the far end of the bar. He motioned with his wine glass toward the French doors that led to the terrace and pressed another button, which illuminated the terrace. "More skiing in the late morning?" he asked, slipping into Richard once more.

Her eyes adjusted to both the absence of light in the library and the presence of light outside. She saw the swirling blizzard and heard the wind howl as it blew thousands of tiny, white flakes across the lit terrace, creating a drift of soft snow against the left-side railing. "Should be the best conditions yet," she said.

"Snow will stop falling by midnight, I should think, and the skies will be clear all day tomorrow." *Still Richard.* He took a sip of wine and stepped toward the French doors.

Perfect.

She followed him.

He was making it easy, for her stiletto was hidden on the underside of the far edge of the terrace's stone railing. She had placed it there earlier in the day, and her plan had been to guide him to that spot, suggesting that they gaze up at the stars while experiencing the chill of the freezing temperature and the rejuvenating inhales of brisk air, which would energize them to return to the warmth of the library and make love on the room's lush carpet or perhaps on top of the varnished bar top. She had learned that the cold-hot treatment she used in college to revitalize her sore muscles after a grueling track meet was also useful in priming and executing a sexual experience; the numbing of the erotic zones made the awakening of them that much more satisfying. On some nights with him, she employed this knowledge to accelerate his orgasm and get the whole thing over with as soon as possible. And the library was one of his favorite places in the chalet to entwine their limbs, which would allow her to leverage the location. Once she had him outside, she would hint at the "afterward" when they reached the railing to direct his mind, hopefully consuming it with his menu of mating-ritual possibilities, while she slid her hand over the railing and took hold of the knife.

Before committing to placing her weapon in its current location, she had identified her plan's main challenge—how to get him onto the terrace and to the railing without giving the appearance of steering him. Ultimately, she had put faith in her training and the record of her superior ability to work him the past few months, first with mind and second with body. The saying, *"You are what your record says you are,"* came to mind when she made the decision to slay him on the terrace. Now that he was approaching the French doors, she assumed to get a better view of the winter wonderland just beyond the glass panes, her task to invite him outside seemed even more manageable.

They stopped just short of the doors and stood side-by-side. Flo took a drink of wine, knowing that this and probably every conversation in the library were being recorded, then said, "I'll have to hope that my favorite author includes a skiing scene in her next novel. I've never been more prepared to read one."

He turned his head and looked at her. He was six feet tall, and she was five seven, but with the heels, she stood almost at eye level with him. "Will you ever tell me who he or she is?"

In order to make her second legend plausible when it leaked, she had been dropping hints that she entertained authors at her beach estate and that she had a favorite one but couldn't tell him who so as not to have that information reach her other author friends. In fact, the subject had become a running tit-for-tat mystery game between them.

"Hughes?" he would say, sometimes as Richard, sometimes as Victor.

"No."

"Atwood?"

"No."

"Morrison?"

"No."

In heavy *Richard: "Good God, not a paperback writer?"*

"I'm not telling you."

She provided the same restrained grin that she had given him each time he had pressed her to learn the identity of the bestselling author. "No. You will just have to attend one of my summer parties and try to guess who it is; there will be plenty of writers to choose from, some of which you have already mentioned."

"So, you might be lying to me."

For a final time, she gave him the mischievous look that got his heart racing.

"But summer is *months* away."

"If I told you now, it would ruin the intrigue. Unlocking secrets always leads to diminished returns. That is why reading a book or watching a film for a second time is never the same as the first." She paused. "Same with shooting up."

This was meant to sting him, knowing that his illegitimate son, who had been the product of Junius's affair with one of his house maids, had been an addict and died of an overdose half-a-dozen years ago at twenty-three. The fact that the young man's relationship with Junius had never been made public was a testament to Worth-Gideon's surveillance and planning division. Knowing and keeping secrets was true power. When you kept them, you were their master; when you told them, you became their prisoner. Junius had lied to her and said that he had never had time for children and that interaction proved invaluable. From that point on, she knew what he looked like when he lied, which gave her a tactical advantage over him and tuned her early warning sensors.

And, now, with instantaneous death awaiting him in minutes, she relied on her ability to read him.

He went to say something but then filled in his indecision with another smooth pull from his wine glass.

He needs to change the subject or else risk having a vulnerability exposed, she thought.

"Agree—" She moved closer to him. *Go for it.* "—Richard?"

His grin widened, and his eyes sparkled. "In principle," he said, as Richard. Reaching out, he ran his free hand through her hair. "Discovering who people are is never much fun, is it? The illusion is what attracts."

And now it was she who sensed a change in the field of energy around them, as if the particles that had been purposely scrambled by her had rearranged themselves and were pulsating around her head, putting immense pressure on her thought patterns.

Something is wrong. He's not talking about himself. He . . . he's talking about me. *But, how?*

I

Hayward Field, University of Oregon, Eugene, Oregon – June, 2001

Three hundred meters left, and then you're all done, Margaret Crandall thought as she rounded the first bend, leading the last lap in the final event of the Heptathlon at the 2001 NCAA Division I Outdoor Track and Field Championships. She was currently in 3rd place overall with a chance of winning, but to do that, her coach figured she'd have to finish first in the 800.

Shouldn't be a problem—she was supposed to *win* the 800.

Margaret had figured it that way too, but for different reasons.

In fact, her coach was a bit disappointed that she wasn't in first or second place going into the final event, but, unbeknownst to her, it was because Margaret had engineered it so. Yesterday, she had eased back in the 200 meters and purposely missed three times in a row in the high jump at a height she usually cleared. Today had been more normal: She was the second-best long jumper in

21

the field, and she finished second; she was the third-best javelin thrower in the field, and she finished third.

Her coach's final instructions before she headed off to check-in for the race were, *"Go out there and give it your all one more time for the maize and blue, kiddo. You're still going to win this thing."* Tears had formed in her coach's eyes. *"You've had a fine four years with us, Margie—proud of you. You're the only one who could have come back after . . . after something like that."*

Margaret had nodded, acknowledging the unsaid words between those lines, which she guessed were, *"At the University of Michigan, we will always be at a disadvantage to those schools whose athletes can train outside year-round,"* and, *"If your dad hadn't passed away in March, causing you to miss a month of the season, you would have slayed the field,"* and, finally, she would have added, *"I feel sorry for you because you were one of the favorites to win the heptathlon at the start of the season, and anything less than that will be a disappointment."*

She was thankful that her coach had not said those things, but, perhaps if she would have, Margaret Carol Crandall, recently-graduated-senior-from-the-University-of-Michigan heptathlete, would have agreed with her. However, what her coach did not know and could not know was that a week ago, Margaret had been approached by a man and woman whom she had never seen before. They were well-dressed, sophisticated recruiters for a small company and invited her to dinner, where they presented her with an offer of a new life with opportunities she would not get anywhere else in the world.

She was intrigued by the offer, even though the man and woman had only glanced over some of the perks—a generous salary with plenty of opportunities for bonuses, the chance to travel all over the globe on the company's dime, and near-complete autonomy over her work schedule. But, most of all, the opportunity to operate in a competitive environment, without politics and bureaucratic red tape, where only the best employees and ideas survive. She reasoned that they had studied her because that philosophy was what Margaret

Crandall valued the most, which was why athletics mattered to her so much, and they must have deduced that the loss of athletic competition after college had been weighing on her.

Naturally, she had looked up the company, Morning Bright, Inc., online, but it was as secretive as a Hollywood talent agency's website—no profiles or content links for *anything*. She had briefly thought of becoming an actress but had dismissed the career path after failing to find anyone in the business to speak with.

There's a reason *they don't give out their information.*

And for that reason, she had been both intrigued and skeptical of Morning Bright and its two recruiters. However, the lure of exclusivity—of joining a private club—and entering a world where there would be no doubt about where she stood at all times based on her merit had sold her on the opportunity. And they had come to *her*, not the other way around. If the job didn't pan out? Well, she was young and had plenty of time for course corrections.

She would fly home to Ann Arbor tonight, and tomorrow, she would meet a private jet at Ann Arbor Municipal Airport that would transport her to the company's offices. Arrangements would be made to pack up her apartment and move her belongings after a trial period with the corporation. No need to waste time and money if she didn't find her footing. But, in the meantime, the company would pay for her apartment in Ann Arbor and take care of her lodging, meals, clothing, and necessities as she began work.

One last race, and she'd be on her way.

There was just one thing that the company needed her to do.

Finish 2nd but no worse than 5th overall in the Heptathlon.

Above all: DON'T finish 1st.

"Everyone remembers who wins, but no one remembers who loses," they had said over dinner. *"We're a very private company, and we purposely recruit top talent. But. We don't want any of our recruits to be in the spotlight. Too distracting—and* nothing *should distract*

from the work we have to do. Now, we know you can win, and so do you. You're supposed to finish in the top five, so it would not be advisable to finish out of the top five—again, we don't want any unnecessary attention paid to you, and that would certainly happen if you finished near the bottom. So, neither get caught up in the glory of the moment nor slack. Finish second through fifth, and you will get to compete in things that few people ever get a chance to compete in, all commencing a few days after your last race. We'll be there, watching from the stands. If you win or finish out of the top five, you'll never see or hear from us again." Then, the woman, who had the coldest eyes she had ever seen, had leaned forward and whispered, *"The irony should not be lost on you that we're requiring you to dial down your competitive nature for two days in order to gain admission into the most competitive environment you've ever been in and* will *ever be in. You see, in our business, everything worth having has a price."* She had then leaned back and taken a sip of her martini. *"And we need to know from day one if you're willing to unconditionally pay it."*

For the last week, Margaret's conscience had been an annoying visitor who wouldn't go away, saying, "To win, you have to lose," at least once an hour. Now, with 200 meters left to go in the last race and event of her career, Margaret heard the voice again as she purposely started to fade. A competitor from UCLA swerved into lane 2 and went around her.

Then one from USC.

And one from Florida.

She gritted her teeth once and pumped her arms and legs faster as she fought off the giant from Arizona who, at six-feet-three-inches tall, made Margaret's five-foot-nine-inch frame look small.

Seated in the stands, high above the track and field, Kerrie Raven watched the race through her binoculars. "She's slowing—told you she wants in."

"Don't be too sure," Jock Gideon replied from the seat beside her. "She's got an incredible kick, could be saving it for the home stretch."

Raven bit her lip. She wanted Crandall and knew that Gideon was lukewarm at best about her joining the company, which, of course, was not the cover name of Bright Morning, Inc. but rather Worth-Gideon, Inc.

He shouldn't even be here, Raven thought. Gideon should be back at the office or in D.C. or at Langley or at the Pentagon or back at his old stomping grounds of Wall Street, navigating the stakeholders and nurturing the relationship between politicians, intelligence agencies, military elite, financial institutions, and, what Worth-Gideon was: a silent contractor for the most secret work that needed to be carried out in the interests, or *supposed* interests, of the United States of America. She fancied herself a better judge of talent than Gideon anyway and often wondered why Byron Worth had agreed to let his senior and more-vested co-owner partner travel to evaluate recruits. Gideon, and Worth for that matter, had to have more urgent and important matters to attend to. She was the director, in charge of all personnel. *"Let me do my job then,"* she had argued last year before the new prospects were evaluated.

She watched as the runners rounded the bend.

"Sonofabitch," she whispered.

Crandall had moved into the second lane . . . and had just passed the runner from Florida in front of her.

"Told you," Gideon said. "She's still a child. We should have gone with UCLA."

Winning means nothing, but losing means an opportunity for a new life, Crandall thought as she passed the girl from Florida and eyed the runners ahead of her. *But if I lose I will never get another chance to be named the best collegiate female athlete in the United States.* Her brain was telling her to slow down, but her body was starting to push harder.

Which destiny do I pursue?

If I win, then I will have something that no one can take away from me, but I will have lost out on something, perhaps, far greater and more long-lasting. She knew that the odds of her making the Olympic team to compete in Athens in 2004 were long. A lot could happen in the next three years. Hell, a lot could happen in six months.

Look at what you just went through.

She knew that she hadn't been the same since returning after her father's death. Yes, in between making funeral arrangements, donating most of her father's limited belongings to a local mission in Shelter Harbor, placing the single box of things he wanted her to have in her brown, 1981 Chrysler Cordoba, selling her father's truck, and selling her childhood home, she had gotten in a few workouts at her high school track, monitored by her old coach, but the March afternoon temperatures had stayed in the high thirties and low forties, and she was unable to practice all seven of her events. In fact, her limited number of workouts ensured that she lost her superior level of fitness in a few weeks. She was a morning person, but the a.m. temperatures—in the twenties—and crushing psychological weight of the tremendous loss she had experienced had kept her underneath the mountain of blankets draped over her in the twin bed in her old room as she slept past ten a.m. most mornings. It had been a month of survival—closing out bank accounts, transferring the small amount of money her dad had saved up for her to her account, seeing old friends and high school teachers at the funeral home along with the few coworkers from the bowling alley where her father had tended bar for nearly thirty years.

The last remaining family member in her life had been taken from her. The last candle in a church of suffering and bad memories had gone out.

Both her high school coach and college coach had said that even making it to this meet would be a miracle.

So, she had fought back and, against the odds, qualified for the final meet of her career. She would make a last stand and celebrate the fact that she had not walked away after being dealt the heavy blow of losing her rock and the light of her life. She would surprise everyone and win the whole goddamn thing for her late father.

And then there had been a knock on her apartment door, followed by the best dinner she had ever experienced. And then there had been the offer.

She passed the runner from USC.

As Raven witnessed Crandall's surge heading into the home straightaway, she thought: *No. Don't do it. You are exactly who we are looking for.*

Crandall hit every marker: no family, no current love life, perfect Myers-Briggs for the work they would have her doing, pure athlete—a heptathlete, which, in Raven's opinion is who the company should continue to target for the position.

"She's going for the win, Kerrie," Gideon said behind his binoculars. "I suspected she wouldn't be able to hold back thousands of years of human conditioning. Not many can at her age. UCLA was the better bet."

Raven wanted to rip the binoculars out of his hands and clobber him on his head with them. "Race isn't over yet." It was a weak reply, delivered with no confidence. She knew what was taking place down there, and a part of her respected Crandall for it.

But, come on. *Just ease up and don't pass anyone else. I don't want the girl from UCLA.*

As the group went around the final bend, the cheers from the stands and infield grew louder, and Margaret strained even more to close the gap between herself and the one runner in front of her.

For half-a-dozen strides, she gained.

You have enough in you to pull this off, she said to herself. *No one has your kick.*

She pressed harder and drew even with the leader from UCLA.

But you have been running from your past for a long time. What you need to do is run toward your future.

27

She was now going stride for stride with the girl from UCLA—the crowd was going nuts—and she waited for the feeling of a frustrating and familiar foe in her legs: lactic acid.

Because she had not stayed in top form the past three months, she had struggled in the final stretch of the 800—her legs feeling like they were full of cement in the last hundred meters. Her times had been decent enough to get her to this meet, but she had lost the feeling of freedom and lightness that she had worked so hard to achieve in February. By mid-March, it was gone, and the lactic acid had once again become a formidable enemy.

Should feel it at any moment now . . .

Then, the giant drew even with them—a three-way battle for first!—and Margaret could swear that out of the corner of her eye, she could see her coach, wearing a blue Block "M" hat and a maize sweatshirt with the words 'Michigan Track and Field' across the front in blue, cheering her on while alternating her view between the stop watch in her hand and Margaret.

Forty meters left.

She pumped hard. The sprint was at an anaerobic pace, which should have taken its toll as her body required more oxygen than her lungs could provide.

But instead of slowing down, she was *speeding up*. From a reservoir deep within herself that she had never accessed before, she found another gear.

The crowd's cheering reached a new height; the stands were one vibrating mass of humanity as the fight for who would reach the finish line first intensified. Margaret's knee and elbow joints felt like they were entering the hot forging process—red hot, and malleable—and she gasped for more oxygen as she made her move.

She edged a yard ahead of the other two.

The track became a blurry mirage of bright colors in front of her, and she realized that it was due to not only the heat of the day but the tears in her eyes as well.

What do I do?

Twenty meters left.

What do I do?

Her conscience answered, *"Run toward your future,"* edging out the reptilian part of her brain that was yelling, *"Push, win,* destroy *the competition!"*

She slowed her arms.

The giant passed her.

10 meters left.

The girl from UCLA passed her . . . but could not catch the giant.

Commit to your destiny.

Margaret eased up even more . . . and crossed the finish line, taking third place.

Normally, after emptying her body of every ounce of effort, she would collapse on the infield, hyperventilating until she recovered from the punishing run. Today, she congratulated the two runners who had beaten her and then took two steps onto the infield. Breathing heavily with sweat spraying into the air with each exhalation, she turned until her eyes found the desired section; then, she stood still and looked up at the man and woman seated near the top of the stadium.

Kerrie Raven's eyes got big behind her binoculars, and the corners of her mouth slid upward, forming a knowing grin. She watched as Crandall held her position for a few more seconds and then walked away. She lowered her binoculars and said, "She's in. UCLA is out."

There was no reply from Gideon. As she turned toward him, she observed him tossing his binoculars into a small backpack and then opening a bottle of Aquafina. They sat alone. The next closest people were seated a dozen rows below them and a section over.

Gideon finished his gulp and screwed the top back on the bottle of water. He did not whisper, but his volume was low enough not to be heard by anyone other than Raven. "You like her because she's the first candidate from your home state."

Not true. I don't like *her at all.*

But, there was a certain temperament of perseverance in Michiganders, born out of the reality of having to live in freezing, snow-covered, and ice-slicked weather for three to four months every year. And, as beautiful as the seasons were up north, the weather was also unpredictable, which forced Michiganders to be, perhaps, the most prepared and resilient residents in the country—having a sweatshirt or sweater within arm's reach was akin to knowing where the refrigerator and sink were. However, preparedness only counted for so much. The true measure of a Michigander dealing with the changes in weather was his or her ability to acclimate to the annoyance—sometimes misery—of never having on the exact clothing to fit the temperature. The concept of layering was a sound one, but eternal layering becomes a hassle in a hurry, and hence, one succumbs early to the philosophy of, "I'm wearing *this*, and *this* will have to do," followed by a calloused shrug in response to a non-Michigan native complaining about it being too hot or too cold or having to change outfits once again.

Raven knew this could be said of other regions of the United States and the world, but there was something about living your whole life in a state like this— surrounded by massive bodies of water, adding their own element to the climate—and experiencing beach-sunning paradise in one hour and treacherous, tornados that could clear-cut a swath of forest in the next. And if you lived in the Upper Peninsula, close to where Worth-Gideon's private training facility was located, the weather delta fluctuated exponentially.

And don't get me started on the roads, she thought.

Crandall had lived through twenty-two Michigan winters. Like Raven, she had been in the metaphorical death chamber that Indy and Short Round had survived in *The Temple of Doom*—their room was just frozen, and the spikes lowering from the ceiling and rising from the floor were jagged spears of ice, ready to impale them and suck the warmth from their bodies. The two other candidates had never experienced temperatures that even neared bone-freezing cold. One had grown up in Southern California, and the other had been raised in Georgia.

There were other considerations: food, water, and shelter. Whether you were a planner or not, living up north forced you to become a survivor, and that meant you always kept your house stocked with the necessities to survive if winter weather came in that eliminated travel.

Raven was a survivor.

Crandall was a survivor.

The advances in technology during the past decade had been nothing short of miraculous. Each day, more and more human beings were connecting with each other via the internet, and a growing number of people now had cell phones. Raven saw the day coming, probably within the next fifteen years, where she would be able to custom order a submarine sandwich from a grocery store on some device, perhaps hand-held, and pick it up or have it delivered to her at a time she designated. And Raven reasoned that when that day occurred, human beings would start to lose perspective on what it meant to be a hunter and gatherer—even a modern hunter and gatherer, which was a grocery shopper: planners of meals, makers of shopping lists, and haulers of food and drink from grocery store shelves and freezers.

We are evolving, my ass, she thought. *What we are doing is being enticed to latch on and never stop sucking on the proverbial teat of technological dependence, which grows by the day.*

She shuddered at the thought of what the Worth-Gideon recruits might look like a decade from now. But the tremor passed as she thought, *I will have left by then.*

"She has the best chance of any of them to handle the challenging conditions," Raven said. "I couldn't care less that we're both from Michigan, but I do care that she can deal with what the last recruiting class couldn't: the weather."

Gideon put down his water bottle and slapped both knees. "You don't know that for sure. No one ever does."

"I like her chances, and you should too. Weren't you the one who told me that you had a former, Michigan-raised associate now living in Florida who called you, laughing hysterically, to tell you that when the first snowflakes had come down a year ago, his neighbors had raced to the supermarket and cleaned the place out with all the other Floridians?"

"Fuck you."

She knew that *he knew* he had no better argument for his choice: the girl from UCLA, who would also not finish first.

"And what was with that little staring act?" he added.

He's still sore that Worth picked Crandall over his Westwood star.

Gideon believed that the heptathlete from UCLA was infinitely more attractive to the company because she was an orphan. And Jock Gideon was obsessed with selecting orphans as candidates. He had even argued that she was a superior orphan because her foster parents had been imprisoned for child abuse after authorities had discovered that the couple had been running a nightmarish child mill in an attempt to get rich under the altruistic auspices of wanting to save abandoned adolescents.

As Worth, Gideon, and Raven had debated at the polished concrete Worth-Gideon conference table prior to the trip to Ann Arbor to have dinner with Crandall, Gideon had exploded at Worth. *"UCLA never bonded with any of her foster brothers and sisters, so no one's going to miss her or wonder about whatever happened to her!"* Raven had interjected, *"Jock, she's just like the crop from last year. She won't last twenty minutes on the island."*

Ultimately, Worth had sided with Raven, and the company had never contacted the heptathlete from UCLA.

Raven raised her binoculars and found her. She was on the infield and had her hands joined on top of her head while listening to her coach. If Crandall would have won the 800 and, thus, won the heptathlon, the chances were good that Raven and Gideon would have shown up in a few days at UCLA's apartment to take her out for dinner. *What a different path you could have had*, she thought, lowering her binoculars and placing them in her tote bag.

Gideon finished his drink and crushed the water bottle. "If I remember, you're the one who argued for our other two candidates, and they're from a state away from here and from fuckin' Georgia of all places."

She put on her sunglasses. "But they've traveled and been kicked around. You know how it is when you get down to picking the last few candidates. It's a lot by feel. Even your pompous ass has said that."

Gideon yawned and then rose and stretched his long, muscular arms. "Kerrie, why do you want to end this nice, young girl's life?"

"I don't," she said, placing her own water bottle on top of a sweatshirt inside her tote—*you can't take the Michigan out of someone*—and then zipped the compartment closed.

He occasionally weaponized the guilt angle, and it had swayed her once before, but, no, not for this candidate. This candidate was different. She stood up. *Hit him right back.* "It's over, Jock. Take a good last look at your girl from UCLA."

She shuffled to the end of the aisle and then started descending the stadium steps. A few rows down, she stopped . . . and then did something she had never done before in her career. She made a prediction. Twisting her head back toward him, she said, "When Crandall makes it, Flo will be the perfect mentor for her."

Gideon stopped stretching, and his cold blue eyes locked with hers.

Not waiting for his reply, she turned around and continued downward.

Landon Beach

She listened as Flo went up the ladder, counting 12 steps. When silence returned, she grasped the cool metal railings and started making her way up. The ladder's steps were also metal of some sort and had grating for grip, which needled the bottom of her feet. She continued to take deep breaths, trying to leverage her other senses to get an idea of the place that she was in. The smell of gasoline, oil, and grease was not as strong, but there was also no trace of comforting scents like cooking or coffee to replace the engine-room stink that hung in the air—the only new odor was something akin to sweaty clothes that had been left in a gym locker for too long.

The temperature was fine. She was neither shivering nor sweating. However, it was December, and if they were anywhere but the tropics, then the temperature outside would be cold. There must be a heating system at work.

Still, she heard no voices.

Is it only me and Flo? Where are the others? Who is driving the ship? Or, was it Flo, and with the engine now at idle, the ship is just drifting?

Core reached the top of the ladder, and Flo handcuffed her hands behind her back once more. The side-to-side motion of the ship was more pronounced now, and she had to use more of the muscles in her long legs to stay upright.

"Fifteen paces until the next hatch," Flo said, taking a hold of her shoulder again, and they began moving together.

Three paces in, a wave a nausea came over her as she smelled fresh vomit. Flo must have heard her sniff and then felt her pause.

"Yes, there is puke on the deck ahead of us. You'll have to walk through it."

She swallowed the bile that was rising in her throat and switched to breathing only through her mouth. A few steps more and she felt her feet squish and then slide on the chunky liquid.

"Keep moving," Flo commanded.

She took another step and was beyond the pool of vomit but knew that both of her feet now had the disgusting, oatmeal-like liquid on them—on the bottom, on the sides, in between her toes, and on top.

She had lost count of the paces, but soon Flo stopped her.

The sound of the hatch opening brought in a draft of air, and she stood up straighter as she chanced a smell. After a few inhalations, the odor of vomit lessened, and other smells became apparent. *I can smell them. They are both in there.*

Flo had her arm again. "Step through . . . and join your trainees."

A few strides in, and the door closed behind her. She could hear breathing.

Now, Flo put a hand on each shoulder and maneuvered her into position. "There. Stay." Her voice had echoed more than before.

We must be in a larger space.

From the smell alone, she was sure that Indigo was to her direct left and Grid to her direct right. The stench of barf was stronger on the left, and she reasoned that it was Indigo who had tossed her insides in the passageway. *Maybe she's never been on a boat in rough weather.*

Core went back to breathing through her mouth only. If one of them spoke, they would all be punished, so she concentrated on trying to determine how many people were in the room, besides the three of them and Flo, based on the number of inhalations and exhalations she heard.

She ended up not having enough time as Flo said, "Open the door."

A few seconds later, a mechanism that sounded like a garage door opening engaged, and an immediate chill came over the room as Core felt the frigid air funnel in and blow against her. She reasoned that they must be in some sort of cargo bay.

"Walk twenty paces forward and stop," Flo ordered.

Core thought that the handcuffs were about control; Flo wanted to know if the three candidates would keep their cool or try to resist, or at least try to take their blindfolds off. The blindfolds were being used to disorient them and surprise them, but were they also a test to see which woman would take the initiative first and try to remove her covering? The past six months had been a learning experience of calculating when to demonstrate initiative or original thinking and when to not act and take a measure of the situation before acting. Right now, Core had settled on the latter of the two approaches. Acting impulsively had its rewards, but it could also lead to punishment or even greater challenges.

Core took her first step while listening to her right and left. She heard the footsteps of the other two recruits. They were almost in sync with hers. *They're nervous, and so am I, but I cannot show it in any way.* She continued to walk.

Her imagination was already running wild with thoughts of being thrown overboard and forced to tread water with no use of her hands and no vision of where she was. The air's frigid temperature told her that the water would be freezing, and with each step, she could hear the sound of the waves slapping the hull.

Five paces . . .

Ten paces . . .

She felt the full force of the wind across her body, and along with the wind came a million microscopic taps all over the exposed parts of her body.

Snow.

Fifteen paces . . .

At twenty, she stopped and spread her legs, using her muscles to balance on the deck as the boat rolled to starboard and then back to port.

Then, she felt hands around her wrists and cuffs, and moments later, her hands were free. She gave a soothing rub to her right wrist first and then to her left.

She did not touch the blindfold.

Perhaps thirty seconds passed, and she shivered as the wind continued to blow an endless supply of snowflakes on her freezing body. *Where are we?*

From a few feet behind her, Flo said, "Remove your blindfolds."

Core did and found herself in between the two other candidates, Indigo and Grid, who were also wearing burlap robes. On the front of Indigo's garment was a stain of vomit. She made a quick scan of the area, not knowing if they would be told to put their blindfolds back on.

They were on a sizable vessel in the middle of a blizzard. Not good. The transom was perhaps fifteen yards aft of her, and beyond that was the dark, churning sea. If she could get closer to the transom or one of the gunwales, then she could taste the sea spray and tell if they were on the ocean or on a body of freshwater. From what she could see, there were no tell-tale signs of rust that came with a vessel that was constantly in salt water, so her initial guess was that they were in fresh water.

She squinted and saw a dark shape on the horizon off the stern. It was difficult to determine what it was or how far away it was because the deck lights shining from behind them were so bright and her eyes were yet to acclimate. Her eyes popped up to the sky, searching for the moon and stars, but all they found was a cyclone of white flurries.

Motion to the left of Indigo caught Core's attention, and she straightened up into the position of attention—they all did—at the sight of Worth-Gideon's Director, Kerrie Raven.

She was dressed in black hiking boots, jeans, a black parka with a black turtleneck underneath, and black leather gloves. She wore no hat. No scarf. Core had never seen her in anything but a black skirt and white blouse or a black suit with black heels during the past six months. There had been few words exchanged as Raven oversaw the training from afar. In fact, other than the first day's induction speech, this was the first time Raven had stood in front of them while they were involved in a training session—what this training session was, Core could only guess.

3

Core watched as Worth-Gideon Director Kerrie Raven approached Indigo and stopped two feet in front of her. The fierce wind had picked up even more, and if there were words spoken by the Director to Indigo, Core did not hear them.

Moments later, Raven appeared in front of Core and studied her body from head to toe with her sadistic eyes. Then, she moved on to Grid and finally disappeared behind them. Thirty seconds later, her voice boomed, "Remove your robes."

The women untied the rope-like belt and let the garment fall to the deck.

And now Core felt the cold gusts touch the parts of her body that had been shielded by the robe, and, against her efforts to control her body, she started to shiver. *I could use the belt to my advantage on shore—as a weapon, a snare . . . a tourniquet?*

"You may not take any part of the covering with you," Raven said. "You are animals. And in our line of work, you will be going up against *animals*. If we have it our way, then your job will never call for you to navigate a scenario like tonight." She paused. "Unfortunately, we don't always have it our way because, at the same time that we are trying to dictate the terms of our engagements, our opponents are trying to dictate the identical terms to *their* advantage." She appeared in front of them again and took turns staring into each woman's eyes. "And I need to know which of you three has the best chance to survive if things don't go our way." She grinned. "I need to know how much of an *animal* each of you really is." She clasped her hands together. "Now, walk until you are two feet from the transom and stop."

Using her peripheral vision, Core saw Grid move first and then Indigo. She stepped off, feeling like Heston and the other two astronauts charging naked through the brush in *Planet of the Apes*. Soon, all three unclothed women had stopped a few feet short of the aft rail. *I don't hear the motor revving up . . .*

Well, fuck. Looks like we're swimming.

Her mind was racing. *Grid will try to disable one of us while we're still on the boat, if not both of us. I'm closest, so she'll probably go for me first. I do not want to get tangled up with her here; if I'm injured, then it takes away my advantage in the water . . .*

The water. I've got to get in fast.

She formed her plan. *Indigo is to my left, Grid to my right. Indigo will head straight for the water because she is physically weaker than me or Grid, so she won't be a problem. Grid, however, will jump directly at me when we get the signal; it's what I would do if I had the advantage of physical strength. She'll anticipate that I'm going to be moving forward, trying to get over the transom and into the water, so she'll dive a little forward of where I am. So, when we are told to start, I'll give a quick fake forward and then do a backward roll. If I guess correctly, she'll fly past where I was and possibly get a hold of Indigo, which would be perfect. I'll sprint to the port gunwale and go overboard there.*

My next move will be key.

I have to stay under as long as possible. One of them may stand on the transom, waiting to see where I come up so that she can dive at me and both hit me and submerge me, so I need to be far enough away to eliminate this option.

She heard two sets of footsteps approaching.

It's going to happen soon. Core closed her hands into fists.

The footsteps stopped.

Flo spoke first. "If any of you quit, I will kill you." She paused. "You finish the course at all costs."

Then, it was Raven's turn. "You have probably guessed by now that we're not dropping you off on the island. You will have to swim there. If you flounder in the water, no one is coming to get you. We will let you die. Now, look at the shoreline." Core listened to the static and then the *beep* of a radio, perhaps only a foot behind her. She heard Raven's voice say, "Turn on the tower light."

A few seconds passed, and then, high above a stretch of beach that was far away from the lighthouse, a white light illuminated.

"Swim toward that light, and you will see your own individual lights as you get closer to shore."

Okay, there's my rally point.

Core thought she heard the sound of a gun being cocked.

"At the sound of the gun," Raven said.

Then, Core heard retreating footsteps.

They're getting out of the way. Any second n—

BANG!

Core gave a jab-step forward and could see Grid already in a crouch, ready to leap. What Core did not expect to see was that, to Core's left, Indigo was doing the same thing. *They both think I'm the strongest overall.*

Core leaned back and executed a perfect back roll just as the other two sprung at her former position. There was a sickening crunch as the crown of Indigo's head met Grid's nose, and blood erupted from her nostrils as both women landed on the deck.

Core's backward roll had given her the clearance she needed to make it undeterred to the port gunwale, and she sprinted toward it through the dark blizzard of snowflakes. To her left, she saw Grid blocking punches from Indigo, who was on top of her. Then, with a hideous scream, Grid bucked her own body, and Indigo fell off.

As Core stepped onto the rail, she saw Indigo reaching up for the transom . . . and then saw Grid leap. Core crouched, pushed off, and sailed through the air toward the water below while Grid's outstretched hands found only air above the gunwale where Core's legs had been just a second earlier; her abdomen hit the gunwale hard, and she bellowed in pain as blood splattered onto the rail.

Core's body sliced into the cold, dark sea. Her angle of entry was more vertical than she had wanted, so she plunged perhaps eight feet under the water before leveling out. The water was colder than any water she had ever been in before, but the adrenaline inside of her was propelling her arms and legs to rise to the occasion.

Okay, now, ten strokes before you come up. She pulled her arms through the freezing water and turned to the right, swimming for five strokes. Then, she adjusted her course to the left and pulled and kicked five more times before coming up.

Her head broke the surface, and she gasped for air, her lungs already burning. Quickly, she took a small taste of the water. *Fresh.* She turned her head on a swivel and looked back at the boat. She could see Raven and Flo at the rail looking at her. Then, her body sunk into a huge trough of a wave, and they disappeared for a second. As she climbed the next peak, she saw Grid and Indigo just aft of the boat's stern. They were crawl stroking toward her; Core still had a lead of perhaps fifteen yards because, one, she had entered the water first and, two, the waves must have pushed the boat's stern to starboard because the island was now off the boat's port beam. To account for the direction, the waves were traveling, she aimed a few points to the right of the tower's white light and then began pulling hard for shore.

Having swum in Lake Huron for her entire life, she was used to swimming in heavy seas—she preferred it to the pool when she was training during the summers for the upcoming track season. A windy day on the lake had always created strong waves, which provided resistance and a better workout. During those sessions, she learned how to keep a straight line toward an objective.

She wondered if the other two had ever swum in seas with large waves.

In any event, she had to reach shore first and enter her paddock. If Grid or Indigo reached their light first, which meant they would reach their guns first, they might try to kill her with their one shot. Likewise, if she reached her light first, she could use her gun and possibly kill one of them, but she would be handling a gun with numb hands and fingers, battling hypothermia. No, it was essential for her to grab the gear, open her gate, and start warming up as soon as possible. Plus, she had not forgotten about the cut on her leg. She needed to be able to use her gun, even if it was only for one shot, to combat whatever was in her paddock.

As Core descended into a trough, she stopped and treaded water for a few seconds, the wind sweeping wave tops and snowflakes against her face. When she started to feel the water lift her up, she looked behind her. Whereas the women had been closer together when she spotted them aft of the stern, they had separated laterally now by about twenty yards. One seemed to be a bit ahead of the other one, but Core did not know who it was. All she saw was splashing, but they both seemed to be having difficulty staying on course. She felt relieved as she had opened the distance between herself and her competitors to around thirty yards.

The swimmers disappeared as she slid into another trough. Core turned around, and the island's coast slowly came into view as she started to ascend once more. While estimating that she had just over one hundred yards left, she began to feel the extreme chill of the waves once more.

Get moving!

She plunged her face into the water and began to pull, her arms feeling heavier and heavier as each one knifed into the water. *Ten push-ups and ten sit-ups when you hit the beach. I don't care where the other two are. You have to warm up.*

She concentrated on each arm stroke as she accelerated down the backside of waves and then hit a wall, stabbing into the rising face of others. Every ten strokes or so, when she felt herself moving upward, she would stop and evaluate her position, making the necessary course adjustment. Each breath of the cold night air made it seem like there was a limited source of oxygen available, and her constant exertions to inhale more air made her lungs feel like they were burning. The effort sapped more and more of her energy.

As she neared shore, her spirits began to rise. *Anything on land will be better than swimming in this*, she thought.

Core could now hear the huge waves breaking on the shore, and soon she was able to stand in the rocky shallows. Straight ahead and soaring over the trees was the white light at the top of the tower. Below and equidistantly spaced along the narrow strip of beach were the three lights. Her red light was to the left of the tower; the yellow was directly beneath it; and the green light was to the right. Her feet were numb, but she did not want to chance cutting them on any sharp rocks littered along the bottom, so Core paddled and body surfed on the waves toward shore until she could reach down and touch the rocky bottom with her hands.

All it took was a few feet of feeling the bed to determine that it was strewn with rocks and boulders of various shapes and sizes. If she stood, her first step could result in a snapped ankle, eliminating her. So, she crawled on all fours, the waves pushing her closer to shore and constantly threatening to roll her over.

At last, she reached land and stood. The wind was even stronger, and the flurries of snow angling down at her body made it seem like she was taking a snow shower. Core turned and saw Indigo and Grid thirty or forty yards offshore. Grid had followed Core's line, but Indigo had drifted to the left, and she was navigating a nasty shoal of jagged rocks that rose a few feet above the waterline.

Core jogged a few yards inland and dropped to the pebbled beach. She did ten push-ups, then turned over and did ten sit-ups. Her body was shivering. *More movement.* She stood and did thirty jumping jacks and then, for thirty seconds, sprinted in place while dreaming of an enormous, hot mug of coffee to warm her sore throat and a down-filled blanket to wrap around her body.

She stopped jogging and then did ten more jumping jacks. *That's enough.* Indigo had successfully avoided the shoal and was pulling for shore; Grid now stood in water that rose to just above her hips, but Core guessed that she came to the same conclusion about the bed that she had and sunk back down into the water and started body surfing toward shore.

Core gathered her shaking hands together, and after taking a deep breath, she blew warm air into them. She flexed her fingers and looked at the three lights. She could reach Indigo's yellow light and possibly have time to run back and throw her key, knife, and gun into the water, but by that time, Grid would be on the beach, and either have a head start toward her own light or start fighting Core right there.

In a split second, she decided not to go for Indigo's cache and sprinted toward the red light.

C ore reached her light and stood, gasping for each breath and stooping over a wooden box with a hinged top. She pulled the top open, and, as promised, inside was a skeleton key on a leather lanyard, a .357 Magnum, and a knife—the Tom Brown Jr. Tracker #4 mini, which was equal parts hatchet, saw, and knife.

She wondered why they had given them the mini and not the Tom Brown Jr. Tracker #1, which was the knife they had all become most familiar with during the past six months of training. She picked up the Magnum and pushed the cylinder release forward. Then, she pushed in the ejector rod and a single, rimmed cartridge landed in her palm. Without the ability to pull the bullet and weigh it, she would not be able to determine the grain. Her eyes glanced at the dark woods.

What's in there?

During one of their first weapons classes, they had been briefed on the .357 Magnum and the various loads—125-grain, 145-grain, 180-grain, etc.—and the differences. The prime example of why the different grains mattered was a story of a park ranger who had fired multiple 125-grain rounds into a bear's skull and not killed the bear because the first few bullets had flattened against the thick, solid bone and failed to penetrate. It had taken two more rounds to finally penetrate, but by that time, the bear had already maimed the ranger. Hence, for the bullets to be effective in killing humans and animals, they needed to penetrate and expand, forming an effective wound channel. She rubbed the cartridge between her numb fingers. For a bear, she'd need a hard-cast 180-grain load. For big cats, humans, and deer, a 145-grain bullet would get the job done.

She trusted that whatever grain the bullet in the cartridge was, it would be appropriate for whatever she would face inside or outside the paddock.

Core loaded the cartridge into the cylinder and closed it.

One shot. Don't waste it.

Movement down the beach grabbed her attention. Grid had not warmed her body up and was progressing toward her light like a drunk trying to walk straight down the center of a wide hallway. Core watched as she stopped, almost falling over, and then started doing jumping jacks.

Indigo was just reaching shore.

Core put the leather lanyard around her neck, and the skeleton key rested just above her navel. *The lanyard is too long . . .* Then, as Flo had taught her, she focused on reading the situation and making adjustments. *Your lanyard is too long, and you have a Tracker #4 instead of a Tracker #1. C'mon! Think!* Her teeth continued to chatter. Then, Flo's presentation on the differences between the two knives came back to her: *"And, because of the size, you can affix the Tracker #4 to the end of a pole, making an effective spear."*

A spear.

She picked up the knife and gun and ran the twenty yards to the forest line. Now, she saw it: a ten-foot-high chain-link fence with razor wire at the top. Directly in front of her was an immense jail-cell like door with steel bars spaced evenly apart through which a person could slide only an arm or perhaps a leg up to the knee. She located the rectangular plate of steel with the keyhole and took her key and opened the gate.

She stepped inside and closed the gate behind her and locked it. In front of her, there was a dense thicket of trees—*spruce of some type*, she thought—and a worn path that twisted to the right. She ran thirty yards down the trail and stopped. Looking back, she could not see the gate anymore and was certain that neither of the women could get a clear shot off on her. Core placed her gun on the ground and began searching the nearby trees for a bough that would be suitable to make a spear. In less than a minute, she found one—a limb of white birch. She stood motionless, her eyes scanning the trees around her. *White birch. I might be home or near it*, she thought.

This could be an island in one of the Great Lakes, or I could be somewhere in Canada. If I am, what kind of predator would be on the island? Bears? Wolves?

She got back to work, and in another minute, she had sawed the bough to a length of approximately six feet and stripped it of any remaining small branches. As she grasped the pole, she thought that the diameter was perfect—it was like holding a large Maglite.

With powerful, smooth, and precise strokes with her knife, she whittled one end into a sharp point.

Next, she pulled the leather lanyard and key over her head and placed it on the ground. She made quick work of it with her knife and soon had a leather bracelet with the key tied around her left wrist. Using the remaining leather cord, she tied the knife to the other end of the stripped branch, making a double-edged spear.

Trust yourself. You've read the situation correctly.

She looked down at her right leg. Blood was still oozing from the wound, and some had already slid down and dripped onto the inch of snow on the ground. With the spear in her right hand and the gun in her left, she stood motionless for another few seconds listening. Other than the wind bellowing through the trees, swaying them to make them seem like they were waving goodbye to her, she heard nothing. With her eyes focused on the path ahead, she started running.

A mile inland from the beach stood Worth-Gideon, Inc.'s Weapons Division Head, Albert Munny. In front of him was the high fence that bordered the northern face of the far-left paddock, which Core was currently navigating her way through. To his immediate left was the first of three kennels that respectively emptied into each paddock. And inside each kennel were three enormous wolves who had been starved and fed only scraps of human flesh for the past few weeks. The human meat had come from a spy whom the company's top agent, Flo Fleming, had killed a month ago.

Other than supplying Flo with the gun that she used to kill the man, Munny had not been a part of anything afterward. He didn't know who had cut up the unfortunate agent, and he didn't want to know. His job tonight was to press the three buttons on the remote-control device he held in his right hand, which opened each kennel door, releasing the wolves into the paddocks.

Well, that hadn't been his only job tonight. Thirty minutes ago, he had slid a t-shirt that had been worn by the respective candidate through each kennel's feeding slot. The shirt also had the candidate's blood smeared all over it. Two days ago, Munny had watched as Flo had taken three vials of blood from the lab's refrigerator at the company's office and prepared the shirts. Then, they had been Ziplocked into labeled bags and placed in a backpack that Munny had worn during his trip to the island.

Even though the outside of each kennel looked like a log cabin, the interior walls and ceiling were constructed of concrete. And even still, he could hear the snarling, snapping, and growling inside. Sliding open the viewing port, he saw the three of them, slender but still formidable with beautiful coats of gray and black fur. The alpha was at the gate that led into the paddock as if he knew they were about to be released into the woods. Munny saw a torn piece of the t-shirt in the alpha's mouth as if the wolf were teething and sucking on the remains of the garment to provide relief. Pink saliva dripped from its mouth onto the concrete floor. When Munny had slid the feeding tray in earlier, the three wolves had pounced on the shirt, fighting for it, and eventually tore it to shreds.

The radio in his left hand vibrated, and he glanced at the screen. It was a private call from Director Kerrie Raven. Munny swallowed. There was no amount of money that he would ever accept for being in a paddock with three starving wolves. He wondered if any of the women would survive. No one in the last group had, and his three bosses were anxious to fill the position that had been vacant for almost two years now.

He raised the device to his left ear and answered, "Yes?"

"Release them," Raven's voice instructed.

"Yes, ma'am."

Munny shut the viewing port and then pressed the button. The gate was slow to rise, but when it had opened six inches, he saw three sets of gray paws appear and start clawing the concrete. He looked down at the remote control's monitor and could see the other two kennel doors opening. The growling became louder, and, at twelve inches, he could see three hideous snouts. Finally, the opening became large enough, and all three wolves bolted into the paddock, their paw prints in the snow as clear as black marker dots on a sheet of copy paper.

He spoke into the radio. "All nine are in the wild."

"Copy," said Raven's voice. "Close the gates and return to control."

Munny acknowledged and then pushed a button on his remote control. He watched the screen, and when all three gates had closed, he hopped on his John Deere Gator and sped off toward the lighthouse.

Core's body warmed up as she ran, her eyes ablaze with determination and the primordial instinct to disable or kill whatever got in her way. She wondered where the other two candidates were in their respective cages. If they had not stopped

She was even higher up than she thought, perhaps fifty feet above the bottom where she had started. Her eyes followed the path backwards from where she had come. There was no movement and no noise.

Nothing coming at me from that direction so far.

Core turned and surveyed the woods on both sides of the trail. The pines had thinned, and now the forest looked like a white carpet with a plethora of sticks extending into the blizzard blowing from above. As her eyes searched for any sign of a wolf or another predator, she wondered if there was anything that she could kill to use as bait.

Her head snapped back front and center as she heard another howl, this one louder and directly in front of her. Able to run again, she pointed the knife-end of the spear in front of her and started down the path.

Kerrie Raven watched as Albert Munny entered the cozy control center located on the ground floor of the lighthouse. She had observed him on the monitor as he had parked his Gator moments before and approached the door.

At least he hasn't fucked up anything so far tonight, Raven thought.

Flo Fleming passed a steaming mug of coffee to Munny, and he joined them in the leather office chairs behind a mahogany conference table. Hanging from the stone wall in front of them was a massive screen that dominated most of the wall's upper section. Underneath it were three large color monitors—one for each paddock—and then three smaller monitors underneath each large one.

"They're each approaching the kill zone," Flo said, looking at her watch. "Much faster than last year's group."

Raven took a sip of her coffee and nodded. "Looks like they'll have a few minutes before the wolves arrive."

"Think any of them will stop when they reach the open area?" Flo asked.

Raven tapped her coffee mug's rim with the tips of her index and middle fingers. "Always hard to predict. But it's one of my favorite parts of the evening—seeing them make their decision."

She observed Munny as he set his mug down and studied the three large monitors. Then, she saw Munny's eyes open wide as he leaned forward and stared at the far-left monitor.

"Core's the only one so far to make a spear. Might have one who makes it out of the paddock tonight." He looked at Raven. "And they're all doing better than the cadre of guys from a few years ago."

Raven shrugged to feign indifference. However, inside, she was alive with anticipation. Core had exceeded her expectations. She was durable, cagey, and able to think under pressure. She had handled the challenging conditions far better than the other two, and now Raven would witness if she could kill in order to stay alive. And yet, Raven couldn't count out the other two candidates. This was by far the strongest group since Flo's five years prior.

As for Munny's fascination with the three candidates, Raven knew it was business only. He could appreciate the beauty and athleticism of the nude, toned bodies moving through the wilderness, but they did nothing to arouse him, for he was mostly asexual. The company had known that on the rare occasion when he wanted to have sex, he preferred men, and, like with any other employee, they permitted him to date but allowed no relationships to enter the sharing-the-same-house arrangement. Even with these parameters, Munny was not a liability. He rarely dated, admitting that the closest thing to orgasm was creating an original, innovative, and superior weapon for ending another human being's life. He was even self-aware enough to recognize the irony of getting off on designing and building weapons to kill but not having the stomach to witness the execution of his cruel inventions. Conscience? He had grown the most in this area since joining the company. Like Raven, Munny now considered the candidates as expendable instruments; long before their clothes had been stripped, the individuals had been stripped of their names. Attachment to candidates? Forget it. She knew that Munny had learned this the hard way as he had become fond of one of the best shooters from four candidate classes ago. In the same chair that he occupied now, he had watched her torn to shreds by the three wolves in her paddock as she had begged for help. As a tear had come down his cheek, Raven had slapped his face and said, *"And now you understand."* He had looked away from the monitors at that point, and Raven had placed a hand on either side of his face and forced him to watch the other two candidates get tracked down and slaughtered. His only reprieve each year was that he got to murder the wolves when the evening was over—from a safe distance, of course—but his victory was always short-lived because it was also his job to dispose of the fallen animals . . . along with any human remains.

As for the men who had perished on the course a few years back, well, Raven *had* found their naked forms attractive. But what did that matter? In the training and evaluating of killers, the rules and judgments of even a perceived civilized society go away. In any event, the challenges had exposed the men's overconfidence and enticed them to make aggressive choices at the wrong times. And, because of those mistakes, they had all died horrible deaths that night—her greatest satisfaction had come from watching Jock Gideon's favorite candidate perish with a whimper. Acquiring the island had been one of the company's smartest decisions. Time and time again, the location—along with the *modifications*—had proven to be the ultimate testing ground.

Through a shell corporation named Wildlife Enterprises, Worth-Gideon, Inc. had purchased Michipicoten Island—17 miles long, 6.2 miles wide with 20 inland lakes—in April of 1996 from Ontario Parks, which had administered any matters dealing with the island, shoals, and waters to within almost 2 miles of its shores since 1986. To provide an additional layer of insulation, Jock Gideon and Byron Worth had first created Thresher, Inc., which was listed as the parent company of Wildlife Enterprises, Inc. All funding for Thresher had come from Worth-

Gideon, but the two were in no way connected. As expected, when the Ontario officials had done some digging into Wildlife, all they found was that it was owned by Thresher and that Thresher was worth over a billion dollars. With a fat check in hand for the island, Ontario Parks had walked away from the negotiating table happy. Other than the sum for the island, their only request was that Wildlife Enterprises monitor the wolf and caribou populations. In the early 1980s, two males, four adult females, and four female calves were moved to the island by the Ministry of Natural Resources. By 1992, the herd population had increased to 89. Then, in the winter of 1992, five wolves traveled over an ice bridge from the mainland to the island. Three years later, the wolf population had tripled to fifteen, and the caribou population had declined.

Wildlife Enterprises had promised to regulate the populations.

The allure of basing its training facilities in Michigan's Upper Peninsula, the island in Lake Superior, and just outside of the Township of Michipicoten, Ontario, was due to the area's remoteness and the privacy it offered. The Upper Peninsula was 29% of Michigan's overall land area but only 3.3% of its total population; the island had no inhabitants, and the population in the Township of Michipicoten had been decreasing steadily for decades. When the gold and iron mining industries ground to a halt because of rising costs, coupled with what some residents predicted as the impending collapse of the forestry industry, the economy had thinned and was struggling to rebound. Hence, the latter had provided the perfect opportunity for Worth-Gideon, through Thresher and Wildlife Enterprises, to purchase a large swath of forested land, fence it in, build a complex of buildings out of sight from the dirt road that ran along the property's western edge, and then announce that the grounds and associated buildings were a rustic business retreat for the company. In the first year, there had been some curious locals, but when they found nothing to report to the local coffee shop, the interest had disappeared. The forty acres of land the company had purchased in the Upper Peninsula were still undeveloped but would be used when the company expanded.

For the island, it had taken the entire summer of 1996 to fence in and grade the paddocks, construct the caribou cages, build the holding pens for the wolves, and refurbish the lighthouse and the buildings that surrounded it. The lighthouse had been established in 1912 and staffed until 1988, and Munny had overseen the gutting of sections of the interior and the construction of the pristine command and control center but also the preservation of stone and wood to maintain a rustic feel. The paddock cameras had been installed in the early fall of '96, and the pier—which the motor vessel that had been used to drop the candidates into the water that night was currently tied up to—had been finished just before the initial freeze of the winter had occurred.

Flo's group had been the first to run the course that December.

In terms of recruitment, Worth and Gideon had a list of shell companies to choose from when Raven and Gideon approached a recruit. This year's company had been Morning Bright, Inc.; when the candidates had started the training course in June, the company had been erased. Gideon would notify Raven of the company title to be used when recruiting next year's group in the spring.

Raven observed Indigo and Grid move swiftly through the woods. Because they had not stopped to make spears, they had almost drawn even with Core down their respective trails.

"All three of our underwater panthers are movin'!" Munny said.

She gritted her teeth. When it was announced that Michipicoten Island would be one of the company's training sites, Munny had researched the island and found out that there was a mythological water being, an underwater panther called Mishipeshu (Mishibijiw in Ojibwe) that supposedly called the island its home and was important to Indigenous North American tribes such as the Anishinaabe, Odawa, Ojibwe, and Potawatomi. And ever since the first group had gone through the island course, Munny had occasionally referred to candidates as underwater panthers. It annoyed her to no end.

Narrowing her eyes, Worth-Gideon's Director watched as Munny took over the monitoring duties from Flo, punching keys until the displays rotated, and the three large displays each showed a flat, treeless area the size of a baseball infield that had a path that emptied into it from the south and an exit path on the far side that disappeared into the woods north of the open ground.

"One caribou in each paddock, correct?" Raven asked Munny.

Munny took a pull on his coffee mug. "Confirmed earlier—all in cages."

Raven made eye contact with Flo, who nodded and said, "This will be better timing."

"Agree." She turned toward Munny. "Release one into each kill zone."

Munny's hands clicked away at the keyboard; the three large monitors blinked, and then each displayed a woodland caribou inside of a cage of steel bars that rose perhaps fifteen feet into the air above a concrete slab. There was little room for the caribou to maneuver, so when the animal on the far-right screen dipped its head, the huge rack of antlers clanged against the bars.

A few more keystrokes and the bars began to lower into the ground. "Jurassic Park is still in business," Munny said.

In thirty seconds, the bars had disappeared, and for a moment, each caribou stood still on the concrete slab.

"I wish you'd quit saying that," Flo said.

Munny shrugged. "Why? It's basically the same set up as the goat in the T-Rex paddock, just less hassle. We don't hold the animal underground, so no elevator to worry about, and there's no post and chain." Flo had looked away from him. "Right?" he said, raising his volume.

Raven watched as Flo ignored him.

Then, on the screen, the animals began to move.

The caribou in Grid's paddock bolted forward and, within seconds, was standing in the middle of the open kill zone.

Indigo's caribou turned around and stepped off, deeper into the woods and away from the kill zone.

Then, Core's caribou, which had stood motionless as if assessing the situation, stepped forward toward the open area. There was perhaps ten yards of forest to traverse until it reached the edge of the kill zone.

Grid has a shot. and so does Core, Raven thought. Glancing at the middle screen, she saw the caribou in Indigo's paddock continue to move away from the open arena. *Unless her caribou turns around, Indigo will have a difficult time.*

Raven took another sip of coffee as she watched Core reach the southern edge of the kill zone.

Core slowed as the woods opened into a sizable clearing. Immediately, she scanned the area for threats. She knew an area that had been clear-cut when she saw one.

So, what's the game? she wondered. Her eyes scanned the far side of the opening and noticed that the trees thinned in one small sliver of the forest.

Okay, so the trail picks up on the far side.

There was movement from the left-hand side of the opening; reflexively, she dropped into a fighting position with the knife-edge of her spear pointed toward the possible threat . . . Core watched as a caribou left the woods and began to walk across the open ground.

From her distance, it looked like the animal could have a white rump patch, but the angle she was at and the weather made it difficult to discern. Both males and females had antlers, but a young bull's and a mature cow's were very similar, so it was impossible to determine the sex . . . unless the caribou decided to urinate. Bulls urinated forward, and females urinated behind the rear legs. Core moved forward, and, still being downwind from the animal, it did not notice her. After half a dozen strides, the caribou took a few steps and then stopped.

It began urinating behind its rear legs.

Core took advantage of the distraction and moved a few more yards toward the female. Then, she laid down her spear and assumed a firing position. If Core could put a hole in both lungs or the heart, fatal bleeding would occur within minutes, and the female would drop to the ground fast. If she hit the thoracic spinal column, it would cause instant paralysis, and the female would immediately collapse. Either way, she needed the animal down so that she could slice it open for the wolves. No doubt her competitors would hear the shot, giving them a tactical advantage over her if they saved their rounds, but she had no choice.

She decided to go for the lungs, thinking that maybe it would run off *toward* the wolves after being hit, which would make things much easier.

Remembering what her father had taught her, she raised the Magnum, aimed 6 inches back from the caribou's front shoulder, and squeezed the trigger—just as the caribou started to move.

The female collapsed, sending a puff of snow into the air.

Core's eyes widened. *Must have hit the spine.*

As she tossed the Magnum aside and picked up her spear, she heard more howling, much louder than before.

They're close.

After a short sprint, she stopped, standing over the wounded animal.

"I'm sorry, girl," she said, unwrapping the leather cord from around the knife, "but you're going to save my life."

In a few more seconds, the knife was free, and Core grasped the handle, raising her arm above the animal. She looked into the right eye and whispered, "Shhh . . ."

And then drove the knife in and began to carve.

Once again, Core secured the knife to the tip of the spear. She had done a crude but effective job of cutting open a channel in the female caribou for the wolf or wolves to tear into and begin to feed. Then, she had reached in and felt the warm insides of the animal before pulling her blood-covered hands out and wiping them on the snow-covered ground, making a short trail in the direction of the gap in the trees where the trail started again. It had taken less than a minute.

Now, she thrust her freezing hands into the wound and experienced the warmth once again. She flexed her fingers half-a-dozen times and then removed her hands, wiping them on the animal's thick coat of fur, and when they were dry and warm enough to grasp the spear again, she picked it up and dashed toward the opposite end of the clearing from which the caribou had emerged, still staying downwind.

Height, she told herself. *Gain* height.

A few yards outward of the clearing, she found a birch with a thick branch perhaps five feet above the ground. Above it were branches every few feet that were thick enough to hold her weight. She reasoned that if she could get seven or eight feet above ground, she could observe the wolves, and when they had begun to gorge themselves, she would drop down and move toward the trail.

After sticking the knife-edge of the spear an inch into the ground, she leaned it against the trunk of the birch and swung herself up onto the branch. Then, she reached over and pulled the spear up. Her feet were numb, and she did not feel the smooth surface of the branch. More than anything, she had wanted to rip open the caribou, pull out the organs and guts, and then climb inside to warm up. It had never been more tempting than when she had first dipped her hands inside to soak them in blood, but her survival instincts had motivated her to withdraw her warm hands and forearms and start spreading the crimson-colored liquid across the light layer of snow—like an artist purposely flicking her paint-soaked brush at a blank canvas and watching the paint splatter in a random pattern, flick after flick.

Core climbed up two more branches until she stood at the desired height. The biting wind blew against her face, and her teeth chattered. She held her spear in her left hand and wrapped her right arm and hand around the tree's trunk. *Stay as still as possible until they find the caribou*, she said to herself.

For an undetermined length of time—perhaps a minute, perhaps less—all Core heard was the shrieking wind as she kept her eyes locked on the far trail entrance. She wouldn't see them until they entered the opening, and there was no guarantee that they would all come from that direction—some could emerge from the woods, but it was the best place to focus her attention. Snowflakes continued to come down in a barrage of angled flecks, hitting her body and then some sticking to it. She blinked, trying to keep alert, and moved her eyes over to the caribou. Even though the snow was coming down much harder now, Core could see the dark bulge above the surrounding white ground, and it gave her relief knowing that she would still be able to watch the wolves approach and start to feed after they had picked up on the scent of the dead animal.

Core had just glanced back in the direction of the trail when she thought she heard a shriek.

Was it the wind?

She closed her eyes and concentrated.

For a moment, the only sound present was the same whistle she had been hearing since she had climbed the birch, that of the wind's ear-piercing wave weaving through the trees. She opened her eyes, believing that she was now hearing things. *My mind and senses are starting to shut down. I cannot stay still for much longer.*

Then, she heard a scream so horrifying that she almost dropped her spear. A gunshot followed, and her head snapped in the direction of the other paddocks. *Was it Indigo or Grid?*

Another scream.

And another.

As she continued to look in the direction that the noises had come from, she failed to notice the three large, dark shapes charging across the open ground in her own paddock toward the caribou.

Munny winced as he saw the second wolf lock its jaws around Indigo's left forearm, which she had raised to block the animal's lunge at her throat. Just before this, the alpha had dropped to the forest floor after being shot in the head, spraying the snowy ground with blood, bone, and gristle. Some of the gore had even landed on the second wolf's thick, grey-black coat of fur.

Now, the third wolf had clamped down on the candidate's right calf muscle.

Indigo yelled in pain and grunted, using her right hand to claw at the second wolf's left eye in an attempt to free her arm; she had dropped the knife when the beast had first seized her wrist. Blood shook all over her face as the snow continued to fall.

Munny looked away and settled his eyes on Raven, who was frowning.

71

"I thought she was the weakest of the three, but, *shit*, I thought she'd last longer than this," Raven said.

"Didn't get to the high ground quick enough," said Flo, "and didn't swing the knife while she was going down to keep the second wolf away." She took a pull on her coffee. "She misjudged their speed."

Munny gave one nod because they were right. Indigo was on the ground at the base of the tree she had planned to climb.

"What I still like about this scenario is that it challenges the candidates' tactical thinking while under life-and-death pressure," said Raven. "Because we've set this up as a race, the hunger to reach the finish line first always blinds some of them from seeing the entire situation. And—" She paused. "—we *have* to know who loses the picture and who maintains it." Raven set her coffee mug down, first looking at both Munny and Flo and then looking and pointing to the screen. "This is the only way to find that out."

A blood curdling scream drew their attention back to Indigo's monitor. Munny watched as the wounded candidate writhed on the ground. Now, each wolf had one of her forearms in its jaws and was violently shaking its head back and forth while pulling each arm away from Indigo's body. She kicked wildly with both of her legs and moaned in agony.

Munny reached out toward the volume knob on the control panel.

"What are you doing?" Raven asked.

With his hand frozen over the knob, he said, "I was going to lower the v—"

"Don't."

He swallowed and brought his hand back to his own coffee mug.

The screaming continued.

7

She's either dying or has broken free, Core thought as she listened to the screaming, which had been so clear and horrifying moments before, start to fade.

Then, she heard the growing sounds of growling off to her left.

The wolves.

As her brain sent signals to the thick ropes of muscles in her neck, telling them to move, Core felt tremendous resistance, as if everything above her shoulders was frozen in place. She realized her mistake. She had been stationary too long, listening to one of her competitors face something horrible. Her teeth chattered, and she attempted to grit them but, instead, heard the loud knocking inside her head as her lower jaw would not stop vibrating up and down.

Core swallowed and then continued her effort to twist her head in the direction of the growling; it was like trying to stretch a heavy resistance band between her clenched fists while working out in the candidates' gym, where the three women had spent at least three hours out of every day sweating and grunting while Flo, at first, *tested* their limits . . . and then pushed them beyond what they thought their bodies could do.

A few more squints of her eyes and she had turned her head far enough around to see three gigantic wolves hurtling across the clearing.

Core exhaled in relief as she observed them altering their course to the right. *They're going for the caribou.*

Within seconds, the three wolves stood in front of the open cavity that Core had created, and then one wolf approached the carcass and lowered its snout.

The alpha, Core thought.

Seconds later, the other two wolves joined in, and soon she could hear the sounds of growling and tearing. She felt a jolt of excitement, and adrenaline released into her system, powering her body back up. Pausing only long enough to watch them begin to feed, she lowered her spear to the ground and leaned it against the birch's trunk once more. Grasping the branch with both hands, she swung down and landed a few feet away from the base of the trunk.

She stood motionless, watching the wolves. Not one paused from eating or even lifted its head. In fact, all three had grown more aggressive and were burrowing deeper within the opening in the caribou's flesh.

Core grabbed her spear, scanned until she had located the start of the trail at the edge of the clearing, and then moved toward the path, alternating her eyes between it and the feeding wolves. If she could reach the far side either undetected or detected and ignored, then she would enter the path and back away until she was out of sight. Then, she would sprint.

Her lungs ached as she tried to take in large, calm breaths of air. Don't cough. She knew that her entire plan depended upon the alpha wolf staying interested in the fallen caribou. If it continued to be absorbed with feeding on the dead animal, then the other two wolves would be too; however, if it became interested in her and gave chase, the others would follow. She had faith in her ability to use her spear to keep them away, but it would require her to stop and devote all of her attention toward swinging the spear until she could back up to a tree and possibly climb up. However, this was equivalent to a death sentence—just a slower one.

on her thighs underneath, which created just enough annoying pain to keep her excitement in check.

She also knew that she should not get ahead of herself because before phase two commenced, there was a test she had to administer. And if the candidate failed it, the training stopped, and Worth-Gideon, Inc. would be forced to wait another six months for the next cohort to start the pipeline.

"Everything ready in the medical room?" she asked Munny.

"Yes, ma'am."

She turned her head toward him, maintaining the pressure on the seams of her pants. "We may need to take care of two."

"Understood," Munny said and stared up at the wall of monitors. "I already have a second table rea—"

Raven's eyes snapped up at the monitors, searching . . .

Everything looked normal . . .

No. There. The two wolves who had been feeding on the caribou in Grid's paddock had disappeared.

Raven looked at Flo and then at Munny. "Where did they go?"

C ore reached the paddock gate. She thought about untying the length of leather wrapped around her wrist to use the key but realized that with some coordination, she could just raise her arm and use her other hand to guide the key into the lock and open the gate. However, before attempting this, she peered back at the trail behind her that wove its way up a sizable, wooded hill. Going down it moments before, she had no idea how high it had been.

No wolves.

The woods were quiet; it had been some time since she had heard the screams, and as she stood there shaking uncontrollably, she wondered how Indigo and Grid were faring. Even though they were her competitors, she wanted them to still be alive.

Do they feel the same way about me?

Core did not know the answer or even have a leaning as to how they felt.

Who was it that I heard yelling?

She struggled to place the skeleton key inside the lock, pain coursing through what she could feel of her fingers, but with enough twisting, she finally pushed the key into the keyhole, turned the key, and pushed open the huge gate.

When there was enough space between the edge of the fence and the gate, she slipped through and then closed the heavy door behind her and locked it. She spun around and scanned the woods for threats. The only sound was the howling wind, and nothing in the gaps between the bare trees moved. Propping her spear against the fence, Core went down on one knee and scooped fresh snow into her mouth, chewing until she could swallow. She was dehydrated and hoped that this little bit of water would be enough to get her to the lighthouse.

After one more scoop of snow, she stood up, did twenty jumping jacks, and then felt a sensation she had been hoping for: the urge to urinate. There would be only one chance to use her pee to warm up her hands and try and bring back some feeling in her fingertips. It was risk-reward because soon the liquid on her hands would get cold and start to freeze. But right now, she could not grasp her spear with any kind of strength, and she needed to.

So, she squatted, cupped her hands underneath her, and soon felt the relief of warm pee running over her hands. This was accompanied by shocks of pain as the nerve endings in her fingertips regained some of their sensation. In one quick motion, she lowered one hand and rubbed both sets of toes with the warm urine, yelling, "Fuck yes!" as her toes came back to life. As she wiggled them, she rejoined her hands and enjoyed the last of the slowing stream until it stopped.

Wasting no time, she rubbed her hands together and flexed her fingers five times. Then, she grasped the spear with a much more secure grip—her eyes ablaze with determination.

Time to finish.

Next to the gate was a path, perhaps ten yards wide, that separated the fence from the woods. Taking a few steps back, she could now see the towering paddock fence line that stretched in either direction. The perfect ribbon of pathway separating the tree line from the fence line was like a strip of tape that had been pulled up after having been used to bisect a piece of white paper that had been spray-painted black. The freshly fallen snow made the path sparkle in the moonlight.

Core turned and started running down the path. She would pass by Indigo's gate and then Grid's. Beyond Grid's paddock was the lighthouse. She had heard one gunshot, perhaps a second, but couldn't be sure.

One of them could have a shot left, she thought.

The path angled down and to her right, and she saw the interior fence that ran perpendicular to the outer fence and separated her paddock from Indigo's. Then, just over a rise, a dark structure inside Indigo's paddock came into view . . . a cabin of some sort, but with no lights on and no smoke coming out of the chimney. As she ran by it, she reasoned that it could have been the holding pen for the wolves and that there was one for each of their areas. The back of the cabin emptied down a slope, and she had not been able to see any tracks.

Core continued on, alternating her eyes between the path in front of her and inside Indigo's paddock. The woods inside the fence were dark, with no signs of life. *Is she still in there? Or has she already exited her gate and started on her way toward the lighthouse? Or is she the one with a shot left in the Magnum and waiting to ambush me somewhere along the fence line?*

As the last question echoed through her mind, she almost ran past the gate. Stopping, she scanned the forest inside the enclosure. There was no sign of Indigo, no sign of any wolves, and no sign of a caribou—just falling snow and trees. She bent down and studied the ground just outside and inside the gate. No tracks.

Unless she climbed the fence, she's still in there.

Core rose and kept running.

Soon, she was at the boundary between Indigo's and Grid's paddocks. Then, she passed by another small cabin. Same as before, no lights and no smoke coming out of the chimney.

uttered. Munny was still sitting on the front six inches of his chair and leaning toward the wall of screens. *He's such a child. One moment, he's weak-stomached about the competition; the next, he's cheering for Core to set a new record.*

Flo was busy scribbling down notes on a Steno pad, her eyes alternating back and forth between the pad and the screen like a light switch being turned on and off fifty times in a row. *Like me, she has seen what a training cycle could not predict,* Raven thought. She knew that when Flo completed her evaluation of what she had seen and was now seeing on the screen, she would share her views with Raven in private.

Raven folded her hands and then twiddled her thumbs for a few seconds. She gave the screen a final glance—Core was still plodding along with Grid on her back. Another thirty yards, and they would be able to see the lighthouse.

She whispered to Flo, "Your record is safe," then said, "Albert and Flo, take the Gator and pick up both women. Get them into our hospital and begin treatment. We need to stabilize Grid before we can load her onto the boat and get her to a doctor on the mainland."

"We're going to save her?" Flo asked.

Munny was already up and moving toward the door.

Raven said, "Yes," and paused.

Finishing his jog across the room, Munny exited through the door that led outside. Seconds later, Raven heard the Gator starting up.

She eased her chair away from the counter and then stood up. Through the room's surround-sound speakers, she heard Grid moaning, followed by Core yelling over her shoulder, *"Hang in there. We'll be to the lighthouse soon."*

Raven put on her winter coat and met eyes with Flo. "I found out what I wanted to know."

10

Worth-Gideon Training Facility – December, 2001

C ore sat behind a simple wooden desk in a room she had never been in before. Other than the desk and chair, there were only black drapes that were drawn across what she assumed was a small window and a standing lamp in the corner opposite the wall with the door. The small room had wooden floors, and the walls were painted white—it was spotless, smelling of Pledge. She wore camouflage fatigues with an olive t-shirt underneath. The black boots that she had spent months breaking in through miles of running and hiking were spit-polished to a glass finish, and she maintained her routine of wiggling her toes inside of them for ten seconds once every minute. Her hands were lathered with lotion, and she constantly alternated between flexing her fingers and making them into a tight fist. Most of the feeling had come back. After the island, her hair had been cut and was now wound in a tight bun. She carried no identification, and the sewed-on nametag "Core" above her right breast pocket had been removed—only a rectangular outline of needle holes remained. There was nothing above the left breast pocket.

There was no clock in the space, which did not surprise her since there were no clocks anywhere in the training complex. She had been told that once she reached a certain milestone in the program, she would be given a watch, but that had yet to occur. Her trainers all had watches, which had given them a certain power over her. For months she had been under their control, given tasks to complete in a certain time while lacking the instrument to monitor her progress. It had been unsettling, but she had eventually come to the conclusion that it had helped to sharpen her focus. If she had to guess the present time, she figured it was sometime in the early to mid-morning. She had coffee, eggs, bacon, and toast in the training bay after a morning workout session of sprints, push-ups, pull-ups, sit-ups, and stretching. After showering, dressing, and going through two meditation cycles in the quiet room, Flo had led her down a dark corridor to this room.

Gone were her fellow competitors, their belongings cleared out of the training center's bunk room that the women had shared. What had become of Grid and Indigo, she did not know. Her last memories of the horrible night on the island was of Flo and Munny arriving in an all-terrain vehicle while she had been slogging down the trail with Grid on her back. Flo had jumped out and announced that the event was over. While she and Munny had taken Grid to the vehicle and strapped her in, Core had collapsed in a shivering mess on the forest floor. Flo . . . or maybe it had been Munny, had thrown an enormous wool blanket over her and . . . picked her up?

That had been . . . a week ago? Over a week ago? She wasn't sure of the exact timeline as she had passed out in the vehicle and remembered only waking up in a hospital bed in a dark room back at the training complex sometime after that. There had been a nurse, whom she hadn't seen since her initial physical right before the training program had commenced, who stayed in the room with her, monitoring her recovery. Core had asked about Grid and Indigo, but the only answer the nurse had provided was *"Shhhhhh"* while patting her arm. Then, after a few long sleep cycles, Flo had entered the room, and Core had asked about her competitors. All Flo had said was, *"They are no longer a part of the program."*

When Flo had dropped her off at this room, she had said to wait and that someone would be along to see her. After Flo closed the door on the way out, she locked Core in.

Who is meeting with me? she wondered. *Flo? Raven? Munny? The nurse? Or someone else?*

Core decided to count to six hundred, which would take approximately 10 minutes. If no one showed up, she would do her stretching routine. Then, she'd count to six hundred again. If she was still alone, then she would take off her boots and go through a meditation cycle. She would repeat this pattern—counting, stretching, counting, meditation—until someone unlocked the door. Without access to time, she had discovered that giving herself structure helped her to feel more in control in situations where, at first, it appeared she had no control. One of the hardest lessons she had endured was the least physically demanding. In week two of the training cycle, she had been locked in a soundproof room with no windows or furniture. She estimated that it had taken her two hours to calm herself down and establish a routine to pass the time.

Since then, she had become hyper-focused on analyzing how she spent every minute of her time, her mind scrolling through various thoughts.

What could I be doing right now?

Should I do this *or that* first?

In doing so, she found that she was more efficient—her preparedness at all-time high levels—but still flexible as Flo constantly surprised them with new, more difficult tasks that were meant to challenge their self-selected systems.

Core began counting to six hundred.

She had just said, *"Three hundred and eighty-nine,"* to herself when the door was unlocked and opened.

Core stood up and held the military position of "attention"—the heels of her boots together and forty-five degrees separating the toes, her arms straight down with her thumbs aligned with the seams of her trousers, her hands cupped as if holding a roll of quarters, her shoulders rolled back, her eyes staring straight ahead but taking in everything, her entire body motionless. A five-foot-nine-inch, one-hundred-and-forty-pound statue.

The sleek and powerful Flo entered, wearing running shoes, jeans, and a black polo shirt. Her hair was pulled back into a ponytail. She also wore her usual utility belt, which had a holstered Glock and radio on one side and a Tom Brown Tracker knife in a sheath on the other. She was two inches shorter than Core, but her authority made her seem a foot taller. She held a plain cardboard shoe box in her hands.

Behind her was the taller—a hair under six feet—more robust Director Raven, who also wore running shoes and jeans but was in a charcoal windbreaker and wearing a plain black baseball cap. She wore no utility belt but still donned her chic glasses that framed her dark brown eyes. Neither woman wore any jewelry except a watch. Raven grew more imposing as she approached Core, eventually stopping just short of the edge of the desk directly in front of her; Flo set the shoe box down on the desktop and moved out of view.

Inspecting my uniform and bearing.

Seconds later, she sensed her mentor's body heat and felt a breath on her bare neck. Flo missed nothing during an examination. No doubt she was making sure that there were no loose threads coming out of the starched collar.

After perhaps thirty seconds, Flo entered Core's field of vision once more and took station just to the left of Raven.

"Immaculate," Flo said.

The icy Director of Worth-Gideon made no acknowledgement of the statement, just continued to stare into Core's eyes.

The room was pin-drop quiet for another half minute, and then the Director spoke. "In the box on the table is a Smith & Wesson Mk 22 Mod 0." Her eyes narrowed and lowered to the box, then pinged back up. "Expand," she commanded.

Core had still not forgotten the 10-page weekly weapons tests. If her mind was processing information properly right now, she recalled that the Mk 22 Mod 0 had been covered in week number two. First, they had examined the weapon in the classroom while Flo conducted a briefing as pictures were projected on the large screen behind her. Because a high school friend of Core's had lost an uncle in Vietnam, one of the pictures stuck in her mind. It was of a Navy SEAL with green face paint, wearing camouflage fatigues and a green bandana standing on a path through the jungle while examining the Mk 22 Mod 0. Flo had said that if she or Indigo or Grid made it through the training, they would be proficient in a variety of weapons, but one handgun would be chosen for them as their signature. Other than the Tom Brown Tracker knife, which was the knife all the agents had to master and carry, the gun that was selected for them would be the one they got to know best—the one to keep them alive. Flo had said that her job was like an assistant in an optometrist's office, helping a person choose the right frames from a wall of them.

The weapon choice made sense to her. It was the one she had felt most comfortable with and the one she had had the most success with, landing tight groupings of rounds—center mass and head—in every human outline on the paper target at the shooting range that day.

"Of course," she said, staring straight through Raven as if she was a hologram. "The Mk 22 Mod 0 is a semi-automatic pistol better known by its nickname, the 'hush puppy.' Raised iron sights so you can see over the suppressor, and it has a slide lock to prevent the slide from moving backwards when you fire it, thus decreasing the noise it makes. The original Smith and Wesson Model 39, which the Mk 22 is based off of, had only an 8-round magazine, but the Mk 22 has a wider grip frame to accommodate a 14-round magazine and was primarily used by SEALs in Vietnam to take out sentries and guard dogs—hence, the name 'hush puppy.' It was last produced in 1983."

"Did the one you fired months ago seem like it was made in 1983?" Raven asked.

"No. I would say it was brand new."

"It was." Raven tapped the top of the box. "The weapon in here is the one you fired. If you pass today's exam, it will be yours for as long as you work for us." She paused. "You will have also earned your name."

Her mind wanted to wander and start guessing the name she would take. She had been "Core" for so long now her prior name seemed to belong to someone else, living a life far away from where she was now. However, she could not allow her thoughts to peel off and travel down winding roads with unseen endings. If she failed today, she would exit the program as Indigo and Grid had before her; she would rejoin society, a ghost. So she maintained discipline and focused her mind on the upcoming task.

"Open the box," Flo ordered.

Core did as she was told and soon held the suppressed, black-finished stainless-steel pistol in her hand. She was not surprised to find that the magazine was missing. Even by virtue of making it through the island course, the torture and stress she had endured throughout the entire training cycle was enough to make her consider doling out payback to her overseers the next time she possessed a loaded weapon. And she was now certain that Raven and Flo knew this too. She would have to show that she had not taken the physical beatings and mental abuse personally; it was all part of the game. And only the strongest survived.

"You will not be given a holster, and you will not remove the suppressor and put the gun and it in your pockets. You will carry it in your right hand at all times until you are finished. Is that understood?"

She looked up from the weapon at Raven. "Yes, ma'am."

Raven backed a few steps away and took a step to the side. "Flo?"

Flo moved into Raven's former position. "You will exit through the door behind me and take an immediate left. Travel down the long hallway until you reach the door at the end. Then, stand there and look directly up at the ceiling. A few seconds later, you will hear a beep. At that time, open the door and pass through. You will now be outside. Walk—do not *run*—on the shoveled path across the small yard toward the forest. When you reach the tree line, you will see a railroad tie that marks the start of a wide trail that goes off into the woods. Stand on the tie. You will hear a whistle. Are you with me so far?"

Again, Core stared straight ahead and said only, "Yes, ma'am."

Flo continued. "At the sound of the whistle, your mission will commence. Here are the parameters. The trail is six miles, and you have forty-five minutes to reach the end of it. We want you to aim for a seven-minute-mile pace. At the one-mile, two-mile, and three-mile marks, you will be given your time. If you do not reach the six-mile mark by forty-five minutes, the exercise will be terminated, and you will leave our program." Flo paused. "At the three-mile mark, there will be a wooden box on a stand in the middle of the path; inside will be your weapon's magazine, filled with 14 rounds. You are to insert the magazine and continue. At the end of the trail is another railroad tie. Next to it will be a stand with a digital clock, giving you your six-mile time. If your time is under forty-five minutes, then you will see it reset, and a three-minute timer will start. Standing on the railroad tie, you will see a one-story cabin just beyond a small clearing. Inside the cabin, chained to the floor, is the human target. The door will be unlocked, and you will meet no resistance from the target once you enter. You are to use your weapon to eliminate the target, and it must be done within three minutes. If you fail to eliminate the target within the allotted time, then you will be dismissed from the company."

There was silence, and then Raven said, "I'll leave the two of you for a few minutes." She turned around and exited the room, her heels clicking like the cold beat of her heart.

Even though Core had hated Flo throughout the training cycle, she had grown to trust her. This was the first time that they were alone since before the night on the island.

Flo cocked her head to one side, measuring her.

A human target.

Core had never killed a human before. And in that moment, with Flo's narrowed eyes seemingly scanning her for any signs of weakness, she discovered that in order to take a life, she would need to know the rationale for doing so. And she wondered if that was why she was now alone with Flo.

Were they expecting this?

Regardless, after months of training, she knew herself well enough to realize that the cost of killing without knowing why would be her soul. She recognized that it was the same philosophy for stopping to help Grid when she could have left her there to die. It had been ingrained in her that if she made the cut and was hired by the company, she would be placed in situations where she would have to react, improvise, and live with those split-second choices, and she was willing to accept that. However, she had also sworn to herself that, if given the time before a major decision or action, she would gather information and weigh the consequences before committing. She doubted her ability to kill for sport if, indeed, this was the kind of test she was being given—she didn't think it was. She was also unsure if she *could* kill without knowing why it was essential that her target be eliminated.

"Why does this person deserve to die?" she asked.

"What does it matter? You've been given an assignment. That's all you need to know."

"I won't work this way. I need to know the reasons."

"So," Flo said, inching closer to her, "after surviving the island course and becoming the sole remaining candidate, are you telling me that you're ready to walk away from the company if I don't tell you why it's necessary for this particular individual to be executed?"

Core took a full breath, held it for a five-count, and then exhaled.

If you don't draw your line now, you're lost forever, and you'll never get this moment back.

"Yes."

After a few agonizing seconds, Flo gave a slight smile. "Quite right. We don't need a mindless killer." She motioned to Core's arms, still pinned to her sides. "You can relax."

Core lowered her chin, shook out her arms, and spread her legs approximately a foot apart.

"Please, sit," Flo ordered.

Core sat down in the chair; Flo moved the box to the edge of the table and took a seat on the tabletop. "Last year, twenty thousand people in our country died from overdosing on drugs. In an operation carried out last week, one of the agencies we do work for caught one of the main suppliers in the United States; if I had to calculate, this person is probably responsible for over half of those deaths and over half of the deaths nationwide for the past six years." She paused, exhaling. "Now, do I assign some of the blame to each of those citizens who knowingly put that junk in their bodies? You bet I do. Minus a small percentage who died due to foul play, each one of those people made a decision to tempt fate. However, there is a large percentage of those individuals who wouldn't have been anywhere near those drugs if not for the fact that someone near the top of the drug empire made it available." Flo tapped the top of the box. "That person is in the cabin."

96

Core nodded. "Thank you. This person deserves to die."

"And now we'll see if you're the person to do it. The Director needs to know if you can kill . . . and if you can handle the aftermath of the kill."

Core had wanted to ask about Grid and Indigo since the night of the island course. Since she had just put everything on the line, she decided she had nothing to lose by asking. She said, "Grid and Indig—"

"You'll never see them. Ever," Flo said, cutting her off. "Don't bring them up again."

"Can I ask why I'm still here since I didn't finish the island course?"

"The Director had seen what she wanted to see."

"Did *you* finish the course?"

Flo did not hesitate. "I did."

"What about the other two members of your cohort?"

By the twitch in her eyes, Flo seemed surprised by the question. She leaned back and stared up at the ceiling. "All I will say is that I faced a similar scenario with one of my fellow candidates as you did with Grid."

"Did you help her?"

Flo lowered her eyes until they met Core's. "No. I left her to die—and set the course record."

And now it was Core who showed surprise—blinking eyes, irregular breathing, and the inability to get her mouth to work properly and reply.

Flo stood, and immediately Core was on her feet too, returning to the position of attention.

"Here are two things I didn't tell you, Indigo, and Grid during training. One, every person you see in this business is a threat. Two, don't ever assume anything about anyone." She turned and walked toward the door, saying over her shoulder, "Never forget those two maxims. If you are successful today and afterwards— well, we'll talk then."

Flo twisted the door handle and exited. The door remained open.

97

From the hallway, Flo said, "Go."

In the control room, Raven sat between the co-CEOs of Worth-Gideon, Inc., Jock Gideon and Byron Worth. The room was three times the size of the lighthouse's monitoring space, and Munny was in a soundproof booth where he would provide the viewing experience for her and the two men—all without Raven having to hear his side comments or witness his emotions. If he wanted to speak to them, he would have to push a button, which would light up a small square on Raven's digital panel in front of her. She would have to press it to give him access to speak. And then, after hearing what he had to say, she, Worth, or Gideon could only reply with a nod or head shake. There was no way for Munny to hear what they were discussing in the room.

Flo had her own private viewing room next to the main room, and at the request of Worth or Gideon, she could be invited to join them for the event or just called over to answer a quick question or give an initial assessment. Raven preferred when Flo was invited to watch the candidate's test because she liked having the primary trainer of the candidate close by, and she liked Flo. Worth was thirty-seven—four years younger than Raven—was professional, had decent instincts, and treated her with respect . . . as he should: She was his mentor at the C.I.A. for five years. Gideon, on the other hand, was a political animal and a monomaniacal asshole. At forty-three, he considered himself the elder statesman whom everyone should defer to.

Usually, the first human kill test was the point where the two men entered the training pipeline evaluation (other than Gideon's insistence that he observe the candidates during the recruiting phase). Yes, they saw earlier training footage whenever they wanted to—they had both watched the last twenty minutes of the island footage since this was the first time in three years that they had a candidate who had made it past the stage. However, they both were not happy with the fact that Core had saved Grid. And so, Raven knew the men would be looking for any weakness displayed by Core during today's event.

The ending moments of the island course, before she had sent Flo and Munny to retrieve Core and Grid, had shown Raven that Core possessed a different complexity to that of Flo. It was not uncommon for candidate groups to become tight with each other, although Raven and Flo had designed the training to be centered around competition and not teamwork. But there is something to be said about people going through a bitch of a weed-out course together. Familiarity is unavoidable, but attachment should be. And that is what Raven had found out when Core had saved Grid instead of homing in on the lighthouse finish line and winning the challenge. Core had become attached to Grid. On the one hand, this was encouraging because when a candidate was officially hired by Worth-Gideon, she became a part of a team, and who wouldn't want a teammate who was willing to sacrifice her own life in an attempt to save yours? But, in the line of work that Core would be involved in, the mission always came first. Fellow employees were expendable. Saving a teammate at the expense of mission success was total failure. Now, this didn't mean that you couldn't help someone out. It meant that you needed to possess the experience to know when to do it and when to not do it—when to save your partner's life and when to let your partner die to ensure the mission would be accomplished. That is what they would have to teach Core, but teaching only went so far. She would need to learn to weigh situations and make life-or-death decisions in a matter of seconds.

And the only way she would learn that was through experience.

But to earn the right to gain that experience, she would first have to display the ability to end a human life. In that regard, Core had been behind Grid and Indigo, who, Raven had no doubt, would have done their best to kill Core before she ever dove off the boat that night . . . if only they had gotten a hold of her.

If Raven was being honest with herself, she had doubts about Core's ability or calculated willingness to kill a person. But she had felt this before with recruits—called it her "Joyce Concern."

In the film *The Bridge on the River Kwai*, one of her favorites, a commando team is being put together to blow up a bridge. During the character Joyce's interview, the colonel responsible for selecting the team members holds up a knife in front of Joyce and says, *"Think about this. Are you quite sure you'd be able to use it in cold blood? Could you kill without hesitation?"*

And Joyce replies, *"That's a question I've often asked myself, sir. It's worried me quite a bit. I've tried to imagine myself . . ."*

And after Joyce is dismissed from the interview, the team leader, Major Warden, chimes in with, *"At least he was honest about it, sir. None of us ever knows the answer to that question until the moment arises."*

And now the moment had arrived for Core.

Could Core—Margaret Carol Crandall—kill a human being in cold blood? Raven wondered.

Ironically, the ending of the island challenge had not prompted this query.

No, Raven had been thinking about it from the moment she had watched Crandall cross the finish line to end the Heptathlon.

6 Months Ago . . .

Landon Beach

11

Somewhere over Montana – June, 2001

K errie Raven sat in her red leather recliner in the cabin of Worth-Gideon's luxury private Gulfstream jet, which was nicknamed "Audible," for, like the term's usage in football, it could be, and often was, used when plans changed after a new development. Raven's shoes were off, and she had taken her hair tie out, letting the silky, black hair spread like a handheld fan on the seat's head cushion as she leaned back. A lone flight attendant known only as Mr. Lobby, pristine in his black tuxedo pants, white shirt, black silk bowtie, and white, double-breasted dinner jacket with shawl collar, walked along the lush black carpet of the jet's cabin and politely smiled as he stopped next to Raven's chair.

"Your drink, Ms. Raven," said Mr. Lobby as he handed her a Collins glass with chilled Kors vodka in it.

She took the glass and felt a shiver as her warm palm and fingers touched the ice-cold surface of the glass.

"May I get you anything else, ma'am?" Mr. Lobby asked.

Raven made no eye contact, continuing to study the clear liquid in her glass. She gave a quick head shake, and Lobby bowed before disappearing down the aisle toward the rear of the jet.

She took a sip and closed her eyes, savoring the smooth, cool vodka as it filled her mouth, then rolled her tongue through the liquor a few times and swallowed. She had had one at takeoff, but this drink tasted better. Per tradition, she would have one more later when they began their descent into the Raleigh-Durham International Airport. Once landed, there would be two midnight blue GMC Yukons at the hangar to escort her and Jock Gideon to their respective homes—Raven's estate in the northwestern corner of Chapel Hill and Gideon's mansion on White Oak Road.

She exhaled.

Tomorrow, she would meet with Gideon and Byron Worth at the company's headquarters to discuss the final candidates selected for the training program, which was designed to weed out two of the three and have one final contender for the new position in the company's Rescue and Sanction Division. Angie Stockman, a heptathlete from the University of Southern California who had graduated a year ago, had already signed her paperwork. And so had Debbie Nunes, the heptathlete from the University of Georgia's class of 1999. The final spot was Margaret Crandall's, the heptathlete from the University of Michigan.

Raven opened her eyes, took another sip, and set her glass down. The cold alcohol numbed her back pain from sitting in the bleachers for the past two days. Reaching over to the seat beside her, she picked up a pair of headphones and selected a playlist of Brahms to listen to. Once the music started, she opened the manila file folder that lay on the varnished mahogany tray table in front of her.

A legal pad was next to the folder, and Raven picked up a gold-plated Cross pen and twisted the barrel until the pen tip emerged.

Centered at the top of the first sheet of paper was the name:

Margaret Carol Crandall

Her eyes began to move down the page:

Born: April 30, 1979

Height: 5'9"

Weight: 140 lbs.

Age: 22

Bi-racial:

Mother – Caucasian, 2nd generation immigrant from Sweden, parents deceased, sister, Connie – age 54, whereabouts unknown

Father – Black, 1st generation immigrant from Abuja, Nigeria, parents deceased, no siblings

FAMILY

Father: Ed Marcus Crandall / Born: February 4, 1952 / Died: March 2, 2001, heart attack

Graduated Shelter Harbor High School in 1970

Shelter Harbor Lanes & Pool Hall

1970-73: Maintenance Man

1974 – death: Bartender

Mother: Carol Ellis Crandall / Born: October 29, 1951 / Died: May 17, 1982, complications from childbirth
Graduated Shelter Harbor High School in 1970
Graduated Alpena Salon Academy in 1971
<u>Shelter Harbor Curls & Boutique</u>
1971 – 1981: Hairdresser
1981 – death: Part-owner

Brother: Thomas Edward Crandall / Born: May 17, 1982 / Died: During delivery, May 17, 1982

Raven paused and looked out the window at the darkening skies to the north. Margaret Carol Crandall was indeed a survivor—a survivor beyond overcoming the loss of her father. She had experienced traumatic loss at the age of three and had been raised by a father who had lost his high school sweetheart and his son on the same morning. While watching Margaret Crandall from her stadium seat the past two days, Raven had wondered what it had been like to grow up in that household. Was it an eternally gloomy atmosphere, or had her father recovered to some extent as the years passed by?

She scanned the next few pages and then flipped back.

There was no record that Margaret or her father had ever attended counseling. Nothing had shown up in the review of their health insurance statements. There was also no record of Ed Crandall ever remarrying. Raven was certain that he had relations with women in the two decades since his wife's heartbreaking death, but there were no accounts of any long-term partners in his

There was no data, and employees were forbidden to socialize with each other outside of the company office unless on official business. Raven knew that Worth and Gideon had drinks together at each other's home on occasion and that it was not because they had to discuss work matters. But they ran the company, and they made up the rules.

She always wondered how candidates would respond to the company's other rules and regulations. No one at the company was allowed to marry. To even be considered for employment, a recruit had to be single and have no children. Following this rule had been easy for Raven; she had no desire to bring another being into this fucked-up world. But, more than that, she did not want to carry the burden of being a parent.

She could have provided a Master Class in operating while being subordinate—and being reminded of her forced subservient station—to the two male co-owners of the company and overcoming the obstacles that their secretive, exclusive, and insulated natures presented to her. However, that was a burden she faced alone and would be instructive to no one else in the organization. Outside of the pre-brief before a mission commenced and a debrief after the mission was over, Worth and Gideon did not see or speak to any employees outside of Raven and the Weapons Division Head, Albert Munny. The select few who made the cut and transitioned from candidate to employee were told during their official induction training that Worth and Gideon did not want to see or talk with them. It was Raven's job to deliver the directive of, *"If you see them in the building, lower your head and either walk away or stay put until they pass."*

It was her job to find, test, and hire the best . . . and then send them on missions where they might die. She taught the employees maneuvers for assuming new identities—*becoming* someone else—and navigating the unpredictable, volatile, and opportunistic nature of the twenty-first century as it applied to the company's mission.

We all wear different masks in different situations at different times.

111

She'd had experience wearing a mask that hid who she was every day since becoming "Kerrie Raven." But that was both a figurative and literal mask that concealed an identity that she had purposely chosen to separate from forever. *Can Crandall and the other two finalists do the same?*

Raven sighed. *You're overthinking again.* Selecting the three finalists always seemed like the most difficult part, but it wasn't. It was the next six months when, at the end of it, there would be only one candidate left standing. And it always comes down to one question.

Can they kill?

She downed the rest of the vodka, savoring none of it, and set the glass down. Then, as if her right thumb and right index finger were a pair of forceps, she clamped them down on a patch of skin above the Rolex watch around her left wrist . . . and pinched until her fingernails drew blood.

Can they kill*?*

She drew in a breath and then exhaled, releasing her squished skin.

The plane suddenly jolted, shuddering as it rode through a strong wind current, but soon settled back on a smooth course, which gave Raven the light, sleeping-on-a-cloud feeling. She picked up a white linen napkin and dabbed it in the remnants of the vodka. Then, she blotted the two puncture wounds with it, feeling the burn from the alcohol. Her eyes glanced down at the file.

Can Crandall *kill?*

6 Months Later . . .

Landon Beach

Her mind scrambled for answers. This was not the first time they had kept her out of the loop, and she knew that it would not be the last. What she could not do right now was show vulnerability or anger.

She sat back and forced a yawn, stretching her arms. Then, she walked over to the wet bar and poured herself a double of The Macallan 25. After she sat down and took a sip, she announced, "Even with the stop, she's still at a seven-minute-mile pace."

Gideon glanced at his watch. "We'll see about that in . . . well, *now*."

When she heard the first scream, she realized what he had done. *That sonofabitch.*

Core froze in her tracks.

The screams were similar to the ones she had heard the night on the island. *Where were they coming from?*

Closing her eyes, she concentrated as another horrifying, piercing shriek echoed through the woods.

Left. Almost straight to the left.

She opened her eyes and used them to search the forest in that direction.

There was snow and poles of gray bark rising to the sky but no Grid and no wolves.

Raven and Flo are messing with you, she told herself. *There's no one out here but you and the person in the cabin.*

But then she heard Grid's unmistakable voice, yelling and pleading. "Core? Core! It's all a lie. I'm tied up, and there are wolves all around me . . . I want to go home . . . Help!"

She heard the howl of a wolf in the same direction, then another howl, and yet another.

"Grid! Where are you? I can't see you!"

There was silence, and then the fading voice of Grid saying, "They're going to kill you! Coooorrr ... It's all a lieeeee . . ."

The woods went quiet again.

Core's eyes searched desperately over the landscape, her vision weaving around the trees. Her hush puppy was raised, and she half-expected to see a wolf with blood dripping from its jaws coming for her at any moment.

Again, she could not make out anything other than snow and leafless trees.

She squinted. *Is there a drop-off beyond what I can see?* Pursing her lips, she contemplated taking a quick jog in the direction that she had heard the howls and Grid's voice.

The snow was at least a foot deep, though. *What if I turn an ankle?*

It would be game over.

What if Grid really is out there . . . and I leave her? Can I live with that?

Then, Core's thoughts turned to Flo and the image of her running past her fellow competitor, ignoring the cries as the wolves tore into her. *"I left her to die—and set the course record."*

Core exhaled and turned, now eyeing the path. *Trust your instincts.* She set her jaw . . . and then *launched* down the trail.

Raven toasted the screen and then threw back the rest of her scotch. The anger of knowing that Gideon had somehow arranged for Grid to be recorded after the night on the island was still pulsating through her body, but she had remained in control, and now Core was on her way again.

"Better," said Worth.

Gideon reached for the red button again. "Maybe we can—"

"Jock," Worth said. "That's all we need to see for this stage."

Raven met Gideon's hateful eyes. "More scotch?" she asked, rising to her feet.

Gideon looked away and continued to puff on his cigar.

Good girl, Raven said to herself as she approached the bar.

Core saw the clearing ahead and sprinted. She was certain that she would make it under the allotted time of forty-five minutes but felt better, more natural, going into her kick as she had done in every race that she had ever run.

Her body had warmed back up, and she felt assured, more in control of her emotions. She had convinced herself that neither Grid nor any wolves had been in the woods. For the duration of the trail, the only sound she had heard was that of her own breathing.

Twenty yards from the end of the path, she could see the railroad tie. As also promised, there was a digital clock next to it. And, in the distance beyond, a one-story cabin.

She reached the clearing and heard, "Forty-two minutes and sixteen seconds," as she witnessed the time freeze on the display.

Goal one achieved.

She watched the clock.

It blinked, and then three minutes appeared. A second later, the clock started counting down.

She turned toward the cabin. There were no windows on the front face, just the large door and thick frame around it.

Three minutes to kill whoever is in there.

She sprinted across the open ground and found that there was no porch underneath the sheet of snow. The hard ground ran right up to the base of the cabin. She stood in front of the door and then put her ear to it and listened. Not a single noise.

Soundproof?

She took a breath and exhaled. "This person deserves to die," she said out loud.

Raising her weapon with her right hand, she turned the wrought iron handle on the door with her left.

It took some effort—the door was heavier than she expected—but she soon managed to crack it open an inch.

Immediately, she heard chains start to rattle.

13

The door creaked as Core nudged it open a few more inches.

"Help!" yelled a female voice.

With a quick and powerful thrust, she pushed the door all the way open and saw a woman in a light gray business suit standing in the middle of the room, and for a few moments, Core ignored her as she swept her hush puppy across the space, scanning for other threats. She quickly cleared the cabin's interior as there were no other rooms; the entire place had been gutted. To her immediate left, there were only elbows of piping coming out of the floor and walls in what was most likely once the kitchen. In the far-right corner, there was more piping arranged to suggest that the bathroom had been there. All of the windows on the side and back walls had been boarded up.

Core turned around and looked up. A foot above the door was a video camera and speaker mounted to the wall.

She closed the door behind her and now concentrated on the human target. There were shackles around the woman's wrists and ankles, and chains ran from them all to stainless-steel anchors set into the concrete floor. Core noticed that the chains were taut—the woman could, perhaps, move her legs, arms, and body

123

a few inches in any direction, but that would be it. Her head still had free range of motion, though.

"Who are you?" the woman cried. "What am I doing here?"

Core took a step closer and observed the target. The black heels she had on were shiny and stood out against the concrete floor like two crows standing a foot apart on a sidewalk. The woman was tall and slender, and the blouse and suit fit her perfectly. However, there was a dark stain around the crotch area that tapered off down each inner thigh. So, she had been here long enough to urinate.

She had a large diamond ring on her ring finger and a gold ring on that hand's pinkie. A gold necklace and golden earrings completed the outfit. She wore no watch, and there was no bulge in her pockets to suggest a cell phone was in there. Her tanned face and blonde hair were beautiful, and the only thing that betrayed her blue eyes was the makeup running down her cheeks from them. She had been crying and had tears in her eyes now. When she had screamed, Core had seen her gleaming white teeth.

Age? She took another step closer, the gun aimed at the woman's chest. There were a few thin wrinkles on the forehead and at the corners of her eyes. The chin and neck were mostly smooth, and it looked as if her hands had been recently manicured. So, anywhere from late thirties to early fifties. Knowing that she was a drug czar made Core lean more towards the latter of the two. In any event, the woman had taken care of herself, and it looked like she was married.

How had she gotten involved—

"Why are you aiming the gun at me? Please, talk to me!" the woman shouted, struggling against the chains. "There's been some huge mistake."

Core thought that a minute had gone by on the countdown timer, which meant she had two minutes left. Which, in her mind, meant she had one. She kept the weapon aimed at the woman's center mass and said nothing.

"Just calm down, okay," she pleaded. "I—I was taken. I don't know how many days ago . . . uh, at least a few. They had me in a cell, wearing no clothes, and I was only given bread and water. But then, this morning, they made me shower and put on the clothes that I had been abducted in. They brought me here and chained me up but said I'd be fine! But now you're here, and I've *never* seen you. Swear. To. God. Never seen you. And you're pointing a gun at me!" She began to sob. "I've got a husband and a law practice and two daughters and a family dog. We're happy. They're wondering where I am. I know they are. You've got to help me get out of here. Please!"

In the control room, Jock Gideon snorted. "Funny how they always tell the truth when their life is on the line." He paused, tapping his fingers on the rim of his glass of scotch. "They just don't tell the *whole* truth."

Raven continued to stare at the screen. Gideon was right—the woman, Misty Gale, was telling the truth. In fact, her family had gone to the police and reported her missing three days ago after she had not come home from work. This was because Flo and another one of Worth-Gideon's operators, Rose Varga, had grabbed her that morning right after she had dropped off her kids at school. From reconnaissance, they had learned that it was the one time of the day that she was not being covertly guarded. Her car had been found on a street that had no security cameras, three blocks away from the school.

Do not fall for it, Raven said to herself, watching Misty beg for help. Last week, the beloved sixteen-year-old daughter of one of Gale's neighbors had overdosed and died from snorting what she thought was pure cocaine but, in fact, was crack cocaine. Her boyfriend had introduced her to the stuff after getting hooked on it at a party where his senior classmate, the recognized high school drug dealer, had first offered it to him. What no one knew, however, was that a dozen people above the dealer in the criminal empire's chain of command sat Misty Gale, Attorney at Law.

Raven's eyes drifted over to Worth, who crossed his legs and took a sip from his water bottle. His gaze was momentarily focused on the countdown clock displayed above the main screen.

It read: 1:41 . . .

1:40 . . .

1:39 . . .

"Kill the bitch already," Gideon said as he walked away toward the bar.

Damn, Raven thought. *He beat me to it.*

"I've got money. *Lots* of money," Misty Gale said. "You just have to get me out of here. I know you can do it. You look young. My two girls are *young*! I don't want them to grow up without a mother! PLEASE!"

I grew up without a mother, Core thought, *but it's because she died giving birth to my brother. He died too. How many mothers, fathers, sons, daughters, brothers, sisters, husbands, and wives have you taken away from their loved ones?*

And all at once, her ears blocked out anything the woman was saying, the target's words becoming an echo of white noise. Core took two more steps forward and stopped, her eyes drilling into the target's.

The target's face became hopeful, surprising Core, and the white noise suddenly stopped. Core heard, "Oh my God, I'm reaching you. You *do* understand me, don't you? Woman to woman."

In a smooth, confident, and swift motion, never breaking eye contact, Core brought the hush puppy up and fired two rounds—*tap, tap*—into the target's forehead.

Thirty minutes later, Core stood at the position of attention outside of a closed door in a hallway she had never been down in the training facility.

Ever since she had been picked up at the cabin by Flo in the John Deere Gator, the words, *"I killed another human being"* had been cycling through her mind.

But those words hadn't surprised her. It was the words that had followed that had surprised her: *"It wasn't difficult."* There was no going backward now, only forward.

The door opened, and Flo appeared. "Come in," she said.

Core followed her mentor into a darkened room, lit only by a soft lamp in one corner. She heard the door click shut behind her as they walked past a dozen people seated in cushioned chairs until they reached a small platform in the front of the room. Flo pointed toward a spot on the floor and said, "Stand there, facing me."

She obeyed.

Perhaps a minute later, the door she had entered through opened, and a shaft of white light entered the room. Using her peripheral vision, she saw three figures enter. Then, the door shut once more.

Soon, Kerrie Raven, Flo, and two men were standing six feet in front of her. Flo gave her a smile and a few nods of affirmation. The others remained still.

One man she recognized as the person who had accompanied Kerrie Raven when they had taken her out to dinner in Ann Arbor. She was also sure that he had been the man seated next to Raven in the stadium during her final heptathlon. The other man, however, she had never seen before. He was almost as tall as Gideon but stockier, more handsome, and a bit younger she thought.

Raven stepped forward and spoke directly to her. "We are gathered here today to congratulate you on finishing your introductory training." She paused, and a door to the left of the platform opened. A woman and a man wheeled a gold-plated coffin over to a position one foot in front of Core. They opened it—the inside was empty except for black velvet cushioning. "Get in," Raven said.

She did.

"'Core' is dead, like Margaret Carol Crandall before her."

The man and woman closed the lid.

Darkness.

127

Silence.

A few seconds passed, and the lid was opened.

Raven stared down at her. "From this day forward, you have earned the right to be called Adrienne Astra."

In unison, everyone in the room said, "Adrienne Astra."

"You have been reborn today, Adrienne. Exit, please, and resume your former position."

She stepped out of the coffin and stood in her original place on the platform.

"Now, look into the empty coffin."

She lowered her head and stared at the black velvet cushioning.

As in the banquet scene from *Macbeth*, a ghost appeared before her . . . the woman she had just killed in the cabin—her eyes were closed but suddenly popped open, and she said, *"Oh my God, I'm reaching you. You do understand me, don't you? Woman to woman."* White noise filled Adrienne's ears. Then, two holes appeared in the center of the woman's forehead, and blood started pouring out. Adrienne blinked, and the coffin became a bathtub full of red water with only the woman's head showing . . .

She blinked again. The white noise stopped; the coffin was empty.

"Your job from now on is to put *other* people in this," Raven said.

The director's words hung in the air for a few seconds, and then the man and woman shut the lid and wheeled the coffin away.

"Your mentor, Florence 'Flo' Fleming, designed your name. Adrienne translates to 'dark,' and Astra translates to 'star.' We hope you will live up to the meaning." She stepped toward her and extended her hand. Adrienne took it. Raven whispered, "Welcome, Dark Star."

"Thank you," Adrienne replied.

Using her other hand, the Director guided Adrienne around until she was facing the employees who were seated. The room was in complete silence. "Adrienne Astra, welcome to Worth-Gideon, Incorporated."

PART II

The Moonlight

Landon Beach

July 14, 1970 entry that set Junius on his voyage with the bard. He had the passage memorized. It read:

. . . no other writer hit me with quite the same impact as William S. What a stupendous God he was, he is. What chance combination of genes went to the making of that towering imagination, that brilliant gift of words, that staggering compassion, that understanding of all human frailty, that total absence of pomposity, that wit, that pun, that joy in words and the later agony. It seems that he wrote everything worth writing and the rest of his fraternity have merely fugued on his million themes.

Even before his plagiarized fascination with Shakespeare, Junius had not been much of a reader . . . of anything—certainly, nowhere near Burton's frenetic pace, at his peak, of three to five books a day. And yet, news via the printed form, which still held sway in Greece during his childhood, was not the medium where he had been introduced to the man who would become, in his own words, "his life's work"—to study him, to read him, to know him, and to *be* him.

The obsession had started at age 12 in 1968 when his father had taken him to see *Where Eagles Dare*. The titular character had indeed seemed larger than life, and Junius had sat on the edge of his seat watching Burton, the seasoned spy, in the prime of his life, outwit and outshoot the most historic and everlasting villains the theater would ever know, a never-out-of-season choice for who the baddies were: the Nazis. And even though Burton's co-star was the up-and-coming-tough-guy-heartthrob Clint Eastwood, it was the powerful Welsh actor with the most recognizable voice, perhaps, that the stage, screen, and radio had ever known who captured young Junius's attention that Saturday afternoon in New York City.

As the son of the Greek shipping tycoon, Galen Orion Junius, Victor had been accompanying his father on a business weekend in the Big Apple when, without warning, his father had asked him over breakfast, "Shall we go watch

133

Burton and Eastwood decimate the Nazis this afternoon?" Victor was not familiar with either movie star's name, but he did know that the swastika meant pure evil. He had responded, "Yes, father," and when the lights in the cinema had vanished and the powerful, charming hero of immense and varied appetites appeared on the screen, the young and impressionable heir apparent to the family's shipping dynasty, Victor Lars Junius, was mesmerized.

Now as he walked through the old cemetery's creaky, gray metal doors in Céligny, he minded his routine of stopping first at the grave of the famed adventure writer Alistair MacLean, who had written and published the novel *Where Eagles Dare* the year before the film had come out that had changed Junius's life. After laying down flowers and rattling the keys in his pocket, saying, *"The vibrating clangour,"* which were the first three words of MacLean's novel, Junius would render a salute and then meander back down the long, quiet plot of land until he reached the jagged headstone, perhaps ten yards from the gate, that looked as if it could have been affixed to the end of a giant's arrow. There, the shipping lord would stand and gaze down at the foot of the headstone. If a Welsh football scarf—blood red with a few thin bars of yellow and green spread down the length, sporting a crest and then ending in a row of yellow tassels—was there, he would wait for his contact to appear within five minutes. However, the scarf had to be rolled up so that only the crest and end of yellow tassels could be seen; this was in case another mourner of Burton decided to leave a scarf, which had happened before. If the rolled scarf was not there, he would recite Dylan Thomas's poem "Do not go gentle into that good night" from memory in his best Burton voice and then leave.

Junius watched as Rex took a device out of her pack and started to sweep for listening devices.

In high school, he had read *Great Expectations* by Charles Dickens and found it ironic that the novel opened in a graveyard, the place where all expectations end. Now, he used the novel's ironic setting to his advantage by proposing that whenever Control wanted to communicate with him through an intermediary, that they meet here at Burton's craggy headstone. Hesitant at first, Control had agreed after Junius had explained that he was a Burton fanatic and had bought and restored Burton's old home in Céligny named *Le Pays de Galles*, which meant "Wales" in English, and stayed there a few months out of the year and not only visited the actor's grave but supervised its upkeep. No one would think it was out of the ordinary for Junius to be spending time there. Plus, there were no cameras and no convenient places to conduct countersurveillance.

Purchasing the house had initially drawn some attention from a few news outlets and the usual home-design magazines, but the mystique of the story and the noise from the celebrity gossip machines had soon subsided, and Céligny and *Le Pays de Galles* (he never changed the name) returned to and retained its reputation of providing the rich and famous a refuge from tax-hounds and prying eyes.

The chalet in Gstaad—again, modeled after his hero's—was less private, as Gstaad was less private. The secret was out, had been since the 1960s when *Time* magazine had named it "The Place." Burton's arrival with Elizabeth Taylor in 1970, when they paused their acting careers for a glorious escape from obsessive fans, producers, and directors, was cause for celebration, but what it did, in Junius's opinion, was announce to the world that Gstaad was now the ultimate destination for the denizens of high society. The years that followed would see the likes of Madonna, Prince Charles and Princess Diana, William F. Buckley, Jr., Roger Moore, Salma Hayek, and Valentino as vacationers and part-time residents. Junius knew many of them and had spent time this past Christmas with a tight group.

Other than private residences, the centerpiece of superstar gatherings was the Gstaad Palace, a family-owned, Old World grand hotel with its lobby bar and GreenGo discotheque—Gstaad's first nightclub—where Tina Turner, Michael Jackson, David Niven, Paul McCartney, Sean Connery, Audrey Hepburn, Sophia

Loren, Diana Ross, and of course, Burton could be found at various times over the past forty years.

But, for now, the chalet in Gstaad could wait. Junius preferred spending half of the summer in Céligny at *Le Pays de Galles* and the other half at his native home in Santorini. He would return to Gstaad in September to attend the town's Promenade Party and settle into his chalet until March. However, he was considering buying property in Puerto Vallarta that was very close to the house that Burton and Elizabeth Taylor had owned.

Junius reached Burton's headstone and stopped; a Welsh football scarf was rolled up and resting against the base. There was not a wisp of wind to be felt in the seventy-degree weather. Rex put the device back inside her pack, said, "Clear," and took up station a few yards away from him and kept watch on their surroundings while he stared down at the gravesite. She had yet to discover a bug, but if she ever did, then they were to exit the cemetery immediately.

Because of his association with Control, he was also required to make occasional appearances, "check-ins" Control called them, at the castle nestled into the mountains above Montreux on Lake Geneva's northern shore. It should not have been a problem for Junius because it was his grand estate that he had built there, nicknamed "Burton's Keep." He was not in favor of how his property and blissful mountain retreat were being leveraged by Control—even the reasons given and projected outcomes were questionable. The castle's remoteness and yet proximity to Lake Geneva, and the security Junius had installed there, had made it an irresistible location for Control to use. Everyone was supposed to be cleared out in another year and change; for him, it could not come soon enough.

Standing here, focusing on the grave of the man he admired most, Junius guessed that the summons to meet today meant that there had been a hiccup in the operations going on at The Keep. If right, he hoped to provide a quick solution from afar and avoid having to make another visit to the estate so soon after his last stay there, which had been two months ago. Naturally, he would not be able to say no to the visit, but perhaps Control would allow Rex to go instead. She held more sway with the trainees anyway. Then again, maybe he was wrong about the whole thing, and matters had changed since the current inhabitants had arrived. There was a slight chance that positive news was about to be delivered.

Ah, well, he thought, running a hand through his thick gray hair, yearning for one of the cigarettes in the pack in his pants pocket.

Sometimes, I spin too much over bloody life.

He broke down and pulled the pack of Gauloises, in the classic blue package with the winged Gallic helmet, from his pocket and lit one of the filtered sticks. He was not a three-to-five-pack-a-day smoker like Burton had been, but occasionally, when he was nervous or wanted to feel closer to the actor from Pontrhydyfen, he would shake out a stick and partake. Rex had warned him that he was starting to creep up on a pack a day, but he ignored her. He felt that he was not addicted and could quit whenever he wanted to.

As he inhaled the rejuvenating smoke into his lungs, he relaxed, attempting to quiet his thoughts, which continued to drift toward his mountain complex and the meeting. Then, Rex gave him a low whistle, and he looked up from the headstone and down the row of graves.

The familiarity of their frames, gaits—and when closer—faces, relaxed him further. Control had sent the same man and woman whom Junius had named Mister Johnnie and Miss Walker after they had greeted him with a bottle of Johnnie Walker Blue Label at their inaugural meeting years ago. They were both in their late twenties or early thirties, dressed in New Balance running shoes, jeans, and untucked button-down shirts. When he had first asked them what their names were, they had just smiled, and so he had taken the initiative, which he had a habit of announcing— *"I'll lead here"* or *"I don't wait"* or *"My natural position is out front"*—and said, *"Well, I'll lead here and call you, sir,* 'Mister Johnnie' *and you, ma'am,* 'Miss Walker.'" Again, all they had done was smile in return. When he had extended his thanks for the bottle of scotch, Mr. Johnnie had said, *"A grocer established this whiskey brand almost two hundred years ago. He was wise. Control thinks you are wise, believes the bottle is an appropriate gift to celebrate the partnership, and suggests that you share this bottle with someone who you think is wise."*

"I will," Junius had replied. And so, he had. That night, in a leather chair in his Céligny home's loft, which Burton had transformed into a library, he drank the neck and shoulders off the bottle with Richard, whom he imagined sitting in the empty chair across from him and drinking from the empty heavy glass on the wooden table that sat between the chairs.

The man-and-woman team stopped just short of Imperia Rex.

Junius could see a slight bulge on the right hip of each of Control's messengers. *Always carrying.*

Mister Johnnie nodded and said, "Miss Rex," then made eye contact with him, nodded once more, and said, "Mr. Junius."

He had done this for each meeting after the first, and Junius did not like the smug way in which he delivered the greeting, seeming to revel in the fact that he knew their names but that neither Junius nor Rex knew his.

Miss Walker followed her partner's hello with smiles and nods, but then her face became a dull, seemingly unfeeling, and uninterested wall of clay as she said, "Would it be possible for both of you to make a visit down south?"

Junius knew it was a command, not a question. She was also speaking in the agreed upon code—south meant *north* . . . the castle, to be exact. Even though the area was clear of listening devices, they still spoke as if the conversation was being recorded; the procedure had been in place since the initial meeting.

Bugger. I don't want to. "Sure," he said.

The grin returned to her face. "Excellent. The company will be most pleased."

"The hotel staff in need of some more training, or will this be a social call?"

More training for the staff meant that there had been difficulty with the trainees. *Social call* was code for "Will I be meeting Control there?"

Perhaps it was playful. Perhaps he was bored. She wouldn't know until she got him on the couch.

"Shall we enjoy the rest of this," she said, raising her glass, "over on the sofa?"

"No dessert?" he asked, motioning to the pieces of chocolate cake that sat on the table in front of them.

She dragged the tip of her tongue across her upper lip. "Possibly later."

He gave a nod and stood, then made his way behind her and pulled her chair away from the table as she stood.

"Thank you," she said. *Continue warming and teasing,* she told herself. *Then, get comfortable and pick your moment.*

With their wine glasses both in their right hands, Adrienne reached her left hand out directly behind her rear, which she had molded into a glorious round shape with her snug, crimson dress that barely covered her bottom. He took her hand, and she rewarded him with a sultry look over her shoulder. She hoped that it would draw his attention away from the six-inch stiletto heels she was wearing, for in the right heel was a *real* stiletto blade. A push of a small button on the sole would release the casing, allowing it to slip off, and she would be able to grasp the leather heel and stab with the exposed knife.

They arrived at the couch and sat facing each other with only inches separating her left knee from his right thigh.

She tipped her glass back, and he followed her lead.

As he lowered the glass, she leaned forward and kissed him—a deep, lose-track-of-time embrace. She sensed he wanted to keep going, but she controlled the parting. "I don't want to get clumsy now," she said, putting her wine glass on the table next to her end of the couch.

"For a moment, I thought you were trying to sabotage my tuxedo shirt." He leaned back and guided his glass to safety on the end table behind him.

She wondered if he would try more conversation or make a move of his own. He had not been an amateur conversationalist either, slipping in an appropriate joke here and there as they searched each other for chemistry or at least commonalities. But now, with a little over a bottle of spirits in him, she didn't know if he would possess the skill to invigorate her with his words, which was riskier, or read the suggestions her actions were giving him and keep the talk to a minimum while using his physical gifts. Either way, he had proceeded in the correct order. Talk, then action. If there was a creepiness factor to him, then he had kept it well-hidden.

She did not know how she would work in the taking off of her shoes if he, for example, became an Arnold Toht from *Raiders of the Lost Ark* and said, *"Now. What shall we talk about?"*

Adrienne decided not to give him the chance.

After giving his hand a kiss, she bent down and unstrapped her left shoe. "I don't think I need these anymore."

He grinned and leaned his head back against the couch's fluffy backrest.

She tossed the shoe to the floor.

"Stay right there," she said, giving him a wink. Then, she eased her chest and head over and began to unstrap her right shoe. Carefully, she pressed the button on the sole with her right index finger, and as she removed the shoe, the casing slipped off, exposing a six-inch blade.

Grasping the shoe tightly in her right hand, she looked up at Hugh, who was staring at the ceiling . . .

In one quick motion, she brought both of her hands up, the left grasping a handful of his hair and the right pushing the stiletto up underneath his jutting chin. She would shove it through the roof of his mouth and into his brain . . .

But she didn't.

With the tip of the blade touching the soft flesh between his chin and neck, she stopped.

For a few seconds, neither of them moved—two wax figures frozen in the dark room, lit only by the fading candles on the table.

Adrienne lowered the knife and tossed the shoe to the floor while letting go of Hugh's hair. She rested back against the cushions, and they made eye contact for a second before closing their eyes.

She heard Flo's voice yell, "Lights!" followed by the throwing of a loud switch. The dark shutter of her eyelids started to glow, and she knew that rows of theater lights running along the top of each of the room's four walls had been turned on. When she had entered the space earlier, she had noticed them, along with the fact that the room had no ceiling. Her eyes had followed the open space above the lights up for twenty feet until she saw the steel trusses and metal roof, realizing that she had to be in the pole barn's closed-off section that she had never been in before.

She had been in the other section of the barn almost every day for the past year, where there was an open bay with a boxing ring and a martial arts square next to each other, making a rectangle in the middle, with every conceivable piece of exercise equipment lining three of the walls around them. The fourth wall, which separated the large bay, was a rock-climbing wall. Indigo had asked about what was behind it one day and had been put in a sleeper hold by Flo—the subject had never been breached again.

Adrienne began counting to thirty so that when she opened her eyes, they would better acclimate to the lighting. She heard a door open and then footsteps entering the room. Two to three people she guessed—one was wearing heels.

Raven, Flo, and . . . who else?

No one spoke.

The footsteps stopped, and next, she heard scraping noises that got louder, followed by thuds that were close. She was sure that the two chairs at the dinner table had just been dragged over and placed in front of the couch; this hunch was all but confirmed when she heard two sets of footsteps shuffle nearby, trailed by two creaks that were like the sound that a seat makes when taking the weight of a person.

She reached thirty and opened her eyes.

Seated in front of her was Director Kerrie Raven, wearing heels and holding a clipboard, and Flo Fleming. Standing by the door was Albert Munny.

Raven crossed her long legs and tapped her clipboard with the eraser of her #2 Ticonderoga pencil—the only writing instrument Adrienne had ever seen her use—and said, "Excellent, Adrienne. This would have been a textbook assassination."

She felt relief. Before the exercise, she had been instructed that the scenario could last as long as she needed to get the job done, which had immediately flooded her mind with visions of having to use physical seduction to disarm the man. *"You mean, I could—"*

"Yes," Raven had said, cutting her off. *"Hopefully, you're better than that— especially since this is a first-meeting type of situation. The promise of sex is much more powerful than the actual act in those situations. Let's see if you can leverage it for a quick, efficient kill. Plus, when one is disrobed during a kill, one always loses time getting dressed . . . and those may be precious seconds—life and death seconds. Establishing and growing a sexual relationship with a target is much more useful in long-term missions—more chances to build manipulation into your routine and weaponize it, especially when you can turn it on and off on command."*

At that point, Adrienne had challenged herself to kill him before having to resort to doing anything more than kissing or touching, which she had succeeded in doing.

Hugh extended his hand, and she shook it. "A first-rate job, really," he said. "Great transition from the table to the couch. I loved that you risked turning away from me, leading me from the table to the davenport, but your quick glance back would have given you enough time to react if I was up to something."

"Thank you."

The only thing she knew about him was that he had helped the company before with this type of training. *"You're going to be in the hands of a pro tonight,"* Flo had told her as Adrienne put on her dress and checked the heel release mechanism on her shoe before Flo escorted her to the room. Adrienne's guess was that he was an assassin from a similar off-the-books agency that Worth-Gideon worked with.

Hugh let go of her hand and gave a polite smile to Raven. "Wonderful meal. Anything else tonight?"

Adrienne saw Raven miss his smile as the Director made a note on the paper clamped to her clipboard. "No," she said, looking up. "One minute and fifteen seconds faster than with Rose Varga."

Rose? Adrienne thought. *What is she talking about?* Rose Varga had been in the class after Flo and was the head of Worth-Gideon's Surveillance and Planning Division.

Hugh stood. "But I killed Rose before I brought out the port. We must have eaten faster tonight. The steak was better. Better wine too—I was tired of being chained to Italy the past few times."

But you didn't *kill me tonight,* Adrienne thought. What was going on?

Raven brought the eraser to her lips and tapped it a few times. "Still disappointed in Rose for fucking you that night."

He exhaled. It was the first time Adrienne had seen him act annoyed. "Are we going to rehash that again, Kerrie? You should have stopped the exercise when it got to that point. I even frowned at the bloody camera while she was starting to undress me," he said, pointing to the camera anchored to the wall opposite the sofa.

"No. The lesson she learned stuck with her better because of it."

His grin returned. "Ruthless." He gave a quick bow to Flo and then said to Raven, "I'll be in my room."

Adrienne felt the tension shift as he walked away. She watched as he shook hands with Munny, and the Weapons Division Head opened the door and studied the tall, confident agent as he passed by.

When the door closed, Adrienne looked to Flo, who was now frowning at her.

"I thought you said I was successful tonight, that it would have been a textbook assassination," Adrienne said to Raven.

And now it was Raven who exhaled before saying, "I did say that, and it *would* have been." She uncrossed her legs and leaned toward her. "If you hadn't already *died* after he poisoned your port."

16

Adrienne watched as Munny wheeled in a television monitor, rewound the recording to just before Hugh brought out the bottle of port, and pushed play.

There is no way he did it.

She focused on her own movements first.

At his suggestion of opening a bottle of port to have with dessert, she finished the last bit of her Chateau Angelus and set that wine glass aside. He did the same, mimicking her. The port glass—narrow-rimmed with a tall bowl to reduce the surface area and minimize aeration, nudging one to take smaller sips—*God, I can't stop it!* For the past half-year, she had loathed studying every wine, beer, liquor, mixed drink, and the preferred glassware to consume each beverage in, along with being forced to taste-test each cocktail in ample quantities to build up her tolerance. An irritating consequence of her studying and sampling had been that every time she saw a glass or a drink, her mind would automatically start analyzing the product. But tonight, she thought that her knowledge and tolerance had paid off.

She gritted her teeth. *It hadn't.*

149

Her mind centered on the screen once more, this time concentrating on Hugh as well as herself.

The port glass rested on the table to her right, and she grabbed the stem, bringing the glass in front of her next to the plate with the rich, warm piece of chocolate cake on it. He copied her again. Exactly. He opened the bottle, and she saw the aggravation in her own face, and then . . .

Oh, God.

She remembered.

As she brought her napkin up from her lap, she witnessed him do the same . . . while he poured her glass.

She stared at the screen in embarrassment and horror as his thumb moved ever so slightly away from the shoulder of the bottle—a minuscule tablet falling just after there was enough deep-red liquid at the bottom of her glass to cushion the pill's fall and avoid a careless *tic* sound if it had hit the empty bowl first.

And what had she been doing during this pivotal second?

Gazing in annoyance at his napkin.

I didn't see it. His well-placed mimicking distracted me just enough.

She watched them toast, followed by her sip of port.

"Sonofabitch!" she shouted.

"Pause it," Raven ordered Munny.

The screen froze with a closeup of Hugh grinning directly at the gathered audience, having just poisoned Adrienne.

Adrienne fumed even more, remembering the camera on the wall directly behind her chair at dinner. She scowled at the camera now. *He wasn't grinning at me. He was grinning at* Raven and Flo.

"Now that you understand your mistake, we're done here," Raven said, rising from her chair. "Flo and Hugh are two of the best agents in the world. And, when you are ready, you will be going up against enemies just as cunning and skilled as they are. After tonight, I hope the following is clear." She pointed at

Hugh's frozen grin on the screen. "You must be able to *kill* the best before they *kill* you. You cannot execute the perfect thrust of a knife into the brain of your opponent if you are already dead." She started to turn away but paused. "Everything else was impressive, Adrienne. Focus on that." Raven glanced at Flo. "No more drinking for her tonight. We don't get sloppy after failure. We get cleaner, better."

The director's heels began to click as she walked toward the door.

Munny opened it and followed her out, shutting the door behind them.

When their footsteps had faded away, Adrienne asked Flo, "Did you beat him?"

"It doesn't matter."

"Did you beat him?" she yelled.

Flo put her face in her hands, exhaled, and then slid her fingers down until Adrienne could see her eyes. "Yes."

"How?"

"I cheated." Flo rose and stepped over to the table. "I pretended that I was choking on a piece of steak, gave one of my best performances, really—tried drinking from my wine, then grabbed my water goblet, acted like I couldn't get any liquid down, got red in the face, waved at him for help with pleading eyes, fell to the floor here—" She dropped down to one knee, "—and, after looking at the cameras a few times, he finally came over, thinking that I couldn't actually breathe. I had left the steak knife on the table on purpose so that he wouldn't think I was pulling a fast one on him. He didn't know about the knife I had hidden in my dress's large bow just above my ass. It was a risk placing it there because I knew I would have to kill him before we got to the couch. He would have explored with his hands and found it immediately."

"But didn't you greet him with a hug before dinner the way I did with him tonight?"

"No, I played hard to get. I didn't even let him pull my chair out for me—wanted his hands and eyes nowhere near the bow."

"So, he comes over to help you."

"And I pull the knife out and put it right where you did tonight," she said, miming the move.

"He surprised?"

"Pissed was more like it," she said, getting to her feet. "As soon as the lights came on, he walked out of the room." She walked over and sat down next to Adrienne. "There are no rules. Remember that."

She nodded. "How'd the Director get him to come back?"

"A guy like that can't end on a loss. Rose was his redemption vehicle. I know he claimed tonight that he tried to stop her from having sex with him, but he was lying. He enjoyed every part of the game that night—even made a big show of it when he climaxed. He was lying on the floor with his head almost touching the sofa's bottom skirt. She was riding him, and her knife was just underneath the couch, maybe six inches away from the top of his head. Anyway, he started to orgasm and closed his eyes while raising his chin to the sky in ecstasy, which, of course, gave Rose the opportunity to pull her knife out and press it against his jugular. He opened his eyes, said, *"Damn—got me,"* and she slid off him. Lights came on, and he dressed and left before the debrief. Probably good that he did. Rose thought he was embarrassed, but that all turned to rage when she watched the video of him placing the tablet into her wine glass."

"The hell with him," Adrienne said.

"Don't be too harsh," Flo said, patting her leg. "Raven's right. He is one of the best."

"You ever worked with him?"

"A few times. Once as a husband-and-wife cover."

Adrienne blinked in surprise. "You ever—"

"Sleep with him? No. Mostly cocktails and conversation, some light chat, some shop talk—the art and science of assassination."

"How many times have you gone through this scenario?"

"Only one other time—with a woman. I lost."

"Why a woman?"

"Because my target was a lesbian. No guarantee she'd be interested in me, but I needed to learn how to seduce a woman in case she was."

"Who played the target?"

"Kayla—another agent from Hugh's company. We were both given the task that night to try and eliminate each other. When we got to the couch and started undressing, she got to her knife before I did." Flo folded her hands together. "I was angry at first, but I respect her: solid professional. If that night would have been real, I'd have been six feet under."

"Did it help you on the mission?"

"I'm here, aren't I?"

"Will I have to go through this scenario again?"

"Depends on your target, but if you do, I hope you get Kayla as your training partner. Hard to beat, but she made my mission easier."

Adrienne gazed at the wall in front of her.

"What's on your mind?"

She looked at Flo. "I've never been with a woman—haven't even experimented with a kiss or touching before."

"Goes with the territory. I'm bisexual, so it's nothing for me. You and Rose are straight, so we decided to start you both out on familiar ground for this scenario."

"But—"

Flo rolled her eyes and cut her off. "Is sex a problem?" She did not give Adrienne time to answer. "We fucking *kill* people for a living—watch them take their last breaths in many instances—and we do whatever is necessary to get the job done—anything and everything . . . unless you don't want to survive."

"I know what I signed up for."

"Then you better know how to leverage it. I'm serious." Then, as if a switch had been flipped inside her, Flo laughed. "Do you read books?"

"Sometimes."

"Well, I read a lot. Blow-shit-up, rip-the-enemy's-beating-heart-out-of-her-chest kind of stuff. Telling assassins not to leverage a weapon at their disposal would be like some worthless agent or fragile publisher forcing an author to make her *villains* politically correct. It would be the end of fiction. No thanks. Don't you remember what Raven said before you jumped into Lake Superior?"

"That we're animals."

"Exactly. Highly-trained, aggressive, independent, kill-or-die-trying *animals*. To be the wolf, you've got to kill the wolf. In our game, PC sheep get slaughtered. Decimated. Destroyed. And you know what? Out there right now, the opposition has a trainer like me telling a trainee the same thing. *That* is who we are up against, and their assassins don't go through sensitivity training. Got it?"

"Has Worth-Gideon ever had a male agent?"

"We had one group of three male candidates a few years back." She gave a wicked laugh. "On the night of the island challenge, one got drowned by another about fifteen yards aft of the boat, but then the survivor was so weak, he only made it halfway to shore before dying. The one who made it to shore grabbed a knife, grabbed all three guns, and strung them together in a bastardized bandolier he made by tying the three lanyards together and then entered his paddock. I thought he would be a shoo-in." She shook her head. "Didn't sense the threat early enough; the wolves were upon him before he could remove the bandolier—never even got off a shot."

"I've been meaning to ask you why this year's group hasn't started training yet? Haven't the candidates already been selected?"

"We're not taking anyone new on this year beyond assistants. You didn't hear this from me, but I think they want to see how you turn out before investing in running another cadre through the pipeline."

"Would next year's group be males if they decide to recruit again?"

"Could be. We've also discussed mixed groups of four—two males, two females—and select one of each to join if they can pass the trials like you did."

Adrienne nodded, wondering what it would have been like to go through the training cycle with men—might be fun to knife fight with a man, especially after her partial success this evening. She looked at Flo. "Will there be another debrief in the morning?"

"No. Hugh will be long gone before we get up at five for our run. You won't see him again unless you're working with him or you take my place as a trainer here when I retire. I don't think Raven will ever use someone else for this scenario as long as he's available . . . or Kayla, for that matter."

"What are we doing the rest of tomorrow?"

"Scuba in the morning—cave diving—and then more knife fighting in the afternoon. You're getting better, and the move you made with the stiletto tonight was one of your best, but you're still too clumsy when it comes to avoiding bone when slipping a knife into someone's flesh. I've got you down for five-hundred stabs after lunch; I've already unwrapped a new dummy since you've basically destroyed the other one."

She was pleased and perturbed. Pleased because the scuba diving would be a nice break from her study of alcohol and the High Altitude High Opening (HAHO) parachuting she had been doing. Flo had been with her for half of the jumps, teaching her how to glide and navigate in the air to land at a specific location. The benefit of jumping at a high altitude—especially at night—was that the target on the ground would not hear the plane and would, hence, not be alerted to anything coming down from above. She could jump, open her chute, and home in on her target, which could be miles and miles away. The chances of her being discovered before landing were not good. She had now completed enough jumps to hit her target on the ground with regularity and had not been looking forward to jumping again tomorrow.

The advanced hand-to-hand combat with Flo, wielding rubber knives while wearing safety goggles, had been intense and exhausting, but she had shown tremendous improvement in leverage and creating opportunities for thrusts. However, her entry angles continued to be off, and Flo would say "bone" each time she performed an inaccurate stab. Tearing into another mannequin tomorrow afternoon for a few hours would not be fun, but the morning's dive would give her enough motivation to get it done, and she suspected that Flo had scheduled the trainings in that order for that reason.

"I'll see you at the start of the trail at five-fifteen," Adrienne said.

"No complaining about the afternoon's agenda?"

"No, I need it."

In the hallway, Flo locked the door behind them, and they exited the pole barn. Outside, the Upper Peninsula summer air was cool and rejuvenating compared to the stuffiness of the mock room. Adrienne stepped off toward the housing building and thought Flo would be right behind her.

After a few paces, she turned around.

Flo was headed down the concrete path in the opposite direction.

Adrienne asked, "Where are you headed?"

Not breaking stride, Flo said, "Good night."

Burton's Keep – north of Montreux, Switzerland

Victor Lars Junius stood at the edge of the terrace and peered down four stories at the half-acre of freshly cut grass on the western grounds of his castle. It had felt wonderful to walk barefoot through it earlier, his mind on anything but what he and Imperia Rex had to do tonight. The towering trees rose all around the edges of the lawn, and there was a path on each of the four sides that leaked out of the yard and disappeared into the thick summer foliage. He had wanted to slip on a pair of walking shoes and take the northern path, a two-mile loop that was his favorite, but Rex had steered him back inside. He had showered, rested, dined, and now leaned on the terrace's stone railing and tapped his manicured fingers on the gritty top. The area and pathway lights were on, and he knew from having observed his domain from a helicopter at night that the estate looked like a massive glowing square with tentacles of lights that extended outward in every direction, passing by smaller lit squares scattered throughout the sprawling plot.

Rex, who had been standing in the shadows fifteen feet away, walked over and surveyed the lawn, woods, and winding snakes of light with him.

"I was never happy with this part of the arrangement," he said.

"I know."

His eyes drifted down the western path toward an area of the forest that glowed in the surrounding darkness. "They're lower than animals." He shook his head. "I said it on the way up here. Even with five of Control's best personnel training them, they're out of control."

"That's why we have to do this. We should be back in Céligny right now."

"I know. I know. I just couldn't do it this afternoon. This place is my stronghold. I used to enjoy spending time here. Did you see how happy the staff was to see me? They *love* me." He clasped his hands together. "Can't one of Control's other pigeons be in charge of this wing of the enterprise?" He turned his head toward her. "I asked tonight, right before coming out here."

"Any movement?"

He shook his head no. "I received a rebuke because we hadn't carried out the order yet, and when I asked if another associate could take over this nasty business, I was given the same line that I've been given from the start."

And he hated the line because its logic was sound and irrefutable.

When Junius had taken over StarLine from his father, he had received an ocean's worth of advice, but his father passed on only one guiding principle that had been the cornerstone of the family business for centuries: He who controls the shipping, controls the world—*"as long as there is fuel,"* he had added with a wink and boisterous laugh. As a matter of record, the word "world" had replaced the word "Mediterranean" when the company had expanded to crossing the Atlantic Ocean. Yes, there had been advancements in motorized land and air transportation, and there would continue to be, but even in 2002, the indispensable industry to the world's economic machine was shipping. Generations ago, StarLine was the constant, trustworthy supplier in the Mediterranean, the King of Greece's seven main ports—Igoumenitsa, Iraklion, Kavala, Patras, Piraeus, Thessaloniki, and Volos.

Long before the compass was invented, the Mediterranean offered a smorgasbord of landmarks to steer by, making it a much more appealing waterway than the oceans for travel and trade. And Junius's ancestors had determined that Greece's location at the crossroads of Europe, Asia, and Africa was the perfect launching and receiving point. But they also knew of the vast ocean that lay beyond the Straits of Gibraltar and that one day human beings would learn how to navigate without landmarks. And so StarLine had evolved as knowledge and technology influenced the business. When different kinds of ships were needed to handle the Atlantic and other oceans, StarLine built them before other companies and worked to establish dominance on the seas. Trading and traveling exploded, becoming a global industry, and StarLine was at the forefront. And, as the beneficiary of his family's foresight—and in some cases backstabbing, piracy, and murder—Victor Lars Junius had accumulated more wealth than he could spend in one hundred lifetimes. And yet, still, he had to innovate. Improvements in logistics and predicting weather could always be made, and he had seen a film last summer titled *A.I.: Artificial Intelligence*, directed by the 800-pound gorilla in the Hollywood room, Steven Spielberg, that had opened his eyes to the future. Someday soon, he predicted, his company would be able to leverage this digital tool to revolutionize his business. The day after he had seen the film, he had called an emergency meeting with his board of directors. *"It's all about A.I., ladies and gentlemen,"* he had told them. *"What the fuck is A.I.?"* an elder board member had replied. When Junius had explained it, most of the members just shook their heads in disbelief. Then, the elder, who considered himself the moral compass of StarLine, leaned forward once again and said, *"Richard—oh, sorry,* Victor, *in that type of game, humans always lose. It never ends well for us."* He then tapped the polished conference tabletop with his silver pinkie ring— a tap for each word: *"It. Is. Not. Worth. It. Case. Closed. Game. Over."* Junius had nodded while giving a forced smile, taking his licks, and the board had moved on to other matters. A month later, Rex paid a secret visit to this elder, and the poor oracle had been found dead the next morning—heart attack. The board members were now starting to come around about A.I.

But principles always mattered, and the StarLine executives from Junius's family tree were not the only people who knew and sought to live by the company's one guiding principle. Control also believed in it, which is why Junius had been approached. But, at first, Control was only interested in using certain ships from the StarLine fleet to facilitate and grow the criminal empire's already lucrative illegal arms dealing. This had been an easy move for Junius as other shipping companies were already doing it, but none of them had a partner as powerful as Control. Figuring that it was all just one big worldwide weapons machine anyway, he agreed immediately and received not only the funds to refit and modify the ships—secret compartments and underwater access to them— that would be used for smuggling but also the funds to refit more than half of his existing fleet that would continue normal shipping operations for StarLine. Within weeks, work had started on the ships, and a few months later, the first vessels carrying the loads of illegal arms left port for destinations all over the world. Also, knowing Junius's fascination with Burton, Control had preyed on his weakness and given him access to the most highly sought-after plastic surgeon in the world and set Junius up with a world-class voice coach to feed his obsession with the man from Wales.

And if that is where the parameters of the joint venture between Junius and Control had stayed, then he would have let the machine run and made sure that it was oiled at all times for maximum efficiency. However, he had underestimated his partner. When someone like Control wanted to expand the empire's covert influence by placing mercenary guerillas anywhere in the world that the empire desired, then ships that were already smuggling arms were the perfect vehicle to do so. Once again, the informal meeting with Control had left him thinking that the smuggling of the empire's soldiers, in addition to the secret, sealed cargo, would be a seamless and invisible evolution. It was no accident that the major cities around the world housed the majority of the world's concentration of wealth and power—the exact locations where Control wanted more influence via more *persuasive* methods. Control's argument was only strengthened by the famous economist Thomas Sowell, who observed that *"Given the vast amounts of food, fuel and other necessities of life that must be transported into cities, and the vast amounts of a city's output that must be transported out to sell, there is no mystery why so many cities around the world have been located on navigable waterways . . . New York, London, Shanghai, Rotterdam . . . Geneva, Chicago, Odessa, Detroit . . . Sydney, San Francisco, Tokyo, Rio de Janeiro . . . Paris."* Junius's father had made him memorize the information because, according to Junius's father, *"Don't ever do anything to jeopardize relations with a major city. That is one of the biggest no-no's in the business."* And his father had been right.

Now, Control was leveraging their relationship and the convenience of having ships that stopped at every major city to covertly deploy trained cadre for various missions and then pick them up when the missions were over. One of the meetings in the old cemetery in Céligny had been to coordinate the expansion of the secret compartments to accommodate the soldiers—racks, a small mess hall, showers, and a head. As before, the money flowed in, and the modifications were made. And if it had stopped there, then Junius would have accepted that these soldiers were just more "arms" in the global engine and that nothing had fundamentally changed in their agreement. If the agents were caught or the arms hijacked or the secret compartments aboard his ships discovered, he would claim innocence, launch investigations, and fire the appropriate personnel who had allowed this to happen. And contingency plans were already in place. If one of the secret compartments was discovered, a signal would be sent to the other ships who had them; immediately—it did not matter if they were in the middle of the ocean—the arms would be dumped, and the soldiers would sanitize the compartment and leave. Then, if a hidden compartment was discovered during an inspection, the captain of the vessel was to claim that these were special quarters for company guests. Again, Junius would claim that he never gave the authorization for the compartments, and the captain would be relieved.

But the requests had not ended there.

Control needed Junius to do one more thing: provide a place to house and train the two platoons that would be used.

Hiding storehouses of illegal arms and transferring them underwater to and from StarLine vessels was easy. Two of the reasons were that illegal arms didn't talk and they didn't stand out in a crowd. However, training 28 mercenaries— two fourteen-member platoons—was another thing entirely. Junius had asked in his best Richard Burton, *"Why me?"*

It had been a feeble attempt at clarification, but again, calm and collected, Control had explained why. With some of the organization's senior associates already under surveillance, a new location was needed. When Junius had inquired *just who these other senior associates were*, Control only told him one: Mercedes DiMera, the daughter of fashion icon Gemignano DiMera. The information was useless to Junius other than providing him with the opportunity to crack a sly grin every time he saw the gorgeous Mercedes on television—the Academy Awards, the Met

Gala, the stock market exchange, and making the rounds on all the cable news networks.

He had been trapped. Control held all the high cards.

And so, he had transformed a portion of his ten-thousand-square-foot rustic lodge, located two hundred yards from the Keep's main castle, into a training facility for Control's mercenaries.

But there had been trouble—irreversible damage—and now Junius and Rex were being tasked with "righting the ship," Control's words, not his.

"Are they all in the lodge?" Junius asked.

"Yes. The instructors think I'm coming over in five minutes to inspect the platoons. They know they've screwed up and have been informed that this will be their opportunity to fix their mistakes."

"I am all for using ex-military, and I don't care where they come from, but I will never understand why Control hand-picked every one of these degenerates from the worst prisons in the world."

"I think she realized that she made a mistake."

How does she know that Control is a female? Junius had been instructed to never say whether Control was a male or female. He was sure he hadn't slipped, and Rex had never met Control. *Or has she? Or did she just make an honest mistake? Or did she slip and say something she shouldn't have?* He kept his thoughts to himself.

"And we're here to clean up the mess." He paused. "You're certain that the ventilation system and doors will do what they're supposed to when I hit the button?"

"Yes. Remember, we already tested it on two employees who were stealing from you."

"But that was two people. We're talking about over thirty tonight." They had discussed this earlier, but he still lacked confidence in the plan. And now that Rex had referred to Control as "she," he was even more unsure.

Control wouldn't double-cross me, would she? No. Erase that thought from your mind.

Rex put a hand on his shoulder. "I'll go into the exhibit hall, greet them, then tell them it is a special evening and that Control is here to perform the inspection. I'll go outside 'to bring in Control,' and as soon as I clear the door, you hit the button. It will all be over in thirty seconds."

"What if it goes wrong?"

"Then I'm in trouble, but you won't be. Stay in the panic room and wait. That's why we put the control panel in there in the first place. Hit the master alarm, and that will tell the castle staff to leave."

"What about you?"

She shook her head. "Everything will work, okay?"

"The next instructors and platoons arrive in two days, right?"

"In two days. I'll handle it. You're leaving tonight."

"What? Alone?"

"No. I'm sending Markus with you. He'll be just outside the panic room tonight and stay with you in Céligny until I arrive in a week. Then, he'll come back up here."

She was the only person in his organization that he allowed to talk to him this way. And it was because he had entrusted his life to her care and protection. He agreed with her choice of temporary bodyguard. He trusted Markus. And he agreed that she needed to be here when the new personnel arrived. Until right now, he didn't know that she had planned on doing so. As was his habit, he always provided a way out even though he knew she wouldn't take it. "Are you sure?" he asked.

"Do you want to be coming up here again in a few months to do this all over again, sir?"

He frowned. "No."

"I'm going to kill one of the new team members the evening they arrive—in front of everyone, the first person who shows any kind of non-compliance. That's the way it should have been done with this group. Then you wouldn't have half of them trying to escape the grounds and the other half plotting to kill the instructors."

He nodded and said, "When tonight is over, I'll tell Control that the appropriate message has been sent and that a replacement is needed."

Rex looked at her watch. "Okay, time to clean things up."

They headed inside, and Rex guided him down a hallway where there were framed posters of every film that Burton had ever been in hung on the wood paneling. A maid came out of a guest room with a duster in hand and smiled at him while starting to clean the oak banister of a stairwell to the left of the room.

He smiled back as they passed by her. *She's so* happy. *Everyone here is.*

They turned down another hallway and stopped in front of a door. Inside was a half-bath . . . and the entrance to a secret passageway that led to the main panic room. There were three others in the house, but this one—just down the hall from the top-floor master suite—was the most equipped and most secret. The staff knew about two of the others—in the master suite closet on this floor and in the one on the first floor. Only Rex and Markus knew about this one, and only Rex knew about the last one, which was located off the conference room on the second floor.

"In you go," Rex said. "I set up everything earlier. Markus will be up shortly and meander around the hallway until it's over."

"See you in a bit."

She nodded and then walked down the hallway.

Junius wasted no time. He opened the bulletproof door to the bathroom, entered, and locked it behind him. Next, he placed his right hand flat against the mirror's surface and held it there for one second as it was scanned. He heard a beep and then leaned forward as his face was scanned. Two seconds later, an envelope-sized piece of the wood paneling recessed a few inches and slid to the right, exposing a keypad. He entered his code, and underneath the keypad, a four-foot by four-foot section of shelving holding folded towels swung inward.

He entered and shut the compartment door. He could hear the wood paneling sliding back into position over the keypad, and when it stopped, red-lensed overhead lights came on. He stood up and started walking.

Junius was in a narrow passage, maybe three feet wide and seven feet high. He felt a shock of excitement as he had not been in here for years, not since the last rehearsal when he used to do them yearly before getting involved with Control.

He reached the end of the tunnel and punched in a code on a keypad next to a door. There was a click, and he pushed the door open. Overhead lights came on, illuminating a twenty-foot by twenty-foot room. There was a door on the left wall that led to a bathroom, and next to the door was a closet that had a week's worth of clothing in it. There was a small bed against the other wall, and in the center of the forest-green carpeted space was a chair with an ottoman. Against the wall in front of him was a desk with a rolling chair pulled up to it. There was a control console, two telephones, a CB radio with headset and microphone, and a walkie-talkie sitting in a charging station on the desktop with a computer screen that sat off-center to the right. Above the station were five large screens mounted on the wall, which displayed live feeds from cameras around the property. One rotated through feeds from every camera at the estate; one rotated through feeds from just around the lodge; one displayed the inside of the lodge's exhibition hall where mercenaries, dressed in black fatigues, black boots, and black caps, were milling around; one displayed the lodge's outdoor entrance to the exhibition hall; and one displayed the lobby inside the door that led to the hall itself.

Perfect.

He sat down and studied the console in front of him. On the left-hand side was "the button" he would be pressing soon. It had a square plastic safety cap over it.

He took in a deep breath and exhaled, looking up at the screens and studying the different views.

A few minutes passed, and he focused on the screen with the mercenaries. *Where are the—*

Suddenly, the group froze as six figures, three women and three men, wearing green fatigues, black boots, and green caps came into view. The platoons immediately got into formation, forming two long rows of fourteen members each and a row in front with the six instructors. They stood at parade rest.

His eyes wandered over to the screen with the view of the outside entrance to the hall. Nothing moved.

Thirty seconds later, the impressive figure of Imperia Rex entered the frame. She walked to the door and paused, looking up at the camera. She gave a nod and then entered the lodge.

His eyes moved to the display of the lobby.

Rex walked across the marble floor toward an opening big enough for a set of sliding doors.

On the screen displaying the exhibition hall, Junius watched as the instructors and mercenaries snapped to the position of attention. Then, Rex entered.

She strode over to the nearest instructor, said a few words, and then turned around and exited.

Junius flipped open the plastic shield over the button.

Rex was almost across the lobby floor when a figure came into view.

"What the . . ." Junius said.

It was one of the male trainers.

"This is not supposed to be happening. *Why* is he following her?" Junius shouted.

His eyes shot over to the screen displaying the inside of the exhibition hall. There was no movement. "Fourteen . . . Fourteen, *Five*."

He looked back at the screen displaying the lobby. Rex was waving the instructor to follow her with her right hand as she continued to walk . . .

She was also looking up at the camera. Junius watched as she raised her left hand in front of her and made a motion of pushing a button. The trainer was a few feet behind her and saw the gesture she was making. He stopped and yelled back toward the exhibit hall.

Rex did a quick turn, pulled out her handgun that had a suppressor attached, and shot. A red and pink mist puffed out from the back of the man's head, and he dropped to the floor.

Junius looked at the screen with the feed from inside the exhibition hall. People were scrambling toward the two exits.

He pressed the button.

Immediately, two huge steel doors raced across the two openings and sealed the room before anyone could escape.

Junius breathed a sigh of relief as he observed Rex run out the front door and lock it behind her.

Inside the room, the mercenaries and instructors were frantically looking at the doors, the ceiling, all around. The handful of people at each door started pounding on the thick sheet of steel while others were searching for a way to open the doors.

Then, he heard the delightful sounds of coughing . . .

And then more coughing . . .

There was also shouting and screaming as some of the personnel were pointing at the vents in the ceiling.

For ten more seconds, there was a beehive of frenzied motion across the room—people clawing, climbing, holding their throats . . .

And then the figures began to fall. Skulls fracturing, teeth chipping, necks spraining, and noses breaking as more and more bodies hit the floor.

When there was no more movement, he counted the bodies.

Thirty-three.

He moved his hands to the right side of the control panel and pressed two buttons simultaneously. Just as his eyes had reached the screen again, he saw the crack that ran down the entire middle of the exhibition room start to open. The bodies that had fallen over the crack slipped into the void below when the opening was wide enough. When there was ten feet of space, the two sections of floor stopped. Then, seconds later, both edges of the crack began to lower, and soon bodies from both sides started to slide down the floor and disappear into the darkness below—after a drop of twenty feet, they would splash into a pool filled with nitric acid.

Eventually, there would be nothing left of any of them.

When the entire room was clear, Junius pushed both buttons at the same time again, and in a matter of minutes, the floor returned to its original position. He pushed another button, and on the computer screen, he could see the shrinking red bar that marked the removal progress of the room's contaminated air.

Just as the level hit zero and the bar disappeared, he heard the door open behind him, and in walked Rex.

"Everything good?" she asked.

Junius pushed another button, which opened the two sliding doors to the exhibition hall. He pointed at the screen.

She nodded, looking at the clear room as if nothing had happened. "Markus is heading over to the lodge to clean up the one loose end we had."

Junius sat back. "What did the trainer who followed you say?"

"That the platoons and instructors had volunteered him to escort me outside to see if Control really was coming to inspect them." She sat on the floor and rested her back against the small bed. "It was smart. But not smart enough. They should have had people stationed closer to the doors. Thanks for closing them earlier than we had planned."

"What will Markus do with the body?"

"Drop it down the outdoor chute. After that, he'll clean up the mess on the lobby floor and get ready to accompany you for your journey tonight."

Junius stared back up at the lobby display. The male instructor's body lay in a pool of blood on the marble floor. "Why did they pick him?"

Rex shrugged. "Not sure."

He flipped the plastic safety cover back down over the button and swiveled in his chair, facing her. "I'll call Control."

"Don't say anything about the hiccup."

"It wasn't our fault, though."

"Control doesn't need to know about it."

He rubbed his smooth chin and then motioned toward the screen showing the dead instructor's body. "Is there any way forward that will allow me to part ways with Control? With this whole mess I've gotten myself into?"

Rex ran both of her fingers through the soft carpet. "Only two ways," she answered. "You either retire and let your brother take over as the head of StarLine, in which case you'll have to let him in on everything and probably hand over Burton's Keep, or you—" She paused, looking at the ceiling.

Junius hated his brother, George, but considered him an excellent businessman. After too many seconds had passed, he said, "Or I what?"

Her eyes met his. "You have Control killed."

He thought she might say this. And he had no intentions of weighing in on the subject. Ever since she had possibly betrayed that she knew Control was a woman, Junius had decided to keep his own counsel, but that didn't mean that he could not probe her for information and try to get a read on his bodyguard. His line of questioning was direct and risky, but in order to have the chance of taking a measure of Rex, he had to push the boundaries. But, also, his question to her was genuine. He *did* want to know if Rex thought he had a way out. He was owned, knew it, and wanted to be free.

"You only kill the head when you want to become the new head, and I don't," Junius said. "The other possibility is the lesser of two bad options, but it still leaves the family business in league with Control."

"George wouldn't stand up to Control?"

"He could, but he won't because I've put the company in such a position that, like me, he has no leverage to bargain with." Junius smacked his lips. "There's still too much about the network I don't know to make a move."

"There is a third option."

"What?"

"You could sell StarLine. Then it's not your problem anymore. Still, you'd have to give up Burton's Keep, but you could build a better one."

He snapped at her. "Out of the question."

The room was silent for a few beats. He had not meant to lose his composure, but the thought of selling the company—taking it out of his family's hands—was unthinkable. And he did not want to give up his mountain estate. It would take years to build another one, and those were precious years of his life that he did not want to spend waiting. It already enraged him that he couldn't visit here to relax when he wanted to.

"I'm sorry," he said, wiping his forehead. "I do not like the position I am in right now. Thirty-three, soon to be thirty-four people are disintegrating in a pool of acid right now on this property. I never wanted to be any part of this."

Rex waved off his apology. "I'm fine. And I know. What we just did is not you. It's me, but it's not you."

Junius shivered, knowing she was telling the truth. It was why he had her as his bodyguard. "Let's get the next group off to a good start and see what happens. Perhaps, Control won't need this place in a few years, and things will be better." He didn't believe a word of it. "Last question. Do you think anyone knows of my association with the organization?"

Rex stood, giving a confident head shake. "No. They'd be watching you by now, and I'd know about it." Once again, she placed a reassuring hand on his shoulder. "Go rest in your room. You'll be back to Céligny and your books and your wine and your films and your voice lessons before you know it."

He pushed up from the chair.

He wanted to believe her, but all he could think about was his seaplane exploding in the middle of the night over Lake Geneva.

17

Raleigh, North Carolina – July 2002

K errie Raven parked her Midnight Blue Chevy Blazer in the parking lot adjacent to the six-story brick building that was owned by Worth-Gideon, Inc. She could afford a vehicle ten times the price she had paid for the Blazer, but owning an expensive ride would have drawn attention to her, which the company wanted to avoid at all costs. And so, Raven leased a brand-new Blazer every few years; her Midnight Blue one was less than a month old and still had the wonderful "new car" smell inside.

It was just before 8 a.m., and she took a sip from her Starbucks cup, enjoying her second coffee of the day, as she exited her vehicle and felt the cool summer morning air envelop her. The golden rays of sunshine cast shadows across the lush and manicured lawn that lay between the parking lot and the entrance.

She locked her Blazer, straightened her cream-colored suit, and began to walk across the fresh asphalt and neon, reflective yellow lines of the empty parking spaces while her heels clicked against the pavement. After a vehicle passed by on the road behind her, the only sounds she could hear beyond her heels were of the birds atop the front-lawn feeder, singing their morning songs. The building's windows were tinted, but there were already a few first-floor lights on as the hygienists in the dentist office that rented half of the floor from Worth-Gideon were no doubt getting ready to start another day of delivering disappointing news to their patients. The remainder of the first floor was a physical therapy institute. An optometrist and a family doctor split the second floor; an ENT and an audiologist split the third floor; and Worth-Gideon, Inc. occupied floors four thru six. Raven had been reminded yesterday by the company secretary that her yearly "day of appointments" with each medical firm was scheduled for Monday the following week, for each of the businesses served all the Worth-Gideon employees. It was convenient, efficient, and Jock Gideon and Byron Worth had made extra investments in each enterprise to ensure that emergency surgery could be performed in a fully-equipped operating room located within each firm.

She traveled down the wide, main sidewalk that led to the front doors, but just before reaching them, she peeled off to the left and entered a private sidewalk bordered by two wrought iron fences, hidden by a row of hedges that were seven feet in height. Five yards down the private walk was a wrought iron gate. Key ring already in hand, she flipped to the skeleton key and inserted it into the lock, and the gate creaked open. Only Worth-Gideon, Inc. employees carried keys to the gate, and they were encouraged to vary their routine of entering the building. Yesterday, Raven had gone through the large, glass front doors. The day before that, she had entered via a door in the back corner. Today, she would use the path entrance.

The gate shut with a resounding *CLINK* behind her, and, by habit, she pulled twice on the bars to make sure the gate was shut. She turned, and to her right was a gray box, partially hidden in the hedges, that looked like it housed two electrical outlets. It did not. One flip of the cover would reveal a keypad, which would allow her to enter a code. And if successfully entered, a sheet of bulletproof glass would rise in seconds from the ground between the hedges and fence. She passed by the gray box, and once again, her heels clicked away as she strode along the winding concrete path.

She was certain she knew what the meeting that had been called for this morning was about. And, as always, she was sure that Worth and Gideon had already made up their minds.

Twenty yards later, she stopped under a black awning and took a sip of coffee. In front of her was the heavy-duty steel door that led inside the building. She placed her skeleton key in a black box to the right of the door handle and turned the key, opening the cover, which revealed a keypad. Everyone at Worth-Gideon had a specific code so that administration and security would know who entered the building through this door and when. She entered her 6-digit code and heard a series of clicks as the door's sophisticated system of locks disengaged. She removed her key from the black box, and the cover automatically slid back over the keypad. She pulled the door open and entered.

The building was designed so that there were three sets of elevators—two that traveled between the first four floors and one express elevator for the employees of Worth-Gideon, Inc. that shot straight up from the ground floor to the fourth and could only be used by its company's employees using their skeleton keys and individual codes. However, only Raven's, Worth's, and Gideon's codes enabled them to use the elevator to reach floor five. Hence, if an employee was needed on floor five, they had to be escorted by one of the top three associates. The access to floor six, the private domain of Byron Worth and Jock Gideon, was via one of two locked staircases. Of course, due to code, there were two corner stairwells that ran from floor one all the way to the roof. However, after the building inspectors had left, Worth and Gideon had hired private contractors to install walls and doors that sealed off floors five and above. However, the additions were built in a way that they could be removed if the inspectors came back.

Raven walked down a private hallway and stopped in front of the express elevator. She turned her skeleton key in the keyhole on the wall next to the closed elevator door, and the door slid open. She stepped inside, and the door closed fast behind her. The quick-closing, bulletproof door was another added layer of safety. Once the door opened, an employee or group of employees had only three seconds to enter before the door closed. Once securely inside, then a code could be punched into the keypad to start the elevator, which is what Raven did now. When the last number of her 6-digit code had been entered, the numbers "4" and "5," illuminated in red light, started to blink. She pushed "5," and the elevator rocketed up five stories.

The butterflies in her stomach calmed down as the machine came to a stop, and the door opened, exposing a darkened hallway. As soon as she stepped onto the soft blue carpet, motion sensors registered her presence, and lights began to flicker down the entire length of the long passageway.

She had seen neither Gideon's vehicle nor Worth's parked in their spots this morning and assumed that, minus the men bicycling into the office, which happened sometimes over the summer, she was alone on the fifth floor. Technically, they could have taken a cab into the office, but she doubted it. Even a cab ride would establish a connection between their residences and the company building. She could check the elevator access log on her computer but probably wouldn't. All that mattered was that they would be in the fifth-floor conference room in another half hour.

Raven reached her office door and opened it. The room's lights came to life as she walked in, and she used her right heel to shut the door behind her. The meeting was scheduled for eight-thirty so she had time to read any classified message traffic that had come in since she left the office last night at seven. She had stopped by Second Empire for a cocktail and light dinner before heading home for a dip in her pool. Stepping out of the shower, she saw that she had a missed call, and listened to the voicemail from Worth telling her about the meeting the next morning.

They want to talk about Junius, she had thought. *There's going to be a mission.*

Halfway across the polished pine flooring of her office, she heard her door open and spun around.

In the doorway stood Byron Worth wearing loafers, blue dress pants, and a white collared shirt. His hair was wet and slicked straight back—just like when he worked with her at the C.I.A. and had dressed and showered after a morning jog.

"Came in early," Worth said, patting his trim waist. "Need to shed a few pounds."

Even with all his training, he's still a poor liar, Raven thought.

"Bike in today?" she said.

"Yes, beautiful ride—wasn't enough, though. Threw on my running shoes and took a two-mile jog on the new path. That building on the corner of Willow Drive and Firethorn is going up fast."

She nodded. "Cut the small talk, Byron. What do you want to discuss that cannot wait until the meeting?"

He closed the door with a sly grin. "How come you can always see through me but I can never see through you?"

"Pretty loaded question to the person who trained you—and at eight in the morning no less. Am I being evaluated here?"

"What? No. Of course not."

She always enjoyed reminding him that she had once been his superior. When he had formed the company with Jock Gideon, and they had hired her on as the Director, she thought that she would be an integral part of the leadership team, a valued chair at the table. It had not been the case.

"No one ever knows the answer to that type of question. Instinct and luck, remember?"

He stood still and remained silent.

She tipped her coffee cup back, finishing the beverage.

Perhaps he knows that he's created an exclusive boys' club on the sixth floor. Perhaps he wants things to change. Gideon doesn't.

From the day Worth and Gideon had founded the company, the two men had met privately to discuss major issues before including her. And many times, they had reached a decision together and then informed her of what the decision was before she had provided input. She loathed Gideon, but he was easy to hate. A Yale boy from old family money who had graduated in 1981 and then again two years later with an MBA, Gideon had rose through the Wall Street ranks for thirteen years until becoming bored with it all and wanted new, more extravagant challenges. And so, in 1995, he had approached her thirty-year-old protégé at the C.I.A and pitched the idea of forming a new company. At first, she thought her three years of mentorship would hold sway with Worth. She could not have been more wrong. For, like Gideon, Worth was also a Yale grad and devotee of Gothic elitism and the romance of past traditions, but, more importantly, he and Gideon were both members of Yale's most exclusive and legendary secret society, Skull and Bones. Yes, *that* Skull and Bones. The organization that currently had one of its members as President of the United States: George W. Bush, Bones 1968. His father, the 41st President of the United States, George H.W. Bush, Bones 1948, was also a member. And there were rumblings in the halls of Congress that another member, Senator John Kerry, Bones 1966, was eyeing a run at the White House in 2004.

She never had a chance of keeping him with her, and after Gideon had paved Worth's exit with cash, Worth had been allowed to leave the Company a month later. Raven thought she would never see her protégé again.

However, she was surprised in early 1996 when Worth called her to meet him for a drink in the Hay-Adams Hotel bar "Off the Record." And that is where the trap had been set. He had talked about the new company, the wealth it would generate, and the interesting work that would be done, but her guard was up, and she thought the conversation would end with them trying to use her. However, he had paused at that point, locked eyes with her and said, *"What we need is someone with more experience than I have working with the intelligence apparatuses around town so that we can copy their methods and then upgrade them to our purposes. Of course, we are looking for someone with connections too."* Then, he had shrugged and looked down into his Martini and said, *"Know anyone like that who wants to get rich?"*

And she had fallen for it. He knew that she had been passed over at the C.I.A. numerous times, and what he offered her in the bar where people go "to be seen and not heard" was a cushy director's job with a pathway to becoming a co-owner with him and Gideon. When he had worked for her, she had thought that he had the best hiring sense that she had ever seen, but she had never imagined that his charm would be deployed to attract her. But that was all long ago when she was a top C.I.A. analyst named Carrie Lockwood, who had mentored a former Marine named Bryan Mercer, who was four years her junior.

Before Jack Wetherington had become Jock Gideon.

And before the three of them had undergone plastic surgery after their previous selves had all perished quietly—Mercer in a car accident, Wetherington by an accidental overdose two months later, and herself after a short battle with cancer one month after Wetherington. None of their deaths had received much attention. Bryan Mercer had been a Marine who died of bad luck; Jack Wetherington had been a man with great promise who had succumbed to the evil vices of working on Wall Street for so many years—his death was an embarrassment to his firm and would have also been to his parents if they had been alive to witness his downfall; and Carrie Lockwood had been a forgettable analyst for the C.I.A. who had perished like so many others to the indiscriminate killer of millions, the dreaded "C" word. The short obituaries in Maine, New Jersey, and Michigan stated that each body had been cremated. Between the three of them, there were no siblings, no parents, and only an estranged aunt and uncle of Wetherington's that he had not seen since he was six years old.

Now, looking at Worth, trying to stand innocently in her office before a big meeting, she wondered if the time was right to drop the bomb that she was thinking of leaving the company. The money had been more than adequate so far, three times what her salary was at the C.I.A., but the lack of involvement in decisions that were made concerning an area of the company that *she* oversaw, missions outside of the United States, was making the enormous salary she enjoyed less and less attractive.

Money without power was sex without a partner.

And she had no one to blame but herself for not seeing the close bond that Worth and Gideon shared until after she had transformed herself from Carrie Lockwood into Kerrie Raven. If she had seen it from the beginning, she would have known that the Skull and Bones bond would never allow them to invite her into their private realm on the office building's top floor and neither permit her to become a co-owner of the company nor a partner who would ever be privy to the reasoning behind many of their decisions. However, she had always wondered why they had sacrificed the exclusive connections and support network available through their membership in Skull and Bones. They had given up a lot by killing their former selves. Naturally, she was closer to Worth and thought she would broach the subject with him when the time was right. But that was before she had seen the endgame. Now, she didn't care what they had forfeited by assuming new identities.

Regardless, for months she had been feeling the guilt of her irreversible decision to alter her body and change her name years before. Carrie Lockwood was dead. There was only Kerrie Raven now. And Kerrie Raven had the perfect teeth and jaw alignment, the perfect cheekbones, the perfect bust, and the perfect hairline with thick black hair that Carrie Lockwood had always wanted. Carrie Lockwood had a set of crooked teeth filled with gaps, unbalanced cheekbones, suffered from a severe overbite, and had a rare case of early female-pattern baldness. Her parents had offered to help with her teeth and jaw when she was young, but she had refused . . . and then been told by her mother, *"There will not be a second chance."* And so, lying on the operating table at 36, her mother's words had run through her brain just before she had been sedated to undergo orthognathic surgery, waking up to a jaw properly aligned with plates and screws. When she had recovered enough to safely have the next surgeries, she had undergone the breast augmentation and started a series of three hair transplants—all under an assumed name and paid for with money from an offshore account that Wetherington had set up. Then, the final round of alterations—cheek and laser eye surgeries—had taken place. A year later, she had looked at herself in the mirror and said, *"Carrie Maria Lockwood is gone forever."* Now, seeing that she would never have an opportunity to join Worth and Gideon as an owner of the company, she found herself daydreaming about becoming Carrie Lockwood again and perhaps joining a university on the staff of its Political Science Department where she could relax and spend the rest of her career teaching the philosophy and mechanisms of democracy that ran counter to the things she had been allowed to witness in the past five years working at Worth-Gideon, things she had now become desensitized to.

Just as she had been passed over numerous times at the C.I.A., she felt that she had been passed over here, which skewed every failure and inaction back to herself. She regretted abandoning Carrie Lockwood for Kerrie Raven. She had wanted to slow down in her mid-thirties and fix the inner Carrie Lockwood; instead, she had "fixed" the outer Carrie Lockwood, and the inner Carrie Lockwood had remained unfinished.

Worth finally spoke. "Flo's training of Adrienne has been something else. You were dead-on when you spotted her, and I cannot blame you since you both originated from the same state."

He was using a classic maneuver—one she had taught him. Lubricating a quick shift in topic with charm to backpedal for a moment before advancing the original line of thought. Center until you feel firm ground. And then proceed.

But just as she was going to parry with her own shift in topic, something clicked, and she felt a rush of heat throughout her body.

Adrienne Astra.

Core.

Margaret Carol Crandall.

She was the first candidate from the Great Lakes State that Worth-Gideon had ever considered recruiting, but Raven had insisted that there was no emotional attachment to the girl's origins. And that remained true. But . . . she now realized that there *was* an emotional attachment involved: Raven to her former life.

Raven had grown up in the suburbs of Lansing, the daughter of a State Senator mother and an Attorney-At-Law father, and, yes, she had attended Michigan State—bachelor's in business, MBA, and then a Ph.D. in Political Science, her dissertation on election fraud. And for the past half-decade, she had stored that information, her past, in a coffin along with the memories of Carrie Lockwood. But for months now, she had sought out those memories and details of her former life and used them as fuel for a possible departure. And yet, until this moment, she had not been able to point to what had led her on this nostalgic journey.

"Adrienne continues to grow," Raven said. "But that's not what you came in here to discuss, is it?"

As he raised his hands in submission, the overhead light reflected off the golden Cross of Lorraine, the double cross, set into the round black face of his gold ring. It was the team ring that Magnum, T.C. and Rick had worn in the TV show *Magnum P.I.* and had caught her attention the first time she met with Worth after she, Gideon, and Worth had recovered from plastic surgery and assumed their new names. Not only had she been a fan of the TV show when she had been Carrie Lockwood, but one of her first cases while working for the C.I.A. had involved a veteran of the U.S. Army's 79th Infantry Division, which had distinguished itself at Montfaucon, in Lorraine, during the first World War and selected the Cross of Lorraine as its insignia; the 79th became known as the "Cross of Lorraine Division." It was also used by the Free French Forces in World War II, becoming a symbol of the French resistance. Worth had been impressed with her knowledge and explained that he watched the show in high school and college and became a Marine officer because of it. He had never worn the ring while serving in Desert Storm but thought it was appropriate now that he was someone else running a clandestine organization.

Gideon also wore the ring. He had no affiliation with or affection for the military and had not been a fan of the show. *"That decade just needs to go away,"* he had said, claiming that his reason for wearing the ring was because of the origins of the "double cross." In fact, he had stood in the hallway outside her office and lectured her and Worth. *"First, if you are going to base your style off what you see on the screen, which is so basic, at least go back further than the ridiculous 1980s. Try* Casablanca. *As a member of the French resistance, Berger wore it and showed it to Lazlo, remember?"* Then, Gideon had waved his hand. *"But forget the media.* Real *history matters. The Knights Templar used it, and so did Joan of Arc."* He had smirked at Worth. *"Long before* Magnum *did."* She had ended the conversation with, *"But, Jock, you didn't come up with the idea of wearing the ring. You just copied Byron."*

As Worth walked across the room, he dropped his hands and let them swing, the ring appearing and disappearing with each pendulum-like motion. He stopped a few paces in front of her and ran the fingers of his right hand slowly across his mouth and chin while squinting and exhaling through his nose—she imagined he was performing a final rehearsal of the words going through his mind before sharing them.

He spoke in an even and quiet tone. "Because of Flo's *situation*, do you think she will be able to handle a few months away, developing a cover, and then another couple of months in Europe?"

And this was why he had come in early to speak with her before Gideon arrived: Flo's situation. It was the one secret they had kept from Gideon.

"Is Jock even going to make the meeting?" she asked. Raven knew that Gideon had been at an annual summer retreat with executives from Microsoft, AT&T, Amazon, Berkshire Hathaway, Playboy Enterprises, Sony, Apple, Disney, the Rand Corporation, ESPN, Google, Yahoo, the *New York Times*, the *Washington Post*, and other top-tier companies.

"He should," Worth replied, giving his Breitling watch a glance.

"Why does he even go every year?" She had never asked because she didn't care. However, having Worth answer her right now gave her more time to think about answering his original question, which she had known he would ask one day. She just didn't think it would be today. Then again, she had trained him to maintain a certain level of unpredictability and to leverage it at specific moments.

"It's the one touchpoint with that circle that we still allow. Those companies might appear benevolent, but one, they're loaded, and two, they have the infrastructure to influence people that our company might want to be influenced."

"But why him and not you? He chose to leave those people."

Worth nodded in agreement. "Simple. He still knows how to navigate that world, and they don't know who he was before. As you know, we've done a few favors for some of the CEOs the past two years—ahem, *Archer, Inc.*—and they make sure our company gets an invite."

"Ah yes, Archer. Almost forgot that the chief rival to Yahoo and Google went under after that fiasco with their CEO and CFO. All Flo." *God Damn him!*

He led me straight into that one. I'm not ready to talk about her yet. Redirect! "But does anything actually get accomplished while Gideon's at these retreats?"

"Not much. The key word is *retreat*, and that is the only word that trumps the word *conference* in terms of not getting anything accomplished during a gathering of professionals. It's all about status. And you get that by being invited. The entire weekend is ten percent meetings and ninety percent summer camp, just with billionaires. Gideon said that most of the informal discussions center around gloating about who wasn't invited to the retreat and the possible reasons why." There was silence for a few seconds, and he rubbed the tip of his left index finger in circles over the top of his ring. "Now, what about Flo?"

His explanation of the annual retreat had given her enough time to weigh the risks and rewards of putting Flo in the field for an extended period. "She'll be able to handle it, and she's the right person to send."

"No reservations?"

"I didn't say that."

"So, you'll keep an eye on things while she's gone?"

Raven scoffed. "Well, you're not going to." She expected a grin of embarrassment in return, and she got it.

"You're right. I shouldn't have asked."

"Who were you going to suggest if I said Flo needed a break? Not Rose Varga, for Christ's sake."

Worth laughed. "Of course not."

Did he mean it?

"I was thinking of Adrienne."

"She's not ready yet."

He raised his eyebrows. "Gideon hasn't been paying attention, but I have. She's close."

"And Flo and I will tell you when that day comes."

"What about when Flo is gone for the next four to six months?"

"I'll be working with her."

"And if we need to use her?"

"Then we'll talk, right?"

Worth straightened the gold-plated Cross pen in his shirt pocket. "Right." He let his hand drop down to his side. "How are the new assistants coming along?"

Typical Byron. Moving back into safe territory after exploring unknown regions. However, what he had asked was important. The company was relatively new, but steps were already being taken to build a structure that would be stable, reward loyalty, and, most of all, *last*. Here, she agreed with the two co-owners. Turnover would be bad, and without an initial fresh supply of young talent, the company would die a slow death. It needed to be self-sustaining and dynamic, and those qualities did not come from hubris or waiting for the right person to come along.

Which was why Raven had been involved in recruiting since day one. "They're fine," she answered. "Rose says that Kristy Cummings is more than capable, and Albert Munny thinks Ulysses King is the only person he would even consider turning the Weapons Division over to when he retires."

"How old is Munny again?"

"Forty-five."

"And King?"

"Twenty-six."

"How serious is it between him and that talk show host?"

"Doctor Michael?"

"Yeah. The guy who ends every show with, 'You've faced yourself today.'"

"Didn't know you'd seen it."

"Fuck," Worth said, rolling his eyes. "Good one. I can't stop watching. Have *you* seen it?"

She hated when he admitted to being one-upped because it meant that he had the self-assuredness to be openly vulnerable, which made him even more attractive than he already was. There had never been anything between them, but that didn't mean that she had never thought about it. And because she was considering leaving the company, it was pissing her off that she was thinking about what a night alone with him might look like. And those thoughts were making her lips betray her conscience with a slight grin. "I've seen the show."

He exhaled, giving the impression that he was relieved. "Then you know what I'm talking about."

"He's a good host, and, yes, I think he and Mr. King will remain a couple for some time. Is that a problem?"

"For me? No. For the company?" He eyeballed her. "Relationships equal distractions, and distractions usually equal death in our business. Agree?"

"Yes," she said, looking away.

"Munny know about King's boyfriend?"

By nature, Gideon was more the gossip hound, Worth the quiet professional. But when it came to personnel within the company, Worth wanted information. The irony, of course, was that he wanted no one to know anything about *him*.

"Yes. He's not interested in King, if that's what you're asking."

"No, it's not. I was just curious." He paused. "Do you think we should have everyone in the company pass the island test?"

Where is this coming from? Does he think the assistants won't be able to handle themselves?

"No. Just the operators in our Surveillance-and-Planning and Rescue-and-Sanction Divisions."

"You sure?"

"Do you want to have employees?" She was starting to tire of standing in her heels. "Look, the assistants are fine. They are all qualified to carry and shoot a nine-millimeter, and they have monthly range sessions to stay sharp. We put them through an abbreviated version of the judo, boxing, and wrestling course that our operators take. They can handle themselves."

"But I've always worried that, if it came down to it, and an operator went down, they couldn't kill—even to save their own lives."

"Having Cummings and King run the course won't tell us that. I mean, could you imagine having Munny try and make it through? All we'd have is a dead Weapons Division Head. Yes, killing is a part of the course, but the main areas it tests are a candidate's mental toughness and her physical abilities. We don't need our assistants to be in incredible shape, and if it ever did come down to them having to kill someone to stay alive, then that mission was already doomed." She stepped toward him and put a hand on his shoulder. "So, let's not change things because something is on your mind." She paused, intensity radiating from her eyes. "What's bothering you?"

"I don't like the setup for the next six months with Flo."

"Because of Victor Lars Junius?"

She could see the surprise in his eyes; his mouth opened as if was a reflex motion. She removed her hand.

"I didn't know you knew about him," Worth said.

"I've seen the message traffic and assumed that's what we're going to talk about this morning. Am I wrong?"

"Scattered breadcrumbs."

"Not to an analyst."

"Well, *this* former analyst didn't make the connections."

"So, Gideon pointed you in that direction."

"Earlier this week."

"Have you seen a picture of Junius?"

"Yeah, his company portrait from around ten years ago. Why?"

"Nothing recent?"

"No. What am I missing?"

"Take a look at a current picture before the meeting and tell me if he looks familiar."

He gave her his short, frustrated laugh, which amused her. "You're killing me. No hints?"

"No hints," she said. "What do you know about him?"

He adjusted his pen again, which Raven thought did not need adjusting. "Instead of spending the majority of the year in his palatial estate in Santorini, the shipping titan spends his time in Switzerland, splitting his time between his home in Céligny, his chalet in Gstaad, and his castle north of Montreux." He took his hand off his pen. "A certain portion of his fleet of ships have spent time in the company's shipyard over the past few years, and when you combine the shipping routes of each of those vessels, well, there isn't an important place on the globe that they don't travel to."

She smiled. "And we'll see what conclusions you draw from those facts."

"I won't get specific here, but Gideon's information has me convinced that Mr. Junius is . . ." Worth drifted, seeming to search for the words.

"A part of something larger?" she said. "Could be."

He rubbed his neck. "Important enough for us to think about activating Flo."

"Sounds like it."

He pursed his lips for a moment. "And you still think she will be committed?"

"Has she ever *not* been committed?"

He gave a shaky "No."

Give him a less-than-desirable alternative, she told herself. *That will center him and nudge him to clarify his position.* "We can try handing this off to Wexler if you want."

"And let them get the intel first? No way. Plus, they don't share information like they should. That's why we agreed to let Flo act as Hugh's wife last year so that we wouldn't be cut out." He had raised his voice. *Good.* "Plus, Jock wants

Flo for the job, and now that I know you do, well, I think it will be a short meeting."

It gave her some satisfaction to see him squirm, but she could not show it. She threw up her hands and said, "What do you want me to do?"

He turned around and walked away. "I don't like the whole fucking thing, but I don't see a different course. If we don't act, someone else will. See you in a few minutes."

He closed the door behind him, and the room was silent.

She did not like the situation either . . . but for different reasons.

Landon Beach

3 Months Later . . .

Landon Beach

18

Raleigh, North Carolina – October 2002

Adrienne Astra sat across from Flo Fleming in her private office on the 4th floor. She had known that Flo would be stopping by the office this week for one last check-in before the second half of her mission commenced but did not think it would be on a Friday afternoon—she was about to leave for the weekend when there was a knock on her door.

It had been over two months since she had last seen her mentor, and it felt good to be in her presence again. Flo exuded confidence and control, and Adrienne had found her to be a woman of tremendous integrity, standards—at least as they applied to the work they did—and a focused professional who was dedicated to her craft and the methods she employed to carry out the directives the company gave her. But today, there were added dimensions to her appearance that Adrienne had never seen before. Flo had a deep tan, and her fingernails were polished. The gray slacks and white blouse fit snugly around her trim, wiry frame, and she looked rested. Her hair and makeup were done to perfection, her bottom row of teeth had been straightened, and both rows had been whitened. The designer glasses and black heels gave her a corporate look, like a younger Kerrie Raven. In fact, the transformation of her gritty mentor and sparring partner had been so complete that it had taken Adrienne a few extra seconds to recognize who was standing in front of her when she had opened the door to her office. Where Flo had been since July . . . she had no idea.

Adrienne shut the door behind them and then opened her arms to give Flo a hug.

However, instead of welcoming the embrace, Flo took a seat on the stiff couch and crossed her legs.

She has a lot on her mind, Adrienne thought. *So would I, if I was leaving on Monday for an indefinite amount of time.*

Their interactions always had an official air about them, but the tension she sensed in the room was abnormal. *It's from her side, but why?* She decided to try and lighten the mood. "So, when do I get *my* makeover mission?"

Flo's face remained still, and her eyes seemed to be looking past Adrienne. "How has the training been with Rose and Raven?"

Okay, retreat. Maybe this is how she gets before a mission. Adrienne sat down in her desk chair. "Fine," she said. "Rose has brought me up to speed on every piece of surveillance equipment ever invented, and I've had the opportunity to practice using a handful of the gadgets. There has also been classroom work—the lipreading seminar was probably my favorite."

Flo gave her a polite nod but still did not make eye contact.

"I've also learned a lot about what goes into planning a mission."

Rose had started her with basic geography, intelligence gathering, and funding. Next were logistics, travel considerations, communications, and assuming different identities. When they covered target packages, Adrienne had been hasty and chosen a garrote as the assassination weapon for the mock agent during one of the scenarios. Rose had stopped the exercise and said, *"You chose that without knowing some important information. There are too many variables. What is the agent's background? What is her skill level? Where is she from? Who does she work for? What country is she in? How did she get there? Who is the target? Does the weapon play into any misdirection? How does she plan to get out after the job is done?"* Rose had taken a sip of coffee at that point, giving Adrienne time to process her embarrassment. Then Rose had frowned at Raven, who was also in the room, and set the paper coffee cup on the table with a *tic*. *"You need to think about the answers to all of those questions and then choose a weapon system accordingly."* After that failure, Adrienne had shown improvement in the next two scenarios, and Raven had been pleased.

"You'll be working with Rose a lot in the future," Flo said. "Surveillance and Planning is the glove; Rescue and Sanction is the fist."

"Raven has been adamant about how much time I need to spend training with her."

Flo's eyes drifted toward the ceiling, and Adrienne waited for her to say more. She did not.

What is going on? Adrienne decided to continue. "Beyond monitoring my physical training, Raven has been teaching me about the various intelligence agencies and apparatuses throughout the world and our company's place in that arena."

Flo lowered her eyes to Adrienne's. "What is your assessment of Munny's assistant?"

"He knows his weapons and even goes beyond what Munny usually says when explaining advantages and disadvantages of different systems. He also has a commercial pilot's license, and Raven told me he can fly anything from a floatplane to a Boeing 727. I'm impressed with King, and so is Munny."

"How do you know that Munny is impressed with him?"

"He told me."

Flo scoffed, "Of course he did."

"Is there something wrong with that?"

"What?"

Adrienne raised her voice and leaned forward. "I said, 'Is there something wrong with that?'"

Flo went to say something but stopped. Instead, she stood while giving her a warm smile. Flo reached out her hand. "Sorry," she said. "Of course not."

As soon as Adrienne's hand joined with Flo's, Flo put her other hand over Adrienne's and gave the union a squeeze. Then, using both hands, she closed Adrienne's hand and provided a soothing rub before letting go.

Their eyes were locked as Adrienne felt the folded piece of paper in her closed hand.

"I'm glad the training is going well," said Flo, "and cannot wait to see where you are at when I get back."

Adrienne nodded. "I look forward to it."

Flo turned and exited the room.

After five minutes had gone by, Adrienne opened her office door and strolled down the hallway, saying a quick hello to Ulysses King, who was headed in the opposite direction. She entered the restroom and, seeing that it was empty, went into a stall and read the note from Flo.

9:30 p.m. your back patio

It was what Adrienne had hoped for. She flushed the piece of paper down the toilet and returned to her office, taking her time packing up for the day.

Ten minutes later, she exited the building and walked across the parking lot toward her Jeep Grand Cherokee Laredo. She wanted answers.

Hopefully, she would get them that evening.

* * *

196

Adrienne sat in a lounger on her back patio under the starlit sky. The glow of the city could be seen in the distance over the row of trees that lined her backyard, and a large square of freshly-mowed and neatly-edged grass lay between the concrete flooring of the patio and the tree line. There were no fences on the sides of the yard—there was no need for them. The forest surrounded her home, and her nearest neighbors were well over a mile away on either side.

It was nine-thirty, and she sipped on a cold beer while focusing on the backyard. A stiff wind whistled through the trees, swaying the boughs; it was as if she was outside a football stadium, hearing the crowd cheering for a home team player making a long run.

Which direction will she come from? I'll see her before I hear her.

Thirty minutes ago, she had swept the patio for listening devices and found none. She had no security cameras at the house, so there would be no video record of the meeting. The company had offered to pay for them, but she had declined. Each employee's house had to have an alarm system, but for assistants, home video surveillance was optional; once you became a Division Head, having a video surveillance system became mandatory, hence, Flo's wish to meet at Adrienne's house.

Her walk through the woods surrounding her two-story, ranch-style house before that had yielded nothing out of the ordinary, and as a cold gulp of beer slid down her throat, she relaxed, feeling confident that when Flo arrived, they would be alone.

However, if there was a situation, an Uzi rested in a hidden compartment underneath her lounger. The back doors were seconds away, and if trouble followed them inside, there was a hidden stairway behind a section of the basement bar that led straight up to her kitchen where a counter would slide out, allowing them quick access to the rest of the house. If they had to go up to the second floor and made it to her bedroom, there was a square section of carpeting on the far-right floor of her master closet, which was the top of a chute that merged with a two-story, circular slide, allowing a slider to reach a landing hidden behind a false basement wall in seconds—the classic double-back with a twist. The features were standard in the homes of Worth-Gideon employees, put in by contractors who believed the homes were for rich artists—actors, musicians, and authors—who wished to remain anonymous but needed "escape options" in the event of over-zealous houseguests. And, of course, there was a wall panel on each floor that, when activated by a hidden lever, opened, revealing a weapons cache. Again, the contractors thought these closets were for a different purpose—a mini-Toys "R" Us of the owner's devices and props used in his or her attempt to understand all facets of the Kama Sutra. Naturally, the contractors had wondered: who *would be escaping from* whom, *for* art *could be both social and anti-social.*

Adrienne had missed her mentor and thought that the goodbye chat at the office would be warm with a hint of excitement in the air. She had been surprised by Flo's off-putting, dismissive, and agitated demeanor. And if it had ended that way, without the note, she did not like what her mind told her she would have done as she replayed the conversation in her head throughout the day, waiting for nine-thirty to arrive.

There was movement near the back tree line, and seconds later, she saw Flo emerge from the forest. Adrienne pulled a beer out of the cooler and used her Detroit Tigers bottle opener to pry the cap off. She had been instructed to have nothing at her house that would even give a visitor a whiff of her prior life, but she drew the line at bottle openers. She could always say it was a gift.

Flo arrived at the patio and took a seat in the lounger opposite of Adrienne. "Red cushions with green stripes?" Flo said, patting the lounger's cushions.

"Matches the new awning," she said, jerking a thumb behind her, "and, what can I say, I'm still a sucker for Christmas."

Flo accepted the beer from her, and they clinked bottles.

"When did you start drinking this piss?"

"Always have. It's cheap. And my—"

She caught herself. They were not supposed to talk about their previous lives, even with other Worth-Gideon employees. However, she was certain that Flo knew her background, which made her think that a seemingly innocent, jabbing question like the one she had been asked could also be seen as a probe to see if Adrienne would break protocol. Their meeting tonight had broken no protocols, but it was irregular, and she wondered if that was the reason that she had almost slipped.

Flo raised her left hand and studied her polished fingernails and added, "Your father tended bar at a bowling alley for almost three decades."

Adrienne took a sip, evaluating the statement.

No surprise.

It was now clear that Flo knew some of her background, but, if someone was listening to their conversation, she noted that Flo's comment betrayed nothing of Adrienne's past. She would follow her mentor's lead and answer with a declaration that also gave nothing away.

Adrienne raised the bottle. "His favorite brand."

Time to see what kind of conversation this will be.

As her mentor took a pull, she asked, "How about your dad?"

Flo swallowed and then stared at her. The wind continued to blow through the forest, and Adrienne set her beer down. She was glad that her Michigan instincts had served her well again as she leaned forward and zipped up her cardigan sweater while waiting for Flo to respond.

Another five seconds passed, and Adrienne sat back and picked up her bottle. Flo was still staring at her. Then, her mentor shook her head and said, "No."

Again, the response did not surprise her, but it did give her a better idea of what the parameters of the conversation would be. And having gained that knowledge, she got right to the point. "What did you want to talk about?"

"Will we be alone?"

Adrienne had expected the question at some point. *Will we be alone* was code for *Have you performed a sweep?*

"I've cleared my schedule."

Code for *I've performed a sweep.*

Flo took a chug and then smacked her lips. "I'm going to tell you something you're not supposed to know."

"Could it jeopardize my position in the company?"

Flo adjusted her seating in the lounger and then said, "If you keep it to yourself, no. If you talk to others about it, then I don't know."

"Understood."

Flo tipped the beer all the way back and finished it.

That was fast.

"Thanks," she said, setting the bottle on the concrete with a *clink*. "No more, please." She sat back and crossed her fingers, resting her hands on her chest. "I'm leaving for Gstaad, Switzerland on Monday."

And now, there was no turning back.

Adrienne had not been cleared to know where Flo had been for the past two-plus months before returning to Worth-Gideon today, and she was not cleared to know where Flo was heading next. All she had been told in July was that it would be a 2-part assignment and that Flo would check-in right before part two and see how Adrienne's training was coming along.

"Gstaad?" Adrienne asked.

"Julie Andrews once described it as, 'the last paradise in a crazy world.'"

"Julie Andrews?"

"*The Sound of Music? Mary Poppins?*"

Adrienne shook her head in confusion.

"Married to Blake Edwards?"

Adrienne frowned. "Sorry, not ringing a bell."

"You must have had a sheltered or lonely childhood."

You already know that. "It was. You ever get lonely?"

Flo seemed to search Adrienne's eyes for a few seconds. "Yes. I'm lonely right now." She paused again. "Surprised at my honesty?"

"Based on how you answered my earlier question about your dad, I am."

"You ever seen *From Here to Eternity*?"

"No."

"You really haven't seen many films, have you? At least none that matter."

"I—"

"You need to." She raised her hands. "I know, I know. We've been watching the *Death Wish* series, which we need to resume when I get back, but there are always exceptions for iconic actors. And Charles Bronson is one of them."

Her face was stone . . . kind of like Bronson's, without the wispy mustache.

"Say his name," Flo commanded.

"What?"

"Say Bronson."

"Bronson."

"And again."

"Bronson."

"We watch Bronson."

"We watch Bronson."

"We always watch Bronson."

"We always watch Bronson."

"We never stop watching Bronson."

"We never stop watching Bronson."

"You're god damn right we never do." Flo smacked her open left hand with her right fist. "Anyway, Montgomery Clift—won't even bother asking you if you know who he is—says in the film, 'Nobody ever lies about being lonely.'" Flo looked away from her and into the depths of the dark trees. "True in real life too, right?"

"Yes. But in real life, people like us lie for a living."

Flo sighed. "Sometimes, I want what my life was like before I started working at Worth-Gideon, but I know that it is no longer available to me. It started with the name change. Once that happened, I had to close off my earliest impressions of the world, and I could no longer provide anyone access to them. We become permanent actors, and performing our different roles is the only real life we come to know." She looked around the patio, motioning with her arms. "I mean, is this real?"

"We're talking on my back porch. Yes, it's real."

"No, it isn't. This is a set, and we're just two actors delivering lines."

"How can you say that after what you just told me?"

Flo returned her hands to her chest. "Working at this company will eat at your soul if you let it, Adrienne. I've trained at length to keep mine, but one of the unavoidable consequences of getting to do what we do is the loss of compassion. And I have found that maintaining a certain amount is essential for living and functioning—especially because we won't be in this job forever. Ah ha, you haven't thought about that, have you? Still excited for your first mission." She gave Adrienne a sympathetic grin. "I remember."

"I've put in a lot of work."

"Of course, you have, and, in my mind, you're ready. Hell, maybe it's you who should be going on Monday."

"You don't mean that."

Flo closed her eyes, inhaling a deep breath. She held it and then exhaled. "I suppose I don't."

"You told me all throughout my training that this life appeals to a certain kind of person, someone strong enough to kill the people who are being trained to kill us. Are you not that person anymore?"

"No, I'm still that person. And so are you."

"What's bothering you then?"

"The real fear, however, is once we get stripped of our legends, then what are we? What will we be the rest of our lives? Every reference point will be inaccessible because one, the people we were *before we took this job* are "officially" dead and buried in cemeteries, and two, the people that we were *while in this job* will be retired when we leave the company. So, we're starting all over again in, what, our thirties, maybe our forties, if we don't take on an admin position. But . . ." she said, eyeing Adrienne. "Do you want to be a Kerrie Raven? I don't know. Maybe you do. But here's my point: Don't let the work we do consume you—always have something meaningful to come back to until you decide it is time to walk away."

"What's that for you?"

"I'll let you know when I get back." She leaned forward. "But don't trust me. In fact, don't trust anyone. Betrayal . . . deceit . . . misdirection—you'll get swallowed up. Trust your gut."

Adrienne stared at her for a few seconds and then nodded. "Any idea when you'll be getting back?"

Flo tapped her lips and then rubbed her chin. "Less than a year is all I can say. Then, it will be vacation time."

"How does that work?"

Flo sank back in the chair. "Make sure you look at your contract when you sign in a few weeks." She must have noticed Adrienne's surprise. "Yes, I spoke with Raven, Worth, and Gideon today after I left your office. I told them that you were capable." She let the last word hang in the air for a moment. "Anyway, in the contract, there should be a section that specifically mentions mandatory vacation time *on the company's dime* after the successful completion of a mission. They'll send you pretty much wherever you want to go, but they own famous property in one location that I never turn down."

203

"Can I ask you where it is?"

"I'll only tell you because it should be in your contract, and if it isn't, then make sure it gets in there. You can tell them that I told you about it. That will keep the heat off you, and believe me, they won't do anything to either of us. On the other hand, if you tell them that you know about Gstaad, well, I've already warned you about that."

"Got it."

Flo smiled. "Do you remember the TV show *Magnum P.I.*? Yes? Hey, you have watched something." She had gone from tense and morose to suddenly uplifted, and Adrienne determined that the mood shift was because there were genuine, pleasant thoughts running through Flo's head in anticipation of the post-mission vacation . . . or she was putting up a front and just using the subject to distract herself.

"Worth is obsessed with the show and bought that luxurious estate located off Kalanianaole Highway in Waimānalo on Oahu. Robin's Nest, remember?" She chuckled to herself. "Through a series of shell companies, ending with *Nature-Eco, LLC,* he purchased it from Eve Glover Anderson, a former member of the Hawaii House of Representatives and the stepdaughter of Cox Communications heiress Barbara Cox Anthony. No big secret, all public record, but, here's what isn't." She laughed again. "Worth actually pulled off establishing himself as a Robin-Masters-like owner of the estate. In the final estate-buying negotiations, he sealed the deal by sending Jock Gideon, under a different name, as a legal counsel of Nature-Eco, to explain to Ms. Anderson that the company represented a wealthy environmentalist who wanted to *remain anonymous* but felt strongly about not only preserving Pāhonu but also supporting the Waimānalo Limu Hui and its mission to replenish the once bountiful supply of limu found in Waimānalo Bay. In good faith, Gideon also assured Ms. Anderson that all the estate's existing buildings would not be torn down but renovated to preserve the historical landmark."

"How do you know this?"

"Two years ago, I vacationed with Raven there for a week. She told me over a few martinis in the estate bar."

"No hiccups in the deal then? And no one knows that the anonymous wealthy environmentalist is Byron Worth?"

"No to both questions. The papers were signed the day after Gideon left, and Nature-Eco's first generous donation to Waimānalo Limu Hui was deposited in the community-based group's bank account the following day. Ever since then, it has been understood that Nature-Eco's executives and family members—everyone from Worth-Gideon—use the estate as a vacation home and work retreat. Worth pays someone for the upkeep, and, for most of the year, it's vacant, so there's nothing for anyone with curious eyes to see. Additionally, every beach in Hawaii is open to the public, so people can walk across Pāhonu's beach and swim in the tidal pool whenever they want. Prying eyes are normal—usually, visitors like to stand in the water, point at the property, and say, 'And that's the place where *Magnum P.I.* was filmed.'"

"Pretty shrewd move," Adrienne said.

"When you have obsessions, money can turn fantasies into realities."

She laughed. "So that's why they pay us so much."

"Maybe," Flo said, "if you stay alive long enough. Mostly, though, they pay us well so that we eliminate people before their unjust, uncivilized, or unethical fantasies become realities." Adrienne observed her mentor's mood grow sour and detached again. The smile and concentration were gone, and the energy had left with them.

"Worth's desire to be Robin Masters seems harmless. But, still . . . billionaire role-playing? Is he obsessed or just bored?"

"That's a fair question. But remember, a part of *our* job is to role-play. In fact, it's the most dangerous role-playing there is. A thespian version of Russian roulette, if you will."

Adrienne wondered if Flo was role-playing right now—she had said they were acting.

"And he's not the only powerful person to be obsessed with another character—real or imagined."

"What do you mean?"

Flo lowered her head and gazed at the ground for a few seconds. "Nothing. I shouldn't have said that."

Adrienne gave her a moment of silence and then decided to bring the conversation back to the post-mission vacation in the hopes of getting "Happy Flo" back. She was uncomfortable with the other side of Flo—perhaps because she wasn't used to it, or perhaps it made Adrienne less sure of the choice she had made to work for and, if necessary, kill for Worth-Gideon.

"Well, however he acquired the estate, if the place is anything like I remember from the TV series, then we're lucky to have it."

Flo raised her head; her smile had returned. "That's where I'm headed when this mission is over—nothing in the world like Pāhonu. I'll be swimming in the tidal pool, sunning on the beach, eating surf and turf every night for dinner, and then drinking fine wine from the cellar or single malts from the estate bar while watching old movies by the fire. In fact, Munny and King just returned from that paradise. Too bad they couldn't enjoy much of it, though. Raven has Munny spend a week there every fall and every spring to check the security and install any upgrades. He took King with him this time to start showing him the ropes."

"So that's where they were last week."

"Yes. You will love it there. Again, be sure it's in your contract. Don't sign it unless it is."

"Okay."

"Have you thought about what you'll do with the money?"

"I haven't given it much of a thought."

"Make sure you have a plan."

"What do you do with it?"

"I save half, use one quarter for living expenses, and split the remaining quarter between travel and my film collection."

"I should have known."

"You've never been in my basement."

"Why haven't you shown me before?"

"No real reason to. You've only been over a few times. If you think the setup in my living room is sweet for watching films . . . well, I'll introduce you to a whole new world when I get back."

Adrienne smirked. "Maybe I'd know more about film if you would have shown me the space earlier."

Flo chuckled, "Oh, fuck off, lady."

"Holding out on me."

"Whatever. Having a healthy obsession is smart in this business, gives you something to focus on when you're not training or on a mission. I think Mond said it best in *Brave New World*: 'You can't have a lasting civilization without plenty of pleasant vices.' Yeah, I don't just read grenades-and-guns-going-off-every-twenty-pages types of books. Get over it already. I am a certifiable cinephile. That's one of my vices. The other, I suppose, is my job. It's a rush, and it's a challenge. I get that, but the reward of being financially able to feed your deep interests is worth something too. My suggestion is that you find out what that is for you. For me, I started with collecting all my favorite films. Most are available on DVD but not all of them yet. Then, I started working my way through the American Film Institute lists and the Criterion Collection. But that's just the basics. Later, I got into projectors and started purchasing every different kind, which set me up for acquiring original prints of some of my favorite films. Now, I've added collecting memorabilia from some of those productions."

"What are you going to purchase after this mission?"

"I'd like to get my hands on anything from *Raiders of the Lost Ark*."

"Now, that's one movie I know. What do you want?"

"For starters, the original handwritten script by Kasdan and the miniatures Spielberg used when he was figuring out his shots for some of the desert scenes." She paused. "In terms of other films, well, I'd never turn away anything that Pam Grier wore. I like artwork too, but I'm picky. I don't always agree with the choices the artist made when creating the poster for a particular film. So what I might do is hire an artist I respect to draw the poster the way I think it should have been drawn, and then I'll frame it and hang it in my sanctuary. No one else will have it."

"I'll have to think about what interests me in that way."

"Consider what you have pursued."

"I was poor growing up. I didn't get to pursue *anything*."

"You're always listening to music."

"Everyone listens to music."

"Yeah, but you're always listening to jazz—might be something there."

Her mentor was right; she listened almost exclusively to jazz music. But she had never dug into *why*. Too busy training. "Maybe I'll dig a little into it while you're away."

"Good," Flo said, standing up. Then, her smile vanished, and she looked Adrienne over as if conducting one of the many inspections she had performed during Adrienne's training. Her eyes stopped moving upward when they reached Adrienne's, and Flo pursed her lips. "Tell me about the last Christmas with your father."

"What?"

"Tell me about it. What was it like?" She leaned over and picked up her bottle. "Did you drink this shit together?"

Flo held out the empty beer in front of her.

Adrienne rose to her feet and took a step toward her mentor and grabbed the bottle. "We were poor. Never a lot of presents. But when I turned 21, we shared a good bottle of wine over dinner together on Christmas Eve. He set the table with a red tablecloth and the best silverware we had. Dined on filet mignon and then finished off the evening with a scotch by the fireplace. He'd been saving up money. It was special."

"What did you talk about?"

"The weather—I know, uninteresting, but we're from Michigan. However, we also talked abo—wait, why are you asking me this?"

Flo's demeanor was penetrating, focused. "Keep going. Don't leave anything out."

She searched Flo's eyes for motive. *What in the hell was this?* Adrienne wanted to keep those memories locked away. Private. But she had never witnessed her mentor be this sincere about matters outside of instructing her how to stay alive and the most efficient way to kill another human being. And so, she gave in, letting her thoughts access a region of her brain she had padlocked since joining the company. "We talked about life after college: where I might go, what I might do. I asked him about his job and how much longer he thought he would stay on at the bar. He said if he had his health, he'd remain there. I understood why. He had built lifelong friendships in that place. However, he knew there was a real possibility that I would leave the state and that he would see less of me. I guess that's the thing I remember most about that night, the duality of my feelings—marvelous joy in sharing an evening with him in adult conversation . . . and tremendous sadness that we wouldn't be having these evenings if I moved away because I had become an adult." She paused. "How's that? Or do you want to know what presents we got each other?"

"No," Flo said and reached out her hand. Adrienne took it, and they shook up and down. "Thank you, Margaret."

Adrienne's eyes opened wide as she felt Flo's hand let go, and they stood, three feet apart, gazing at each other.

"I won't call you that again, I promise. But how did it feel?"

She felt an onslaught of emotions: detachment—like the name belonged to someone else; happiness—because, in a word, she was reminded of her one-time simple life; loss—because that life was gone forever. *Damn. My eyes are becoming glassy.*

"For the longest time, I have wanted someone to call me by my real name—just once more," Flo said.

Adrienne wiped her eyes. "I can do that for you."

Flo put a hand on her shoulder and squeezed. "Maybe when I get back." She let go. "Remember everything I told you."

"I will."

"Shoot first." Flo pivoted away and started across the patio toward the backyard. Right before her shoes touched the first blades of grass, she said over her shoulder, "I never knew my father," and kept walking.

2 Months Later . . .

Landon Beach

19

Raleigh, North Carolina – December 2002

"Cummings and Tipler have the bodies," Raven said, slamming the red-colored phone's handle into the receiver that sat on the conference room's concrete table in front of her. "They'll use our contact in Geneva to have them cremated."

She still couldn't believe this was happening. *Flo's gone,* she thought. *And Munny's gone.*

"I want them flying out of Marseille tonight," Worth said.

"I already told you I arranged that," she snapped back.

"Who gives a shit," said Gideon, punching keys on his laptop. "Tell him again."

"Fuck you, Jock!"

Gideon ignored her and looked at Worth over the top of his computer's screen. "The money has already been transferred from the account I deposited

213

it in, and I have the Geneva police chief's assurance that the report will be sanitized." He exhaled and rubbed his eyes. They had all been awake for almost forty-eight hours straight. "We should be fine now."

Raven wheeled her chair back from the table and then stood and walked over to the coffee station, attempting to divert her attention from wanting to strangle Gideon.

"When do they fly out, Kerrie?" Worth asked.

She took a breath and then exhaled as she began unscrewing the top of her stainless-steel thermos. "They'll observe the cremation in around thirty minutes. The process will take a little over two hours to take the bodies down to around five pounds of ash each. Once they have a visual on the piles of ash, they'll leave. By the way, you're welcome for my arranging it so fast."

Both Worth and Gideon stayed silent.

"Then, they'll head over to Geneva Airport and be on their flight within two hours—about twelve hours of travel accounting for a connection. That puts them in Raleigh around six a.m. tomorrow."

Worth nodded. Gideon's eyes stayed on his computer screen.

The first indication that something had gone wrong was two days ago when Munny did not contact Worth-Gideon after he was supposed to have picked up Flo in Gstaad. The trio of Raven, Worth, and Gideon had sat in the very conference room on the fifth floor where they were now—and had not left since—and waited for Munny to call. At first, the three senior associates were not worried. A winter storm could cause delays or broken communications. However, they did delay the message traffic to be sent to StarLine. They needed confirmation that Flo had successfully sanctioned Victor Lars Junius and gotten away before they started the misdirection. And so, they had stayed at the table, anticipating the next check-in, which was when Munny and Flo would reach the cabin that was a half hour from the French border.

No contact—they continued to delay the message traffic to StarLine.

They waited for the next check-in—when the pair would reach the safe house in Marseille—and did not receive a call. They delayed the message traffic again and sent Cummings and Tipler, the two "Kross, Inc. employees," over to the safe house.

The house was empty . . . and stayed empty for the night and the next day. They canceled the message traffic. *Something has happened.*

Then, just over twenty-four hours ago, the bodies of Flo and Munny had been found in a small cabin cruiser, floating on Lake Geneva—eighty miles away from Gstaad. A year-round ferry had hailed the boat as it was in its way, but there had been no response, and no one had been topside on the cruiser as it continued to drift. The authorities had been notified, and a boat had been dispatched. An hour later, the police had found what appeared to be the gruesome result of an argument between a man and a woman that had gone wrong below decks and involved two handguns. The man had been shot three times in the chest and the woman twice in the forehead.

Worth had ordered Raven to immediately deploy Cummings and Tipler to the police station while he started negotiating with the chief to keep things quiet.

"Jock," Worth said. "Is there anything else we need to do before tomorrow morning?"

There is, Raven thought, *but I have to speak with Worth about it alone.* She finished filling her thermos.

Gideon shut his laptop. "No. Whoever killed Munny and Flo is not going to make a move on anyone else in our company right now. The message has been sent and received."

"Shouldn't we let everyone at least know what's going on?" Raven said, sitting back down at the table. She poured a fresh cup of coffee into her paper cup and then sealed her thermos.

"Yes," Worth replied, "but we'll do it tomorrow."

"We done for now?" Gideon said.

"Kerrie?" asked Worth.

She nodded *yes*.

Gideon picked up his computer and stood. "I'm going home. See you tomorrow morning."

"Let's make it eight. I want to see Cummings and Tipler first thing—they can sleep on the flight over. Then, we need to speak with Astra and King."

"Eight it is," Gideon said directly to Worth, seeming to ignore Raven's presence. He exited the conference room, slamming the door.

"He was out of line," Worth said. "But. He's also upset about Flo and Munny."

She gave a dismissive wave of her hand. "It's nothing. I can take care of myself."

Worth pressed his palms together and rested his joined index fingers on his closed lips.

She took a sip of her coffee.

"You know what's on my mind, don't you?" he said.

"Two things. First, you had concerns about Flo taking on this mission. Jock and I thought she was ready. It was two against one, and she went. Now, we're all low because we just lost our best asset along with our weapons expert, but you've wanted to tell *me*—" She paused and looked over at the conference room door. "—and *Jock* for the past two days that you 'told us so,' but you haven't because reminding us of your doubts would not bring them back and because you're conflicted—Flo produced a valuable amount of intelligence from her operation. In fact, if she was alive right now, you'd be thinking that Jock and I were right."

"But she's not alive," he said.

"Bringing me to the second item, which we're both a part of."

Worth covered his face with his hands and then slid them down until they were pressed against each other once again, and his chin rested upon his index fingers. "Any thoughts on how we should proceed?"

"I stand by our decision not to move them the past two days. We have enemies, and Flo had enemies, but it stops there. Children and caretakers are off-limits; I think Jewel and Eleanor will be fine."

"Agreed. The more I thought about it over the past forty-eight hours, the more I figured that if Junius had known about them and wanted to kill them, he would have done it already."

"So what we're really talking about is their future."

Worth reclined and looked at the ceiling for a few beats. "I suppose we are."

And now Raven had to face the question that had been on her mind since the entire situation had started almost three years ago: What happens to Flo's daughter and nanny if Flo dies?

In her first two years with Worth-Gideon, Inc., after finishing the training cycle, Florence "Flo" Fleming had assassinated thirteen people. After the final one, an assassin who was in the final stages of planning a hit on a powerful U.S. Senator, Flo had taken a vacation in Key West. A month after returning, she missed her period and found out she was pregnant, which she told Raven about over dinner at Flo's house. Naturally, Raven had been confused since Flo had signed a contract stating that she would take birth control, but accidents happened, and Raven offered to set up the abortion appointment.

And that was when Flo had surprised her, stating that she wanted to keep the baby.

There had been no talking her out of it because Flo held all the cards. If she could have the baby, then she would continue working for the company. If the company was not going to allow her to have the baby, she would quit.

"But why do you want to have the baby?"

"After the last killing, I didn't feel anything, and I should feel . . . something."

"What do you mean?"

"I've taken life—a lot of them—and I agree that it had to be done. But, Kerrie, I've become desensitized, empty. I noticed something after the first half-dozen sanctions, but the last one made this clear to me: Becoming soulless makes killing easier. It's advantageous in my line of work; there's clarity—a start and an end. But there will come a day when that lack of feeling will turn itself on me, and I'll either be killed or never be able to walk away from what I'm doing for the company. On my time away, I felt the insatiable need to create life—to feel something, to find balance."

And so, faced with losing her best operator, Kerrie Raven had arranged a meeting between herself, Flo, and Byron Worth. Gideon was too by-the-book and would have pushed for firing Flo. But Raven's protégé, Worth, was more open to creative solutions when it involved top talent. No one could argue with Flo's results, and when Raven presented her plan at the meeting, Worth had approved it. Raven and Worth, using their personal checking accounts, purchased a modest, 3-bedroom house ten miles away from Flo's home, and Flo found a sixty-five-year-old widower, Eleanor Groff, with no children and no in-laws to be her future child's nanny. Working around Gideon was easier than they had expected. He agreed with them that after having performed so many successful assassinations for the company, Flo deserved a leave of absence. Worth had also nudged him to expand the company's informal networking, and Gideon spent much of the last year of the century traveling. Flo had her baby, and she, Jewel, and Eleanor lived in the house that had been purchased until Flo was back in shape and ready to return to work. It had been a gamble, but after Flo performed three more assassinations and spent months early last year undercover as Hugh's wife gathering intelligence, the decision to keep her on had proven to be the correct one.

In fact, Worth had pulled Raven aside after one debrief and said, *"She's even better now."*

Flo had never shared the identity of Jewel's father, but she had decided to name someone as Jewel's godfather.

Hugh.

Raven heard Worth say, "Kerrie?" and then repeat it, and she came back to the conversation.

"Sorry," she said, leaning forward. "Eleanor is sixty-seven, and Jewel is two. By the numbers, we'll need to find another nanny at some point, but right now, Eleanor is in good health. Because she thinks Flo was an entry-level business consultant who had to spend a lot of time away from home, we'll tell her that Flo died in a freak skiing accident, falling into a crevasse, making it impossible to recover the body. There will be no service, but we will explain to her that the current arrangement will remain the same, and she will continue to be paid a salary and will still get thirty days of vacation a year. I'll find another nanny to cover for her when she takes her days."

"Who delivers the news?"

"I think it should be you, Byron."

"When's the last time you visited them?"

"Last month. You?"

"Late summer—when Flo was in North Carolina. I brought Jewel a large inflatable, big turtle. Eleanor told me that she takes her to the community pool just about every day."

"That was good of you."

"What does she call you?"

"Jewel?"

Raven nodded.

"Uncle Bee. How about you?"

"Aunt Birdie."

"We're pathetic."

"Why? Because we can't give her our real names so we disguise them as something else? Bee is easy for her to say. And for me, a raven is a type of bird. Besides, Eleanor thinks your name is Ben, and mine is Beatrice."

Worth frowned and then raised his eyebrows. "Flo used her original name around them."

"So?"

"Yeah, well . . ." He leaned forward, almost getting jumpy. "And we are certain that no one else at the company knows about any of this?"

"No one." Raven sat back and took a sip of coffee. "However, Flo may have company equipment at the smaller house that should be retrieved. I propose that you deliver the bad news right after lunch tomorrow. Then, have Eleanor take Jewel out for a few hours, and I will go over and collect anything that needs to be removed."

The room became silent as Worth studied his fingernails. "Christmas is next week."

"You want to wait?"

"Should we?"

"No. Eleanor will know to wait, and she'll know how to phrase it when she does decide to tell her. Okay?"

"Okay," Worth replied. He began to slouch but then sat straight up as if something had just dawned on him. "If Eleanor's salary isn't going to come from the sale of Flo's house, where will we get the money from?"

She thought it was obvious, but she had always had more stamina than he did. After being up for the first twenty-four hours straight, he had still been sharp, but the last twenty-four hours had punched him in the face and rattled his brain. However, his question wasn't without some merit as Flo had been paying Eleanor's salary out of her own account. "The money from the sale will go into our main employee account, which Gideon will see, but when we close Flo's bank account, which only I have access to, I'll transfer a million to the joint account we've been using to cover the situation. Gideon will only care that the money from the sale of her house made it into the company account. He'll have to take our word on how much got added from Flo's personal account."

"How much is in it?"

"Seventeen million as of a few hours ago."

Worth raised his eyebrows at the figure but then frowned. She knew he would trade all the money to have Flo alive again.

The sale of the house would be straightforward. Part of each employee's contract stipulated that they would get to live in a house of their choosing—up to a $400,000 home for assistants and a $750,000 home for division heads—but that the properties would be purchased and owned by the company. This was so the company could sell the house in case something happened to the employee. If the employee retired, then the agreement was that the profit from the sale of the house would be split between the employee and the company but that the employee would get to keep everything in his or her bank account.

But there was a loophole there as well.

Until the employee officially retired, Kerrie Raven was a co-signer on the account. Since it was a seller's market right now and the house had already been paid for, she estimated that they would clear close to a million when they sold Flo's house.

In terms of the joint account that she and Worth had been using to manage Flo's situation, once Raven had transferred the million from Flo's personal account into the joint account, Raven would arrange for automatic transfers to be made to Eleanor's checking account at the beginning of each month, and Worth and Raven would continue to give her a year-end bonus every December.

"Tonight, I'll leave here and go to Flo's main house," Raven said.

"Why?"

"Just in case she has anything there that would link her to Jewel, Eleanor, or the other house. There shouldn't be anything, but you never know. If I find anything, I'll remove it. Then, after we tell the company tomorrow morning of Flo's death, we can send over a team to clean out the house without the fear of them finding anything. After it's been cleaned out, we'll have it prepped and then put it on the market."

Worth rubbed his eyes and said, "Oh, right," as if in admission to being tired and foggy-brained. "Do we still keep Jock out of the loop?"

"I don't see any reason to include him at this point. Do you?"

Worth studied the ceiling again. "No." He lowered his eyes to hers. "What about Hugh?"

"I'll call him tonight."

"What are you going to say?"

"That Flo died on a mission. He'll ask about it, and I'll tell him I can't say anything right now. He'll ask about Jewel, and I'll say that I think it would be a good idea if he stayed in her life. Then, I'll set the hook."

"What?"

"I'll tell him that when the situation settles down, I may be able to give him more information about who killed Flo."

"Why would you do that?"

"For two connected reasons: one, we want Junius dead; and two . . . Hugh is Jewel's father."

"You're kidding."

"No."

"Why didn't you tell me?"

"It wasn't important until now."

"How did you know?"

"He was on leave at the same time Flo was down in Key West. I did some digging around and found out he was there."

"But why would she name him Jewel's godfather?"

You're acting attentive now but still can't pick up on the obvious. "I think that was more for us and Eleanor. Flo and Hugh knew the truth all along, but they used their working relationship to set him up as Jewel's godfather so he could occasionally visit her."

"Think he'll talk?"

"No. He'll be hurt when I give him the news because I know he cared for Flo, but he'll keep his mouth shut while he waits for me to give him more information."

Worth sat up. "Then, you'll use him to go after Junius."

"He's the best that Wexler has, and when the time is right, I'll feed Hugh the intelligence about Junius . . . and we'll sit back and watch."

"They'll send him to assassinate Junius?"

"Hugh won't stop until they do. And if need be, I'll talk to my counterpart there to ensure that they send him."

"He won't be emotionally compromised?"

"If they sent him tomorrow? Absolutely. But Junius is going to be expecting some sort of retribution, and his guard will be up for a while. So . . . we wait. When his guard starts to lower, we unleash Hugh on him—win-win, Byron. Junius dies, and Hugh avenges the death of his lover. Then, I'm going to push him to retire so he can help raise his daughter."

"So, that stuff about a replacement nanny was made up?"

"No. Hugh might not want to retire."

"But why don't we send someone to take Junius out before Hugh does? I don't trust Wexler."

"Because Flo was our best, and our best just got killed."

"What about Adrienne?"

"Not before Hugh gets his shot. Plus, King needs time to get settled into his position. Could you imagine us sending him and Adrienne to kill Junius in a few months? No way."

Worth shook his head in frustration. "I feel like we're reliving the past six months. I'm outnumbered again—Gideon loves Hugh, and you'll both push for him to be given a shot while we stand by."

He needs something real, she told herself. "Byron, I'm *devastated* by the loss of Flo. Everyone else in the company will feel the same when they find out tomorrow morning." She paused. "Now, we'll recover, but this is a monumental setback. To send Adrienne and Ulysses to Switzerland right now for revenge would be to permanently cripple this company. Promote them? Yes. We have to do that, and we *will* do that tomorrow morning. Trust me. Let the situation with Hugh play out."

Worth went to say something but then closed his eyes and rubbed the bridge of his nose. "Okay. Let's see how he takes the news and how the situation develops over the next few days."

"I think that's a wise move." She stood. "I'm headed over to Flo's. See you in the morning."

20

Adrienne watched as the light above the conference room entrance turned green. Raven stood next to her and opened the door, ushering Adrienne through. There had been a buzz on the fourth floor that something was going on, because the big three had been spending a lot of time at the office over the past few days. Adrienne thought that it might have something to do with Flo's mission, and she had looked for hints in Raven's demeanor as the Director had fetched her from her office a few minutes ago and escorted her to the fifth floor. However, Raven maintained a neutral demeanor, and Adrienne could ascertain nothing about why she was being invited to the conference room.

The space was as she remembered it when Raven and Flo had given her a brief tour when she first arrived in Raleigh and was settled into her new house. It had been shortly after she had been inducted into the company through the weird coffin ritual that still crossed her mind from time to time.

The lights were dimmed, and Worth and Gideon sat in two large leather chairs opposite of a spot on the table where there was a stainless-steel thermos, leather padfolio, and pen set in front of a chair, which she assumed was Raven's.

Worth greeted her; Gideon typed on his laptop.

"Coffee? Water?" Raven asked Adrienne, pointing at the station in one of the room's corners.

She saw the two coffee makers, the stack of cups, the bowl full of sugar packets, and the tray of wooden stirring sticks. There was a small fridge underneath the table where she had seen milk, half & half, and bottles of water when she grabbed a bottle on her tour.

"No, thank you."

"Brave," said Worth.

Of the two men, she had always considered Worth more personable. He had a relaxed demeanor and always greeted employees. Gideon was aloof and, she suspected, mean. It didn't bother her, but if they were all part of a cohesive team that specialized in leveraging resources and intelligence to eliminate other human beings, she did not understand why he wasn't more neutral, like Raven.

The Director backtracked from her path to the station and said, "Suit yourself." Then, she arrived at the seat behind the material that Adrienne had spotted and waved her over to sit in the chair beside her.

Adrienne sat, and Raven slid a yellow legal pad and black ballpoint pen in front of her.

"Adrienne," Worth said. "We're about to share the following news with the company but wanted to speak with you about it first."

He paused, and she felt the triangulated stares of her three superiors. Whatever the news was, it seemed serious. However, the pause and stares were clearly components of power dynamics in motion.

Adrienne stared straight back at all three, making eye contact with Raven, then Gideon, and finally locking eyes with Worth. She said nothing.

Worth looked away for a beat and then said, "Flo Fleming and Albert Munny were killed during an operation."

The news was worse than she could have imagined.

Flo? Dead? Munny? Dead?

She continued to look into Worth's eyes. It kept her emotions in check.

"We know that you met with Flo in your office in October," said Gideon. Adrienne continued to stare at Worth. "Hey. Over here. I'm talking to you!" Gideon shouted.

She closed her eyes and then shifted her gaze to Gideon.

"I'm sorry, does it bother you to look someone in the eyes when they're addressing you?" Gideon snapped.

She didn't hesitate. "You tell me."

"Wha—what did you just say?"

This time she grinned. "You tell me."

Gideon exploded. "Get out of here! Get the fuck out of here right *now!*"

She leaned forward. "Have you run the island course?" Her pain at the loss of Flo was converting to rage. "You saw how I did. I don't think you'd make it to shore." She was on her feet. "And I bet you want to fight me right now. Teach me a lesson. Good," Adrienne said, dragging the last word out. She leaned farther forward, taunting him. But while all eyes were focused on her face, she had slipped her right hand behind her back and underneath her sweatshirt. She felt the handle of her Tom Brown Tracker knife. "So, come on," she said. "Come on!"

In a second, she had her blade out in front of her, the tip aimed right between the eyes of Gideon.

He saw the point of the blade and flinched, driving his head back into the leather chair's headrest. The force, along with the push from his feet, rolled the chair back, and he sat there hyperventilating.

I knew it. He's weak.

In a smooth motion, Adrienne slid her knife back into its sheath, never breaking eye contact with Gideon. *You're done treating me that way.*

Raven put a hand on her forearm. "Calm down. We're all feeling the loss—"

227

Gideon stood up, his knees shaking and his chin vibrating.

Adrienne bore her eyes into his. *Get the fuck out of here.*

He grabbed his computer and walked out.

When the door shut, she said, "I think I'll have that cup of coffee now," and walked over to the station.

By the time Adrienne returned to the table with her cup, neither Worth nor Raven had said a word.

She sat down. "Sorry about that." *No, I'm not.*

Worth rubbed his chin. "Okay. Let's start over."

Adrienne gave a grin of satisfaction. *Let's do that, Byron.*

"What did you and Flo talk about the day that she visited you here in October?" He brought his pen out of his shirt pocket and rested the covered tip on his pursed lips.

Was he only going to ask about the first meeting? Does he know about the meeting we had later that night? Maybe he'll ask about it as a follow-up question. Flo's words came back to her.

"Don't trust anyone."

"It was a quick meeting," Adrienne said. "She came in and asked me how my training with Director Raven and Rose was going, and I told her what I had been working on. If you both remember, she was looking tan, fit, and rested, so I joked with her and asked when I got to go on my 'makeover mission.'"

Worth slid the tip of his pen below his chin, said, "What did she say to that?" and then slid the tip back to his lips.

"Nothing. She ignored the question and asked me what I thought about Munny's assistant, Ulysses King."

Raven readied her pen over her open Padfolio and asked, "And what did you think about Mister King?"

Adrienne said to both, "I told her that his weapons knowledge was intimidating and that he was more thorough than Munny was when explaining certain systems to me." She took a drink of coffee and turned her attention to Raven. "I also told her that you had mentioned to me that he had a commercial pilot's license and could fly anything from a floatplane to a Boeing 727, which I was impressed with."

"Why do you think she asked you about him?" Raven asked.

"She's our primary trainer and works hand-in-hand with Munny. Because King is his assistant and a relatively new hire, and the fact that she had been gone for a few months, I suppose she wanted to know how he was doing from someone other than Munny." She sat back for a beat. "But that's just a guess. She never told me why she was asking about him."

Adrienne watched as Raven and Worth exchanged a nod.

They both scribbled on their pads for a minute and then Worth asked, "Anything else? Did you circle back to her mission at all?"

"No. After asking me about King, she wished me well and said that she looked forward to seeing me when she returned from her mission." Adrienne looked down at the table, and the room was silent for perhaps thirty seconds.

"Never told you where she was headed?" Worth asked.

Gstaad, Switzerland—and I want to know why, she thought. "No. Never mentioned it. I wasn't that interested anyway."

"Why is that?"

"Because I wanted to know where she had been. She looked five years younger."

"But she didn't tell you."

"No. The subject did not come up again after she ignored my first question about it."

Raven unscrewed her thermos and poured herself a cup of coffee then spoke while screwing the lid back on. "So, she comes in your office, you ask her about her mission, and she says nothing about it. Then, she asks you about your training and what you think of Mister King. Finally, she wishes you well while she's away, and the meeting ends. That sum it up?"

For that *meeting,* Adrienne thought. "Yes," she said. Before they asked more, she added, "She was a great mentor. I'm lucky to have had her."

Worth tapped the covered tip of his pen against his lips twice and then cocked his head to the right. "Did you have any contact with her after the meeting?"

If he, Raven, and Gideon had indeed been spending a lot of time up here the past few days, she guessed that they had known about Flo's death for longer than the past day, which meant if questioning her was a matter of timely importance, they would have brought her in before this morning. And, they had not asked her directly about her second meeting with Flo. Again, if it was important, they would have cut to the chase. Her instincts told her that this interview was more in the lane of standard procedure after there had been an incident. Additionally, there was no reason for them to suspect her of foul play as Flo had been her mentor and Adrienne had yet to go on a mission.

"No," she said.

Raven set down her pen and swiveled her chair to face Adrienne. "Did you know anything else about her?"

Once again, she heard her mentor's voice say, *"Don't trust anyone."* The sentiment certainly applied to Gideon, but could she trust Worth and Raven? *Perhaps, in time,* she thought. If she told them some of the things she had learned, she could pass the knowledge off as having been from earlier conversations with Flo.

"Always have something meaningful to come back to until you decide it is time to walk away," Flo had said.

"What's that for you?" she had asked.

"I'll let you know when I get back."

Maybe Worth and Raven already knew what that was for Flo—maybe they didn't. Adrienne doubted that she would ever find out what it was. But . . . could this 'meaningful thing to come back to' have something to do with her death? She could not rule it out. Also, the night of Adrienne's failed test to kill Hugh in the dinner scenario, why had Flo walked away from the housing building? Where had she gone that night?

She pondered the questions for a moment but then settled on one of her original arguments for not telling them anything: *They waited to see me,* she said to herself.

"We did chitchat from time to time over lunch about surface-level topics like movies we enjoyed and books we had read and particular brands of scotch we enjoyed, but I never knew anything about her personally beyond that," she said. However, they had been to each other's home for dinner, and at least Raven could know that because technically she had access to Flo's home security video camera recordings since the company co-owned the house. So, Adrienne added, "To prove my point, I have been to her house a couple of times for dinner, and she has been to mine a few times. We talked a little bit of shop—mostly her critiquing something I had done wrong during that day's training session—had a few drinks, and then watched a movie. In fact," she said, giving a laugh in remembrance, "we were working our way through Charles Bronson's *Death Wish* series. But in the year and a half I knew her, we only made it to *Death Wish III*, so that tells you how many times we got together." She paused. "As a side note, I think *The Mechanic* is better than all of them."

Worth gave a slight grin. "Anyone else attend the movie nights?"

"No."

"And during them, you both never talked about anything else, correct?"

"I did ask her once about vacations after missions, and she told me about Pāhonu." She eyed Worth. "Impressive. I hope to go there after one of my missions."

Raven rolled her eyes. "Let me guess. She told you to make sure it was in your contract, right?"

Adrienne played along. "How did you know she did that?"

"Because she did that with everyone."

"Can't blame her," Worth said. "It's your favorite vacation spot too, Kerrie."

Raven gave him a grin, but it vanished just as fast as it had appeared. "Nothing else was discussed between the two of you?"

Adrienne took a gulp of coffee. "Nothing more than what I already told you. To be honest, Flo was boring company."

It was a lie, but she hoped that she had provided enough half-truths to end the discussion.

Worth put his pen back in his shirt pocket. "Thank you, Adrienne. You're going to find out a lot more about the situation in the coming days as we are promoting you to Flo's position." He reached out his hand. "Highly irregular since you haven't completed a mission yet. But, well, you're it. Congratulations, you're our new Rescue & Sanction Division Head."

She shook his hand and then shook hands with Raven, who said, "Congratulations."

Before she could process what had just happened, Worth continued. "There will be a team at your house later this morning to set up your video camera surveillance, supervised by Mr. King. He'll show you how to use the system when you arrive home. No mystery that he's going to be promoted today too. Tomorrow, we'll need both of you here early to start working on what happened to Flo and Munny." He paused. "As long as you don't threaten to kill one of our CEOs anymore."

I can't promise that, she thought, but didn't say it out loud.

"You have my word, sir," Adrienne said.

✳ ✳ ✳

Raven watched the door close, and then turned to Worth. "Let's try and avoid putting her in the same room with Jock for a while."

"Did you think she would have injured him?"

Raven shrugged. "I don't want to think about it." She shook her thermos, guessing how much coffee was left in it. "He doesn't need to like anyone here, but he needs to respect the work they do, and with that comes not treating them like garbage in every face-to-face interaction." She unscrewed the lid and poured more coffee into her cup. "We can keep them separated for a little bit, but she's a division head now."

"Will she be ready to start training people this summer?"

"We'll lean on Rose at first, but, at some point, Adrienne will have to be ready . . . if we even have a group this summer."

"I was thinking about that too." He stared at the table.

"What is it?"

He peered up at her. "I thought we had a James Bond with Flo."

"We did."

"Flo's mission was the first time we have gone on the offensive. We have had our personnel be ruthless and do unpleasant things since the formation of this company, but we built our reputation on being sound defensively—no one gets into the inner circle, and we perform sanctions always on our terms. Our clients need to appear peaceful. We don't. We just can't make any headlines."

"We're lucky our enemies did not decide to turn our employees' deaths into a headline this time."

"In the end, it's still all about communication—the sending and receiving of messages. For years, Flo delivered many to our opponents. This time, we received one back."

"Maybe we dial it back and just focus on sanctions—not undercover operations."

"No other option, at least in the short term, but we still need intelligence gathering, right?"

"Maybe we keep that in Rose's lane and abandon the hybrid idea of assassin-agent. That's how we envisioned it in the beginning, anyway. Flo was just . . ." his voice trailed off.

"Something special," Raven said. She pulled a pack of cigarettes from her cardigan's inner pocket and shook two out.

"I guess it's that bad," Worth said, accepting one of the white sticks. "Where were these a few days ago?"

"Didn't want to share with Jock." She pulled out a lighter and lit her cigarette, then tossed the lighter to Worth.

"He only likes cigars."

"I'm not so sure about that."

Worth looked surprised. "Huh . . . Ah . . . Do we still have ashtrays in here?"

She walked to the wall cabinet above the coffee bar, opened it, and returned with two heavy glass ashtrays.

"Reminds me of our old days together," Worth said.

The comment stung a bit, but she let it pass. She put the top back on her thermos and moved it to the side. "Look, our experiment was always based on the question: Could we take the best athletes in the world and train them to pull the trigger? We put a premium on athleticism because they needed to be able to have the stamina and physicality to operate in any realm of the world and under the most challenging and physically demanding circumstances that the Earth can offer. Remember? You also understand well our more complicated considerations: Are they controllable? Can we trust them? And if they passed muster, then we would use them as assassins—target package, weapon selection, insertion, kill, extraction. Simple. Then, we met Flo."

He cut her off. "And she evolved our vision: develop a cover, study the subject or subjects, insertion, gather information, kill if necessary, extraction."

He set his right fist on the table. "I had dreams of developing an assassin-to-agent pipeline."

God, he can't let it go. "I admit, it was a nice option to have when we had Flo. And I know that Flo's death is forcing you to evaluate your dream."

He took a long drag on his cigarette and then blew the smoke toward the ceiling. "I suppose I'm asking, Can Adrienne become a Flo?"

She needed to give him hope but also a healthy dose of realism.

He used to grasp for silver bullets when things went wrong at the C.I.A., and he's doing it again.

"No one will 'become a Flo.' Now, could Adrienne grow into an agent? Maybe. We'll have to see how she does on a real mission first."

"I wonder what Jock thinks."

Jock only cares about two things: leveraging power to make as much money as possible, and sticking it to his old Wall Street buddies every chance he gets. Hell, Flo's second mission was to assassinate one of his rivals who had double-crossed him on a deal long ago. The man was also trading financial secrets for money from a terrorist organization, but Jock considered that secondary to his main reason of revenge. Of course, she could say none of this to Worth right now. "I wouldn't know what he thinks," she said.

"What about counterintelligence?"

Where did this come from?

But she remembered that he also had a habit of switching topics when he was stressed. "What about it?"

"Is there any chance Flo was betrayed from within our walls?"

She inhaled the glorious smoke deep into her lungs, savoring the relaxed feeling. She was back up to a pack a day and wondered if anyone knew that she was smoking again. She exhaled and broke off the tip of ash into her ashtray.

"There's *always* a chance. We've known that since our C.I.A. days. You should ask, How much time do you want to spend looking into it?" She finished her coffee and crushed the paper cup. "Why do I feel like I'm about to be volunteered for something?"

"Not necessarily. Doesn't it all feel wrong to you, though? How could Munny and Flo walk into a trap? Junius was about as easy of a target as they come."

"Maybe one of them made a mistake. Maybe Flo was thinking about home. She wasn't infallible, Byron."

"You're right, of course. That could have happened. But we could also have an internal problem. Now, I'm not talking about an all-out mole hunt. I would just like you to poke around a bit."

"Anyone in particular?"

"How about the man we're about to call in and promote?"

"King?"

"Munny was showing him the ropes, and that meant he had access to our server."

She sat back and stretched her long legs. "That shouldn't be a problem, but I don't think we have a leak. Flo would have been killed long ago, and we wouldn't have the intelligence that she gathered."

"That Junius is part of a larger organization?"

"Exactly."

"His death was supposed to give us the opportunity to sit back and watch them scramble, learn about *their* response methods."

"Like you said, we're the ones who received the message this time."

Worth stubbed out his cigarette and stood up. "Let's take a fifteen-minute break and then talk to him. We won't mention any of this. I want him feeling confident after we promote him."

"Anyone else you want me to check up on?"

"Not at the moment." He started to walk toward the door. "I'll get Gideon back in here." He stopped and looked at his watch. "We need to be quick with King if I'm going to make it to Eleanor's house around noon."

She inhaled from her cigarette one last time and then put it out in the ashtray. "In ten minutes, I'll go downstairs and fetch King."

They both exited the conference room, and Raven entered her office and closed the door. She walked to the floor-to-ceiling windows, stopping to look down at the snow-covered ground that had been a lush, green carpet four months ago . . . when Flo was alive and preparing for her mission. She remembered when Flo had emerged from the coffin, eyes radiating intensity, during her official welcome to the company. Raven lowered her head, and a tear slid down her cheek.

Then another.

Then another.

Through glassy eyes, she beheld the bare line of trees that lined the property and the charcoal-colored sky above them.

Ulysses King. Of course. Why hadn't she thought of him before?

21

Gstaad, Switzerland

"I didn't know when she was going to make the attempt, Control!" Victor Lars Junius said into his burner phone. "We should have had better intel."

"You're a stupid sonofabitch," Control replied. "You could have died."

"I *let* her go."

There was a pause. "You're lying. If she would have had her weapon on her, we wouldn't be talking right now. You had a few hours beforehand. Rex should have killed her before she even made it to the library!"

She was right, but, at the moment, his pride would not allow him to apologize. He had been feeling his Burton confidence at an all-time high that night, and so what if he wanted to act on it and get a measure of himself as a killer? If the agent was so powerful, then why *hadn't* she finished him off before leaping from the terrace?

Huh? What about that, *Control? You megalomaniacal, micromanaging bitch.*

"We can always look back in hindsight and see how it might have gone down differently."

"Hindsight? If that's how you continue to see, then we have a major problem that needs to be addressed. I need you to see with *foresight*. We recovered a few evenings ago because we knew where Munny would be. But your theatrics almost cost us. What if she would have gotten away?" There was silence for a moment, and then he heard what he thought was ice clinking in a glass. "So, tell me, Victor. *Do* we have a problem?"

He walked across the carpet to the library's bar and poured himself another glass of Lagavulin. The clinking he had heard had actuated his thirst for more scotch. Fuck that Pavlov guy, fuck his dog, and fuck Control. After a calming sip, he said, "No, we don't have a problem."

"Good," Control said. "Worth-Gideon won't come after you again for a while, if at all, but an agent from another company might. Be more prepared next time."

The phone call ended, and he buzzed Imperia Rex into the library.

"Here," he said, passing the phone to his bodyguard.

"Did it go as expected?"

He took another drink of scotch and resumed his Burton persona. He had tried speaking like his idol to Control once, and she had destroyed him on the phone. His confidence shattered, it had taken him months to work up the courage to resume his voice lessons. Tonight, he was dressed exactly like his glorious Richard had been in *Who's Afraid of Virginia Woolf?* Slip-on Oxfords, wool slacks, white collared shirt, tie, cardigan, and dark, thick-rimmed glasses. He even had a corner of his library set up exactly like Burton's corner study in the film and had sat there for hours earlier, thinking about the attempt on his life. The rest of the room was covered in elaborate Christmas decorations—wreaths and bows, strings of lights draped on the walls, an enormous tree with ornaments on every branch and bubble lights and strings of beads and popcorn, and there were enough presents underneath it to fill a quarter of the floor space. In fact, every room in the chalet was decorated as such, and Junius planned to go from room to room on Christmas morning, wearing his festive pajamas and robe and open the presents, for they were all for him.

Before the call with Control, he had said to Imperia Rex, *"Everything in its place, Martha. Everything in its own good time."*

"Nothing I couldn't handle," he said to her now. "A trifle of concern, that's all."

"I apologize if something I did led to that conversation."

"No, not at all. Rubbish. We handled matters." He rubbed the glass in a circle on the oak bar's top. "Of course, you do know that 'they'll' be back for another visit at some appointed hour."

Rex approached the bar and filled a Collins glass with ice water. "Vic—"

He raised his index finger.

"Richard—"

He smiled.

"—I know you could have handled her. But, please, let me know when you hear from our source *earlier* than you did this time."

He removed his cardigan, as his idol had in the film, and wondered at the glass of scotch. "As if my life depended on it."

"Thank you." She started to walk away.

"Say it again, dear. Just once more."

"You have the voice of a sorcerer."

"Not that bit. The other line, if you please."

She stopped, the wall lights illuminating her like an angel. She turned around slowly—*God, how he wanted to ravish her on the floor in front of his presents!*—and said in an annoyed tone, "If you existed, I'd divorce you."

He took a drink. *Better than before—still needed work, though.* He gave her a sly look. "You've been advised, Martha."

She winked in affirmation and then stepped out of the room.

Landon Beach

7 Months Later . . .

Landon Beach

22

Raleigh, North Carolina – July 4, 2003

Kerrie Raven stood on the home's small front porch, removed her sunglasses, and rang the doorbell. She looked left and then right, impressed by the freshly cut grass that ended in a wooden fence on both sides—the sprinklers were up and going *twitch-twitch-twitch* as water spread across the two sections of lawn. A few seconds later, drops hit the corners of the brick porch, and judging from the glazed surface, she guessed that the watering had been going on for a while now. It was 9 a.m., and the parade would be starting in two hours. It was also a day off from work for Raven, and the corner of the porch's wet surface reminded her that she was looking forward to a relaxing day on her pool deck, soaking in the warm July sun, drinking a margarita, and occasionally cooling off with dips into the cool, crystal-clear water. Later, she would sit on the second-floor balcony to her bedroom and watch the fireworks.

There was much to reflect upon as the flames of freedom continued to burn: the war in Afghanistan was well into its second year, and a U.S.-led coalition had invaded Iraq in late March, the President of the United States giving a televised speech two months ago from the Aircraft Carrier *USS Abraham Lincoln* (CVN-72) with the White House-produced banner that said *Mission Accomplished* mounted on the carrier's island behind him.

But first, a check-in visit with Eleanor and Jewel before they headed downtown for the annual festivities.

She heard footsteps, followed by the sound of a deadbolt being unlocked and a chain lock being slid across the channel and then dropped. The door opened twelve inches to a confused Eleanor, dressed in white tennis shoes, a blue skirt, and a red tank top, which Raven thought exposed too much cleavage.

"May I help you?"

Raven gave her a smile and watched as the nanny's eyes opened wider in recognition.

"Why, Beatrice. I . . . I didn't recognize you with your hair tucked under the ballcap and the jogging suit and waist pack. Big change from your usual suit."

"Day off. Heading to the gym before the parade."

Eleanor gave her a smile and opened the door wider. "We'll be at the parade too! But I didn't know you'd be stopping by today. Ben was here yesterday." She stood in the doorway with one hand on the knob and the other holding a brown mug of coffee.

"I know. It's why I'm here. He told me about the lovely visit, and I felt so guilty since I haven't been here in forever. Is it okay?"

"Heck *yes* it's okay. Happy Fourth! C'mon in."

Raven gave her arm a pat. "Aren't you looking festive?"

Eleanor closed the door behind her. "All-ready for the big celebration. You should see Jewel's outfit. I just laid it out on her bed—like dressing up a doll. Going to be Little Miss Patriotic today."

"Where is the little munchkin?"

"Just drying off after her bath. She was outside playing in the front sprinklers for the past half-hour, which reminds me . . ." She pushed up a row of blinds covering a living room window and peered out. "Yep. I forgot to turn them off." She dropped the blinds and turned back toward Raven. "Gettin' old, Miss. Ah, well, if the lawn gets an extra-long drink, it's not the end of the world." She shrugged. "Anyway, the girl wants to go to the playground, then the parade, and then back through the sprinklers when we get home. I swear, it is from one thing to the next with that ball of energy."

"Keeps you busy."

"Always."

She waved Raven through the living room, and they entered the kitchen as was their normal procedure. The house was the same as always. Spotless. Not even a dish in the sink, and Raven noticed that the tile floor had been recently mopped and the cabinets wiped with Pledge—the tell-tale smell was mixed with the aroma of coffee as she took a seat at the small table.

Eleanor joined her and placed a blue mug of coffee in front of Raven while she took a swig from her own mug. "We had a lovely visit with Ben yesterday. He's so good to Jewel—especially since . . . well, you know."

"Yes. Sorry for not giving you any notice, and sorry it has been so long since I was last here. Work, you know?"

"Oh, don't you worry." Eleanor gave a politician's smirk of pride, like she had just delivered the words *"a job well done"* to some poor sonofabitch who would never see her again. "I've been keeping up with everything—bills, cleaning, Jewel. Hard to believe that preschool is only about a year away." She laughed. "But we'll be er-ready."

"I know you will," Raven said.

She heard a door open down the hallway.

Eleanor turned her head and yelled, "Jewel, get dressed, sweetie, and then nanny's got a surprise for you!"

Taking advantage of the distraction, Raven set her coffee cup on the floor.

"Can I come see?" a tiny voice said.

"Not yet! Get dressed, and then you can come out!"

"Okay!"

Raven heard footsteps bounding down the hallway, followed by the sound of a door opening and then closing.

"She will be so excited to see you," Eleanor said.

Raven slid her hand down to her waist pack and unzipped it. She grasped what was inside. "I don't think so," she said, almost in a whisper.

Eleanor set her coffee cup down, her smile replaced by narrowed eyes and a cock of the neck to the left. "What?"

Raven pulled out her pistol with a suppressor attached, aimed it at Eleanor's forehead—Eleanor's brown eyes just starting to open wide—and fired two shots.

As the dead nanny's body slouched back against the kitchen table chair, Raven stood and stepped back carefully from the table. In a matter of seconds, she had stripped off her hat, jogging suit jacket and pants, and her running shoes and socks, exposing her tan shorts and a white t-shirt that she had on underneath. Opening her backpack, she removed a pair of flip-flops, a blonde wig, and a pair of latex gloves, all of which she put on. Into the backpack went her jogging suit, hat, running shoes, socks, and waist pack.

After picking up her mug from the kitchen floor, she walked to the corner of the living room and poured her coffee into the soil that filled a ceramic pot holding an ugly houseplant. She placed the mug into her backpack and then set the open backpack by the front door.

With the gun in her right hand, she turned and walked down the hallway.

As she stopped just short of the door, she could hear "Dit, dit, dit, did, dit-Dora. Dit, dit, dit, dit, dit-Dora."

Raven knocked on the door. "Jewel, it's Birdie, your buddy. I couldn't wait any longer. Can I come in?"

There was a pause, and Raven imagined the two-year-old's mind at work, searching for a visual image of a person named Birdie and, once acquired, matching it to a memory of her voice. "Birdie! I gettin' my shoes on! Come in!"

Raven raised the gun and opened the door.

"My budd—"

Pop-pop.

23

"Are you sure you weren't followed any of the times you visited them?" Kerrie Raven asked Byron Worth.

Worth's eyes were red. An opened bottle of Woodford Reserve sat on his living room coffee table next to his filled glass. A minute ago, she had arrived at his house and told him the horrible news that someone had shot and killed Eleanor and Jewel. "There's no way. I—I used classic tradecraft." He took a pull from the glass and swallowed. "How could this have happened?"

"I don't know. I haven't been there for months."

Worth set the drink down and then put his head in his hands. "Oh, Jesus. It might be because of me."

"Don't say that. If anyone made a mistake, it was Hugh."

For a moment, Worth regained his composure and lifted his head. "Eleanor did tell me that he had spent a weekend there a few weeks ago." He reached for the glass of bourbon. "People make mistakes when they're emotional, and he was definitely attached to Jewel." His head fell back into his hands. "Oh, that sweet little girl."

Raven started to sniffle. "I went to the parade, and since I was close to their house, I—I decided to drive by. Didn't plan on stopping, but you had me so jealous from your fun visit yesterday, and I just wanted to see her—"

She broke down in tears for a good minute.

He rubbed his eyes and then reached out, putting a hand on her shoulder. "How long did it look like they had been dead?"

"I would guess since last night. What time did you leave there yesterday?"

She already knew his answer.

"Around four. They wanted me to stay for dinner, but I declined. God— maybe if I would have stayed. . ."

She wiped her eyes and sat up straight. "Byron, stop that talk right now. I want you to stay here while I go and clean the place up. Whoever took out Eleanor and Jewel could be gunning for you next. Or Hugh." She locked eyes with him. "Where is he?"

Worth removed his hand from her shoulder. "His hit on Junius is in two nights. He left for Geneva yesterday. For Christ's sake, we're the ones who started that whole chain of events." He shook his head. "Do you think what happened at the house is some sort of warning?"

Triumph.

She had known the mission was in the works for some time, but Worth and Gideon had been keeping the exact date to themselves. This past week, Worth had been in contact with Igraine Wexler, the head of Wexler, Inc., but Worth would still not mention specifics to Raven. If anything, he was still mad that another company was going to take the glory away from Worth-Gideon.

This had forced her to play her high card today, and it had worked. She would now be able to tell Control, and Junius and Imperia Rex would be ready when Hugh arrived at *Le Pays de Galles* in Céligny to sanction Junius. After Raven disposed of the bodies and cleaned the house, she would not leave Worth's side for the next few days. Hence, he would be less likely to suspect that she had compromised the mission, and she would start to plant hints that the leak had to be from Hugh's end, which would force Worth to stay in contact with Igraine Wexler. Paranoia would reign at Wexler, giving Raven the perfect opportunity to tell Worth that her investigation into Worth-Gideon, specifically Ulysses King, had yielded nothing unusual. She would say to him with great confidence, *"Our house is clean."*

She shook her head as if his suggestion were ludicrous. "No. The timing is too coincidental. They cannot possibly know that he is coming. Think of it. If they knew that Hugh was on his way to kill Junius, they wouldn't do something like this to jeopardize the trap they had set for him. In fact, this might actually work to Hugh's benefit, but he cannot afford any delays." She sat back against the couch's puffy leather cushions. "This hit means that they somehow found out that Flo was the girl's mother, and they're trying to close the loop on that failed mission of ours, which would be a message to us. Or . . . they followed Hugh a few weeks ago, or during his visit before that, and thought they were sending a message to him but not knowing that he was leaving to kill Junius."

"Faaahhhck." Worth inhaled and then blew out a breath. "So, what move would you suggest I make?"

"Nothing until Hugh returns. You and Igraine do not want to do anything to compromise the mission. Also, if Hugh were to find out before he heads to . . . Gstaad, right?"

"No," Worth said. "Junius is somewhere else right now."

"I won't even ask," she said. "It's just you said Geneva, and I assumed . . . well, bad memories from Flo."

"I'll tell you when it's over, okay?"

She rubbed his arm. "Okay."

"Well, if Hugh knew that his daughter had just been killed, then he'd be emotional, and that's a no-no before a mission like this."

"Agree. We'll break it to him when he gets back." Worth swallowed. "But he won't get to see her body, will he?"

Raven looked away from him. "No, he won't."

He tipped back his whiskey glass, finishing it. "Sure you don't want a small one before you go?"

"No."

"Shouldn't I go with you to help or provide cover?"

"No. I am expendable. You're not." She stood. "Now, stay here and keep the doors locked, and don't drink any more of that stuff until I return. I'll have one with you then." She looked at her watch. "It'll be late, but I'll call you when I'm on my way."

He stood next to her.

Time to plant another seed. "I'm staying in one of your guest bedrooms until Hugh's mission is over, so get it ready. We're not going to let anything mess this up."

He nodded. "What about the C.I.A. wanting to hire us for that mission in Basrah? We've got to put Adrienne in the field sooner or later. Jock's unsure about it, though."

"They can wait for now and so can Jock. We shouldn't even be in that corner of the sandbox right now. However, if Hugh's mission is successful, and it should be, we'll discuss it then. Don't talk to anyone today. You have to seem like everything is normal and you're enjoying the next few days off. I have to as well."

"I'll have the guest room ready for you."

Good. Because I'm going to fuck your brains out in it tonight.

"Thanks," she said.

He was a means to an end—everyone at Worth-Gideon had become that to her. In the very best of times, she had been treated as an expendable object; in the worst of times, an outcast, a nonconformist, someone to be ignored and marginalized because she didn't think as they did—she wasn't *one of them*. And when she had learned that she would never fit in or be accepted by those in power, Raven had set out to eviscerate them, burn the whole thing down. Turn the tables. Trade in lies. Use the boogeyman argument. Make up intelligence and leverage it against those in charge who would keep her at arm's length. Embarrass them. *Destroy* them. She understood that until other spies were highly placed in similar institutions, there would be the disadvantage of not being able to use the peer-review system to verify her circular arguments—her conclusions appearing within their premises. But now, there was such a peer planted at Wexler, and the time was coming to use that relationship to her advantage.

Raven had not started her own company. Too hard. Instead, she had joined a new company—Control's—where her skills were valued . . . while still being able to cut down the company, which she was still a part of, branch by branch, sacrificing others for herself along the way—never for advancement, for it was impossible. Her motivation had not been born out of boredom, creating an in-vogue desire to create a new area of study, tied, or not tied, by a thread to the previous body of work. And her motivation had also not come from some 3 a.m. realization that the fault lay in her because she was unable to reach the plateaus of excellence that her predecessors had, relegating her to the hard truth that she would forever be a second-rate citizen in the intelligence game, the spy realm. No, her drive had always been revenge, unclouded and uncomplicated. Flo and Munny had been expendable. Gideon was expendable.

She looked into the tired eyes of Byron Worth and gave him a sympathetic grin along with a loving squeeze and then a rub of his right arm. Worth was expendable.

Hugh was expendable.

And, one day, Adrienne Astra would be expendable.

She left the estate and headed for home. Before she cleaned up the nanny's house, it was time to call Control from the burner phone that should have been placed in the shed on the far side of her property by now.

24

Céligny, Switzerland

Victor Lars Junius reclined in his leather armchair on the upper floor of the annex to Le Pays de Galles' main house. The annex was a large barn with a loft that used to house pigeons, and Burton had converted the loft into a spacious and beautiful library with a gabled ceiling, knotty pine walls, and floors that had to be reinforced because of the weight of the books. There was an outdoor staircase that led up to the entrance of the library and a balcony that extended out from French doors at the other end.

Upon entering the library from the stairs, there was a beautiful stone fireplace to the immediate left, and facing the French doors, one saw a scattering of easy chairs, tables, and couches. Burton had kept a typewriter on his desk, and so Junius had one on his desk, although he had never punched a key. There were bookcases that swung out from the shadows all along the right-hand side and framed duplicates of Richard's seven Academy Award Nomination certificates hung on the strip of knotty pine above the swinging bookcases; when the shelves were positioned inward, three cubby spaces were formed under the sloping ceiling. Burton's third wife, Suzy, had put in the shelves, which had transformed the room from a mere study to a reader's dream space, and when Junius purchased the estate, one of the first things he did was fill the empty shelves with most of the books that Burton had possessed. He'd even special-ordered a large, two-handled luggage bag made of black leather and gray fabric to resemble Burton's famous monogrammed "book bag" that he always traveled with, loaded with new books to satiate the actor's enormous reading appetite. However, Burton kept some mainstays in the bag—*The Complete Works of William Shakespeare*, *The Book of Common Prayer*, the Qur'an, and the *Dictionary of Slang and Unconventional English*—and so, Junius bought copies and kept them in his "VLJ"-monogrammed bag as well, although he bored of them easily. He lacked the discipline to work through master prose and eloquent poetry to reap their rewards, usually cracking open a detective novel after twenty minutes with W.H. Auden, Ted Hughes, or even Evelyn Waugh. Even though he would profess an incurable curiosity and thirst to look up new words and therefore expose himself to new ideas, Junius usually bowed out of leafing through his array of dictionaries after studying a word or two or when his mind drifted to wine, his shipping empire, or women.

In another hour or so, he figured that the American assassin would arrive and attempt to kill him. "Poor fool," he said. However, Junius agreed with the location the assassin's company had chosen for the attempted sanction. Le Pays de Galles gave the good lad, Hugh, the best chance. The chalet in Gstaad had too much security for him to penetrate, and his castle, *Burton's Keep*, in the mountains north of Montreux, was impregnable. Also, a training cadre had just arrived, and the signs were that this would be the best group yet. Ever since the "bad group" had been disposed of, things had gone smoothly, and graduates of the training were now performing clandestine missions from the bowels of his fleet of ships.

Still, it did not matter that his estate in Céligny could be penetrated by the dashing Hugh. Having Kerrie Raven on the inside of Worth-Gideon, Inc. had proven useful once again. In his mind, she had justified every cent of her salary with the latest intel about Hugh's mission; that could be because he was, yet again, the target. However, he had never second-guessed his decision to recruit her years ago, and because he had brought her into Control's circle, he thought that the high lady was a bit jealous of his hiring insight. Then again, perhaps not. It didn't matter. Sir Hugh would be meeting his end on this perfect summer evening.

Junius slid out of his armchair and poured himself a snifter of brandy from the bar that had been built between the windows on the side of the library facing the main house and guest chalet that Burton's brother Ifor had built and stayed in. Snifter in hand, he walked toward the open French doors. On cooler, breezy summer evenings, he liked to keep the glass doors open and enjoy the sweet scents wafting in from his flower garden.

"I wonder what the poor of the world are doing this very moment?" he said, stepping onto the wooden flooring of the library's balcony. He felt light in his sandals, linen pants, and V-neck t-shirt. "*Summer garb,*" his mistress had called it. He knew she was waiting in the main house for him to be done with this business tonight so that he could join her for a bath by candlelight to relax his tense muscles and calm his nerves from the inevitable excitement that accompanies observing a trap being set. She was a decade younger than he was, came from money, and knew what she wanted. And he liked all those things about her, but a part of him—the part that even "Richard" could not penetrate—still missed the beautiful agent that Rex had killed in December. Finding out that the agent named Hugh, who was coming to be his executioner tonight, had been involved with the agent had upset him when Control had delivered the news a day ago. He shouldn't be jealous, but for some reason, he was.

Ah, well. It will be a joy to watch him killed tonight. He looked down at the wooden flooring. *Should be right about here, I think.*

The wind ran over the hair on his arms and swept the gray hair off his forehead for a moment. The plugs he had surgically implanted months ago had filled in his thinning hair nicely, and upon inspection in the mirror before leaving the main house for the annex earlier, he thought that the surgeon had done a first-rate job of matching his hairline with Burton's at age 40, which had been the target. *"I want it to look like Richard's when he starred in* The Spy Who Came in From the Cold. *Can you manage it?"* he had said in his best "quiet, conspiratorial" Burton with a penetrating stare, only broken by a shift of his eyes before and after. *"Can you manage it?"*

And indeed, the surgeon had.

As Junius took a rejuvenating sip of brandy, he observed Imperia Rex leave the guest chalet and make her way over to a spot almost directly beneath him.

"The seaplane has just landed. It's time to get you inside the main house."

Hugh had arrived in Geneva a few days ago, and they had permitted him to scope out the grounds with cameras—one with a telescopic lens—binoculars, and night vision goggles from various positions outside the property. He was good; if they hadn't been looking, they never would have noticed him. And he performed surveillance at different times—before dawn, during lunch, mid-afternoon, after dinner, and at two a.m. in the morning. They were also entertained by some of his disguises: the jogger, the tourist, the farmer, the repairman, and the bird watcher—only in the middle of the night had he looked like a professional, wearing all-black clothing. He had never carried a sniper rifle, so Rex had allowed Junius to put his daily rhythms on display for the assassin—especially his nightly visit to the library after dinner. Rex had found out that Hugh and another agent named Sharkey, who also worked for Wexler, Inc., were staying in a small house just outside of Geneva. Sharkey was a pilot of a seaplane owned by one of Wexler's shell companies, and Rex had guessed that the plan would be for the two men to fly north from Geneva to just offshore of Céligny tonight, anchor the seaplane, go ashore, travel the half-mile from the water to Le Pays de Galles by foot, and then Sharkey would position himself to provide cover if Hugh's retreat became hot.

Rex would have the chalet's porch lights on, along with a few interior lights. She would also have lights on in the upstairs and downstairs of the main house. As for the barn, only the library lights would be on. After observing Hugh's movements, she knew this setup would force him to approach the barn from the other side of the property. If she had left the chalet dark, like she had on purpose last night, then he could have come from that direction as well. But tonight, she wanted to direct his movements, which is why she would also leave the French doors open on the library's balcony and have jazz music playing. Hence, the most efficient way for Hugh to reach the second-floor library undetected would be to climb the closest of the two posts which held up the balcony and then go over the spindled railing.

But that is where trouble would start for the supposed superstar agent Hugh. And when trouble started for Hugh, trouble would find Mister Sharkey.

"How do you think they're planning on getting out of the country?" he had asked Rex yesterday morning over coffee. By noon, she had the answer.

"They'll leave the property, hike it back to the seaplane, and my guess is that Sharkey will fly it south to Montpellier. Control's man in France said that Wexler owns a mansion there that is right on the Mediterranean—perfect place for a seaplane to land. Then, they'd leave the Montpellier–Méditerranée Airport for Paris or London or Berlin and then fly back across the Atlantic."

Junius peered down at Rex. The dress rehearsal was over. It was now time for him to take refuge in the wings and for the illusion to take center stage. He said, "Right. The other me is in position," and then walked back through the library, heading for the exit and outdoor stairs.

Hugh moved swiftly along the fence that ran the length of the right-hand property line of Le Pays de Galles. Sharkey was a few yards behind him. Lights were on inside the chalet and main house, and the chalet's front porch lights were also illuminated, which had eliminated the approach vector from that side of the property. Hence, he would go over the fence at a point that faced the backside of the barn, and Sharkey would travel farther down the fence line to a point where he had a clear field of fire that covered the open area stretching all the way from the barn to the chalet. If anyone came out of the barn, main house, or chalet and threatened Hugh's exit, they would find themselves on the receiving end of his sniper rifle that had been left hidden in the bushes down the road from the estate last night.

Hugh heard the rumble of a train in the distance and smiled.

Right on time.

Across the street and only a hundred yards from the house were train tracks, and he had hoped that the train would not have a delay and pass while they were getting into position. Everything was happening as it should happen when one performed a proper surveillance and had top-of-the-line intelligence.

As the sound of the train grew louder, they quickened their pace, and just as Hugh arrived at his desired position, the train roared by in the distance. From the other side of the property, they had observed that the only lights on in the barn were from the second-floor library. His target was a creature of habit, and that would be his undoing tonight. Hugh was sure that Junius's bodyguard, Imperia Rex, was somewhere on the estate, perhaps even with him in the library, but killing her was not a necessity tonight. Junius was the target. Rex would only be eliminated if she became a target of opportunity or if she interfered with his mission. This bothered him because they both deserved to die for what they had done to Flo. And in that life-taking, they had stolen one of the two most precious things in his life. The other was back home and should be getting ready to have dinner right now—perhaps her favorite: macaroni and cheese with hot dogs and Kool-Aid. He had wanted to give Junius a drawn-out and painful death, but it would not be possible. A quick death would have to do.

His lean muscles were taut underneath his black pants and long-sleeved, black shirt. He had shaved his head today and had applied camouflage face paint to his neck, face, and head in a moonlit clearing by the train tracks that they had scoped out the day before. On his feet were black moccasins that resembled slip-on aqua shoes; they were quiet, and the soles had excellent grip.

Sharkey was dressed similarly, and Hugh watched as he moved past him, heading to his place farther up the fence line to set up his field of fire. From their rehearsal last night, it would take him thirty seconds to get there and settle in.

Hugh lay flat on the ground and moved his left hand down the fence post until he found the black piece of string that he had tied to the bottom of it the previous evening. The string ran along the ground all the way to Sharkey's position, and if everything was a go when Sharkey was set, then Hugh would feel one short tug. If it was not clear for Hugh to proceed, he would feel three tugs, and Sharkey would soon rejoin him and tell him what was up. If they were in immediate danger, he would feel five or more tugs, and that meant to haul ass out of there immediately.

He waited and focused on his breathing, calming himself for the choreographed athletic moves he was about to make. With his right hand, he felt the gritty grip panels of his 9mm that had a suppressor attached and was in a holster on his right hip. If there were five or more tugs on the string, he would remove the gun and be ready to shoot as he sprinted away; if there were three tugs, his hand would not move; and if there was one tug, he would release his hold on the 9mm and start his planned maneuver.

The seconds ticked away in his head.

Three . . .

Two . . .

One.

A moment later, he felt one short tug and put on his gloves, which were pebbled with rubber to aid his grip while scaling the post and railing.

In seconds he was over the fence and had reached the side of the barn. Carefully, he slid around the corner and crept along the side, keeping his eyes on the lit chalet.

Then, he was at the post and could hear jazz music—Sinatra singing *"Guess I'll Hang My Tears Out To Dry"*—coming from the open doors on the balcony above.

Fuck this guy. He doesn't deserve to listen to Sinatra.

But I'm glad he is right now.

The inseams of his pant legs, from mid-thigh down to mid-calf, were covered with rubber patches, and using these patches along with the soles of his shoes and special gloves, Hugh ascended the wooden post and then reached up and pulled himself up over the side railing.

He went flush against the open door, out of sight of anyone in the library. The music was louder now, of course, and he recognized which part of the song was playing. His eyes scanned the open area between the barn and the glowing lights of the chalet. He saw nothing.

The layout of the library came into focus in Hugh's mind—bookshelves on the left, windows on the right, fireplace at the far end . . . in between, tables, couches, and chairs.

He inhaled.

Smooth entry, shoot anything that moves, but, at all costs, make sure to kill Junius.

He exhaled.

Taking in a large breath, he heard the song reach its crescendo with Sinatra belting out, "Oh, WELLLLLLLL . . ."

Hugh started his exhale and turned into the library. There was no movement in the room, and his entrance was quiet.

Immediately, his eyes located Junius. The shipping tycoon and murderer was seated with his back to Hugh on a couch at the far end of the room in front of the fireplace and stone chimney. The room was considerably darker at that end.

He took three steps and put Junius's head directly in his pistol's sights. But simultaneously, his brain sent him a message that said, *"This is too eas—"*

The bookshelves! They were all swung parallel to the left wall!

It was the last thought he ever had.

From behind the second bookcase, Imperia Rex watched as Hugh dropped to the floor, his head a mess of blood, bone, and gristle.

She pulled the case toward her and moved around it, still training her weapon on Hugh's body. In another beat, Rex was standing over it, and she fired a shot into his heart.

The figure seated on the couch did not move as it was a mannequin of Richard Burton that, through several cutouts, Rex had paid $100,000 to a Greek movie studio to make under the guise of it being a gag birthday gift for Junius a few years ago. The truth was that Junius wanted it not only to gaze at and have private conversations with but also as an insurance policy of sorts when he started working for Control. He never imagined that he would actually need it to save his life, but Rex had just put it to good use because, even from the front, it looked real. Junius would be overjoyed that it was not damaged.

There was no time to lose, and she took the radio off her belt, keyed the mic, and said, "Number one sanctioned. Your turn."

She stood still and put her faith in the sniper that Control had sent them two days ago. In her mind, she saw the woman putting the radio on the ground while still looking into the night vision scope on her rifle . . . taking aim at Sharkey, who sat across the property by the fence and had his weapon trained on his field of fire, waiting for Hugh to emerge from the library at any second . . . the center of the crosshairs freezing on a point in the middle of his forehead . . . her finger squeezing the trigger . . . and her watching through her scope as the bullet entered Sharkey's forehead, a green mist expanding behind his skull.

Five seconds later, her radio crackled to life, and she heard, "Number two down. Heading over for sanction shot."

A minute later, Rex's radio came on again, and the sniper said, "Number two sanctioned."

PART III

The Blue Hour

5 Months Later . . .

Landon Beach

25

Raleigh, North Carolina – December 2003

"I'm ready, and you know it!" Adrienne shouted at Kerrie Raven.

"I know you are," she said, crossing her long legs, which bunched up her gray skirt, "but you and I don't get to make the call. Please, sit back down."

Adrienne paced back and forth once on the lush carpet and then obeyed her boss.

They sat on black leather couches across from each other in a corner of Raven's office—the only light came from the rays of sun streaming through the large wall of windows. Raven opened a glass jar on the coffee table between them and pulled out two tea bags. After dropping one into each of the red China cups in front of them, she poured scalding hot water from a turquoise-colored teapot over the bags, filling the cups. "You could have at least let me make tea before yelling at me."

269

Adrienne exhaled. "I'm sorry. I shouldn't have taken my frustration out on you."

Raven waved her statement off. "Maybe you should have. We've delayed this thing long enough."

"I'm in the best shape of my life—better than in college."

"Your skills have never been sharper, I might add. And there does come a point when you need to be given the opportunity to display those skills."

"The last six months have felt like I've been going to track practice every day but not allowed to compete in any of the meets."

"What can I say? You're right."

Adrienne nodded her thanks and pulled a folded piece of paper out of the front pocket of her jeans. "Take a look at this," she said, handing the paper to Raven.

Raven opened it and placed it on the table. It read:

The multitudinous seas incarnadine,
Making the green one red.

MACBETH: Act II, Scene II, Lines 60-61

Tomorrow and tomorrow and tomorrow . . .

MACBETH: Act V, Scene V, Line 18

Our revels now are ended . . .

THE TEMPEST: Act IV, Scene I, Line 148

Cap a pi . . .

*This last line is unfinished. Most likely from HAMLET: Act I, Scene II, Line 200:

Armed at all points exactly, cap-à-pie,

cap-à-pie = head to foot

Raven said, "What is this?"

Adrienne picked up the paper. "*This* is how deeply I have been preparing for the mission." She folded it and slid it back inside the right-front pocket of her jeans. "In the final pages of Melvyn Bragg's biography, *Richard Burton: A Life*, he wrote that when the guests had left after Burton's funeral, his fourth wife, Sally, began cleaning up their house and noticed that he had written something on the scribble pad that he always kept on his bedside table. The writing was in red pen—red was his favorite color—and the words on the paper I just showed you were the ones he wrote before going to bed for the last time. As you saw, the last line was unfinished, but I searched possibilities online, and I think it's from *Hamlet*. My handwritten notes you saw were the other Shakespeare plays he quoted before drifting off—word-for-word snippets from three plays." She sat back. "Shakespeare was his favorite writer, and he loved to quote him."

Her boss titled her head and seemed to measure her for a moment. She had not given Adrienne a look like that in a very long time. "I see you've been thorough."

"I want this mission."

"You want revenge."

"I want the truth."

Raven scoffed. "Good luck finding that in this business."

"You want revenge too. We all do. Flo was the best of us, and I cannot believe she walked into a trap. In the month since you all finally read me in on Junius and the two failed missions to sanction him, I've come to believe that."

"I know what Flo was, Adrienne." She paused. "But our adversaries are tough. Flo, Hugh . . . *no one* is immune to being outflanked, especially on the enemy's turf."

Adrienne shook the statement off. "It doesn't add up."

Raven smirked. "When did you finish the biography?"

There she goes, changing the subject again. Adrienne had noticed that Raven was doing it more often in the past few weeks since Byron Worth and Jock Gideon had announced to Raven, Adrienne, Ulysses, and Rose that, *"There* might *be a mission."* Hearing Raven's replies reminded her of the time she had seen a TV crew capture two politicians engaged in a conversation; one politician asked, *"What about the investments you made when it was going on?"* and the other had smiled, put his hand on the man's shoulder, and said, *"How's your family? How's your boy?"* Adrienne replied, "I finished the biography yesterday. We're wasting time."

"We're being careful."

"He's in Montreux," she said. "Right. Now."

"I know that."

"And you, Worth, and Gideon know that it's more remote and not as well defended as the chalet in Gstaad and Le Pays de Galles. And it's winter."

"What does that have to do with anything?"

"It's December."

"So?"

"Every December, he always stays in the chalet in Gstaad."

Raven looked down at the tea. "Go on."

"Junius is a creature of habit, has his routines. He's obsessive, not only about becoming Richard Burton but about his schedule. And he is always in Gstaad this time of year."

Raven's eyes raised up to meet hers. "What do you think that means?"

"There could be a meeting taking place right now, or one is about to take place, which would make now a prime opportunity to not only kill him but to gather intelligence. Or . . . something could be wrong, and he's hiding out there while he deals with it."

"Not something wrong with the shipping company, right?"

"Correct. The numbers on StarLine have never been better—we saw that in the briefing two days ago. What I meant was that something could be going on in the organization he works for."

"Not a bad theory."

"If I'm right, then now is the perfect time for me to go. There will be no way to get him when he reaches Gstaad."

Again, Raven looked at the cups of tea.

I want answers. You sidestepped me once already. It's not going to happen again. "Want to know why their failed missions don't add up for me?"

"What?" asked Raven.

"I told you that something wasn't right with the way those missions ended."

"Of course. They both died."

Her answer had a hint of annoyance. *She looks off-balance.* "That's not what I mean."

Apparently not wanting to wait any longer, Raven picked up her tea. "Well, what do you mean then?"

Her tone had recovered to an even and cool one, *a pragmatism about her born from years of playing the spy game,* Adrienne thought—*dodge and parry, wait, redirect, dodge and parry again, wait, act.*

"I mean that Flo and Hugh were the best. Flo had a week-long window to kill Junius, and she received a message a few hours before she died that changed the location of her pickup point."

"Because of the weather," Raven said.

"I know, but that shouldn't have thrown her off. She wouldn't let it throw her off."

"Your point?"

"What if she was set up? What if Hugh was too?"

Raven grinned and took a sip of tea. "You have more in common with Worth than you know."

"Worth?"

"I'm going to put your mind at ease, okay?"

Where is she headed with this?

Raven set her cup of tea down. "You should try this." Then, she closed her eyes as if what she was about to say had been repeated fifteen times before. "After Flo and Munny died, Worth assigned me to see if there was a mole at Worth-Gideon. You can ask him if you like. I've been searching for months now, including investigating you."

Shit, I walked right into this one.

"You certainly like your Bar and Grill restaurants and your daily jogs. A movie here and there, but what is up with the stereo equipment, jazz records, and books about jazz?"

"I found my vice."

"Your vice?"

"My drug. Jazz music is my drug. Do you know what it is like to listen to an Ella Fitzgerald record on a recording-studio-quality sound system?"

"No. I just get CDs. Less hassle."

"Completely different experience."

"Not much of a love life, I noticed. No prospects in Raleigh?"

Adrienne picked up her cup of tea. *It's not ready, but the hell with it.* She stared at Raven and shrugged. "Not interested right now."

"Jazz over sex? Well, I hope that changes at some point. Celibacy will dull your edge after a while." She took a sip of tea. "You're in your twenties. Break some hearts."

She wanted to ask about her and Worth; there had been rumors that they were more than co-workers, but that was a bridge too far to cross. The conversation would end. However, it was her turn to deflect and bring the conversation back on point. "And I'm guessing you haven't found a mole."

"Thankfully—no. Our house is clean." Another sip, and Raven crossed her legs the other way. "But that doesn't mean that Wexler's house is clean." She set the cup down. "And now I'm going to tell you something that doesn't leave this room. Agreed?"

Adrienne nodded.

"Hugh and Flo were romantically involved during their husband-and-wife mission."

The mission case file was one of the first things she had read when she had been brought into the fold a month ago. It had been fascinating to read the report and aftermath of their success. However, in no document was there ever a mention of them being lovers. Flo had lied to her. Why?

Raven said, "Everyone has their secrets, Adrienne."

"I guess so."

"She never told you?"

"Not in so many words."

"Expand, please."

If she told Raven now what Flo had said to her right before the doomed mission, she would be admitting to her boss that she had not told the entire truth when Raven and Worth had questioned her in the conference room months ago. *Was there a way to soften it?* Yes. "First, she told me that they were not involved. I guess she lied."

"Perfectly understandable. But what did she say?"

275

"It's nothing. She stated, 'Make sure you have something to come home to.' But she said that to me a million times during training, so I'm not sure it had anything to do with Hugh." It was a half-truth—Flo had only said it once—but it allowed her the opportunity to explain the statement away.

She now had Raven's full attention, and the Director did not move for at least thirty seconds as if she were in a trance of deciding whether to believe her or not. Finally, she took a sip of tea and then set her cup back down and said, "What do you think she meant by that statement?"

"Probably physical structures, tangible things—a house, a job, maybe a community, and I guess that's where Hugh could have come in since he helped with the 'dinner trainings' throughout the years, right?" When Raven did not respond, Adrienne decided to run with it a bit further. "And, as you have observed, *all I have* are objects to come home to. Haven't built up much human capital, but we're all just renting space, right? What *is* lasting?" She mimed Raven and gave a dismissive wave of her hand. "Well, maybe I need to get out a little bit more." *Let's turn this around on her.* "What do *you* think she meant?"

Raven cleared her throat and managed a grin that was almost warm in nature. "You're probably right. Her home was her sanctuary. I suppose, on some level, she could have been referring to Hugh, but that seems unlikely. They were discreet."

"But am I following your line of thinking that, because they were involved, it may have played a part in both of their missions going off the rails?"

"If there is a leaky faucet at Wexler, then, yes, it could have led to both disasters, and I have told my counterpart so. I hope there isn't, but we can't rule it out."

"And that is why Worth and Gideon are being careful?"

"Not because of that. Wexler knows nothing about your upcoming mission, and we will keep it that way. They would think we're crazy anyway. My counterpart there called me when her boys' bodies were found and said, *'Kerrie, if*

Hugh couldn't get him, then no one can.' And half a year later, they are still devastated by the loss. Not even training anyone new. I wouldn't be surprised if they announced that the company was dissolving. Not many can recover from a blow like that—it's like having a limb lopped off."

"We did."

"Barely. And now we're considering rolling the dice again with you."

"It has to be now."

Raven leaned forward and tapped her fingers on her bare knees. "I'll talk to them this afternoon."

Adrienne sensed a bit of hope. "So, you're behind me on this?"

Raven clasped her hands together. "Let's say that I'm not against you going . . . But . . . I want to know why you didn't bring up what Flo had told you when we interviewed you after her death."

"As soon as the words left my mouth a few minutes ago, I thought you might ask that." She laughed; Raven did not. "And the truth is, I never gave it a second thought after I completed the training cycle—just believed it was some sort of mantra that she used with everyone. I was also too raw when you interviewed me, *shocked* at the news of Flo's death."

Raven shifted her gaze to the window, and after Adrienne had taken a sip of tea, her boss nodded and said, "That makes sense." Then, she locked eyes with her. "Would you believe me if I said I was *still* shocked by it?" For the first time ever, Adrienne witnessed Raven's eyes become glassy.

"I believe you," she said.

"And that is why when we send you, we must make sure you come home. When you go there, *you* don't exist; the mission doesn't exist; and if you get into trouble—get cornered or captured—*no one* is coming to get you." She paused. "Well, if you *are* captured, someone will be coming, but they'll be coming to kill you so that you don't talk. Understand?"

"I understand. And I *will* come home."

"You better. But I'm taking my vacation either way, and I would prefer to sit on the beach at Pāhonu, sipping a frozen margarita, knowing you're back in Raleigh and hunting men in a different way." She paused, raising a finger to her lips. "Or it might be nice if you were on the beach next to me, watching the turquoise water roll over the tidal pool wall and talking about . . . possibly we wouldn't even need to talk."

The thought of Raven soaking up rays, knowing that Adrienne was dead and that a third mission to assassinate Junius had failed, unnerved her. Their business necessitated the strict limits placed on social interactions, keeping personal views and histories buried deep beneath the surface. And she had accepted those limits, but the Director's statement had delivered a moment of pure, unobscured insight, revealing who Kerrie Raven was, and yet, in perfect sync, had also dropped the everlasting curtain from the rafters to the stage, hiding who Kerrie Raven was forever.

"Naturally, I prefer the option where I survive."

Raven stood. "You are a master of death. I am convinced of that, and we can't wait forever to utilize your skills. We're outside at three in the morning, navigating the moonless, starless, pitch-black environment of Junius's organization and his role. But," she said, raising her right hand and extending her long, slender index finger, "the blue hour may be upon us."

"The blue hour?"

"It's just my metaphor for us potentially coming out of the darkness we've been in since Flo and Munny were killed. Let's say that midnight represents when that happened. Well, we've been fumbling in the night ever since, searching for lights." She smirked. "Even perhaps for a 'dark star' to suddenly illuminate and light the way for us."

"I've *been* ready."

"Of course you have." Raven curled her index finger and lowered her hand. "The blue hour is a period, usually lasting between twenty and one hundred minutes, that occurs right before sunrise or right after sunset when the sun is far enough below the horizon so that the sunlight's blue wavelengths rule. Forget right after sunset because that would mean we're headed back into the shadows. If we focus on the pre-sunrise blue hour, then my metaphor holds merit. With a successful mission . . . The Blue Hour Sanction . . . we would finally escape the terror of night and head toward sunrise. We'd be able to understand who we're up against and work to dismantle their ambitions."

"Can you convince Worth and Gideon that this mission is overdue?"

Raven shrugged. "One thing I cannot do, even after all these years working with them, is predict their behavior."

"What about using your metaphor? I think it's decent."

"They'd only poke fun at it." She cocked her head. "Did you see the latest photograph of Junius in the case file?"

"How recent?"

"I'll take that as a no." She stopped and brought her hands together as if she were going to pray. "Forgive me. It may not have been uploaded yet. The lead team saw it only yesterday afternoon." She cleared her throat again. "It was of Junius out and about in Céligny a few months ago, lazing through a market with his mistress, a basketful of fruit in his hand . . . Anyway, that's not important. What was of note was that the photograph was taken from only a few yards away and offered a side profile of excellent quality." She narrowed her eyes. "He's had surgery lately. Somehow, he got a doctor to *add* pockmarks to his face. Can you imagine the pain?"

"Pockmarks . . . Oh, similar to Burton's? I never thought he'd go that far."

Raven raised her eyebrows—Adrienne sensed in satisfaction—and said, "Now you know something you didn't. Like all billionaires, he lost *himself* a long time ago, but, in his case, he has now lost himself *in becoming* someone who has been dead for a quarter of a century." She turned away. "He deserves to die."

"And so does his bodyguard."

She turned back. "Hard not to believe she had a hand in killing Flo, Hugh, and Sharkey."

Adrienne let Raven's words hang in the air and then, as if by osmosis, brought them into her soul, squeezing and releasing them at first and then strangling them. From deep within herself, she found a new level of calm and regarded her boss with an unfeeling, thinking-of-something-else kind of stare. The words came out of her mouth as if pre-programmed. "I'll kill her. I'll kill them both."

26

**Burton's Keep, north of Montreux, Switzerland –
December 2003**

Victor Lars Junius walked down the grand staircase of his castle dressed for war. The uniform—black army boots, full camouflage fatigues, camouflage scarf, olive t-shirt, and maroon beret—had arrived a few days beforehand. Since then, the boots had been spit-polished to look like glass, and the clothing ironed and starched to crisp and razor-sharp crease perfection.

Five minutes ago, with the help of his butler, he had donned the outfit and assumed his persona as Richard Burton, starring as Colonel Allen Faulkner in Junius's production of *The Wild Geese*. Of course, divergent to his character in the film, he carried no weapons as he had no need to. He could stay in la-la-land directing false troop movements from afar, which also ran contrary to the cutthroat-lead-from-the-front character his shining star on a hill had played in the 1978 film.

Imperia Rex and the cadre of mercenaries in the lodge would do the real work in an hour. The staff had been reduced to only security, maybe half-a-dozen nutters who would die for him if need be. The butler, cooks, and maids were all sleeping soundly in Gstaad, awaiting his arrival.

He had just gotten off the phone with Kerrie Raven—*sigh*—and she had informed him that Adrienne Astra, the latest twist in a line of his failed executioners, would be approaching from the southeast in exactly one hour. Along with her would be two other pillocks, Rose Varga and Ulysses King, who would also find heaven tonight.

But wait. Junius was lying to himself, for he did have a weapon this evening. Slung across his body on a black nylon shoulder strap was . . . was . . . a machine gun of some sort. He'd forgotten the name, but these things didn't matter because, *one*, it completed his outfit, and *two*, it was a fake. A toy made to look like the real deal, which was just as well because he had nearly killed a waiter at his chalet in Gstaad when he had been given a fully-loaded one a few years back. Now, a pistol, he knew it inside and out, could fire the bloody thing at anybody if need be. But the bringer of death hanging across the front of his fatigue jacket right now? No, it was better that it was a fake—didn't even fire blanks. Nonetheless, it gave him great joy as he could move with it freely, train it on any person without fear of harming an innocent staff member around the grounds of the Keep. In any event, he would not be engaging in the real battle. He was much too valuable to Control, and maybe after the stomping his people gave the assassins tonight, the companies would stop sending them.

But Junius could not think about that at the moment. A bout of melancholy had taken hold of him earlier, which he would address with brandy and a cigar once he reached the first-floor library. The reasons the monster had him in his grip? There were two. The first—he was lamenting the fact that Burton had died at fifty-eight in 1984, just as he was about to reprise his role as Colonel Faulkner in *The Wild Geese II*. And the second—he knew that Burton, whom Elizabeth

Taylor had called "the Frank Sinatra of Shakespeare" during their whirlwind relationship, had been edging near the role of King Lear when he died, and Junius was beside himself. For he knew that he would never get to see his beloved RB play the role he was destined to own. That particular fissure in his happiness had actually appeared a week ago, when he had cried to his then-mistress, *"But I'll never see him as Lear. No one will ever see him as Leeeeaaaarrrr! The entire world should still be in mourning! But . . . there is hope! I almost have the part memorized, and I progress through my acting classes like the thunderbolt I am, a comet of cosmic potential. I shall play Lear at The Old Vic, and you shall be with me!"* Then, he had begged her in his most vulnerable yet Wales-against-the-world Burton, *"Please consider the surgeries, Old Snapshot, Quick-take, my little Twitch, my girl, my 'Ocean.' I have the finest team of plastic surgeons ever. In a year, you could be my* Elizabeth. *They could do it!"* She had left him the following morning, and he was single once more. A loathsome outcast. A muppet. A prat. A gone-to-the-dogs performer and man.

As he stepped off the bottom step onto the polished wooden floor and marched through the great hall toward his realm of books, he thought, *Tonight, I will rebound. Reclaim my rightful place. Get even with myself.*

But, had he deceived himself again? *Fie, for shame!* For he just might engage in the war tonight as Rex had promised him that he could execute Adrienne Astra if she were taken alive. *God, how I hope it comes to pass.*

He reached the library's enormous doors and paused outside of them, faux machine gun in hand, ready to shred the imaginary intruders that had entered the sanctuary he was about to access with the twist of a brass door handle.

He said, "Relax, old boy," and let the toy gun hang down once more.

It would all start in another half hour or so when his platoon of mercenaries would leave the lodge and get into position along the southeast corner, waiting for Adrienne and the two other maggots who had lost the plot to come sneaking into the Keep. *Lucky them.* He entered the library and closed the door.

However, unbeknownst to the Colonel, the curtain on tonight's play had risen early. The platoon of mercenaries was already dead.

Adrienne Astra, dressed head-to-toe in all-white fatigues, hid behind a drift of snow in the forest to the north of Burton's Keep. In her right hand was her hush puppy; in her left the special radio that Ulysses King had given to each of them before the mission, on which only she, Ulysses, and Rose could transmit and receive.

She had it against her ear, waiting. Their mission radios were turned off as the actual mission wasn't supposed to start for another hour. She was taking a huge risk, but when Raven's message had arrived two hours ago, saying that they should approach from the southeast instead of from the north, Adrienne had trusted her gut and disobeyed the order. Knowing that the last two missions to kill Junius had failed and that a message had been sent to Flo, changing the pickup location that night in Gstaad, she sensed something was not right. Thus, she moved the timetable up, and they proceeded with an alternate plan.

Now, she was waiting to hear if a major part of that gamble had paid off or would lead to disaster.

Thirty seconds passed. Nothing on the radio.

Thirsty seconds more.

Then, Ulysses said, "Everyone in the lodge is asleep forever. Zero exits through the west and south sides."

"Zero exits through the north and east sides," Rose said.

They did it. Thirty-some fewer enemy troops to deal with. She breathed a sigh of relief. "Copy," she said. "Move to your next positions. I'm taking out the two Cane Corsos now."

Their quick study of the lodge had paid off, for the plans had only arrived after Raven's last call. Again, Adrienne's gut told her that the plans had been delayed by someone at Worth-Gideon to dissuade the team from attacking the estate from the west. The intricate system of ventilation shafts and vents had been the key, along with the two kennels built on one side of the building, which Ulysses had detailed the past fifteen minutes to her over the radio.

He had a way to enter the attic from the roof, but his inspection of the kennels had provided access to the lodge as each enclosure had a swinging door that let the dogs travel between the kennel and the inside of the lodge as they pleased. Of course, the dogs were not in the kennels or chained outside of them tonight. They were being used as a decoy of sorts to deter Adrienne from entering the property from the north, making it seem like the southeastern approach really was the preferred route to assault the Keep.

The Worth-Gideon Weapons Division Head had accessed the vents and, wearing a gas mask, pumped cyanide gas down through the ceiling vents, flooding the mercenaries' living quarters. Rose had been covering the north and east sides of the building with her sniper rifle, and once the gas had been released, Ulysses had quickly moved outside to cover the west and south sides. And that was what she had last heard from them until Ulysses's report.

Not a soul made it out of the building.

Now, Rose would be swinging around to set up a field of fire just south of the castle, and Ulysses would be heading northeast to meet her at the woodpile.

Her boots sunk deep into the white powder with each step, but she still moved swiftly through the pitch-black forest as heavy snow continued to drop from the sky. In just under two minutes, she arrived at the northern edge of the property. The rich, calming smell of smoke coming out of two chimneys was much stronger now, and she imagined the roaring fires in the hearths within the enormous castle. The surveillance pictures and the view from the flyover did not do the structure justice. The dark wall of the castle's north face was dotted with rectangles and squares of light from an array of windows. Square towers rose forever into the air, and circular spires and cones stabbed the sky, forming a jagged vista far above the snow-covered grounds.

She surveyed the yard. A patio with chairs around a large, snow-covered table was to the left, and there was no movement across the bare yard or beyond the easternmost edge of the castle. The dogs were chained outside the main back entrance, which was roughly in the middle of the face and next to a shed full of firewood. From their study of the photographs, they had estimated the shed to be twelve feet in width and twenty-four feet in length; in person, the dimensions seemed about right. She had seen similar stacks of wood, albeit shed-less, in the photographs of Junius's residences in Céligny and Gstaad. *How the man loves his fires,* she said to herself. As for lighting, there was only a single light above the double doors of the main entrance, which was casting a yellow glow onto the dark fur of the Cane Corsos.

The dogs had been barking on and off for the past twenty minutes as she had seen, through her night vision goggles, a few deer wander onto the property and then leave. Her plan was to get to the woodpile and take her shots from there.

She flanked right until she had cleared the western edge of the castle and was out of view of the dogs. She altered course to the south and made her way through the forest until she was directly across the estate's western lawn from the back side of the woodshed. She stood motionless behind a large pine and listened. Ulysses would be coming this way soon.

The dogs had gone quiet, and the only sound was of the wind pulling the blizzard through the trees. Snowflakes flew almost horizontally into her face as the gusts were still coming from the east, which was a lucky break as it would help mask her approach.

Adrienne took half a dozen careful steps, weaving around the bare trunks, and reached the outer edge of the castle's western lawn. After one scan with her night vision goggles, she gripped the hush puppy firmly in her right hand and started sprinting across the yard.

* * *

Junius reclined in a leather chair with his legs propped up on an ottoman. He held a large Cuban cigar in his right hand and a snifter of Henri IV Dudognon Heritage Cognac Grande Champagne, priced at two million dollars a bottle, in his left hand. His secondary bodyguard and pilot, Markus, standing a few feet away, put the silver-and-gold-plated bottle back on the rolling-cart bar that he had wheeled over at Junius's command.

Junius took a sip of the brandy, and his spirits soared. If any drink on the planet was worth the amount he had paid, then this was it. The smoke hung in the air above his cigar, and he felt relaxed, calm, and in control.

"Well, is it everything you had hoped it would be?" Markus asked.

"That and more," Junius said as Burton. He vowed not to break character tonight. It was his show, his spectacle, and he intended to deliver. "Markus," he said, raising his glass, "may I deliver an appropriate line for this occasion from *The Wild Geese?*"

"Of course, sir."

Junius tapped the cigar, and a chunk of ash fell into the 24-karat ashtray that sat on the table next to his chair. "Of course, *Colonel.*"

"Of course, Colonel."

He gave Markus a grin and raised his glass in a toast. "There's a special clause in my contract which says that my liver has to be buried separately, with full honors."

Markus gave polite applause.

Junius put the cigar in his mouth and inhaled. *He knows I've been drinking too much lately. Everyone around this place knows it.* He eyed the bottle. *I'll only have one more before the shooting starts.*

The doors to the library flew open, and Imperia Rex rushed in with her 9mm drawn.

"Rather a dramatic entrance, I must say."

"Markus, stay with him, and lock the doors once I've gone."

In an instant, Markus pulled out his own 9mm. "What's wrong?" he asked Rex.

"Yes, what *is* going on?" Junius added.

Rex had already started retreating from the room. "I am almost certain that everyone in the lodge is dead. Our company arrived early and not from the direction they were supposed to."

Before Junius could say anything or grab his toy weapon, she had slammed the door shut and was gone.

Adrienne reached the edge of the woodshed. She would not climb up and onto the metal roof and crawl along it, so there were only two other options to move forward and position herself for the shots: the narrow alley between the shed and house and the other side of the shed that faced the open yard and woods. The alley was the most covert approach, but if trouble arose, which could happen at any moment, then she would be trapped.

She chose the more open side.

But first, she turned around and glanced at the tree line through her night vision goggles. No sign of Ulysses yet.

After seeing no one in her scan of the castle and the northern lawn, she made her way down the side of the shed.

The stiff wind continued to blow in her direction, and she could smell the dogs now. A quick peek around the corner revealed the large canines pacing back and forth, their chains sweeping the snow on the ground with each pass. She raised her hush puppy, took in a breath, and on the exhale, turned around the corner and shot the first dog, then the second. Both animals fell to the ground, blood sprayed on the snow around their heads.

She sprinted to the back of the woodpile and found Ulysses there.

"All good?" he asked.

She nodded and brought the special radio to her mouth. "Both dogs down, Rose. Ulysses is with me. We're about to head inside."

Ulysses spoke into his radio. "Misdirection explosives and flares in place. Shout if you need them."

Rose said, "Copy. I've got the front and drive covered. There is a snowmobile at the entrance to the service road. Could be useful later. There were footprints by it, headed back toward the lodge, so be ready."

"Don't answer anything from Raleigh," Adrienne said.

Ulysses nodded; Rose responded with, "Roger that."

They put their radios away.

Adrienne was about to motion them back toward the main entrance where the dead Cane Corsos were when an array of spotlights came on from above, illuminating the entire northern and western lawns.

"They know," she said. "Get ready."

27

They both went flush against the back of the shed, the overhanging roof keeping them hidden in the shadows. Only a few feet from where they stood was the start of the gleaming blanket of white snow, lit from the lights on high. Adrienne assumed the eastern and southern lawns had spotlights shining down on them too.

She heard the main entrance doors open. Then, the voice of a man.

"Aw, fuck. The dogs are dead."

Adrienne gave a quick nod to Ulysses and then slipped in between the shed and the house, the overhang still giving her concealment and Ulysses covering her rear. In a few seconds, she reached the shed's front edge and flattened her body against the white snow, camouflaging herself. She held the hush puppy in front of her and waited.

"Damnit," the man said. "Damnit, damnit, damnit."

There was silence for a few more beats, and then one of the doors creaked, and a different man emerged from the house and walked right in front of and then past her lumpy figure in the snow.

He spoke. "Bloody hell. The old boys probably never saw what hit them. I'll go tell Rex."

"The hell you will. You're staying here with me. She told us to guard this entrance."

"We're sitting ducks, lad. No chance. I'm heading in."

For a second, both of their backs were turned in her direction as they looked out over the lit sea of white . . .

It was all the time she needed. In one seamless motion, she came to one knee and then stood.

The first man was turning back around. "Perhaps, you're right. I'll hea—"

Pop, pop. Adrienne shot twice at his head.

Before the other man seemed to register what the red liquid was that had just sprayed across his face, there was another *pop, pop*, and Adrienne watched as his head came apart, the remains shrouded in a red mist. The first body had fallen on top of one of the dogs, and the second body fell backward onto the snow, flakes spreading out as if the man had just landed on a bed of feathers.

She felt Ulysses at her side.

All the intelligence they had gathered told them that Junius would either be in the main library located on the southeast corner of the first floor or the smaller library on the second floor of the castle's western side. At first, they had been told by Worth-Gideon that he would be in the smaller library, but then "new intelligence" had suggested that he would be in the larger library, which made the southeastern approach more attractive as it opened the possibility for Adrienne to use her sniper rifle and take Junius out that way . . . if the drapes were open. If not, then she'd have to enter the castle from a variety of southern or eastern entrances that she could choose from.

Right now, her gut told her that he was in the large library, probably expecting to watch her and the team get slaughtered after approaching the castle from that direction. It would be the first room that she and Ulysses checked. The only problem . . .

It was on the other side of the castle's first floor, and his protectors may have moved him already.

"Main library first," she said to Ulysses and turned toward the door. "In we go."

Raleigh, North Carolina

Kerrie Raven sat at the conference room table across from Byron Worth, who had just taken his seat.

"Jock is on his way," he said. "All ready?"

She gave him a smile. "This is going to work tonight, Byron. The southeast approach is the way to go."

"Definitely puts some distance between them and the mercenaries in the lodge."

"Adrienne will have killed Junius and be on her way off the property before they even know that something is wrong."

"So, you're still thinking a sniper shot?"

"If the drapes are open, and we have every reason to believe they will be . . . Byron, she takes the shot."

"If she misses, can she get out of there in time?"

"It's why we hired a heptathlete, remember?"

"Tell me again what her move is if the drapes are closed?"

"She'll pick a convenient entrance and try to enter the library that way."

"And you feel good about her knowledge of the floor plan?"

She exhaled. "How many times do I have to tell you that the model we made in the building up north was exact? And she ran through it thousands of times. She'll get to the library quick."

Worth swallowed. He had beads of sweat on his forehead, and his face was already pale.

It's going to get a lot paler in about a half hour, she thought.

"It's going to be okay." She looked back, making sure that Gideon was not entering the room. The door was closed. She turned and winked at Worth. "And we're going to *celebrate* later tonight."

He took in a breath and held it, puffing out his cheeks . . . He exhaled, and his cheeks collapsed as if they were a balloon that had just popped. "I hope you're right."

"Trust me," she said. "We've done everything we can. Our source in Montreux, who told us about which library to go after and the way to approach has been verified through Wexler. They've used him before in different European countries. I'm just glad that he was able to help us out with the plans for the lodge and the intelligence about the library." She paused. "You saw it. We've set Adrienne up for success."

It was a lie, of course. There was no such man in Montreux. Her contact at Wexler worked for Control, so it was the perfect situation to provide Worth and Gideon with peace of mind that the source had been verified. Now, would there be a man found by Worth-Gideon's cleanup crew in a few days or weeks? Yes. A man had already been killed earlier in the afternoon and was now rotting in a cabin miles from Burton's Keep. It would be seen as a double-cross, and both companies would learn, yet again, the hard way that being a field agent was risky business.

She had told her bosses that the location of the contact was known only by Wexler, and Wexler did not want to share the information in case there was a leak on the Worth-Gideon end. Raven had also waited to play the Wexler card with her bosses because she knew that they distrusted the people there, especially since the whole Hugh-Sharkey debacle. But, when she delivered the information to them that there was a Wexler operative who had information about the estate in

Montreux, they had authorized her to make contact. The intelligence the man had was what Worth had called *"A game-changing gold mine."* She had played it off as doing everything in her power to make sure the mission succeeded because she knew how stressed her lover was.

More than once today, he had squeezed her hand and thanked her.

There had also been the quickie in his office, which she had stated they both needed after preparing for the mission non-stop for the past few weeks.

"Are we in contact with them?" Worth asked.

"They were on their way the last time I spoke to them, which was . . ." She looked at her watch. ". . . almost two hours ago. I was waiting until you and Gideon got here to contact them."

"Well, let's not wait for Jock."

She grinned. "I'm starting to like this job." Another lie.

She called the team on the radio.

No reply.

She called them again.

No reply.

And now it was she who started to sweat.

Adrienne and Ulysses sped down the hallway that emptied into the atrium where the grand staircase was located, her focusing on what was in front of them, him covering their rear with his Uzi. It was just as they had practiced at the training facility. When they reached the atrium, there would be two more arteries that branched off, one to the right of the staircase and one to the left. The one to the left was the lengthy hallway that ended with the doors to the library on the right-hand side, and that was the only way to enter or exit the library. However, there was a room off the library, whose use they had been unable to determine. And because of that, they had marked the room as important.

They reached the end of the passageway, and she signaled for them to stop. The enormous chandelier high above the atrium's floor was a conglomeration of crystals, lamps, and brass fixtures that cast a shadowy glow on the space below.

"Okay, like we rehearsed. I'll cover the stairs and the hallway to the library. You cover the other two hallways."

Ulysses nodded his understanding.

In a burst of controlled energy, they moved across the room, eyes scanning, weapons training. No one in sight.

They passed by the staircase—no one was coming down.

"Keep it tight," she said over her shoulder.

They turned into the darkened hallway.

Suddenly, two figures appeared in front of her, not ten yards away.

Adrienne aimed center mass and shot both in the chest. They fell, but the concentration devoted to eliminating those threats had caused her to lose her peripheral focus for a moment, and a door swung open, knocking the hush puppy from her hand. She spun and saw Ulysses turning to fire on whoever was in the doorway, but he was too late as a large figure emerged and, too close to train his own gun on Ulysses, hit him on top of the head with it.

Adrienne watched as Ulysses fell to the ground. The man started to lower his weapon, but Adrienne had now checked her momentum, and in a lightning-fast move, she spun and kicked the gun out of his hand.

In seconds, she had withdrawn her Tom Brown Tracker knife and thrust it into his neck. The man let out a cry, but then there was someone else coming out of the doorway—a gigantic woman aiming a 9mm at them. Adrienne pulled on the knife and swung the man around just in time for the front of his body to receive the bullets from the 9mm, shielding her.

She could see the surprise in the woman's eyes, and with the power of her legs, Adrienne thrust the dead man straight at her.

It was enough to force the woman to shift her concentration away from Adrienne and deal with the large man falling on her. When the woman moved the hand that was holding her gun to push the body away, Adrienne seized the opportunity and attacked that hand.

The woman, who Adrienne was convinced was Imperia Rex, dropped her weapon, and Adrienne twisted her arm around behind her and swept her legs. *You may be a bodyguard, but you are not an assassin.*

She fell flat to the ground, and Adrienne, her eyes full of fury, landed on top of her, attempting to hold her down while Adrienne reached for her own knife. But the woman was strong, and she bucked wildly underneath her, throwing Adrienne off balance to the right. And she saw in a split second that if she tried to correct her motion, the woman would be able to buck once more and flip her, thus gaining the initiative. But. To Adrienne's right was Ulysses' Uzi on the floor. If she went with the motion she could grab it, roll, and fire.

Trust yourself.

She leaned into the fall and soon felt the Uzi in her hands. Completing her roll, she aimed and let loose on the woman who had just picked up her 9mm and was swinging it toward Adrienne.

The woman's chest erupted in a shower of blood as a track of holes appeared, starting from the belly and heading north toward the neck. Adrienne did not stop, holding the trigger until the woman's face was unrecognizable.

She pulled her finger off the trigger and watched the body fall backward.

Footsteps in the atrium behind her!

She had the advantage as she reasoned that they would hesitate before shooting because their people were in the hallway too. Adrienne turned and shredded the four men as they entered the hallway, their automatic weapons falling from their hands.

She put her back against the wall and looked left and right, left and right, waiting for more enemies to approach. The house went quiet.

Quickly, she snapped a fresh clip into the Uzi and, holding it in her right hand, she used her left hand to rouse Ulysses, who moaned at first but then jumped up when he saw the bloody bodies around him.

His eyes flinched, and he grabbed his head.

"Can you cover us for a few seconds?" she asked.

"Yes," he answered.

She handed him the Uzi and took her backpack off. From inside, she removed a small canteen of water and 4 tablets of ibuprofen from a zippered compartment. She took the gun back from him, and he swallowed the tablets with half the water from the canteen.

She handed him the Uzi again. "Your head's not bleeding. Now, can you go on?"

He nodded.

She re-sheathed her knife and picked up her hush puppy, and they made their way swiftly down the corridor to the library and stopped outside the doors.

"Ready?"

"Ready."

Adrienne took a step back and, with one massive exertion, kicked the doors in.

She was in the room in seconds and immediately recognized the four pillars stretching to the ceiling high above. To her right was a man in full fatigues wearing a maroon beret, trying to squeeze into a door that was sliding open. He was yelling, "There's not a one of you who can do what I do!" Next to him was a younger, taller man, who was now diving for cover behind a couch. And he would have had a good chance at making it, had he not been trying to shoot his 9mm at her while jumping, which exposed his chest. All of this had registered in her brain when the doors had blown open, and through pure instinct and reaction, she had aimed her hush puppy at the man and squeezed off two quick rounds. She watched as they both hit him in the chest before he disappeared behind the couch. His shots had gone way wide of her and splintered the wooden paneling on the opposite wall.

As she ran toward the couch, she heard Ulysses yell to the soldier attempting to enter the room, "Stop!"

She reached the couch and threw a cushion over the back of it to see if the man on the other side could still shoot. There was no shot, and she swung around the far side and fired immediately, hitting the man between his shoulder blades as he was lying face down on the floor.

Adrienne stood over him and shot him in the back of the head.

"Move away from the door," Ulysses ordered the soldier.

The soldier obeyed.

Adrienne ran toward him, and as she saw his face, she marveled at the resemblance: Richard Burton . . . also known as Victor Lars Junius.

And to add intrigue to her observation, the man pleaded to her in Burton's voice. "Oh, God, you've sent Markus to the undiscovered country. Please. please. No more. I'll cooperate. I swear by my sword."

She reached him and punched him in the face. Down he went.

"Watch the corridor."

"Got it," Ulysses said and moved into the hallway.

"Rex! Rex!" Junius shouted from the floor.

Adrienne kicked him in the ribs and then bent down over him. She grabbed his ear, pulling his head around to make eye contact with her. Adrienne growled "I killed Imperia Rex. She died with her *intestines* in my teeth."

He started to cry but still spoke as the famous actor. "Why? Why must you taunt me with *Equus* references?"

She dragged him over to one of the pillars. "Hug the pillar, and put your wrists together if you want to survive."

He did it in seconds.

Then, she pulled out a zip cable tie from a pocket in her white fatigue pants and zipped his hands together. Then, she patted him down. No weapons.

"What are you doing?" he asked.

She took off her backpack, opened it, and removed a pair of pliers. She waved them in front of his face. "Teeth or fingernails?"

His chin began to quiver. "There's no need. I'll tell you everything."

She cocked her head to one side. "Who is the mole at Worth-Gideon?"

His eyes looked left and then right.

"Okay, it's fingernails."

28

Rose Varga looked through her rifle's scope and saw the body on the ground twenty-five yards away. The man had just attempted to run across the front lawn of the castle, and Rose had put him down.

Is he the man who was on the snowmobile earlier? she thought.

She scanned her field of fire with her scope, moving from right to left across the yard.

Nothing ther—

Crack! Crack!

Snow exploded next to her right elbow, and she rolled to the left.

Crack-crack-crack!

She continued to roll.

Then, a light illuminated her, and she heard the roar of a big motor.

A second snowmobile. He must have been waiting to see where I was!

Rose got to her feet and ran for the nearest tree, snow puffing all around her as the man continued to fire from his machine.

10 yards away from the tree.

Crack-crack-crack!

Five yards away.

Crack-crack!

She made it.

The roar was getting louder.

Reaching into a pocket in her fatigue pants, Rose removed a flare. *I have one shot at this.* She lit it and then threw it as high as she could into the open.

Crack-crack-crack!

Knowing that he had reacted to the flare did not stop her motion of bringing her rifle up, peering into the scope, and centering the crosshairs on the man driving the snowmobile. He was almost to her. She fired . . .

And watched as the man dropped his weapon and reached for his chest. Then, his other hand came off the throttle, and the machine slowed after sailing past Rose and the tree, missing it by yards.

She dropped the rifle and pulled out her 9mm from her shoulder harness. The machine came to rest, and the man slumped to the right and fell off. She approached and put two rounds into his skull for insurance. Then, she turned off the snowmobile's lights and returned to her rifle.

After a complete 360-degree scan of the area, Rose resumed her original position, establishing her field of fire once more. "Who's next?" she said.

Adrienne clamped the pliers down on the fingernail of Junius's left index finger. "Who is the mole at Worth-Gideon?"

"Anything but that," he begged. "I can't—"

She ripped off the fingernail.

And that took him out of his character, as his scream was his own.

He crumbled, but since his hands were around the pillar, he fell awkwardly, and she thought she heard a pop in one of his knees. He howled in pain.

She wasted no time and squeezed the pliers down on the same hand's pinkie fingernail.

"Okay! Okay!" he yelled. "It's Raven." He sobbed. "It's Kerrie Raven."

An unstoppable wave of anger and sadness passed through her, and a fissure split her soul. She pulled the fingernail off and screamed above Junius's yell of pain, "Ulysses! It's FUCKING RAVEN!"

Junius's screams became moans, and Ulysses stepped into the doorway, his face pale. "Raven? I never saw it, Adrienne. Thought it would be Worth or Gideon."

"We'll do a call with Rose in a minute. Keep covering our exit."

He nodded and disappeared back into the hallway.

She dropped down next to Junius's head. "More fingernails? Or are you ready to talk?"

And the floodgates opened. He told them about what happened to Flo and Munny, how he was recruited by Control . . . everything. And the wonder of it all was that it had only taken ten minutes.

As she stood, looking down at him, she was rather disappointed with his lack of more important knowledge, like *who* Control was and what her ultimate plan entailed.

However, he had told her what room he was trying to access when she had busted open the library doors: the secret communications room.

"I'm due to call Raven and Control soon after the three of you are eliminated."

"And we do that from there, right?" she asked, pointing at the open door.

"Yes."

"Last chance. Is there anything else you can tell me?"

"Please don't hurt me when I tell you this."

"I can't promise that, but I can promise that I will go on hurting you if you get button-lipped now."

He swallowed. "Raven killed Flo's daughter."

"Flo's daughter?" And it immediately made sense. *Always have something to come home to.*

302

"Control told me about it. The father, Hugh, was the second assassin they sent."

My. God. Hugh.

"Why would Control tell you that Raven killed Flo's daughter?" She could barely believe the words that were coming out of her mouth.

"To make me fear Raven. The hell with that. She's a bloody cur, and that's all."

"Why are you telling *me* about it?"

"So you can take her out, of course. Me? I'm done. *Through.* You have my word that I'm resigning my position with Control. The whole thing will fall apart when I'm gone anyway."

She stared into his eyes, and she believed he was telling her the truth about Flo and Raven.

Adrienne turned around and started walking toward the opening to the hallway. His Burton voice had returned, and at full-force. "Where in the devil are you going?" he said.

She glanced back at him. "I'll be right back, Richard." She thought she registered a crooked grin but wasn't sure.

In the hallway, she pulled out the special radio once more and dialed Rose. When she answered, Adrienne said, "I've got Ulysses here with me in the hallway outside of the library. Junius is tied up inside, and I'll deal with him in a few minutes. You?"

Rose then detailed the snowmobile chase and said that she had seen no one else.

Adrienne acknowledged the report and then said, "Bad news, Rose. Flo, Hugh . . . *all of us* were set up by Kerrie Raven."

"That BITCH!" Rose shouted. "She's been trying to reach me on the other radio for the past five minutes."

"Me too," Ulysses added.

Adrienne handed him her Worth-Gideon radio. "Demolish this along with yours."

He gave her a thumbs up.

Then, she spoke into the special radio once more. "We'll talk it all over once we're done. Right now, we have more work to do. Rose, you've got to sell this for us. Call Worth-Gideon in one minute and tell them that Ulysses and I are dead and that you've been shot in the chest and are bleeding out. Then, I want you to act like someone has found you and is about to execute you. Say some desperate last words to them and then destroy that radio. Then, call me."

"Got it," Rose said.

"After that, commence Plan Bravo."

"Done." There was a pause. "You were right about us getting double-crossed. Sorry for disagreeing with you."

"Forget it. Dark Star, out."

Adrienne slid her special radio into her pocket and turned toward Ulysses. "Get the van and pick me up at the gate."

"I'll be waiting for you."

She watched him sprint away and then entered the room, finding a shaking Junius on the floor. "I'm going to get you up in a few minutes."

"And then what?" he asked.

"You'll see."

Raleigh, North Carolina

"Rose? Say again, Rose," Raven pleaded. On the inside, she was cheering. Finally, someone had called, and it was not good news.

"Chest shot. Bleeding out. Astra's dead. King is dead. I'm not . . . going . . . to . . . make . . . it—"

"Goddamn it! Keep her on the line!" Gideon yelled.

"Rose? Can you move?" Worth asked.

No answer.

Raven's eyes welled up.

What a turn of events!

Worth started pacing, saying, "Oh my God. Oh my God."

"Rose!" Raven screamed through tears.

"Dir – eck – tir. He's uh – proaching me. Going. To. Finish. Me. Off."

"Do you have a fucking weapon?" Gideon roared into the speaker.

There was a pause.

"Sah – ree," Rose said.

The line went dead.

Worth stopped and placed both of his hands on the concrete table. "It's over."

Gideon picked up a chair and slammed it against the floor.

Raven sensed it was her moment. Her Blazer keys were already in her pocket. She executed. "I've got to get out of here. I've got to get out of here!"

And she did.

She bolted out of the room, ran down the corridor, and entered the elevator before she heard the conference room door open. Whichever man it was, he would be too late.

The door closed . . . and then opened on the first floor. She exited the building and raced for her Blazer.

She would take her predetermined route, which only entailed two minutes of driving, and stop. Then, she would exit and wait for Junius's call. After receiving confirmation, she would return to Worth-Gideon, apologize, and start the cleanup process but then drop the bomb that she was leaving for Hawaii on the red-eye. It had all been her fault, she would claim. They would disagree. She would act distressed, broken, in need of escape. They would try to dissuade her.

She would not let them. Worth would offer to come with her. She would say maybe in a few days. She needed to be alone.

Her eyes opened wider as the Blazer came into view. *I did it. I did it!* she said to herself.

Adrienne's radio beeped, and she answered.

Rose's voice said, "Done."

Adrienne acknowledged and slipped the radio back into her pocket.

"Done *what?*" Junius asked.

She knew Raven would need time to get away from the office to be able to take the call from Junius, so Adrienne answered the great Burton impersonator by kicking him in the ribs. Then, she waited ten minutes, while listening to him whimper.

After one last look at her watch, she cut the zip cable tie around his wrists and said, "Get up."

After another series of moans, Junius finally stood, favoring his right leg.

She grabbed his hair, walked him across the polished library floor, and shoved him through the open door of the secret control room. With a tremendous pull, she sat him down in a chair behind the communication center. He cried in pain, and she pressed the end of the suppressor against his temple. He cried more.

"Now, sit and deliver the two messages. Raven first and then Control, right?"

Junius nodded. Tears streamed down his face, and he punched buttons, flipped switches, and adjusted dials until a green light started to blink on the far-right panel below a digital readout. No more than five seconds later, the blinking stopped, and the bulb's green glow was constant. He took a breath and gathered himself. "Raven is now on the line. I'll say my bit, and then you'll hear her reply."

Adrienne pressed the suppressor harder against his skull. "It better be convincing."

He picked up the headset, took in a breath, exhaled, keyed the mic, and spoke in his own voice. "It looks like an unfortunate climbing accident has taken place on the Eiger, and two female climbers and their ground man have both disappeared."

A few seconds went by.

Then, she heard the cold voice of her boss. "Sorry to hear. What are the chances of locating them?"

Junius keyed the mic. "Not good at all."

Raven replied, "Understood. Will be out of contact for a few weeks while the search party is deployed."

The light below the digital readout turned red.

"She's off," he said.

"So, our bodies were never going to be found, right?"

"Correct," Junius said.

She hit him across the head with her hush puppy, knocking his beret off, and then pressed the end of the suppressor against his temple once more. "Now, Control."

"It won't be her voice that we hear."

"Whose will it be?"

"One of her many cutouts."

"Proceed."

Again, he went through his routine, only this time punching more buttons, flipping extra switches, and adjusting three additional dials—including one underneath a false screen. At the very top of the control panel, three bulbs began blinking green.

They waited more than a minute for the lights to switch from blinking to a steady glow.

Junius keyed his mic. "Three successful sanctions. Cleaning complete. Zero losses. Situation normal. Leamas notified."

The response was immediate. "Understood. Next contact in twenty-four hours. Site B."

The three lights turned red, and Junius removed his headset.

Using her foot, she swung him around in the chair and took a few steps back.

"Raven is Leamas?"

"It's the name I proposed to Control for Raven, which Control accepted. Burton played Alec Leamas in the 1965 film *The Spy Who Came In from the Cold*, which was based on John le Carré's novel."

"Surprised you didn't want it for yourself, Rich."

He looked at the floor, apparently hurt. "I did. She said no."

"*Control* is the head of MI6 in that movie and runs throughout le Carré's fictional spy universe. Did Control steal the name for herself from that world too?"

"I asked her once, but she never answered."

"What's Site B?"

"My chalet in Gstaad."

She stood, processing for a few seconds. *That might give us enough time.*

"Okay, I have done as you asked," he said. "Could you please hand me my beret?"

She stood motionless, her hush puppy aimed at his forehead.

"If the call is not placed in twenty-four hours, what happens?"

His chin began to tremble. "Why would you say that?"

"If I tied you up for instance and left you here?"

She saw relief in his face. "Oh." He took a breath. "Well, they'd have someone here soon. No problem, though. I can survive without food and water for twenty-four hours."

"How soon?"

"Maybe a few hours—maybe less."

Twenty-six hours. It's worth a shot. She picked up the beret and tossed it to him, then lowered her gun.

He straightened it, admired it, and then put it on.

She studied him. "I must admit, you look just like him."

He cleared his throat and delivered, "You think so?" in a near-perfect Burton voice.

"You've had a lot of work done."

He rubbed the pocked marks on his cheeks. "Worth every bloody shilling." Still Burton.

She waited a few seconds, staring him up and down, and said, "Passion, you see, can be destroyed by a doctor. It cannot be created."

At first, a squint and then a blooming of the eyes. He gasped and then whispered, ala Burton, "*Equus*, again." Tears were back in his eyes, and his voice became a booming Burton. "Did you know that Sidney Lumet shot the eight great monologues for the film in a single day? What a beast I was!"

She raised the gun once more and aimed right between his glassy-yet-fierce, popping eyeballs.

The realization hitting him, he dissolved into the scene, delivering the *Equus* lines to her as if she were a member in a global audience of admiration. "The boy's in pain, Martin . . . Yes . . . And you can take it away . . . Yes . . . Then that has to be enough for you."

Adrienne said to the pleading thespian, "It isn't. But it will have to do." She pulled the trigger twice, and Junius-as-Burton-as-Colonel-Faulkner-as-Doctor-Dysart fell to the floor.

In minutes she was to the service road that cut across the property, eventually ending in a gate that opened to the main road, which wound its way down to Montreux. She felt a sigh of relief as the snowmobile was still there next to the start of the road, which was covered in at least six inches of snow. Now, if it started, she would not have to backtrack and take the other one that was still in the middle of the southern yard.

Adrienne grabbed the goggles that hung on the machine's left handle and put them on. Then, she hopped on the snowmobile, started it—*YES!*—flipped on the headlights, and raced off down the road, a beam of light cutting the hilly forest in two.

Right now, Rose would be executing Plan Bravo by stripping herself of electronics and destroying any identification. She would change her appearance, assume her alternate legend, and take the second rental car southeast and dump it, finding new transportation. Adrienne had made sure they all had alternate legends to use that the rest of the company did not know about. Rose would pay with cash, so there would be no money trail. When she felt that no one could track her, she would check into a hotel for a week-long stay and wait to hear from Adrienne and Ulysses.

Snow needled Adrienne's cheeks as she sped through the night, the snowflakes in the headlights making her feel like she was in a *Star Wars* movie going into hyperspace. The road bent to the right, and she slowed around the tight curve. Then, it straightened, and she accelerated, the machine leaping ahead and plowing through the freshly fallen snow.

Raven had betrayed them; it made her sick. She thought of Flo. She thought of Hugh.

She thought of Flo's daughter.

"How could she?" she yelled into the cold air.

She tried to calm down, but all she felt was rage. Not even killing Rex and Junius had diminished it. However, she was alive; her team was alive; and her instincts had served her well. Flo had told her to trust her gut, and she had done that by meeting secretly with Ulysses before the mission and telling him her theory that someone at Worth-Gideon was compromising their people. And so, believing her, he had loaded extra gear in the company plane and transported it to Oahu last week when Raven had sent him there to prepare Pāhonu for Raven's vacation after the mission was over.

Under a different name and paying with a different credit card, he had rented a large cabin cruiser for three weeks and ferried the gear from Oahu over to Maui, and placed everything inside a beach house in Paia that he had also rented for three weeks with the card. After setting up the house and laying out the gear, he had driven the boat over to Lahaina Harbor and put it in a slip he had rented. Then, he had caught a short flight back to Honolulu.

At the time, Adrienne had not been certain that there was a mole in Worth-Gideon, but setting up the safe house in Paia as a base of operations seemed like the best option. If the mission was successful and they were not able to discover the identity of the mole, then there was no harm done. Ulysses would travel under his alternate legend and clean everything up while on vacation. If they discovered that there was a mole but didn't know who it was, they'd be in the same boat.

Then, there were the specific mole scenarios. If the mole was anyone but Raven or Worth, the safe house gave them a place to hide and plan their next move. If they needed to use the house, they would use their alternate legends to fly commercial to Maui. If the mole *was* Raven or Worth, then the house might come in useful because of its proximity to Oahu. They knew that Raven would be vacationing there, and if the rumors were true, Worth might not be far behind. So, if they discovered that either of them—or both of them—was the mole, and if Raven or Worth knew the team members were still alive, then they could play dumb and withhold the fact that they knew who the mole was, attend the debrief in Raleigh, and find a way to approach, in private, Jock Gideon and either Raven or Worth, depending on who had betrayed them, and let them know what was going on. However, they would not tell them about the safe house unless it made sense for an operation to be conducted.

And then there was the scenario playing out right now.

Calculate! she told herself. *Figure it out!*

They had discovered that Raven was the only mole, and Raven and everyone else at Worth-Gideon thought they were dead. Raven was heading to Pāhonu. Ulysses had checked. She was on the red-eye to LAX, and, accounting for the time change and layover, she would touch down in Honolulu around 6 a.m. Hawaii-Aleutian Standard Time. Ulysses and Adrienne were booked to fly out of Geneva at 5 a.m. Accounting for time change and layovers, they would arrive in Maui around 2 p.m. Hawaii-Aleutian Standard Time, which was around twenty-six hours from now . . . two hours after Junius would have failed to call Control. The problem was that Adrienne didn't know how soon Control would act.

Thus, she focused on this question: What would Control decide to do when she found out that Junius was dead and that, most likely, Adrienne Astra and her crew were still alive? She would realize that Junius had lied to Raven, which would tell her that someone had found out that Raven was the mole. Hence, there were two probable options. One, Control could try to contact Raven at Pāhonu and tell her to disappear. Two, she could have her killed, fearing that she was about to be kidnapped and interrogated and also because she was no longer useful.

When Adrienne and Ulysses arrived at the beach house in Paia, they would be able to tap into the estate's security cameras immediately. If Raven had split, then there was still a chance they could track her down because, at most, she would have had only two hours. She could only leave via boat, plane, or helicopter, and with Ulysses's contacts, those would be quick to check. If Raven was still there, then they could monitor her, and if it looked like she was trying to leave in a hurry, they could call the local police and have them stall her until she and Ulysses arrived. At that point, they might need help from either Worth or Gideon, but Adrienne would make her decision then. If Raven was still there and *wasn't* leaving, then they would put their plan into action, which would be to come over to the estate later that night and abduct Raven for interrogation.

There was only one possible problem with that plan. If Control did want Raven dead, she would send an assassin or team to do the job. The wild card was that Adrienne did not know how close the team would be to Oahu. She doubted that they were already there because if something had gone wrong with the mission and Raven had been found out, then Control would have killed her in Raleigh before she ever took off for Hawaii. That meant that there was probably an assassin or a team in Raleigh. However, now that it appeared that everything had gone to plan, would Control keep them there? Were they always there? Or would she direct them to some other location to take care of a different situation?

Or . . . Did she have an assassin or a group that was closer to Hawaii than Raleigh that she could deploy? Not knowing the answer to any of these questions bothered Adrienne. In the end, though, she went with the most likely scenario, and that was that the assassin or team was in Raleigh, and if Control deployed them as soon as Junius failed to call and they flew straight to Honolulu, then they would still get to Pāhonu *after* Adrienne and Ulysses had already abducted Raven and left.

But it would be close.

The service road made a final bend to the left, and as Adrienne came out of her turn, the gate appeared before her. Ulysses was there, his Uzi hanging from a strap slung over his shoulder.

The van was nowhere in sight.

She stopped the snowmobile. "Where's the van?"

"Too much ice. Couldn't get it up here."

She eyed him for a few seconds, gripping her hush puppy. *If he raises the gun one inch, he's dead.* Her eyes darted left, then right.

All clear.

"Everything okay?" he asked.

Keeping him in view, she hopped off the machine and jumped over the gate. "Yes. Let's go."

313

They started to sprint down the road and had made it twenty yards before he slipped and fell. She helped him up. "You weren't kidding."

"Told you. It's worse by the van."

She breathed a sigh of relief. *Okay, he's not leading me into an ambush.*

Five minutes later, they made it to the van and climbed in the back. Ten minutes after that, they had changed into their disguises and assumed their new identities according to their alternate legends. Adrienne started the vehicle, and Ulysses poured them each a mug of coffee from the thermos he had put in the van before the mission had commenced. She smiled at his preparedness and took a sip.

As the vehicle moved along the road toward Geneva, Adrienne reviewed the scenarios with Ulysses. The Weapons Division Head listened intently, sipping on his coffee and occasionally nodding. When she finished, he was silent for a minute, and the only sound in the van was of the wipers going across the windshield, struggling to give them a clear view through the blizzard outside. Then, Ulysses said, "You're forgetting one other option that Control has."

"What's that?"

"What if she directs a team to show up at Pāhonu when we're there and attempts to take Raven and us out all at the same time?"

You smart little bastard. How did I not think of that?

She gritted her teeth and focused on the road. A few beats later, she looked at him out of the corner of her eyes and said, "Then, we need to be ready for the fight of our lives."

"Affirmative."

She thought of Flo's daughter once more, and her stomach cinched. Knowing what Raven had done was a secret Adrienne knew she could not keep inside.

She told Ulysses.

He almost put his fist through the windshield. "The hell with taking her hostage. Let's just kill her."

She continued to stare ahead at the road. "We will eventually do that. But first, I'm going to make her suffer."

29

Pāhonu, Waimānalo, Hawaii

Adrienne Astra kicked five feet below the surface using her Dräge rebreather, which produced no air bubbles that could alert someone scanning the ocean's surface that a diver was approaching. She navigated by underwater compass and trusted it, not using a dive ligh to sweep the sea in front of her, which would be another giveaway to someone posted on top of the estate's massive concrete seawall. The only thing in he hand was a speargun.

By her calculation, she should arrive at the tidal pool's rock wall at any secon now, and so she ascended. High tide was not for another four hours, so the toy stones of the five-hundred-foot long and fifty-foot-wide wall should still be visible above the surface. In her study of the area, she had learned that the 8,900 square-foot estate was constructed in 1933 and named Pāhonu as a tribute to the ancient Hawaiian turtle pond—the tidal pool—that was used to trap sea turtles which were a delicacy for high-ranking chiefs. She had also watched a few episodes of *Mangum P.I.* and seen Magnum, played by Tom Selleck, swimming in the tidal pool. This night, she hoped that she would not be the sea turtle, "honu" in Hawaiian, that got trapped and killed.

Crouching on the ocean's sandy floor, she rose until the glass plate of her mask broke the surface.

There was the rock wall, perhaps twenty yards away. To her left, beyond the tidal pool, beach, and sea wall, were the lights of the main house glowing above the shrubbery and palm trees. She grinned as she was only ten yards right of the opening that would allow her to swim into the tidal pool. There was another opening on the left-hand side of the wall, but Ulysses had said, *"If you swim down that side of the wall, it will make no sense to enter the tidal pool because you'll almost be to the beach. However, if you land on the beach there, then you'll be close to another property line and lose some of the protection of the seawall. Go straight in through the center gap."* And so, she had set an appropriate course to swim through the rock wall's center opening.

Seeing no movement in the water or on the estate's glowing white strip of sandy beach—the estate had over five-hundred feet of ocean frontage—she submerged, altered course to the left for a few kicks, and then straightened, heading directly through the gap and into the pool. Even in the winter, the daily high was near eighty degrees, and the water was warm to swim in compared to the extreme temperatures she had just endured in Switzerland.

She paused in the middle of the pool and slowly raised her head above the surface again. The beach was clear.

Adrienne went under and kicked until she was within ten yards or so of the shore. She took off her fins and quickly exited the water, sprinting toward the beach. To her left, the seawall rose in three separate tiers. She took off her diving equipment and unzipped her wetsuit, exposing her black, one-piece bathing suit underneath. From the camouflage dry bag that had been secured to a clip on the side of her Buoyancy Control Device, she removed a coil of rope, a pair of slip-on sneakers, a pair of night vision goggles, a Tom Brown Tracker knife, a tranquilizer gun and six darts, a hush puppy with a suppressor attached, a handheld VHF radio, and a pair of shorts with a belt threaded through the top that had two spare clips for the hush puppy, a thin case with the extra darts, a sheath for her knife, and a holster that would hold either her tranquilizer gun or hush puppy, depending on which she was not using.

She turned on the radio and watched as the black number '27' became illuminated by a glowing green background. She said, "Landed, over."

After waiting a few seconds, she heard, "Copy. Standing by, out."

She turned off the large handheld and hid it along with the dry bag and speargun in the brush.

She geared up.

With her night vision goggles, she did a quick scan of the shoreline in both directions and then surveyed the top of the seawall. As Ulysses had told her on the hour-and-a-half boat ride from Maui, the Worth-Gideon vacation estate had no exterior safeguards other than the chain-link fences, stone walls, front gate and cameras; there were also no interior cameras. Worth did not want the estate's safekeeping and trespassing deterrents to look any different from the other beach houses lining Kalanianaole Highway. Hence, there were no security personnel assigned unless Worth or Gideon were visiting—they used to bring Munny but brought Ulysses now, and Raven preferred to be there alone or with Flo. But that could change if the rumors were true about Raven and Worth. Perhaps Worth was on his way here right now.

The only stations to monitor the outdoor cameras were in the library and the basement communications room next to the wine cellar. Ulysses had suffered there for most evenings during Byron Worth's visit a few months ago, staring at the bank of monitors, unable to enjoy any of the fine wine located thirty feet away. Raven had not come on that particular trip, so maybe there was nothing going on between them.

In terms of Adrienne's approach to the estate tonight, Ulysses had informed her that there was a rough path through the shrubbery beyond the top tier of the seawall that opened into a rectangular-shaped strip of grass bordering the northeastern face of the house. Then, he had added that during Worth's visit, Worth had casually mentioned to him on Ulysses's way down to the communications room to man his post, *"Raven told me she never monitors the cameras when she's here. Can you believe that? Of course, she usually brought Flo with her. Ah, well, enjoy your watch. I'll be in the living room."* And so, before they left the house in Paia, Ulysses had accessed the security system and had frozen the images on the cameras that covered the beach and tidal pool and the ones that covered everything from the path through the shrubs to the northeastern side of the house. Once they were on the water, Ulysses would not be able to access the system and, therefore, would not be able to assist her by being her eyes from the yacht. He had wanted her to wear a headset so that they could maintain comms, but she did not want the distraction as she performed her mission.

She had told him, *"If you can't see the monitors on the yacht, then you can't warn me of anything. All I'll be able to do by wearing a headset is ask you for help if something happens, and by the time you get here, I'll either be dead or have taken care of the situation myself."*

Neither of them knew if Raven would change her routine, but Ulysses reasoned that if only a few of the black-and-white displays were frozen, they wouldn't look that different from the numerous other feeds if Raven took a quick glance. Additionally, if she still thought Adrienne and Ulysses were dead, it was doubtful that she would change any of her routines.

It had been a quiet day so far, which left only a few scenarios in play. *Will we be able to get her and get out of here quietly? Does Control have an assassin or a team en route to kill her right now? Have they been told to kill us too? Are they already on the property?*

The Weapons Division Head had agreed with her that Raven would not change her routines. Then, he had briefed her on the Director's movements. After learning that Adrienne and Ulysses had been killed, Raven had left the office and flown from Raleigh to LAX on the red-eye and then grabbed a connecting flight from LAX to Honolulu, arriving at the beach mansion that morning. Per usual company protocol, she had contacted the Worth-Gideon office from the estate's communications room and checked in with Rose Varga's assistant, Kristy Cummings. There had been no communications sent since. Both Worth and Gideon had been adamant that, beyond them, Ulysses be the only one with access to all the company's technology, as they had mandated with Munny before him. Now, being presumed dead, Ulysses was exploiting this weakness. Cummings was serviceable as an emergency software and hardware technician and systems administrator, but she was probably reeling from the supposed death of Rose, and neither she nor Worth nor Gideon knew how to monitor what Ulysses was doing remotely. And they wouldn't be looking since they were wrapped up in dealing with the fallout from his and Adrienne's supposed deaths, which was basically waiting for the bodies to be found like Flo's and Munny's had. The company had no active assets in Europe, so it was doubtful that they had found out that their three employees were still alive.

From a review of the estate's security cameras, groceries had been delivered later in the morning, and Raven had taken two swims in the tidal pool. Other than those trips to the beach and having lunch and a drink later in the courtyard Raven had not left the house. The only additional pieces of intelligence that Ulysses had been able to gather were that Raven enjoyed spending time at night either reading in the library or sitting by the fire in the living room and that she slept in the bedroom on the second floor that had the terrace with the ocean view After dinner, she never left the estate. The last footage of Raven outside was from the camera covering the courtyard—she had finished a glass of wine at one of the round tables two hours ago and headed inside. Right before they had left Maui, Ulysses told her that the company's black Mercedes-Benz S500, license plate ECO 2, and blue Ferrari 360 Modena, license plate ECO 1, were still parked in the two open garages.

Once Adrienne reached the house from the backyard, there was one window where she could see into the library, two windows that provided views of the living room, and three windows attached to the corner suite—one in the bathroom and two in the bedroom. On the seaward side of the building, she could enter the living room through a set of French doors, and at one end, there was another set of French doors that led into the bedroom suite, and at the opposite end, she could enter the house through a door that led into the bar.

She had to avoid the courtyard and its entrances because those cameras were still on.

If she found that Raven was not in any of those rooms, she had three primary options to access the second floor. One, she could head back outside and travel the length of the seaside wall until she was below the terrace and climb up using the vines and by looping her rope around the terrace's corner post. Two, she could use her rope to climb up onto the sitting room balcony and enter the suite that way. Three, she could stay on the first floor and hug the wall under the arched loggia and enter the stair hall leading to the second floor. Then, she would take a right and follow the outdoor hallway until she reached the terrace suite, which had a sitting room with an ocean view and the bedroom with two ocean-view windows and the terrace. A secondary option was to take the small stairway near the front entrance up to the sewing room on the second floor and then head down the open hallway. Last resort options included accessing the eastern-side balconies and terraces, but that would expose her since Ulysses had not turned the security cameras off that covered that side of the main house.

She liked her options but would only commit to peering through the ground-floor windows first to get a lay of the land. Anything beyond that, she would have to rely on her situational awareness along with trusting her gut.

Adrienne turned seaward and scanned the horizon. Directly offshore of the estate, in deep water beyond the reef, she saw the yacht's lights with Rabbit Island looming on the horizon. There would be no communication between her and

Ulysses until she tranquilized Raven and radioed him from the communication center. He would then speed in toward shore on a rubber dinghy equipped with a powerful outboard motor and pick her and Raven up on the beach. Once onboard the yacht, they would cruise back to Maui and transfer Raven into the basement of the house they had rented. Then, Adrienne would call Worth and Gideon, explain everything, and have them send an interrogation crew there to question Raven.

She placed the night vision goggles and the hush puppy on the top of the seawall and then scaled it. Standing up, she walked across the top, holding on to the chain-link fence, and soon arrived at the highest tier. There, she stopped and strapped the night vision goggles to her head and did a scan of the property. The estate's Spanish Colonial Revival-style main house was beyond the shrubs in front of her. To the right and in the distance was the gatehouse; farther to her right was the private tennis court; and to the right of that, the boathouse. She took a few more steps until she reached the point Ulysses had told her about, scaled the fence, and then left the wall, having found the narrow path toward the house. She was thankful that there were no "Zeus" and "Apollo" to greet her, but if there had been, she would not have hesitated to provide another example, as she had in Switzerland, of why her preferred weapon was nicknamed the "hush puppy."

As she reached the edge of the shrubbery and the start of the back yard, she turned the night vision goggles off for a moment, flipping the sights up so that she could behold the scene with her own eyes. The beauty and majesty of the estate overwhelmed her for a moment. Seeing it up close for the first time, Adrienne understood why Byron Worth had wanted the property and why it had come with a steep price tag. The 3-acre estate was the perfect mix of gardens, trees that had been planted when the home was constructed in 1933, and the graceful, European style of the structures—modernity tempered by nature and class. The low-pitched clay tile roofs gave the L-shaped main house an understated look as if it had grown out of the foliage that surrounded it, and although she could not see these now, she was aware of the house's famous arcade and the lava rock walls that lined some of the perimeter.

If I survive this tonight, I am coming back here.

There was light coming out of the library's window and the two living room windows. The first-floor bedroom windows were dark as were the windows on Raven's second-floor suite in the corner. Adrienne flipped the sights on her night vision goggles down, turned them on, and scanned the area. She saw no movement in her field of vision and determined that, after repeated sweeps, there was no one concealed in the shrubbery that lined the yard.

Trusting her surveillance, she made her way diagonally across the lawn until she was underneath the terrace. There, she hid the coil of rope in the tangle of vines and then moved along the wall, looking in the darkened windows of the first-floor bedroom. She turned the goggles off again and flipped up the sights, letting her eyes adjust.

She moved to the living room windows and saw no one inside. There was an empty snifter on an end table next to one of the couches, but that was the only sign that someone had occupied the room. But how recently?

She moved to the library window and peered inside. Again, no one.

Do I enter the house here, or do I climb up onto the terrace?

She decided that the terrace plan was too risky—Raven could be sitting in a chair that was back from the railing, looking out at the ocean. As soon as the rope went up, she'd see it, and if she was armed, Adrienne would have no cover. Her observation of the terrace earlier had only revealed that Raven was not standing anywhere on the terrace where she could be seen.

So, it would be the bar entrance.

Adrienne went around the corner and listened at the door to the bar. There was no window, so she waited, trying to determine if anyone was in the bar room. After a minute, she picked the lock and pulled the door open an inch, the barrel of her hush puppy's suppressor aimed at the opening. There was no tell-tale shaft of light that leaked out and no noise to suggest movement inside.

She opened it another few inches, saw and heard nothing, and then opened it enough for her to slide inside.

Moving through the bar, library, and living room, she cleared the bedroom suite and followed her plan, exiting the living room to find herself underneath the arched loggia. She moved past a bedroom and then picked the lock to the stair hall.

Inside, she cleared the space and sped up the main staircase. At the top, she entered the outdoor passageway and looked out over the beautiful courtyard. A cool wind blew through the palm trees, and their swaying fronds made a whisper sound as she moved down the hall toward the corner suite.

She paused outside the door that led into the sitting room portion of the suite and loaded a dart into her tranquilizer gun. Carefully, she put the gun back into her holster and held the hush puppy with her right hand as she slowly turned the doorknob.

It was unlocked.

She opened the door far enough for her to slip in and gently closed it behind her. The room was dark, and she flipped down the sights once more on her night vision goggles and turned them on. To her right, the door to the bedroom was ajar, and she could hear the soothing roar of a box fan. Growing up, she had slept with one every night, even into college, but Flo had broken her of the habit during the training cycle. *"Your ears are your best friend when you are sleeping. They may mean the difference between life and death."*

Adrienne stepped toward the door and nudged it open with her left hand, the hush puppy raised for action with her right.

Six inches . . . she could see the nightstand.

Twelve inches . . . she could see the head of the bed and Raven's black hair spread on the pillow—she was lying on her side, facing away from Adrienne.

Eighteen inches . . . she could see through the glass door that led to the terrace.

She froze.

On top of the railing were two grappling hooks . . .

A second later, she saw a hand reach over the railing.

30

Adrienne opened the door and transferred the hush puppy to her left hand. In two steps, she was at the bed with the tranquilizer gun out, and she fired the dart into Raven's buttocks.

Her eyes were already fixed back on the railing as she heard an "*Ow*" followed by an "*Uhhh*."

Raven was out.

As Adrienne holstered the tranquilizer gun and transferred the hush puppy back to her right hand, she saw a hand holding a gun with a suppressor rise over the railing next to the hand that was already there.

Then a new hand, next to the second grappling hook, latched onto the railing.

Her mind was a flurry of assessment. How many assassins were coming up the grappling hooks? At least two. How many were on the property? Had they followed her? *No, they would have killed me already. They must have come from another direction, and it is just luck that I got here first.* Were they coming up from multiple directions? There was only one entrance to the bedroom from the terrace. The door from the sitting room to the bedroom was open, but the glass door leading to the sitting room's small balcony was closed, as was the door to the hallway. She'd hear it if anyone came in that way . . .

But only if she turned off the fan.

I need it on for one more thing first.

She pulled Raven off the bed, pushed her underneath it, and threw the covers back over the pillows. The mess couldn't have settled better on the bed; it still looked like a figure was underneath the covers.

There was now a head and shoulders to go with the first two arms on the terrace, and the second person's other hand—also holding a gun with a suppressor—was now over the railing too. The first person was a man with a thick beard, and he was wearing a headset; however, he was not wearing night vision goggles, which still gave her the advantage . . . so long as the lights stayed off.

There was a light switch by the open door and one by the terrace door.

She turned off the fan and watched the terrace, her hush puppy raised.

The two figures made it all the way over the railing and now stood on the terrace. The second assassin, who was also wearing a headset, turned, giving Adrienne a profile, and she saw that the person was a woman. She also had no night vision goggles on.

Adrienne watched as they spoke into their headset mics, but she did not see either of them lean back over as if to talk to someone on the ground. Even though they were communicating via headsets, it still would have been a natural movement for one of them to give a quick glance back over the railing if someone was down there. So there is at least one more person around—in the house, on the property, in a car outside of the gate, on a boat offshore . . . somewhere.

I'd come in from both sides if it was me planning the operation.

She heard a jingling in the sitting room like someone was unlocking the balcony door.

How many?

She positioned herself against the wall between the windows so that she had a clear line of fire when the two from the terrace came in from her left, and the assassin or assassins came in the bedroom from the sitting room on her right Even if someone appeared in the bedroom doorway, it would be difficult for him or her to see Adrienne.

The female assassin on the terrace motioned the male toward the door, and Adrienne watched him look through the window at the bed. He said something into this mic and then put a gloved hand on the door handle.

To her right, she heard the balcony door open, then the soft sound of footsteps moving across the floor. She listened for a second pair but heard nothing.

Okay. Three of them.

The terrace door was locked, and the man quietly worked it while the female killer behind him trained her weapon on the bed.

Adrienne heard a click as the man successfully unlocked the door; the footsteps in the sitting room stopped.

The handle of the door started to move.

An arm with a hand holding a gun with a suppressor rose in the open bedroom doorway . . . while the person's other hand reached for the light.

She could see the head, and Adrienne committed.

She fired two shots into the assassin's skull, and the figure fell backward; the door to the terrace opened, and she fired two shots into the man's head, a green mist forming in the air around it. Seeing her partner's head come apart, the woman jumped back, but Adrienne was quick and took advantage of her surprise. In one smooth motion, she took a step forward, aimed at the woman's head, and fired two shots—another explosive green mist spread into the air as the woman fell to the terrace floor.

Adrienne dropped to one knee and trained her weapon on the open bedroom doorway.

There was no movement and no more sound.

She ran to the first assassin she had shot. It was a man—a man with two holes through his forehead. He was not wearing a camera. She removed his headset and listened.

"Radar one, two, or three, do you copy, over?"

It was a woman's voice, and she repeated the question once more. After no reply, she said, "Radar one, two, or three, this is Radar four, over."

There was a three-second pause, then Adrienne heard, "Radar one, tw—"

A man's voice broke in. "Radar four, go to protocol alpha, out."

The line went silent.

At least two more of them left—a woman named Radar Four and a man.

Adrienne assumed that Protocol Alpha was to switch to a secondary means of communication because of the possibility that the primary means had been compromised, which it had been.

Okay, they are either going to make one more attempt or they'll head out. I need to get to the communications room and tell Ulysses to get here and that the zone is hot. But how do I do that?

First, she ran over to the other two dead assassins.

No cameras.

Adrienne ran back to the bed and, keeping an eye on both the terrace and bedroom door, she weighed her options. She could reach the first floor by rappelling down using the grappling hooks and line, but one of the two remaining assassination team members could be watching the terrace and would kill her even if she just peered over the side. Same thing for going out the sitting room balcony. Those ways were out, which left her with one option: exit the sitting room and sprint across the exposed outdoor hallway and stop in one of two rooms. The closest would be the stair hall, but when she arrived at the bottom, she would have to travel through a few more rooms to get to the small staircase that led to the basement. All the way down the outdoor hallway was the entrance to the sewing room, which provided access to the small staircase on this level. Then, she could take it all the way down.

What she hated was that she would be leaving Raven unguarded. However, she was certain that the two remaining enemy team members did not know that she was on the property; they would think that Raven had killed their team members. If Adrienne was seen while moving to the basement, she needed to draw their attention away from the corner suite. And there was only one way to do that.

She knelt next to the bed and pulled Raven's body out. The pajamas.

It just might work.

Adrienne took off her shoes, shorts, and night vision goggles and then stripped the pajamas off Raven and put them on. They were a bit big for her, as Raven was two inches taller and a few pounds heavier, but they would be fine. She rolled the ends of the sleeves once and put her shoes back on. Her skin tone was darker than Raven's, but the hallway was darkened and the only parts of her light brown skin that would show would be her hands, face, and neck. The hair was a problem, though, as there was no way that her light color would pass for Raven's silky black mop.

However, if I had a . . . she looked at the dresser, and on top was a black ball cap with a white swoosh on the front. She raced over, held her hair up, and then put it on.

She would only take her hush puppy; everything else, she would stow under the bed.

Kneeling, she pushed Raven's naked body back underneath the bed along with her gear, but not before inserting a fresh clip into her weapon and placing the half-used clip on her shorts' belt.

She crouched low and made her way through the sitting room. Then, she cracked the door open enough to peer into the courtyard. Everything seemed calm. She opened the door a little more, and now she could see that the hallway was clear. The right side was, of course, all open-air; on the left side, she would pass by a linen closet, a bedroom door, the opening to the stair hall, and another sitting room door before entering the door to the sewing room at the end.

You cannot wait forever.

After taking two calming breaths, she sprinted all the way down the corridor, covering the doorways and openings along the way, and made it to the sewing room. There were no shots fired at her, and she had no idea if she had been seen. A part of her hoped that she wasn't; a part of her hoped that she was. Either way, she wasted no time and sped down the narrow staircase, ready to kill anyone in her way.

The bottom of the steps opened into a stone-walled atrium with three doors. One led to the communications room, one led to the wine cellar, and one led to a full bathroom that Worth had installed when he purchased the property.

After sweeping the area, she punched the access code into the keypad next to the communications room door, and the door *beeped* open.

She entered and saw an entire wall of monitors on the opposite wall, giving the dark room a glow that was enough to see by. She quickly studied the monitors and saw no signs of the two assassins. To her right was about every conceivable piece of high-tech communication equipment on top of or affixed to a table-and-wall combination station that ran the length of the room and had three chairs pulled up to the tabletop. To study the different means of communication in her training modules was one thing; to see everything all in one place was another. Before contacting Ulysses, she followed his instructions and watched as the displays that had been frozen went live. *I will need every advantage now to get out of here with Raven.*

Next, she turned up the volume on the VHF set and picked up the mic. After turning to channel of 27, she keyed the mic and said, "Robin is ready. Nest is not, over."

Less than five seconds later, she heard, "Copy, out."

Good, he'll be on his way, and he knows we've got trouble. Now, how do I get Raven to the beach?

As the thought crossed her mind, one of the far-right monitors caught her attention. She walked over and leaned toward it. On the screen was the courtyard . . . and the remaining female assassin was moving across it toward the stair hall entrance.

31

She's coming after me, Adrienne thought.

On the opposite wall was a large safe that she knew contained a variety of weapons and gear, and, for a moment, she thought of opening it and seeing what was in there, but if she did, she would lose the advantage over her opponent. If she moved now, she could claim the high ground.

She left the communications room and bolted up the narrow staircase, arriving in the sewing room in seconds. She cleared the room and then crept up to the door she had left open to the outdoor hallway but stayed far enough into the room that no one could see her from below. If the assassin came up the grand staircase, Adrienne would kill her when she reached the top. If the assassin decided to come up the narrow staircase, Adrienne would hear her and go kill her here.

She listened, but the wind was making the palm fronds whisper again. A minute passed. Then another.

A sound.

Where was it?

She closed her eyes and concentrated.

There it was again!

Footsteps.

Behind her.

She's coming up the narrow staircase.

Adrienne turned and crept back across the room and took a left in the back corner. She could hear the steps now as she paused at the final wall of protection out of sight of the top of the narrow staircase.

The steps stopped for a moment, and then . . .

Creak.

Adrienne took in a breath.

Crrreeeaaak.

She slowly exhaled . . . Crouching low, she spun around the corner.

The woman was two steps from the top when she saw Adrienne and tried to lower her gun to account for the surprisingly lower target.

It took too long.

Adrienne squeezed off two rounds, *pop-pop*, and watched the assassin's head burst as the woman fell backwards down the stairs.

At least one left.

She ran down the steps and grabbed the headset off the body and seconds later heard, "Radar four, do you copy, over?" Then, "Radar four, over . . . *shit!*"

She listened for a few beats, but the line remained silent.

Where is *he? If they were working as a pair, then he could be coming up the grand staircase. If not, he could be anywhere on the property.*

She returned to the open door and studied what she could see of the courtyard and the entire length of the outdoor hallway. The courtyard looked still, and there were no sounds coming from the stair hall.

Same position as before.

She calmed her nerves with two breaths and then sprinted across the opening covering the doorways and opening as before. Once again, there were no shot fired at her, but that did not mean that he had not seen her. Adrienne entered the bedroom and cleared the suite. The three bodies still lie where they had fallen. She looked at her watch. Ulysses would be to the beach in five minutes.

She got to work and, in two minutes, was geared up and had Raven back in her pajamas. Her mind had been working on the problem of how to get Raven safely to the tidal pool since she had relayed her message to Ulysses. It was down to one option. She would use the fireman's carry to transport Raven to the stair hall, then drag her body down the stairs, and use the fireman's carry once again to get her to the tidal pool. There was only one other option, and that was to kill Raven right now and get to the beach, but after Raven's betrayal, Adrienne did not want to give her the easy way out. She wanted information. The company would want information.

With her night vision goggles strapped to her head and her hush puppy in her right hand, Adrienne hoisted Raven up and over her shoulder and took off for the opening to the stair hall.

The rubber boat sped through the tidal pool opening, and Ulysses cut the engine. Seconds later, the bow glided to a stop on the beach, and he exited, wearing night vision goggles and holding a suppressed Beretta M9 in his right hand. An Uzi submachine gun with a 25-round clip inserted hung on a shoulder strap, and there were spare clips for both weapons on the ammo belt that he wore. Munny had hated the Beretta, but Ulysses loved it, a true workhorse that fit his style.

While traveling all the way in from the yacht, he had seen no other crafts in the water, and before his rubber boat entered the tidal pool, he had surveyed the estate grounds and found nothing out of the ordinary—no sets of scuba gear and no landing craft. Whoever had made Robin's Nest hot had come by land. Standing on the beach, he surveyed the area again and listened for voices and sounds of gunfire or movement.

He saw where Adrienne had kicked sand, covering her tracks on the beach. Even if she hadn't, the tracks would be gone by morning after high tide.

There were no other tracks.

All was still and silent.

Using a pair of bolt cutters, he cut the padlock on the beachfront gate and opened it, giving Adrienne a clear path from the lawn to the boat.

Then, he scaled the lowest tier of the seawall and did another scan of the property, moving from right . . . to left . . .

Suddenly, he saw movement near the main house, and he snapped his head toward it.

There she was, carrying Raven over her shoulder and running away from the bar door exit and across the grass.

His eyes opened wide as he searched the area around her.

She was now twenty yards away from the open gate.

Fifteen yards away.

Ten yards—

A figure came into view, running across the courtyard. Ulysses leapt onto the beach and sprinted toward the open gate.

Adrienne could see the open gate to the beach now as she gritted her teeth and continued to carry Raven. Her lungs burned, and her legs felt heavy as if she was in the final stretch of the 800 meters.

C'mon, PUSH, she told herself.

No one had made a move on her in the house, and she had not seen anyone on the grounds during her scan from the bar door—perhaps, the man had left.

A figure came sprinting through the open gate. It was Ulysses . . . and he was pointing behind her with his finger . . .

And aiming his pistol.

Before she heard him yell, "Behind you!" she dropped to the ground.

And saved herself, but not Raven.

As her knees and forearms touched the soft ground, she felt Raven's body lift off her back and go past her head. For a precious second, the Director lay motionless, face down on the rich, thick lawn of the estate. Adrienne was already rolling and bringing her hush puppy up to neutralize the threat when she heard *pop-pop* . . . followed by a *splat-splat* as they hit Raven's head and turned it into a mess of goo.

At nearly the same moment, she heard *pop-pop-pop-pop-pop* and saw the assassin fall back as bullets from Ulysses's Beretta entered the man's chest.

She stood and ran with rage toward the man on the ground. Within seconds, she was standing over him, her foot on the hand holding his gun and her hush puppy aimed at his head. Three wet spots were growing on his chest, and the man spit blood as he tried to breathe.

"Who are you?" she asked.

The man took a second to give her a bloody smile; then, his eyes began to close. She put a round in his forehead, finishing him off as Ulysses arrived at her side. She bent down and tore the headset off the man and listened. There was only silence.

"We have to go," Ulysses said, looking around with his night vision goggles. "There could be more of them, and we've lost Raven."

Adrienne ignored him and ran back to Raven's body. She ripped off her night vision goggles and knelt on Raven's thighs, facing her chest and what was left of her head. Her hands sprung out and grabbed the lapels of Raven's pajama top and pulled her slumping form near her face. "Why did you do it?" she growled.

"Adrienne?" Ulysses said, putting a hand on her shoulder.

She shook his hand off with her shoulder and then took her right hand off the lapel, made a fist, and slammed it into Raven's chest. "Why?" she yelled, shaking Raven's body back and forth with her left hand. She felt flecks of the former Director's blood, bone, and gristle hit her face, neck, and arms. "I wanted *answers!*"

She pushed the body away and watched it hit the ground, with more blood and gore hitting the grass around Raven's head.

Ulysses's hand gained a much firmer grip on her shoulder this time as he said, "Adrienne. We must go."

She turned toward him—he had flipped up his sights so she could see his eyes. They were serious.

Hers were starting to get glassy. "I—*we all*—deserved . . ." She shook her head. "She got off *easy!*"

He leaned over, picked up her night vision goggles, and handed them to her. "I know, but she paid for what she did. C'mon."

A minute later, the two of them were seated in the boat, heading out of the tidal pool. Adrienne's camouflage bag, speargun, and handheld VHF radio rested on the boat's wooden deck. As Ulysses helmed, she sat facing the estate and scanned the water and property as it started to get farther and farther away. No lights had come on in the two adjacent estates.

"I screwed up," she said.

"No, you didn't. It was one on five; you got four. I don't think they were here to kill us. We surprised them. They were here only to kill Raven."

"I should have—"

"Done nothing differently. If we had not acted on our own, we would have never found out the most important piece of intelligence gathered tonight."

She scoffed. "What is that?"

His eyes met hers. "That the people she was working for wanted her dead faster than we did."

"I hope you are right about leaving her body there."

"Part of Munny's turnover with me entailed him explaining the concept of a 'cleanup crew.' Trust me. In no more than an hour, the organization that sent that team will send another one to clean everything up."

"And we let them?"

"Yes."

They were too far away from the estate's shoreline now for the night vision goggles to be of any use in surveying the property, so she did one three-hundred-and-sixty-degree scan, saw nothing but their yacht, and took the goggles off.

Ulysses opened the throttle up, and the boat cut the flat, dark surface with ease.

The sound of the motor provided enough noise for Adrienne to consider what might have been. She had wanted to confront Raven about Flo and Flo's daughter more than anything she had ever wanted to do in her life before. Perhaps it was because of the things Flo had said before her final mission. Perhaps it was because Raven had betrayed them, betrayed everyone, and compromised all that the Director had claimed she stood for. And perhaps it was because Adrienne had lost her brother—an innocent child like Flo's daughter—and thought that they both deserved to live the lives that were taken away. Who would they have become, and what would they have done? These things would never be known. And it was the finality of *never* that meant the injuries from those losses could not—and would not—ever heal.

And if I had followed Raven's message, the same questions would have applied to me. Flo's advice saved me, but will it be enough to keep me alive long enough to bring down the entire organization?

Adrienne took one last look at the estate, shrinking in the distance. As she thought of Raven's body lying in the cool, tropical grass of the night, she realized that something had changed inside herself.

She turned her head away from the shoreline and motioned for Ulysses to throttle down.

He did, and she said, "Turn the motor off."

"What for? We're almost there," he replied, pointing at the yacht a few hundred yards away.

"Trust me."

He shut the motor off, and after a few seconds, the rubber boat lay nearly motionless on the moonlit water. "What is it?"

"We don't stop until every one of them is dead."

"The people that Junius was working for?"

Adrienne nodded. "All of them. I want to kill Control personally."

Ulysses sat motionless for a few beats, but he did not break eye contact with her. "Might take us a while to do that."

"However long it takes."

He reached out his hand. "However long."

They shook and then broke the grip.

"We'll take a look on the monitors when we get back to Maui. If you're right about the cleanup crew, we'll call Worth and Gideon tomorrow morning when the place is clean."

"And if I'm wrong?"

She raised her eyebrows. "You won't be." She paused. "I never thanked you for tonight."

"Just doing my job." He started the motor and put his hand on the throttle. "Ready?"

She set her jaw and said, "Born ready."

Ulysses throttled up, and they sped toward the yacht . . . and toward their destinies.

EPILOGUE

Raleigh, North Carolina – February 2004

J ust before nine in the morning, Adrienne Astra stood below the green light bulb illuminated above the heavy door that led into Worth-Gideon, Inc.'s conference room on the fifth floor. She turned the steel handle and entered the darkened and spacious cavern. The room smelled of fresh coffee from the station in the corner, and she walked over and poured herself a cup before taking her seat between Rose Varga and Ulysses King at the room's immense concrete table. She had been notified of the meeting via Byron Worth in the late afternoon yesterday and was looking forward to it. The first operation to investigate someone in the United States who was possibly connected to the organization that Raven and Junius had worked for was in the works.

Adrienne set her full paper cup down to the right of a red-colored manila file folder on the table in front of her. There were also folders in front of Rose and Ulysses, and two folders had been placed in front of the chairs across the table for Worth and Gideon when they arrived.

341

The trio greeted each other and then sat silently.

She admired her co-workers' attire—sharp, appropriate, and serious.

Worth, Gideon, and the three division heads had agreed upon a formal dress code for all official conference room meetings, and the two bosses had given Adrienne, Ulysses, and Rose each $100,000 to upgrade their wardrobes. Today was the first gathering according to the agreed-upon norms.

Rose sat tall and proper, wearing a navy pinstriped Alexander McQueen suit and the glossy, crimson polish on her perfectly manicured fingernails shined like mirrors under the dim lamplight above the table. She yawned and twirled an emerald-colored Montblanc fountain pen with her slender fingers, two of which had gold rings on them that seemed to glow in the murky space.

Ulysses was in a black Armani suit with a black vest, white shirt, and black tie littered with tiny white polka dots. His Gucci glasses rested on his folder, and he closed his eyes, rubbing the bridge of his nose.

Adrienne wiped the sweat from her forehead with the end of her white blouse's sleeve; the room's temperature was frigid, but her body was still warm from the five-mile run an hour earlier. The blouse and her charcoal suit were Ralph Lauren, but she had resisted upgrading her writing tool, staying with her BIC Round Stic pen with blue ink. She removed it from the inner pocket of her suitcoat and set it on her folder, glancing at the printed label at the top:

Samuel Ingraham Michaelson

From the short pre-brief yesterday, the three of them had learned that Michaelson was a hedge fund manager living in a luxury high-rise in the Chelsea neighborhood of New York City. Some of Gideon's digging in his old stomping grounds had yielded financial ties between Michaelson and Junius's StarLine shipping company. Adrienne could sense from the look in Worth's eyes before she left his office that she would be heading to the Big Apple soon.

She took a sip of coffee and blinked, saying, "Strong."

Rose laughed and raised her cup. "Wake up, Astra."

"Too strong," said Ulysses, continuing to rub the bridge of his nose.

Rose swallowed her sip and said, "Drink up, you little shit," to the slouching Weapons Division Head.

He flipped her off. "Next time, you can join us for the rest of the mission instead of spending a week on the French Riviera."

"You're still sore about that? I was just doing what Adrienne instructed me to do."

Ulysses flipped her off again.

Adrienne looked past him to the large space beyond the end of the long table. The wall that had once separated Raven's office from the conference room had been removed, and everything in Raven's office had been taken out. After a team had swept for listening and surveillance devices and found none, the inside of the space had been renovated to make it a seamless part of the new, expanded conference room. She could see the outlines of the hefty leather chairs, round tables made of pine, and the lengthy bar that sat on the room's dark carpeting. She still felt out of place on the fifth floor, which she, Rose, and Ulysses now had access to. Before, it had been the Co-CEO's and Raven's primary domain. Now, it felt like an upper floor in a haunted house. The few times she had come up here during the past month to ask the men a question, she had found the conference room empty and the other office doors locked. After the failed attempts to touch base with them, she learned that Worth and Gideon, when they came in the office at all nowadays, spent most of their time on their exclusive sixth floor. The betrayal had shaken the men and made them retreat into themselves even more than before. However, after bringing Rose into the circle of five who knew what had really happened to Raven, they all decided to publish a lie to the rest of the company.

The decision was made to avoid the paranoia that would spread if other knew that the person who was third in command and had hired them was double agent who had betrayed the institution, leading to the deaths of Flo Munny, and Hugh. Better to let them believe the reframed fictions that (A) Flo Munny, and Hugh had died heroically uncovering a corrupt global conspiracy and (B) After helming a successful countersanction mission, carried out by Adrienn Astra and Ulysses King, Director Raven had decided to sail off into the sunset o obscurity.

And then there was the secret held only between Adrienne, Worth, and Ulysses: Kerrie Raven had murdered Flo's child, Jewel, and Jewel's nanny Eleanor. Adrienne would never forget the sight of Worth's face or the stench o his vomit after she let him know what Junius had told her. His reaction told he that he and Raven had been lovers and that he had known Jewel.

In early January, Worth and Gideon announced the Director's retirement and issued a joint statement, praising Raven for her leadership and wishing her a lon, and content life out of the shadows and into the light of afternoon naps, happ, hours that started, well, whenever she wanted them to, and walks along sand beaches with no cell phone on her hip. They stated that they had attempted t cajole the Director into letting them throw her a going away party, but Raven ha respectfully declined, desiring to melt and disappear into her new part. A expected, there was little questioning about the departure. Most employees a Worth-Gideon, Inc. did not envision staying in touch with each other after thei time at the company was over—certainly not with the cold and aloof Director.

Before the announcement, Adrienne had torn down all the security camera at her house that the company had installed and had put in her own system, whic the company did not have access to. After what Raven had done, just the though of someone inside the company being able to watch her at her own house mad her stomach turn. Visiting Pāhonu for vacations in the future would be one thing but at home, she demanded privacy.

The door to the conference room opened, and in walked Byron Worth and
ock Gideon, both wearing dark suits.

"And, perhaps one day, *we* will have a yacht with underwater compartments
where we can run sea-to-shore operations. We'll say we're a yacht with divers
loing some treasure hunting." Worth locked the door, which Adrienne knew
made the light outside the conference room turn red.

Gideon walked to the coffee station. "You'd need a builder, a marina to
berth it, and then a captain and crew to pilot and operate it—and probably
nother crew to guard it when it's in port. Nah . . . too much hassle."

Worth waved a dismissive hand at him and approached his seat at the table.
Good morning," he said.

They all returned the greeting, and Ulysses put his glasses back on.

Other than the light verbal jabs, she sensed tension between the men—in the
books they gave each other and the way that Worth had avoided talking about
Gideon when Adrienne and Ulysses had called to notify him about Raven's
betrayal and the failed mission in Hawaii to bring her in for interrogation. At
irst, he had hidden his embarrassment with anger, but then he had acted with a
lear and decisive mind. It did not hurt that Ulysses's prediction about another
eam returning to the estate that night had come true. He and Adrienne had
vatched the efficient operation from the beach house in Maui, and before the
un had come up, all the bodies had been transferred to a van at the front gate,
nd everything had been cleaned up and fixed except for replacing the broken
lass in the second-floor bedroom's terrace door. Worth had then ordered
Adrienne back to the company office and assigned a team of his own, headed by
Ulysses, to sweep the entire estate for bugs, fix the terrace door, and upgrade the
ecurity. Only after he had spoken to them and given his directives had he called
Gideon to bring him into the loop.

Adrienne watched as Worth sat down and sipped from a bottle of water while
e looked at the file folder in front of him, not touching it. She liked his tie, red

with black grid lines and knotted in a perfect double Windsor. The company had suffered a tremendous setback, and together they needed to right the ship. And it would all start with this meeting.

She took the top off her Bic pen and slid it over the end.

Worth set his water down and eyed her for a few seconds; she gave him a nod and took a sip of coffee.

Gideon arrived at the table with a cup of coffee and took his seat next to Worth. He neither greeted nor looked at any of the division heads.

Worth removed his glasses. "Look, we're going to be tied up in Afghanistan and Iraq for a long time. I know that's not the information being released to the public, but I trust the word on the ground, and the word is that we might be in both places for years." He wiped his glasses with his shirt sleeve, inspected them and then put them back on. "So, contractors and special companies like ours are not going to be out of a job anytime soon. However, I have let the powers that be know that we're focused on what I believe to be something bigger." He licked his top lip, then his bottom lip, and finally smacked them. "And they agree with me."

Gideon sat staring at the table.

I wonder what he thinks about this, Adrienne thought.

"So, that's where our focus will be." Using his right hand, Worth tapped the top of his red file folder. "Samuel Ingraham Michaelson." He paused and made eye contact with everyone in the room, holding his stare with Gideon the longest. "Let's begin."

Jock Gideon arrived home to his sprawling estate forty-five minutes after the meeting had concluded. After changing into running shoes, jeans, sweatshirt, and winter coat, he emerged from his walkout basement and strolled across the snow covered yard until reaching the start of the teardrop-shaped, two-mile trail that vent into the woods, made a loop, and then merged once again to the original path, ending where he now stood: at the beginning.

The meeting had been a *beginning*, the beginning of a new chapter at Worth-Gideon, and he was indifferent to the insight, suggestions, and questions presented. Varga didn't concern him; King, he didn't know well enough yet; and Worth, well, he talked too much at meetings and seemed to be warming to the idea of allowing the division heads more access to the co-CEOs. Worth had even approached him afterward about relocating the division heads to the fifth floor, while the two of them moved permanently to the sixth floor. *"We should also consider giving the three of them access to that floor,"* Worth had said.

Gideon hated the idea, but he could still maneuver around Worth and manipulate him when he needed to.

As he stepped off and began to move down the path, he thought about the real threat to his position and his power:

Adrienne Astra.

He had watched her operate that night at Pāhonu. Flo had trained her well, perhaps too well. She was sound in all facets of assassination and survival. But what had kept him up at night for the past few months was the fact that she was instinctual about her work, and that was the one trait that could not be taught. No island course or any other test the company devised could measure how an operator would react when put in the kind of situation she had found herself, both inside and outside of the beachfront estate. Hearing her recount the specifics of every move she made and why she made them had gotten his attention. When someone was good in this business, it got his attention. Until she survived the mission to assassinate Junius, he had not wanted to believe in her abilities. Now, he couldn't stop thinking about them.

She was supposed to have died on that mission according to the trap tha Raven had set. So was King. And, yet, they hadn't. Then, she and King had disappeared and emerged in Hawaii . . . a few minutes too early, in fact, a Control's assassination team had learned.

Control.

Well, she had missed a golden opportunity to kill Adrienne Astra but had no missed the occasion to eliminate Raven. In fact, he had wondered how earl Control had known that Adrienne Astra and Ulysses King were still alive and tha Junius and Rex had been killed. But those conspiratorial thoughts had vanishec when he reasoned that if she had known any earlier, then she would have had Raven killed immediately to prevent her from talking. The situation must hav just evolved naturally with the convergence of the two parties occurring that nigh at Pāhonu. Control certainly hadn't told him anything about it. The only reasor he knew about the events was pure curiosity. He'd gone home and was ready to start dinner when he decided to check the security cameras at the ocean-fron estate. And what a show he had seen.

In any event, Control had manipulated Gideon, and it did not sit well with him. By having him and Raven both planted at the company, she was able to receive 2-source verification on all important intelligence passed to her. H should have seen it earlier, but he had been arrogant—he was arrogant—and had pressured Worth to keep Raven excluded from the all-boys club on the sixth floor. He had always considered Raven a lesser being anyway and had no ide until she had been killed why Worth had warmed up to her in the past year. H had fumed at the beginning of his first call with Control after the debacle or Oahu. She should have trusted him and *only him* to keep an eye on and, wher necessary, steer events at Worth-Gideon. Just when he was ready to put th exclamation point on his tirade against Control for not letting him know tha Raven was also one of her pigeons, she had said, *"Did you know they were sleepin together? No? Then you're a fool. She's been feeding me information before you have for th ast six months. I was even beginning to think she would be more valuable to me in the future than you, but now that she's gone, unfortunately, you're all I have left. And don't ever speak to me the way you just did. You don't know where I live, but I know where you live and work."*

At that point, he had retreated. When playing the long game, one needs to know when it's time to bend the knee and when it's time to bend the knee and then spring up and cut the head off the queen. He had also come to the awful conclusion that by having two spies in the organization, Control had a built-in assassin right there to silence the other one quickly if he or she was found out and one of Control's own assassins was too far away. It was brilliant. He had shuddered at the thought of what would have happened if he had been found out—possibly Kerrie Raven showing up at his front doorstep wondering if he had time to talk with her over a quick drink . . . and Raven killing him when he invited her inside.

What made sense to him now, though, was why Worth had insisted on going with Raven to Oahu after thinking that Adrienne and Ulysses had been killed. *'onofabitch wanted to get laid!* And, in hindsight, Gideon admitted to himself that Raven had been impressive when she had rejected Worth's proposal, delivering her lines to him right in front of Gideon in the conference room—*"The cleanup crew is on their way to Montreux. Join me in a few days. You too, Jock. This was my ball, and I dropped it. They're dead. I need to be alone. If you want my resignation now, I'm happy to provide it."* And Worth's response! *"Go ahead. You need time and space. We'll supervise the cleanup, and then I'll join you, and we'll talk about your future."*

At present, matters had somewhat simplified for the company but gotten a lot more complicated for him. Worth trusted Adrienne Astra—the chemistry between them during the meeting was obvious to his trained eye—and Gideon could see that he would not be able to cut off her access to Worth easily. But . . . no one was on to him yet. If they were, they would have acted already. Yes, Worth had waited forever to tell him about what was going on, but Gideon reasoned that it was out of embarrassment from not seeing through Kerrie Raven. Gideon doubted that King would ever be able to discover that he had been watching the events play out at Pāhonu in December; Control's tech guru, who had shown Gideon months ago how to access the monitors at the estate without anyone knowing, was superior in every way to the geeky expert Gideon had stared down at the conference room table today.

No, the problem was, and would continue to be, Adrienne Astra.

Gideon reached the split in the path and took the right-hand trail. After fifty yards, he stopped in front of a small wooden bench just off the path. There was a thin layer of snow on the seat, and it took a few brushes with the sleeve of his coat to clear a space to sit.

He reached into his jacket pocket and pulled out a pair of binoculars and then sat down. For the next five minutes, he surveyed the entire area of woods around the bench, from the ground all the way up to the tree tops, acting like a man who was one with his surroundings—enthralled by the beauty of winter in the woods of North Carolina.

When he was convinced that he was alone, Gideon put the binoculars down and then bent over as if to tie his shoes. His right hand slipped back toward the bench, and he slid it underneath the wooden seat until his fingers found what he was looking for. With a slight tug, he removed a burner phone that one of Control's associates had placed there yesterday before the heavy snowfall.

He sat up and looked at his watch.

11:58 a.m.

There were two times he could call today: one was at noon, the other at four p.m. Thankfully, the meeting had ended in time for him to make the noon phone call. It had taken every ounce of his patience to wait for Byron Worth to finish his speech when the men were alone afterward. If he only knew what Gideon was about to do and had been doing for the past two years after Control had approached him on a trip to Berlin.

When the 1990s, the so-called decade-long "holiday from history," had officially ended with 9/11, Gideon had sensed, for the first time in his life, that the world order could be upended. It would take time, but technological innovation, highlighted by advances in A.I., would provide an organization with the ability to choreograph the assassinations of the old-world centers of power. To the naked eye, it would appear that each one was falling from within. But in reality, the entity controlling the high-speed, interconnected highway of information exchange and innovations that would replace human beings as the earth's dominant labor force at an exponential rate would be the architect of the epic downfalls. Junius had been limited in his world-conquering view. For him, being the tsar of the world came down to his simplistic proverb: He who owns the seas owns the world. He saw the potential for A.I. to revolutionize his business but didn't expand the concept. For Control, owning the world came down to one thing: being able to dominate the entire tech sector.

Providing people with access to connected, digital platforms, which knowingly and unknowingly encouraged moral and political corruption would con humans like a fish trap that had been purposely severed from its line and buoy, sinking to the bottom. Fish would continue to enter the trap, looking to feed on what was in the trap, and then become food for other fish that would enter the trap, and on and on. The killing would not stop until the trap was removed.

The concept was nothing new to Gideon. Human beings had always been the designers of the advancements that increased their quality of life, while concurrently inventing more powerful and more efficient weapons to depopulate the earth. And, in an irony that only fallible human beings the world 'round could appreciate, those inventions had, time after time, eventually turned on the inventor.

With the entire world about to be connected in ways that were unfathomable in years past, Gideon had two questions for Control: one, Did she possess the technological edge to one day leverage A.I. against her opponents? Put another way—Did she control the traps? And, two, Would she be powerful enough to take charge of the population after the world order had been rearranged to her design? Put another way—Would she be able to govern the traps, considering the potential for a world of fish with an irreversible dependence on the success of her organization?

She had provided him with her answers in Berlin. After "careful consideration"—an overused phrase for celebrity divorce announcements—Gideon had come to the conclusion that the answers to both questions were *yes*. And Control's disclosure of some of the company's financials had removed all of Gideon's doubts. For he had learned long ago when reading Eric Ambler's book *A Coffin for Dimitrios,* that, "The important thing to know about an assassination or an attempted assassination is not who fired the shot, but who paid for the bullet."

However, for a good portion of his meeting with Control, he had thought about walking away and being a part of the team that would assassinate *her* and terminate *her* organization. After all, Worth-Gideon, Inc. had been formed to make sure that the proverbial "fish traps" didn't get anywhere near someone who had the means to deploy them—better yet, destroy the "traps" before they made it to the "boats"—better yet, destroy the "trap" factories.

But, in the end, Gideon had found his answers to the questions of the future in the past. A few years ago, in a moment of what he tried to convince himself was weakness, he had wandered into a bookstore and bought a copy of the newly released *Norton Shakespeare.* But on his drive home, he had realized that weakness had not steered him to the bookstore and book; strength had. No amount of money or other distractions could distance himself from his love of literature and reading that had been ignited in him by Yale's legendary Sterling Professor of Humanities, Harold Bloom, whom Gideon had taken a course from in his undergraduate years. And so, that evening Gideon had thumbed through the book and stopped at one of his favorite plays, *As You Like It*. But before reading the play, he had read Jean E. Howard's introduction, which had reminded him of *why* he liked the play. In fact, he had been so struck by some of her commentary, that the words appeared to him as he was contemplating Control's offer:

As You Like It *invites its characters and its audiences to suspend the rules of everyday existence and to imagine different realities . . . What if we could have the world "as [we] like it?" Shakespeare's title invites us to contemplate that very question. What do we like? What do we desire? And by extension, how could the world be rearranged to accommodate those desires and wishes? . . . The relationship of the "natural" to the "artificial" is a topic fundamental to pastoral; that is, are what human beings have made—cities, gardens, systems of social hierarchy—preferable to the simplicity and lack of artifice supposedly found in rural settings and communities? Such debates continue today, as we frequently long for simpler, slower lives but find it hard to wean ourselves from all the sophisticated conveniences of modern life. The choices weren't easier in the early modern period, when courts and cities had pleasures and attractions as well as vices and corruptions.*

Gideon had decided that tech would ultimately win. And, thus, Control would win.

However, the past had also taught him that one person could make a difference—Adrienne Astra could be the fatal flaw in Control's plan.

He exhaled. Control still wanted her dead, but Gideon had explained that if Astra was killed now, then Worth would not hesitate to bring in the larger espionage and law enforcement apparatuses of the United States government to join and start investigating the organization and hunting its members. *"You do not want that kind of* heat *right now—especially because Junius just died,"* he had told her.

Besides, he thought, *I want to be the one who gets to eliminate that annoying little bitch.*

His watch beeped the arrival of noon, and Gideon dialed the number he had memorized for this one call—the number changed every time. After four rings Control answered.

Gideon listened for a minute and then said, "I understand your concern. I'm still as surprised as you are that your team didn't get her in Hawaii . . . Yes, I think Worth respects Astra . . . Am I worried about her? No. As we discussed before she's on borrowed time, but the Junius fallout needs to quiet down before we move on her or Worth . . . I'm aware that time is an issue. You have to understand that it will be more difficult for set-ups now . . . Why? Because Worth has taken over mission communications, and he wants to give the division heads more access . . . Well, our goddamned people will just have to be better than she is won't they? Victor Lars Junius was an idiot and Imperia Rex proved to be no Gardell Valorous." He smiled. *Time for some charm.* "I'm still jealous that you get to keep her. Bodyguards like that come around once every generation . . . No the plan hasn't changed. Tell Baron, Cashmere, and DiMera to calm down They're not in danger. I've steered Worth-Gideon to start with Michaelson. He's small. Expendable . . . Yes, I know that he could lead them to Cashmere, but it's better than the other two, agree? . . . *Of course,* I'll eliminate Worth at some point but right now there is too much to be gained by keeping him alive . . . Take over the company? No, being top dog could tie me up with too many meetings dinners, and hours of administrivia. Much better to stay junior partner in the endeavor . . . We'll kill the other key personnel when the time is right—might even get a few of them to turn—then offer the remaining twits severance packages, and, finally, disband the corporation . . ." His grin widened. "Yes Control. I look forward to our rendezvous too."

The call ended, and Gideon replaced the phone underneath the bench Control's associate would retrieve it once he was out of sight.

She has no patience, he thought as he stood and reached his hands to the sky *And one day, that will be her undoing.*

The bright sun warmed his face around his sunglasses, and the muscles in his arms began to burn as he stretched them and spread his fingers even more.

And that day is coming soon, ma'am.

He let his hands drop to his sides.

After a leisurely scan of the bare woods that surrounded him, he turned and started to walk back down the path, the freshly fallen snow crunching under the weight of his running shoes.

AUTHOR'S NOTE

Thank you for reading or listening to *The Blue Hour Sanction*. As an independent author, my success greatly depends on reviews and referrals. If you enjoyed the book, it would help me out if you left a quick review and then passed on the recommendation. If you would like more information on upcoming books and discounts, please sign-up for my email list through my website (landonbeachbooks.com) or follow Landon Beach Books on Facebook, Twitter, or Instagram.

The Blue Hour Sanction. This is the first action novel I have written, and I now have a new appreciation for authors who write in the genre—it was a challenge to write but rewarding to finish. Coming up with a character's origin story is something that has always interested me. I just never thought that when the time came for me to tackle the job that I would be writing the origin story for a character created by a fictional author whom *I* had created! Nevertheless, it was fun, and I hope you enjoyed the ride. In terms of Adrienne's adventures in Hawaii . . . what can I say, I am a huge fan of the original *Magnum P.I.*, and have always thought it would be fun to set an action sequence at the fabled and fictional estate of Robin Masters, which, in real life, was the legendary Anderson estate named Pāhonu in Waimānalo. Since that section of *The Blue Hour Sanction* is set in 2002, the descriptions of the tidal pool and estate are accurate. However, if you are thinking of visiting Oahu and checking the place out, you will find that every building except for the boathouse, which served as the exterior of Thomas Magnum's quarters in the guest house, has been demolished . . . replaced by a modern, mega-estate, owned by a former president. However, every beach in Oahu is a public beach, so there is nothing to stop you from taking a swim in the historic tidal pool—but, be ready for the secret service to take an interest in your movements!

A few books and films that stood out during my research phase of writing the novel were: *Secrets of the Tomb: Skull and Bones, the Ivy League, and the Hidden Paths of Power* by Alexandra Robbins, *America's Secret Establishment: An Introduction to the Order of Skull & Bones* by Antony C. Sutton, *Wealth, Poverty and Politics* by Thomas Sowell, *The Richard Burton Diaries* edited by Chris Williams, *And God Created Burton* by Tom Rubython, *Richard Burton: A Life* by Melvyn Bragg, *Rogue Warrior* by Richard Marcinko with John Weisman, *Action* by Robert McKee and Bassim El-Wakil, *A Coffin For Dimitrios* by Eric Ambler, *The Wild Geese* directed by Andrew V. McLaglen, *In From The Cold: The World of Richard Burton* directed by Tony Palmer, *Who's Afraid of Virginia Woolf?* directed by Mike Nichols, *Brave New World* by Aldous Huxley, *Where Eagles Dare* written by Alistair MacLean and later directed by Brian G. Hutton, *Equus* directed by Sidney Lumet, and **The Norton Shakespeare*.

*Jean E. Howard wrote the Introduction to *As You Like It* in the 1997 1 edition of *The Norton Shakespeare* (this author's college textbook). However, in the novel, I quote from Dr. Howard's revised Introduction to *As You Like I* from the 3rd edition of *The Norton Shakespeare*, published in 2016. Although some of the wording remains unchanged from the 1997 edition, most of what quote is from the 2016 edition. Hence, it would not have been available to Joc Gideon during the fictional timeline of the book. But, the material in the 201 revised Introduction served the purposes of my story, and so I used my artisti license to quote from the 3rd edition as if the quoted material had all appeared in the 1st edition. Note: if you noticed this while reading the last few pages of the novel and were about to call me on it, then we are definitely friends who have not met yet!

Okay, time to finish this series with *Huron Sunrise*. Then, I will finally close out the Great Lakes Saga with *The Bay*.

Many thanks to MB, EL, DB, MM, RR, JT, JBx2, JG, and TK who a provided helpful comments on early drafts of the manuscript. A giant hug t my wife and daughters who continue to allow me to "make stuff up" for living.

Happy Beach Reading!

L.I

If you enjoyed *The Blue Hour Sanction*, expand your adventure with *The Cabin,* a stand-alone espionage thriller in The Great Lakes Saga. Here is an excerpt to start the journey.

THE CABIN

Landon Beach

PROLOGUE

BERLIN, DECEMBER 2005 – PART I

The spy was late. CIA Officer Jennifer Lear sat inside a toasty café drinking a cappuccino, *Die Welt* open in front of her. She was at a table for two against the front window and right next to the door. Outside, the snow fell as if there was an unlimited supply, and Berliners wearing dark heavy overcoats and knitted hats made their way along the Kurfürstendamm. She felt a hint of sympathy for her partner who was outside weathering the freezing temperature a block away. A feigned yawn and stretch gave her the opportunity to glance at the clock on the wall above a booth with two loud Germans arguing over a game of chess. 7:02 p.m. Her agent, Sari, had never been late, which would give Lear the grounds to call off the meeting right now. But, Sari would be doing a surveillance detection run, and the weather might be slowing her down. Lear and her partner had decided on a 5-minute window. Sari now had 3.

She moved her toes up and down inside her hiking boots. Her feet were sore from her own hour-long surveillance detection run with her partner, performed to make sure that no one was following them before she entered the café. First, they had driven around for a half an hour to spot anyone tailing their car. Then, she had gotten out and started to walk while he parked the car up the street in front of a bookstore. As soon as he exited the car, a third officer emerged from the store, took the keys from him, and drove the car out of the city. For the next half hour, Lear had strolled the shopping district while her partner followed from a distance.

The door chimed, and Lear took a sip of her cappuccino to see who had entered. Damn. It was a heavyset grandmother with a scarf over her mouth. The woman shut the door behind her and moved toward the café's bar. Lear set her cup down. *Where was her agent?*

CIA Officer Brian Turner shivered beneath his wool coat. The wind whipped against the snow on the ground, dusting it up like a snow blower and then scattering the flakes in a narrow blast pattern. He crossed the street and began to look in store windows. He pondered, he nodded, he abruptly stopped and acted like the deal he saw advertised on the storefront was too good to be true, and he kept watch on his surroundings to make sure that nothing interfered with Officer Lear's meeting. He had last seen their agent at the rendezvous six months ago, and he wondered what information she would have for them this time.

The corner of the awning above the storefront he was currently "browsing" gave way, dumping a pile of snow directly on his neck and coat collar. As he brushed the snow off with his gloved hands, some of it slipped under his shirt and ran down his back—*Jesus, it was cold*. The summer meetings were much more pleasant. Why did he keep getting assigned to winter meetings? Lear only handled one summer meeting and one winter meeting a year; the rest of the time she was probably at her cover job or working as an analyst at Langley. He was stationed in France, which made it easy for him to accompany her to Berlin. They were posing as tourists for a week and were being treated to all Berlin had to offer: the Gendarmenmarkt, the Brandenburg Gate, the Reichstag, the Berlin

elevision Tower, the Berlin Cathedral, Museum Island, and the Berlin Wall
Memorial and Documentation Centre. Then, on a pre-arranged day and time,
they would meet up with their agent. The usual protocol called for Lear to live
in Berlin under the cover of some state job at the U.S. Embassy. Once the CIA
had an agent for her to run, she would coordinate all of the meetings using
classic tradecraft—dead drops, chalk markings, the opening of a window at a
certain time, etc. But in the last decade, this had become more difficult to pull
off since most foreign countries now watched *every* employee of the embassy.
Updated techniques were needed to effectively run agents and gather
intelligence. Using officers once or twice a year for the face-to-face meetings
had proved effective. The Berlin station personnel would set up the meetings,
but when the meetings actually took place, known officers were followed and
unknown officers like Lear and Turner were not—allowing them to slide into a
café or take a stroll in a park to meet with their agent. They would exchange
money and other items for information, forward it to the Berlin office, then go
on acting as tourists for a few more days.

Turner entered a store directly across from the café. The warmth inside
restored him. He took off his gloves, smiled at a salesperson, and meandered
through an aisle of clothes until he was facing the window. He could see Lear
sitting at the table. The other chair was empty. Something was wrong.

He turned toward a rack of men's coats and picked up the sleeve of one to
study the price tag, which also gave him an opportunity to glance at his watch.
:04. Four minutes late. If Sari didn't show in one minute, they would leave. A
no-show agent was a pain because of the time devoted to the meeting's set up,
communication, and surveillance detection run, but it didn't necessarily mean
that anything was wrong. Perhaps the agent was being followed and had to
bort. Not a problem, they'd set up another meeting. But still...

He let the coat sleeve go and gave the street a quick survey as if to check
the conditions outside. The snow continued to pour from the sky as shoppers

walked the Kurfürstendamm. The agent was nowhere in sight. Less than a minute left. He felt uneasy.

Officer Lear finished her cappuccino and dabbed a napkin across her lips. Convinced that her agent was not going to show up, she started to slide her chair back away from the table. It had only moved a few inches when the door to the café opened and Sari entered.

Lear bent down and tightened the laces on both of her hiking boots. The floor looked like it hadn't been swept in months, and the snow tracked in had turned the dirt into a wet grime. She sat up. Placing her elbows on the table top, she rested her chin on her hands and stared out the window disinterestedly as if she'd be there to pass another hour.

Sari joined her at the table.

"Guten Abend," Lear said, still looking out the window.

Sari affectionately rubbed Lear's right arm. "Alles klar."

Lear turned her head and released a smile. "Ja, alles klar, danke." She took out a handkerchief and surveyed the café as she wiped her nose. Nothing seemed out of place, and no one was paying attention to them. Lear put the handkerchief back in her pocket.

Sari had spotted the folded newspaper on the table. After a pause, she laid her large purse next to the paper and began to search the middle pocket with her left hand. With precision and timing, she slid her right hand between the folded sections of *Die Welt*, as if to stabilize the purse, and then removed it, joining her other hand in the search of her purse's contents.

Lear pretended to be annoyed with Sari's searching until Sari finally pulled out a pack of gum. Lear's face said: *about time.*

Sari offered her a stick, which was accepted, then took one out for herself.

Lear said, "Danke," and put the green piece of gum into her mouth while Sari placed her purse on the floor. Lear slid the newspaper into her backpack with her right hand. With her left hand, she took a small cookie tin out of her coat pocket and placed it inside Sari's purse. The tin was filled with cash. When they had started exchanging information, Sari had asked for more specific items—an original Michael Jackson Thriller record, two cartons of Treasurer cigarettes, a Gucci scarf—but now she just wanted cash.

"Bitte schön."

Lear relaxed. The Berlin exchanges were always quick, and the signal that everything was fine was communicating in simple German phrases that any tourist would know. If there was anything wrong and they needed to split, Lear was to say a long sentence in English, and, if there was anything wrong on Sari's end, she was to say a lengthy sentence in German. Lear didn't know why Sari was late, but she was convinced that, whatever the reason, all was well. She made eye contact with her agent and then, using her right index finger, rubbed her watch face in two slow circles.

Sari patted Lear's arm. It was time to get going.

Lear rose from the table and pushed in her chair. She said, "Gute Nacht."

"Bis dann," Sari replied.

Lear put on her backpack and headed for the door. The two Germans playing chess had escalated their insults as Lear slid by their booth. She pulled on the door handle and heard, "Wir fahren morgen mit dem Zug nach Hamburg, wenn ich dich wider sehe, lieber Freund." *We'll take the train to Hamburg tomorrow when I see you back here, dear friend.*

Lear looked over at Sari, gave her a nod, and then exited the café.

Outside, she noticed Turner leaning against a lamppost across the street. After tilting her head back and looking at the sky, as if pondering whether to venture out or head back inside, she took a pair of reading glasses out of her right coat pocket, examined them, and then put them in her left pocket.

* * *

Turner's heart started to beat faster, and his situational awareness became even more acute. Lear had just signaled him that something was wrong. But what was it? It appeared that the meeting had gone smoothly; it definitely hadn't been rushed. Surely, Sari would have signaled trouble as soon as she entered the café, but the two had sat down like old friends. Had Lear seen something after the meeting? He put his hand inside his coat and felt the handle of his 9mm. He slid his fingers down the barrel and felt the silencer attached—the pockets were extra-large to accommodate the handgun. At the same time, his eyes swiveled left and right, then up and across the rooftops. Nothing seemed out of place. He looked through the café window. Sari sat, reading a paperback. She seemed in no hurry.

His eyes met Lear's, and she turned left out of the café. This was the direction they had agreed upon if there was danger. He let her get a block ahead and then began to follow. In another block, he would cross the street and—

There. A man wearing a driver's cap and carrying a shopping bag from an upscale clothing store entered the sidewalk from an alley. He took a little too much time searching the crowd of fellow shoppers until he spotted and began to follow Lear. Trouble.

Turner kept his eyes on the man. After a few paces, the man made a second mistake and turned his head to the right, keeping it fixed for a moment in the direction of another man who was across the street. The second man was half-a-block ahead of Turner and walked with a smooth, confident stride. He had on a black overcoat with a scarlet scarf, and his mop of salt and pepper hair blew in the wind.

Then, the second man veered off the sidewalk and entered a store; the other man continued to follow Lear. Turner saw his opportunity and crossed the street, cycling his eyes between Lear, the man following her, and the storefront where the second man had disappeared. As he passed the store, he

id not see the man inside, but he only had a second to scan. There was no
me to double check, and he could not reveal himself by stopping and looking
1 the storefront window. He focused his attention solely on Lear.

From a corner inside the store, the man with the overcoat and red scarf
atched his fellow agent follow the woman. He waited an entire minute until
1ey were far away down the sidewalk. He approached the window and
canned both sides of the street. Confident that he had not been seen or
pllowed, he exited the store and headed back toward the café.

Turner began to close the distance between himself and the man following
.ear. Up ahead was an apartment complex, and if he could walk past both of
1em like he was in a hurry to get somewhere, then he could warn her. It was
is only chance. He sped up.

Lear saw the apartment complex looming two blocks away. Should she
art into the main office, take an elevator up, walk all the way down the hall,
ıke the stairs down, and then exit out the rear entrance? It was a simple
vasion technique, and they had discussed it last week when they arrived and
3ain this morning. She wasn't sure if she was being followed, but Turner
ouldn't be far behind. He would join her in the building and they would go
om there. The one thing she could not do was turn arou—
"Apartment plan," a voice said next to her, and before she could turn her
ead, she saw Turner running past her. Ten yards ahead, she saw him look at
is watch, shake his head, and then swear loudly in German. He continued to
in—past the apartment complex, past another store, and across the next
ıtersection.
Now she knew something was wrong. Twenty yards until the entrance of
ıe apartment complex. She maintained discipline, never speeding up or

looking around, and her hiking boots continued to crunch though the freshly fallen snow.

Ten yards.

She put her hand inside her coat pocket and fingered her own 9mm with silencer attached—she hadn't fired a gun since the range, right before she left the United States for the mission. She had never fired at a human being before

She reached the double glass doors and entered the apartment building. Then, she picked up her pace and strode toward the elevator—same luck! The doors were just about to close. She slid her hand between the doors, and they opened. An elderly German couple frowned; she apologized. The doors closed, and she saw the 11th floor's button was lit. The elevator started to climb; she pushed the button for floor 3.

Turner watched as the man followed Lear into the apartment complex. Then, he stepped away from the outdoor restaurant table he had slid behind and scooted around the space heater before heading back toward the apartmer complex's back door where he would take the stairs up to meet her.

Lear exited the elevator and made her way swiftly down the long hallway. At the far end was a door with the sign reading "Ausgang" above it that led to the stairwell. Almost clear. She would go down the stairs, out the back door, and head straight for the waiting car, which would be two blocks away. She knew the car would be there because if everything had gone as planned, they would have already been picked up on the other end of the Kurfürstendamm; her team would have switched to the alternate pick-up location immediately when she and Officer Turner hadn't shown up. She continued to hustle towar the door.

* * *

Turner entered the stairwell and was already on the second flight when he heard the door below crash open. He looked down and saw three men with guns drawn enter the building. They saw him and started racing up the stairs. Then, he heard something that made his insides turn: They were shouting at each other—in Russian. He ran up the last flight to the door numbered 3.

Lear grinned as she moved to within ten feet of the stairwell door. *Piece of cake.* Then, the door burst open. It was Turner.

"Run!" He said.

She stopped, confused. "Brian—"

"Now!"

She turned and sprinted away down the hall.

STATE HIGHWAY 250, NEW YORK
THURSDAY, JUNE 29, 2006

"We're almost to our little bungalow, babycakes," Iggi Hilliar said to his wife as he tapped his fingers on the steering wheel. "Gonna seduce your ass before our company arrives."

Maria Hilliard's large sunglasses stayed focused on the *People* magazine she held in her hands. "Keep dreamin'," she said. "Plus, you just got some last night, and you're lucky you got that." She grinned. "Don't you need a few day to recover?"

He started to roll up his window.

"No," Maria said. "I like to feel the breeze while we drive by the lake."

"C'mon. A little AC, please? It's hot out and not even 9am."

"No," came the final answer behind the magazine.

He rolled his window back down and then observed his reflection in the rearview mirror. His brown forehead was dotted with perspiration, and the black hair that rose four inches from his scalp became wet as he wiped the sweat from his forehead through his hair. His thick full beard was helping to hide the tell-tale signs of weight gain on cheeks and neck. Monday nights filled with beer and snacks at the bowling alley followed by all of the goodies each press box included during football weekends hadn't helped. His playing days were long gone, but now he got to do the next best thing: get paid to watch games, get fed free, mostly delicious, food while he watched and took notes, mingle with prime-time coaches and players and sometimes interview them, and then write it all up for the *Democrat and Chronicle*. "So my thirty-three-year-old body doesn't look like Donovan McNabb's anymore," he said. "I recover just fine."

Maria let out a giggle, "You're damn right it doesn't. You've got your own bowling ball starting to form." The wind blew through her black wavy hair. "This air is heaven."

Iggi took his left hand from the steering wheel and began to rub his belly, which, he had to admit, was out over his pants and close to the wheel. He was getting though; when he stood up, it all evened out. At least that's what he told himself. "Didn't you notice last night, how I used this to my advantage? It kept my rhythm smooth like a pendulum." He pointed to his gut. "This thing is a weapon."

She dismissed his argument with, "Uh huh," and kept flipping through her magazine.

The road curved to the left, and the trees began to thin out as lakeside houses began to sprout up. Beyond the properties, Lake Ontario was a sheen of cobalt. A few triangles of canvas were spread out on the water like signposts on a road that stretched in every direction. *You'd never get me on a sailboat.* Too slow. Too boring. Too much work. Powerboat or nothing. Slam the throttle down and let's go already.

Maria put the magazine back in her tote bag.

Shoot. She's going to start talking about the weekend.

She looked past him at the lake. "I can't wait for you to meet Cal."

"How come I've never met him before?"

"Well, he's been a little busy since 9/11, don't you think?"

Right. He was a cop. A Detroit cop. "I forgot," Iggi said.

"Well, he's my friend," she said. "So be nice."

"I can't promise that," said Iggi. "He's got to prove himself."

"Why?"

"I can't believe you're asking me that."

She took off her glasses and looked out her window at the passing road signs. "I'm sorry," she said. "I promise he's good."

Iggi exhaled. What does *good* even mean? "We'll see."

She gave his right forearm a quick rub and then put her glasses back on. "Haley isn't seeing anyone right now."

Man, she switches topics fast—always has. "The birthday girl is single, huh?"

"Ridiculous, right? But she's so introverted, I don't see how she's ever going to meet anyone," she said. "I mean, I'm her one friend at school, and if I didn't go down to have lunch with her once a week, I think she'd just stay in her physics lab and no one would ever see her."

Iggi rubbed his beard as he thought. He'd been distracted the past few weeks going back and forth with his editor on the phone over the book manuscript. The editor wasn't pleased with what he had called the 'nuclear missiles' Iggi had shot in the opening chapter about the culture of losing in the Detroit Lions's locker room and the irony of a fierce man-eating lion serving as the franchise logo. The editor was also unsure of the title: *Not with a Roar but a*

Whimper: Three Decades of Ineptitude. He wondered why Iggi didn't write a book about the Bills instead—at least they *had gone* to the Super Bowl four times in a row. Iggi had replied, "New York is where I make my living, Robert, but Detroit is where I'm from. I don't shit where I eat." Anyway, he hadn't had time to think of this weekend—let alone the guest list—until they were getting into the car.

Usually, they invited Maria's college roommate and her husband to stay with them over the July Fourth weekend, but the couple was unavailable. Like the professional athletes he covered, Iggi liked routine. Maria liked to say he needed someone to give him a routine. Left to his own devices, without some game or season to prepare for, his daily journey became unpredictable and inefficient. Now, he was being asked to help host two people he didn't know. Of all years, why did the Fourth have to be on a Tuesday this year? That meant that the guests would be arriving on Friday and departing on Wednesday. In sports parlance this was like playing man-on-man defense for the entire season and suddenly being asked to play zone defense in the championship game—and the championship game was going to take three overtime periods to decide. And why *these* two people? Well, he could somewhat understand Maria's invitation to Cal. Some childhood bonds lasted a lifetime. But Haley? The quiet-as-a-mouse math and physics teacher whom he had seen only once? Twice? Anyway, the last time had been at a bar last year during a boring end-of-the-year faculty get together, which he had escaped by inventing a work emergency while using the restroom and then delivering his lines with feigned regret and surprise to the huddled group of worn out teachers.

Great. A Detroit cop and Haley. Wait a minute.

"I know what you're up to," he said, giving the steering wheel a tap like a coach giving a player a pat on the butt for a good play.

"And what is that?" Maria said.

"You're at it again. Trying to play matchmaker with our guests."

Maria picked up her plastic cup of Starbucks iced coffee and took a sip through the straw. "We'll just have to find out about that."

"Jesus," Iggi said. "Is that all this weekend is? Some booty call?" He paused. "Are you sure Steve and Val can't make it?"

"Let it go," she said.

Iggi shook his head in frustration. "I just want it to be like it always is. Besides, you're leaving me in another week to go 'teach for America' for a month. Can't we have one summer where someone else goes and helps the damn kids?"

"Not a chance. I need my time away doing the Lord's work."

"What about when we have kids? Will you leave then?"

She grinned. "So, now you're thinking about us having kids again?"

"Anything to get my mind off this weekend. I really don't wanna hang with new people."

"You know my girl is beautiful, but her life is so damn boring! I've gotta get her out of her funk. Being with us and meeting Cal will be a good thing. And Cal? His divorce was finalized this past fall, so he's back in the game."

Iggi cracked a smile.

She took another sip of her coffee and then set it down. "What?"

"You know you make my ass weak when you use sports to describe life," he said. "This weekend is going to be a disaster."

"It's going to be fine." Maria checked her watch. "Besides, tonight is all ours."

Their SUV climbed up a hill and then started down the other side. At the bottom, the woods thickened around them as the road curved away from the lake.

Maria's family had immigrated to the United States from Cuba over one hundred years ago, initially settling in Tampa, Florida, before moving north.

The towering log cabin had been in her family for three generations, set in the middle of three wooded beachfront lots, and had been constructed by her grandfather Miguel Ernesto Torres in the spring of 1961 after Kennedy's narrow election win, for which Torres had helped get out the vote and was compensated with manila envelopes stuffed with cash. As a fellow World War I veteran and Roman Catholic, Torres had wept tears of joy when it was announced that Kennedy had won, and he had wept tears of sorrow when it was announced that JFK had been shot and killed in Dallas. These were the only times that Maria's father had ever witnessed his father cry, and it had become a family legend—brought up, quietly shared, and then passed down within the log walls of the cabin: "El padre dos veces lloró"—the two times father cried.

Miguel Torres had wanted a home for his family that would serve as its heart—a pulsating center where celebrations would be held, yet also a sanctuary that would sustain them through life's challenges. However, he had warned that the physical structure alone would never sustain them. 'A house on the beach does not solve any of life's problems,' he had said. What would sustain them was gathering at the cabin and drawing strength from each other. This had been his vision, and the house he had built for it was also an architectural masterpiece.

The log home's great room had floor to ceiling windows that allowed for a sublime sight of Lake Ontario, and there were three bedrooms upstairs all with lake views. Besides the great room on the first floor was a den, kitchen, walk-in pantry, and dining room. The addition had been built in 1987 and included a first-floor master suite, entertainment room, wine cellar, and sun room.

Her grandparents were gone, and the house now belonged to her parents. But they lived in Boston and rarely used it, whereas Maria and Iggi lived only an hour away from the cabin and spent almost every weekend there. Some weekends Iggi would be away covering sports, and she would have time to herself. She rarely had company as her younger brother and his family didn't like the water and had no interest in visiting what had been the family's rallying point for forty years. They were in Boston too, and, as much as her two nephews loved Aunt Maria and Uncle Iggi, they had been spoiled—ruined?—by the fast pace of Boston compared to the solitude of the cabin. If her grandfather had still been alive, then he might have cried a third time knowing this. Friends? There had been a few teacher retreats there, but those had tapered off when her colleagues started having children. The advance from Iggi's book had provided them with enough money to buy the house from her parents. Maria suspected they would be willing to part with it because there were good memories there, but too many echoes whenever they visited. Perhaps because she was another generation removed, she didn't have her grandparents' presence haunting her down the hallways, up and down the staircase, or in every doorway. Her father wasn't an emotional man, but she knew it hurt too much for him to be there with his parents gone.

The woods surrounding the cabin extended for fifty yards toward the road and around thirty yards to the right and left. The neighbors had not sold their extra lots. The houses could not be seen; only by sitting on their beach or swimming were they aware that they had neighbors, and that was only if the neighbors emerged from their residences or had company. The closest town was Bay Harbor—five miles away and far enough to make it a pain if an item had been left off the grocery list by accident. While sitting on the back deck looking out at Lake Ontario in complete silence, she often thought that if there was ever a stretch of property for a celebrity to disappear from the spotlight, this was it. She teased Iggi that he needed this place to hide when angry fans read his honest column every week. He joked back that if the Lions fans ever found the cabin, they might burn it down.

Her routine during the past school year had become more of a Friday countdown every week—watching the clock like the students until the final bell rang. After trying to convince young 12th grade minds that books like *Beloved* and *One Hundred Years of Solitude* should be cherished and pondered, she would exit the brick fortress moments after the bell and speed out of the school's back lot. It took fifteen minutes to navigate the city traffic until she hit State Highway 250. Once on 250, it was just under an hour to reach the grocery store in Bay Harbor where she'd stock up for the weekend and then travel the final miles to her getaway. If the weather permitted, she would lower the windows and turn up the radio. She wished a nurse could be sitting in the passenger seat taking her blood pressure at that exact moment.

Iggi parked the car in the handicapped spot closest to the big doors that welcomed shoppers into Danny's Market. From the glovebox, he removed a white and blue press pass encased in plastic with a black lanyard wrapped around it. He unwound the lanyard, found the knot he had tied to shorten the length, and then used it to hang the press pass from his rearview mirror.

"Cha Ching," Iggi said.

"You're ridiculous."

Iggi whistled the theme to Monday Night Football as they exited the vehicle. "If a cop happens to drive by, it looks just like a permit."

Maria adjusted the purse strap on her right shoulder. "How long have you been doing this?"

Iggi patted his round stomach. "Ever since this little guy started to form."

Maria peered around the parking lot, expecting a patrol car to pull up any minute and arrest them. The lot was quiet. "Let's get this done," she said, pushing his hand away as he tried to hold hers.

Iggi shivered as they crossed through the A/C boundary and approached the grocery carts. His hands hovered over a cart's handles.

"Oh, C'mon!" Maria said and grasped the handles.

Iggi pulled his feet back just in time to avoid them getting run over. "Shit's cold in here," he said.

Recently, 'Beer Caves' had started to sprout up in gas stations across the country, and Iggi got a kick out of going in and freezing his ass off for a minute while grabbing cold beer—*nothing* beat cold beer—and watching his breath escape into the atmosphere. But Beer-Cave temperatures in a grocery story? Guy must be paying a fortune to keep the place cool.

"Let's *go*," said Maria, looking back at him.

They made their way down the familiar aisles with Maria maneuvering the cart around other shoppers like a racecar driver. *She's worried about my press pass being used to park in handicapped parking. Such a rule follower. Relax, girl.*

He walked alongside the cart and nodded as items like steak, hamburgers, hotdogs, chicken, and bratwurst got added to the cart. *Hell, yes. Time to grill. Thank God Maria tackled everything else in the kitchen.*

She threw in spaghetti, garlic bread, Caesar salad, potato salad, baked beans, macaroni salad, Ruffles potato chips, pickles, lunch meat, bread, onions, mushrooms, bacon, eggs, ingredients for homemade waffles, a massive bag of Dunkin' Donuts coffee (his favorite), vanilla ice cream, and—his eyes got greedy—ingredients for Maria's special raspberry pie.

They turned the corner and went down the final aisle—drinks.

Non-negotiables first: He lifted two cases of Bud Light and a 12-pack of Pepsi (Coke could go to hell) into the cart, while Maria put in a 12-pack of Diet Pepsi and directed him to load up two cases of bottled water.

They paused. "Now, what wine should we go with?" Maria said.

"Don't tell me they're wine snobs," said Iggi. "This is the Fourth of July; beer is where it's at."

She rolled her eyes and walked past him.

"What? Am I right or am I right?"

She picked up two bottles of merlot and two bottles of chardonnay and put them in the cart. "It's what our *guests* want that is important. Cal will drink beer with you, but the wine will go with dinner."

"There isn't a thing in this cart that beer doesn't go with."

"Waffles?"

"Watch me," Iggi said.

She looked at their full cart. "Let's check out and head next door."

"What's next door?"

"Dorne's Liquor Store. Cal likes Scotch and Haley and I are having margaritas on the beach." She maneuvered the cart around a young couple arguing over a bottle of wine. 'It doesn't finish well.' 'Not enough body.' 'They've probably never even tasted a Malbec.' *Christ.*

Iggi shook his head. "I thought you said he'd have beer with me."

They reached the end of the aisle. "He will," she said over her shoulder. Seeing the coast was clear, she crossed the main aisle and arrived at the checkout counter. Iggi took a *Sports Illustrated* off the rack and put it in; Maria grabbed *People*, *Bazaar*, and *Redbook*.

"These won't be around too much longer will they?" Iggi said looking down at the magazines.

"I'm afraid not," Maria said.

Iggi started loading items onto the register's conveyor belt. "Want me to go next door while you pay?"

She searched her purse for the checkbook. "No, let's go together."

"What were you thinking for dinner tonight?" He said while hoisting one of the cases of Bud Light out from underneath the cart's basket.

"I was thinking about a spinach smoothie."

Iggi's eyes narrowed. "What?"

She pinched his arm. "Just kidding. How about we pick up pizza and wings from Miss J's?"

He picked up the second case of Bud. "Now you're talkin'."

They exited Dorne's Liquor store and headed for the SUV. The sun was rising higher and the muggy heat was suffocating.

"What was all that shit about single malt versus blend the owner was talkin' about in there?" Iggi asked, pushing their overflowing cart.

Maria held a side of the cart with one hand and a black plastic bag containing the scotch, tequila, and margarita mix in her other hand. "I don't know," she said. "Just that the single malt was better or something."

"It sure was more expensive," he replied. "What in the hell does that guy know? And since when do people introduce themselves by giving their age and middle name?"

When the towering figure had approached them in the store, Iggi had momentarily slipped into his sports reporter character and asked if he had ever played football.

The man had rubbed his beard—every bit as big as Iggi's—and said, "No. In my forty-seven years of life, I've stayed away."

Maria said, "Great, Mister—" and searched for a nametag.

"Rick Gregory Dorne at your service," he said.

"Okay, Mister Do—"

"Rick," he cut her off.

She nodded. "We're in need of a little help selecting a bottle of scotch for friend."

With his hands behind his back, the right wrist held by the left hand, Rick thoughtfully nodded and said, "If I'm asked."

Iggi and Maria looked at each other and then back at Rick. "Um, you're asked," she said impatiently. "What should we get?"

This was the wrong question to ask. Rick went on a three-minute-long istory of scotch peppered with bar war stories of him drinking particular rands of scotch until closing time at hole-in-the-wall establishments in New ersey. It was, "I'm an old bar horse myself—grew up in 'em," and "I know my vay around a bar stool," followed by, "It was three against one, and I kicked all neir asses." His last tale ended in a wide grin and the triumphant declaration, I *know* how to navigate a bar." Simultaneously, he placed a seventy-five-dollar ottle of The Macallan in Maria's hands. Iggi had watched, mesmerized. Rick ad placed his hands behind his back once again and said, "A Detroit op...Yeah, in my humble opinion, he'll love this, darlin'."

"You have got to be kidding me!" Iggi shouted as they neared the vehicle.
"Uh huh," Maria said. "And *you're* payin' for it."
Underneath the driver side windshield wiper blade was a yellow ticket.

ABOUT THE AUTHOR

Landon Beach was born and raised in Michigan but now lives in the Sunshine State with his wife, two children, and their golden retriever. He previously served as a Naval Officer and was an educator for fifteen years before becoming a full-time writer. Find out more at landonbeachbooks.com.

Made in the USA
Columbia, SC
29 August 2023